THE LAST OF THE FIREDRAKES

THE AVALONIA CHRONICLES

by

FARAH OOMERBHOY

WISE *Ink*
CREATIVE ★ PUBLISHING

THE LAST
OF THE
FIREDRAKES
THE AVALONIA CHRONICLES

ISBN: 978-1-940014-70-8
eISBN: 978-1-940014-72-2

Library of Congress Catalog Number: 2015944123
Printed in the United States of America
First Printing: 2015
19   18   17   16   15   5   4   3   2   1

Cover design by Scarlett Rugers
Interior design by Kim Morehead

Wise Ink Creative Publishing
837 Glenwood Avenue
Minneapolis, MN 55405
www.wiseinkpub.com

To order, visit www.itascabooks.com or call 1-800-901-3480.
Reseller discounts available.

*To my father, the most courageous man
I have ever known. Rest in peace.*

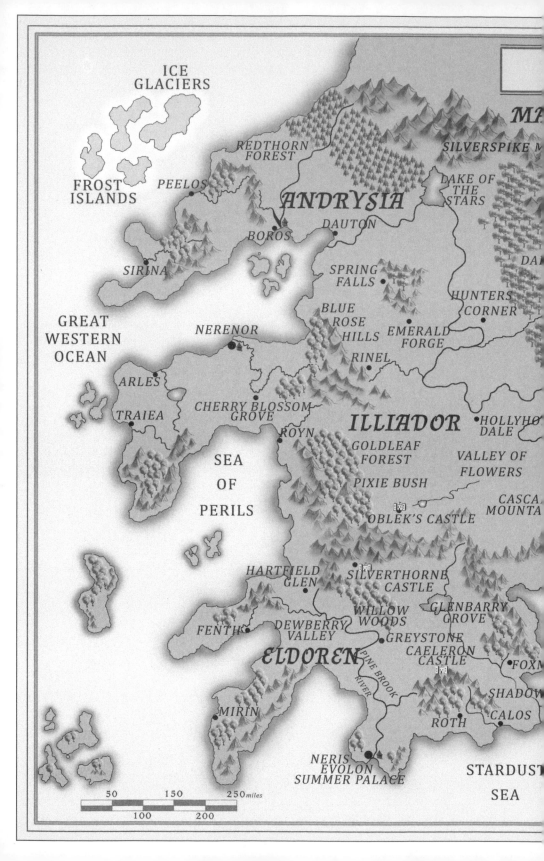

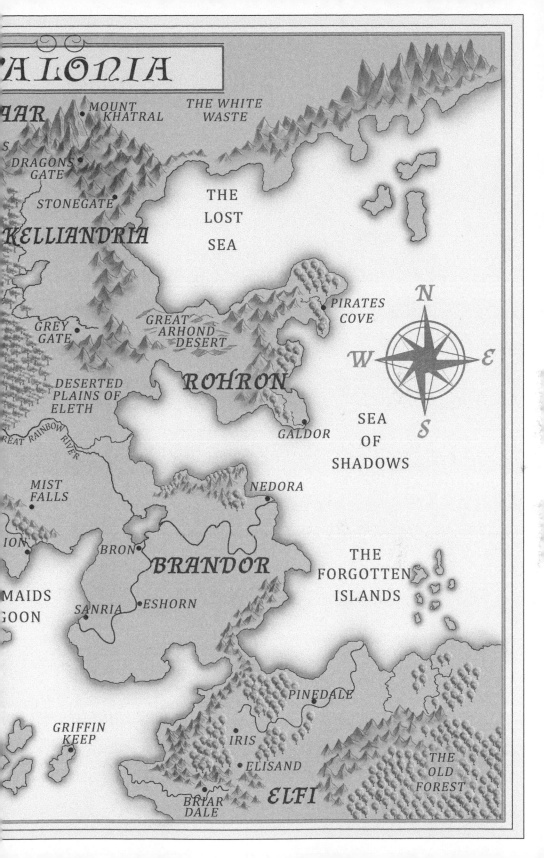

1
CHANCE

"GET UP!" said a familiar but thoroughly irritating voice. "Get up, you freak, and stop that awful shrieking."

I sat up in my bed, sweat pouring from me, my heart beating so fast it was as though I had just run a race. I knew it was only a dream, but it always felt so real, as if I had really lived through it.

I turned my head to see my angry cousin Cornelia glaring straight at me. Her perfect blonde hair was neatly brushed and pulled back with a silver headband. She was already dressed for school, with her uniform and coat on.

"It's eight o'clock, Aurora," Cornelia said. "Get up. We are so late. I don't want to get into trouble because of you again. We already missed the bus; Ms. Holden is going to have a fit. And, for God's sake, stop this screaming thing that you do every night. I just can't bear it anymore." She huffed and preened at herself in the mirror.

"Maybe you need to see a shrink," she added as an afterthought, glancing at me and turning back to her perfect reflection.

"Okay, okay, I'm up. Give me five," I muttered as I rolled

out of bed and jumped in the shower. Maybe I did need a shrink. I couldn't control the nightmares, and I had no idea why I kept having the same dream over and over again.

It all started a few months ago, on the night of my sixteenth birthday. Every time I closed my eyes, I could see my mother running down a dark corridor, carrying me in her arms. I could actually feel the heat of the flames that licked at her heels as a woman she called Morgana came rushing towards us with a gleaming dagger raised to strike. But I never knew what happened next; it always ended the same way, with a flash of light and me screaming.

I could never remember anything about my birth parents. But now this dream had started—and I couldn't understand how I knew that the blonde-haired lady in my dream was my real mother. I was adopted when I was barely two years old and was fortunate that the clothes I was wearing had my name embroidered on them when my adoptive parents found me; otherwise, I wouldn't even know what it really was.

The warm shower shook off my fears, and I struggled to get dressed as fast as I could.

Cornelia was pacing up and down the small room as I quickly pulled on my ill-fitting uniform, which consisted of a white shirt tucked into a pleated green skirt, under a moss green blazer. I wore my scruffy black shoes and gathered my books and papers from my bedside where I had left them last night. I hadn't finished my homework, and my side of the room was an absolute mess.

"Come on," Cornelia said impatiently. "Mummy sent me back up to get you."

"Where's the rest of my homework?" I asked, frantically looking around for the lost sheets of paper.

Cornelia shrugged. "The piles of crumpled sheets lying on your desk?" she asked, putting her hands on her hips.

I glared at her and nodded slowly.

"I threw them out with the trash last night after you went to sleep. Mummy said to clean the room, so I did," she said, grinning slyly.

"But those were my notes," I ground out through clenched teeth, trying very hard to keep my anger in check.

"Well, you shouldn't leave them lying all over the place if they are so important," Cornelia said, dismissing me with a wave of her hand.

"They were not lying around. They were on my desk," I said, raising my voice.

I was so angry, but there was nothing I could do. I had long since discovered that arguing with Cornelia never got me anywhere. She always wanted to have the last word and would go to any lengths to make sure that she got the better of me.

Sighing, I resigned myself to the fact that I would have to make up some plausible story about my lost homework. My history teacher was not going to be pleased.

I looked in the mirror. There was no point in bothering

with my unruly black hair, which had now grown so long it was touching my waist. Just tying it in a rough ponytail would have to suffice.

"Mummy's going to drive us to school," Cornelia said as we rushed downstairs. "You know how she hates to be kept waiting."

Aunt Arianna was standing in the kitchen, drumming her false fingernails on the counter, looking extremely irritated. Her dark, wispy hair was pulled back in an elegant bun, and her sharp, beady eyes glared daggers at me when I walked in.

I was in a bad mood myself, so I just gave her a sulky nod.

"Can't you ever be on time, Aurora?" said Aunt Arianna scathingly. "For the life of me, I cannot figure out why my husband agreed to take you in. If it were up to me, I would have sent you back to the gutter you came from."

Cornelia just smiled and nodded her head, agreeing with everything her mother said.

I flinched at her harsh words but chose to ignore them. It was too early in the morning for another fight. I knew my aunt hated me and didn't want me around. I had tried being nice and helpful, and I cleaned my room and helped with the chores, but she was still mean to me whenever she got a chance. After a while I had given up trying.

So I kept my mouth shut and got into the backseat of Aunt Arianna's battered blue Volvo. My aunt handed me a piece of toast before she started the car.

"Don't want you fainting in school because you had no

time to eat breakfast," said Arianna Darlington, shooting me a withering glare.

"Thank you," I said, taking it. I was surprised that she had even bothered.

"Don't thank me," said my aunt, meaning every word. "I didn't do it for you, I just don't want to be called into school to pick you up later today. I have a very busy day ahead, and I don't have any time for your silly fainting spells."

She started the car, as unruly tears welled in my eyes. I brushed them away quickly.

It had been two years since my adoptive parents died in a horrific car crash, and I had been staying with my father's brother, his wife, and his daughter at their London home ever since. I guess I was lucky that they agreed to be my guardians; I don't think they really had to, since I was not actually family, just adopted. But anything was better than being put in the foster system.

I couldn't wait to turn eighteen; only then would I be free of the tyranny of my Aunt Arianna and Cornelia, both of whom were also probably counting the days until I left their house. It was not for another one and a half years, and it seemed like a lifetime.

School was a disaster.

I had to hand in an incomplete homework assignment because of Cornelia, and I got a week of detention because of it. I knew Cornelia hated me just as much as her mother did, but she was much more clever and sly about it.

As the day trudged on, things got steadily worse. I failed my algebra test, got my ass kicked in basketball, and, to top it all off, I had no friends, so I had to eat lunch on my own. Just a usual crappy day.

I was sitting in the school cafeteria, minding my own business and moving a piece of dried-up meatloaf around my plate, when a mousy girl with huge glasses whose name I couldn't remember came up to my empty table and handed me a note. I took it and looked up at her, confused.

"What's this?" I asked. No one had ever given me a note before.

The girl looked embarrassed but didn't say anything. She just avoided my eyes and walked away.

I opened the note and glanced over it hurriedly. I couldn't believe this was actually happening—this was no ordinary note. It was from Alex Carrington, the most popular boy in school.

I scanned the crowded lunchroom quickly. Alex was sitting at a corner table, chatting animatedly with a group of his friends, all part of the football team. His hair was blond and cut stylishly short, and he had the bluest eyes I had ever seen.

Suddenly he looked up, and our eyes locked. He was a little taken aback, but he gave me a small smile, which I could only interpret as reassuring. I looked away quickly, embarrassed that I had been caught staring at him.

Inside my chest, my overjoyed heart started doing somersaults; I was ecstatic. Could it be possible that Alex Carrington had actually noticed me? I had had a crush on him ever since the seventh grade, but he never gave me a second glance. Until now, I thought, with a silly smile on my face.

His note said that he wanted me to go with him to Kimberly Walden's party on Friday night. But why would Alex send me a note? He could have just come over and asked me himself, since he didn't seem the note-passing type. But I could be wrong, and I wanted to get a moment alone with him. I gathered my courage and waited outside the cafeteria, preparing myself to finally talk to Alex.

He walked out of the school lunchroom surrounded by his friends and a gaggle of giggling girls, whom I recognized as some of Cornelia's friends.

"Hi Alex," I said abruptly, as he passed by me standing awkwardly alone in the hall.

Alex stopped and turned. "Well, hello there," he said, his boyish charm utterly disarming me.

"Um, I got your note," I said, a little flustered, looking down and shifting from one foot to the other. This was the first time I had actually talked to him, and I desperately wanted to make a good impression.

He raised his eyebrows. "My note?" he said, looking slightly amused.

"Yes," I said, peeping up at him.

I figured that maybe he was a bit shy and he didn't want his friends to know about us yet, so I lowered my voice and spoke quietly.

"To go to Kimberly's party on Friday," I said softly. "I just wanted to tell you in person that I would love to go with you."

To my utter dismay, Alex started laughing at me.

"Why would I go to Kimberly's party with you?" he said between guffaws.

"But the note?" I spluttered.

I fished out the note from my scruffy blue knapsack, still confused, although a growing dread had started to creep into my bewildered mind.

Alex took the note from my shaky hand, stopped laughing and scanned it quickly. Finally, he looked up.

"I didn't write this. I'm sorry, but I don't even know your name," he said, more gently this time. "I thought everyone knew I was going with Cornelia to the party."

Suddenly raucous laughter erupted behind me. I looked around, with my heart beating a thousand times faster than normal. Someone had played a cruel joke. And it didn't take a genius to figure out who it was. Cornelia and her friends were laughing their heads off at my utter humiliation.

Unshed tears welled up in my eyes and threatened to spill down my cheeks. I turned and fled down the school corridor, disappearing into the girls' bathroom, with the dissipating sounds of Cornelia's evil laughter ringing in my ears.

I was crushed, my already wobbly confidence stamped beneath Cornelia's perfectly manicured feet. I was never a popular girl in school, even when my adoptive parents were alive. But now I would be the school joke, the person everybody whispered about behind their back.

After an hour of crying and feeling sorry for myself, I finally managed to dry my tears and wash my face. I had to try and pull myself together so I could get to my next class. I looked in the mirror. My face was all blotchy, and my usually bright green eyes were dull and tinged with red.

I dragged myself out of the bathroom and managed to slip into my English class. I sat at the back, where I would not attract undue attention, and tried to listen as Mr. Roberts warbled on about the significance of Shakespeare's *As You Like It*, but my mind was elsewhere.

I knew my grades had slipped drastically, and I was working on it, but there were some days that I still could not function properly. I would just lie in my bed for hours, thinking about my adoptive parents and all the good years when I had a real family. They may not have been my birth parents, but they cared for me as if I was their real daughter.

My mind was filled with memories that I held on to like a lifeline. Picnics in the park, holidays by the sea, people who actually loved me—and then I would realize that it was gone, that I was all alone and nobody wanted me. And I would cry into my pillow at night, muffling my sobs so that Cornelia would not hear me.

I had long ago given up wondering about my birth parents: who they were and why they gave me up. No one ever had any answers, and soon I stopped asking altogether. But now I was having this dream, and I didn't know if it was a real memory or just a figment of my imagination. I tried not to think about it, but the mysterious woman in a crimson cloak who held a dagger to my mother's heart seemed all too real.

The medallion I wore around my neck was my only link to my birth parents, and I never took it off. It was all I had with me when I was adopted. I turned it around between my fingers. It looked like a small gold coin. But the carvings on it were in a script that I could not recognize. It was my lucky charm, and, although it wasn't much, just having it with me made me feel safe.

"Aurora Darlington," came the crisp voice of Ms. Holden, the headmistress of my school, snapping me jarringly out of my reverie. I looked up. I hadn't even noticed her come into the classroom.

What had I done now? I wasn't exactly the best student these days. I knew that. But I had made it a point to scrape through just enough to stay out of the headmistress's office until now.

"Aurora, I'd like to see you in my office," said Ms. Holden. She nodded perfunctorily at the bespectacled Mr. Roberts, who looked utterly terrified of her, and walked out of the room.

I gathered my books and bag and got up from my desk. A few girls sniggered behind me, but I was used to it. Ever since my parents died, everyone spoke to me in hushed voices, as if I might crack any minute, or they talked and whispered about me behind my back. I had learned to ignore it and move on.

Nothing, however, could be worse than the humiliation I had experienced earlier today at the hands of my horrible cousin. Now I knew exactly what they were laughing about. I hung my head and hurried out of the classroom.

Headmistress Holden's office was much smaller than I had expected. As I closed the door behind me, I noticed a man was sitting in one of the chairs with his back towards me. Ms. Holden went and sat down opposite him and directed me to the chair near the man. I walked forward and turned to stare at the familiar face of my uncle, Christopher Darlington.

He had a long, angular face, with dark brooding eyes hidden behind horn-rimmed glasses. His hair was a dirty blond color, like wet sand. He was wearing his usual grey pinstripe suit and was dabbing his sweaty forehead with a crumpled handkerchief, which he dug out of his pocket.

What was he doing here? Was I in trouble?

"Good afternoon, Aurora," said my uncle.

I nodded at him.

Christopher didn't hate me like my aunt and cousin, but most of the time he treated me like I wasn't even there. He

11

wasn't mean to me, but he never stood up for me either. We barely said two words to each other, and I only saw him at dinnertime. He worked at a bank or something and was out of the house before I woke up.

Ms. Holden cleared her throat before she began.

"Aurora, my dear," Ms. Holden said, in a voice so different from her usual rude, clipped tones that I was momentarily taken aback. She always had a sour look on her face, as though she had just eaten a whole bowl of lemons. I had never even seen a flicker of a smile on her face, and now she was grinning away like her life depended on it.

I stared at her and back at my uncle. What was he doing here? What had I done now?

"Now Aurora," said Ms. Holden, "your uncle has requested for you to take a leave of absence from school."

"What! Why? Right now?" I blurted out. No one had said anything about this.

"Let me finish," said Ms. Holden sternly. "Your grades have been steadily slipping and you have barely passed most of your classes this year. Nevertheless, I have decided to grant you leave this time, since your uncle has explained the circumstances."

"Which are?" I asked, looking at my uncle, who remained quiet.

"I am sure your uncle will explain it to you," Ms. Holden said.

It was strange; my uncle hadn't mentioned anything last

night at dinner. I decided I would ask him later. And I wasn't too disappointed; after all, missing so many days of school would be great. And that meant I would be away from all the pointing and whispering, which had been happening since the whole school heard about my incident with Alex Carrington.

Ms. Holden and my uncle stood up and shook hands.

"Thank you," said Uncle Christopher to my headmistress. "You have been most helpful. I will have her back in a few days."

He walked across the room and opened the door. "Come on, Aurora, we have a busy day ahead," he said, exiting the principal's gloomy office.

I remained silent, gathered my things, and followed my uncle out of the school. I had no idea what was going on, but I was sure I was going to find out soon enough.

2
REDSTONE MANOR

As SOON AS we got home, I packed my meager belongings—a few jeans and T-shirts, an old tracksuit of Cornelia's, a pair of pajamas, and my toothbrush—in an old duffel bag that Aunt Arianna had found for me from the attic. It was splitting at the seams and the handle was torn, but somehow I managed to lug it down the stairs and out onto the street.

My uncle had explained that we were all going on a trip. He and the family had been invited to his boss's country house for a few days, and Uncle Christopher insisted that we leave immediately.

This was why I was pulled out of school? What was so important that it couldn't wait until the holidays? And how come they were taking me with them?

The last time they went away, Aunt Arianna left me with Mrs. Haversham, who lived across the street. She had two uncontrollable little children, and, in way of payment for my room and food, I had to babysit the little devils. It wasn't that I didn't like children, but seven-year-old twin boys were a bit more than I could handle.

A big black Range Rover was parked outside the house.

Uncle Christopher was sitting in the front passenger seat, and a chauffeur in a hat got out and opened the door for me to get in. I handed the chauffeur my luggage and got into the roomy back seat, where Aunt Arianna and Cornelia were waiting.

We drove at a leisurely pace at first, due to the traffic while leaving the city. But within half an hour I could see Windsor Castle rising up in the distance above the treetops, and soon we were in the countryside. Uncle Christopher had said it was going to be a long journey, so I closed my eyes and decided to nap.

When I woke up with a crick in my neck, we were driving past meadows and farms and acres of woods. I had no idea which part of the country we were in. It had suddenly become colder, and there was a nip in the air. Although it was spring, the weather was temperamental. I looked out at the trees whizzing past and shivered a little as I pulled my favorite brown leather jacket closer around me.

It was a cold and gloomy spring evening. As we finally neared our destination, a light mist rolled around our car as if searching for a way to get in. I peered out of the backseat window. No house in sight! Not that you could see much with twilight just setting in.

We must have been traveling for hours, and I was exhausted.

"Another few minutes and you will be able to see the house," said Uncle Christopher chirpily, as if the long journey hadn't affected him in the least.

Cornelia didn't even bother to look up; she just huffed and continued texting away on her new iPhone.

When the house finally came into view, I was taken aback. For the first time, I had to admit that Uncle Christopher was right to get so excited. The "house," as my uncle called it, was not just a house—it was a massive, centuries-old structure called Redstone Manor.

As we drove through the gargantuan iron gates and up the long gravel driveway lined with old spruces and ancient oak trees, Uncle Christopher chattered on in his irritating nasal voice.

"Redstone Manor was built three hundred years ago, and it has been in my boss's family ever since," he said proudly, as if he had something to do with it.

It was a huge pile of high walls, turrets, massive pointed gables, and pinnacles with ornate chimney stacks. It looked more like a mini castle than a house. Ivy and creepers climbed the walls, and massive arched windows embellished with decorative panels lined the sprawling structure. It was absolutely enchanting.

"Welcome to Redstone Manor," said my uncle.

As we drove up to the massive front door of the house, I was excited. I had never been inside a real English manor house before, and I was looking forward to exploring the property.

A thin, stern-looking lady with spectacles and a severe white bun was standing at the top of the steps to greet us. She introduced herself as the housekeeper, Mrs. Pitts. Standing to her right was a portly man, smartly dressed, with his shoes polished to perfection. He was Mr. Martins, the butler.

"Welcome to Redstone Manor, Mr. Darlington," he said.

"Yes, yes, glad to be here," said Christopher, puffing out his chest. He was obviously feeling very important right about now. I wondered what his boss was like. His house was nice, that's for sure.

Uncle Christopher cleared his throat. "When will I be able to meet Lord Oblek?" he asked.

"His Lordship was delayed. He will meet with you tomorrow when he returns," said Mr. Martins.

"Follow me and I will show you to your rooms," said Mrs. Pitts crisply. "I will have some food brought up to you, as you must be tired from your long journey. The footmen will take your luggage up to your rooms."

My uncle and aunt nodded and beamed as if they were walking into Buckingham Palace. We followed the housekeeper up the broad stone steps and into the massive house.

The great arched wooden doors opened into a massive foyer, which had a grand staircase that led to the upper floors. Statues and huge paintings lined the walls of the mahogany-paneled corridors, but I hardly noticed. I just fiddled with my medallion and followed Mrs. Pitts, my mind on other things.

I couldn't understand what we were doing here. Uncle Christopher worked at a bank. Did he really work for the person who owned this house? And why did the butler refer to this Oblek guy as His Lordship? Was he a lord? An earl? A duke? It was all very strange. How would my uncle know a lord of the realm?

Mrs. Pitts showed me to my room and left me to unpack and freshen up. Cornelia and I had a whole suite of rooms, with two bedrooms and a large comfortable living room.

My bedroom was beautifully decorated with green-and-pink flowered wallpaper and matching curtains. Cornelia's room, which was even bigger than mine, adjoined the living room on the other side, opposite my room. I didn't want her presence to spoil my experience here. I had already decided that I was going to make the most of this place. I liked history and being in a house this old made me very curious to explore.

I wandered around the room and sat on the edge of my bed. I wished for the thousandth time that my life were different, that somehow my adoptive parents hadn't died in the car crash. I even wondered occasionally what my life would have been like if my birth parents hadn't given me up. Definitely better than this, I was sure. But it was no use wondering; it was not going to bring anybody back.

There was a tray laid out in the living room, so I had a little of the tomato soup and two of the chicken sandwiches, which were very good.

I left my mobile phone on the bed and went for a shower. We had been traveling in the car for most of the day, and I was tired. I couldn't sleep, however, without reading for a while, so I decided to go and look for a book after dinner. Surely a house this large and old had a library.

After I had my bath and changed into my pajamas I put on my pink fleece dressing gown and resolved to wander around the house.

I walked quickly down the long corridors of the massive manor house, occasionally passing white-capped maids in uniform shuffling busily out of rooms, arms laden with linens or clothes. Moonlight streamed in through the windows, and the corridor ahead was illuminated by a spectral white sheen. Finally I stopped one of the maids and asked for directions. I was pointed towards another, darker wing of the house.

It was eerie in the east wing, and cobwebs hung in the corners of the shadowy corridors. I tried a few doors and found myself in various stuffy rooms with white dust covers that obscured the furniture. This part of the house looked like it hadn't been lived in for a long time, and the rooms smelled musty and unused.

I nearly gave up my search when finally I came across huge wooden double doors at the end of the corridor. I pushed the heavy door open slightly and peered inside.

This was it, the library. Great, finally! Now if only I could find a good book.

The beautiful, oak-lined library was a remarkable space. It was the only room in this part of the house that looked like it was cleaned every day and pristinely kept. A first-floor gallery ran along one side of the gigantic room, adorned by an intricately crafted, church-like ceiling. Two large leather armchairs were placed on opposite sides of a small round mahogany reading table, and the wooden floor was covered with plush Persian rugs. Along one wall, two immense bay windows, both hosting a comfortable cushion-covered window seat, overlooked the vast manicured gardens of Redstone Manor.

Perfect for reading.

As I walked further into the gigantic library, I looked over to the wall at the very end of the room and was immediately mesmerized. The entire wall at the far end was covered with a huge tapestry that dominated the whole space. It was a delicate and elaborate weave, depicting a dark forest surrounding a crystal-clear lake, with a magical castle glistening in the distance.

Now I was positive that this was my favorite room in the house. I turned back to the bookshelves. Redstone Manor had an excellent collection.

Where to start? The walls of the enormous room were packed from top to bottom with shelves, filled with a seemingly countless array of books. Some were newly bought, and some looked as though they must have come with the house many centuries ago. This was like a dream come true.

Just as I found the complete Chronicles of Narnia, I heard someone at the door. I don't know what came over me, but I panicked and dove behind one of the large leather armchairs. I knew I was not doing anything wrong—just borrowing a book—but I still felt spooked.

I peered out from behind my hiding place, feeling immensely stupid.

It was my Uncle Christopher. I tensed. Maybe he had come down to choose a book himself? That seemed like a reasonable explanation. I was about to come out from behind the chair and announce myself when I realized that he wasn't going towards the books, but towards the tapestry.

What was he up to?

My uncle stood unmoving in front of the tapestry and stared at it. I stayed where I was because I had no idea what he was doing and I didn't want to startle him. He might get angry. I looked over towards the double doors of the library. They were shut, and there was no way I could leave the room without Uncle Christopher noticing.

So I crouched and waited.

My uncle was definitely acting very oddly. That was clear when he held out his arms, palms facing outward and touched the tapestry. As he did that I felt a breeze enter the room.

I turned to the windows, but they were shut. A rustling noise startled me and I looked back towards my uncle. My mouth fell open, as I stared mutely at the scene unfolding in front of my eyes.

The tapestry on the wall was shimmering like moonlight on water, while the rustling noise and the breeze were coming from inside it. I spotted the bushes in the tapestry moving slightly, and sudden, strange ripples started forming in the fabric, expanding from the middle, like when you throw a pebble in a pond. Quite unexpectedly, a big booted leg and an arm came through the tapestry. Slowly, finally, a whole body emerged.

I had to clap my hand over my mouth to prevent myself from gasping aloud. I couldn't believe what I was seeing. A big, bearded, rough-looking man in a battered fur-lined black cloak, with a patch over one eye and a massive sword that swung at his rather large waist, had just stepped out of the tapestry, and into the library of Redstone Manor.

Everything happened so quickly, I couldn't even think. I knew I should say something and excuse myself, but then my uncle might think I was spying on him. So I decided to remain where I was for the moment. In fact, I was too fascinated to do anything more than crouch behind the large leather armchair and see what happened next.

Finally the stranger spoke. "Christopher, do you have the girl?" he said, his voice a deep rumble. He looked mean, with a patch over one eye and numerous scars, which crisscrossed his bearded face.

For a moment I wondered what had happened to him

to disfigure him so. But then my thoughts whirled quickly back to the main question clamoring in my head. How on earth did he appear out of the tapestry? Then more questions whirled through my confused mind. What was on the other side? Who was this man? And what girl were they talking about?

"Lord Oblek," said Christopher, bowing slightly to the black-cloaked man. "I have brought her."

The rough-looking man called Oblek stared at my uncle, his one good eye widening in expectation. "Is she here, in the house?" he said.

"Yes," Christopher replied, quickly stepping back.

I could tell my uncle was nervous.

I couldn't understand who or what they were talking about, but I started to get a really bad feeling that I wasn't going to like it.

"Are you sure she's the right one?" Uncle Christopher asked.

"Yes, of course I'm sure," said Oblek, in a condescending tone. "Would I have wasted years of my life searching for her, only to find the wrong girl? Come on, Christopher, you know I am smarter than that. Imagine my delight when I found out she was your niece. Well, your adopted niece anyway."

My uncle Christopher nodded and dabbed his perspiring head with a purple handkerchief.

I couldn't believe what I had just heard. They were talk-

23

ing about me. Uncle Christopher had no other nieces that I knew of. Why would this strange man be looking for me? This made no sense.

Oblek grinned and clasped his hands together. "Finally I will deliver the girl to the queen and she will reward me beyond all imagination."

"Yes, yes, you can do what you like with her," smirked Christopher, "but not before you pay me my fee. It has become quite considerable now, seeing as I will have to answer many questions about her when she's gone."

Gone? Where was I going?

"You'll get your money," said the wily Oblek. "But only after I have the girl in my possession. When is the earliest you can get her to me?"

"Arianna will bring here down here at midnight," said Christopher.

I wasn't surprised to learn that Aunt Arianna was involved in this. She wanted to get rid of me ever since I moved in with her, but I thought Uncle Christopher liked me. I couldn't believe how wrong I was. There was absolutely no one I could trust.

Suddenly my foot cramped. I gasped, clutched at it, and started rubbing, but I had to change my position. I moved ever so slowly, adjusting myself behind the armchair, but it was a futile attempt. My shuffling had created a noise, and I knew I had been heard.

"Someone's here," said Oblek, whirling round, his hand

on the hilt of his massive sword.

I moved backwards, but there was nowhere to go. I was trapped.

Christopher came over quickly, grabbed me by the arm and pulled me up from my crouching position.

"Don't you know that it's bad manners to eavesdrop, young lady?" said my uncle, angrily. His floppy gold hair was a mess; he was fuming, and his glasses were steaming up.

"What have we here?" asked Lord Oblek, his one beady, black eye fixating on me with a scrutinizing glare as he walked slowly towards me.

"It's the girl you have been searching for, my lord," said Uncle Christopher, with a slimy smile on his reddened face. He pulled me along towards Oblek, clutching my arm with his bony fingers, which bit into my skin like needles.

"Hey, that hurts," I said, trying to pull my arm free from his grasp, but he didn't let go.

"So, it seems your work has been done for you, Christopher. She has been delivered to us of her own accord," said Oblek, his arms crossed across his chest.

"I'm not a package to be delivered anywhere," I said through gritted teeth. "You have the wrong girl. I don't even know you."

"Ah, but I know you, Aurora Firedrake," said Oblek.

"What nonsense. That's not even my name. I'm Aurora Darlington," I insisted. "I told you, you have the wrong girl."

Lord Oblek ignored me and spoke to my uncle. "She has

25

a strong likeness to her father—the same dark hair and green eyes of the Firedrakes. She is definitely the one. I don't know how she stayed hidden all these years, but she is Azaren's only child. I am sure of it."

My mind reeled with the implications of this revelation. I longed to know who my real parents were, and this person here seemed to know them, however dangerous he looked.

"Let go of my arm," I said to Christopher, trying to twist out of his vise-like grip.

He just laughed at me and held on tighter, so I punched him in the stomach, and he released me, momentarily stunned as he bent over. I took my chance and made a dash for the door, but my uncle recovered quickly, caught me again and slapped me across my face. My neck whipped to one side with the force of the blow. I had lost my chance, and Uncle Christopher dragged me back to Oblek, who stood watching all this calmly.

"Interesting!" said Oblek, coming closer to me and staring me down. "A feisty little thing, isn't she? I must get her to the queen immediately; there is no time to waste."

What queen? What the hell was this guy going on about? Why was he after me? And where did he want to take me?

He stepped closer to me, and I instinctively shrank away. His breath was rancid, and his rotting teeth grinned at me through the mess of his black beard.

"You're not taking her anywhere until you get me my money," Christopher said, holding on to me like a lottery ticket. He started edging away from Oblek, towards the door, pulling me along with him. "I want what I was promised."

"And you can't take me anywhere I don't want to go," I added for good measure. Not that it was any help.

"Oh, you'll get what you deserve," said Oblek, an evil grin spreading across his hideous, scarred face. Faster than I could follow, Oblek raised his right hand, and white bolts of light shot out from his palm, hitting Christopher squarely in the chest. His grip loosened immediately on my arm, and my uncle crumpled to the floor like an empty sack.

Oblek closed the space between us in a trice. "And you, my dear, don't have a choice," said Oblek, as he closed his big, beefy hand around my arm.

I stared at the crumpled form of my uncle on the floor. He looked dead. Did this weird guy just shoot white light from his palms?

"You killed him?" I gasped, still shocked at what I had witnessed.

"It doesn't matter. I just needed him out of the way," said Oblek, not giving Uncle Christopher another thought.

All this was happening so fast; I couldn't understand what this had to do with me. I wanted to find out more about my real parents, but I didn't want to go anywhere with this horrible person. Who knows what he had planned for me?

"I'm not coming with you," I said, trying to pull away from him. "You're a monster." But he held my arm in an even tighter grip than my uncle had.

Oblek laughed. "You haven't seen anything yet, girl," he said. "Where you're going, monsters will be the least of your problems."

"What do you mean?" I asked, my voice cracking. My legs felt shaky, and I was now bordering on the edge of panic. Where was he taking me?

"You will find out soon enough," Oblek said, grinning.

He pulled me towards the tapestry that shimmered as soon as he touched it with his palm.

I felt like my life had just shattered all over again. My parents were gone, my uncle had just sold me like a slave, and there was no one to help me, no one on my side. I was alone, I was in trouble, and I had absolutely no idea what to do. It was all too much, I couldn't help it; I burst into tears just as Oblek yanked my arm and pulled me into the magical, shimmering tapestry.

3
KIDNAPPED

FOR A SECOND that felt like a lifetime, everything stopped; I felt like I was floating in nothingness. Then I blinked, and, when I finally opened my eyes and focused again through the tears, I couldn't believe what I was seeing.

I found myself standing at the mouth of a small cave situated on a hill and overlooking a quiet, moonlit valley. On my left, a dark forest stretched out as far as the eye could see, treetops glistening silver in the light of the full moon. The hills around us undulated into wildflower-filled meadows that lay sleeping in the dewy night.

Far down in the valley, I could see a little village, its lights twinkling in the distance. To my right, a waterfall splashed playfully into a small river that ran down into a lake, next to which the little village was built. The moon here was fuller and larger than I had ever seen it, and the night sky was awash with a fantastic array of glittering stars.

Had I passed through the tapestry? Where was I?

I looked around, disbelief clouding my judgment. I was still trying to get my bearings after that strange moment when I had been inside the tapestry and nowhere at the same time. It gave me a funny feeling, as though I had been lifted out of my own consciousness and then put back into my body.

A warm breeze brushed past my face and played with my hair. Gone were the cloudy grey mist and the cold, nipping wind of the English countryside. I drew in a sharp breath— the air was crisp and clear, sweet smelling, and fresh. The moonlit valley was filled with fruit trees, wildflowers, and rolling meadows.

"How did we come here? Where are we?" I asked, still confused.

"You really are ignorant," said Oblek, glancing at me. "I take it your uncle didn't tell you anything?"

I shook my head and looked down. Oblek had tied my hands with a rope he had with him while I was still dazed and looking around. It was humiliating, and the rough ropes cut into my wrists, rubbing them raw every time he pulled me forward.

I had to find some way out of this. And, at the moment, the only thing I could do was discover more about where I was. Then, when I got an opportunity, I could escape and find my way back up to the cave on the hill, where we had arrived out of the tapestry.

But then what?

Christopher was probably dead, and Aunt Arianna would doubtless blame me for everything since I had disappeared at the same time. I had no idea what to do. I didn't really want to go back, and, now that my adoptive parents were dead, I had nothing to return to.

I was starting to panic. I had nowhere to go, and my mind was imagining an array of horrible outcomes of my kidnapping. My palms had become sweaty, and my racing heart was thundering in my chest as I half-walked and half-ran, desperately trying to keep up with Oblek's giant strides.

"Why are you doing this?" I pleaded with my kidnapper.

But Lord Oblek said nothing. He didn't even look at me. He just kept walking ahead and dragging me along behind him, with no more explanations as to what he was planning to do with me.

I was terrified, and I had no idea if I was going to survive this. But I tried to be brave. Maybe I could talk my way out of this?

"You do know that this is called kidnapping?" I said, trying to reason with Oblek.

He didn't bother to answer.

"What will happen to me now?" I squeaked, my voice breaking, as I tried not to cry.

"Queen Morgana will decide what is to be done with you," said Oblek, finally.

Queen Morgana! The woman from my dream? It was not possible that this, too, was a coincidence. It must be the same Morgana, the one who had tried to kill my real mother.

Who the hell was she?

Suddenly all of this seemed extremely scary. I hoped that

I was still dreaming and that there was no way I had actually traveled through a magical tapestry into some strange land. It all seemed very exciting in books. But actually being kidnapped and then hauled around like an animal, traveling deep into a land I knew nothing about, was not my idea of fun.

I had to get away from this horrible man, and fast.

I wanted to find out more, but I was getting tired as I trudged along behind Oblek. My legs were aching, and my fluffy slippers were wet and dirty. I wondered how much longer we would have to walk.

"Where are you taking me?" I pleaded, running helplessly behind him. "Please, you don't have to do this, just let me go. I won't go to the police, I promise. Just let me go."

Oblek suddenly turned towards me to say something. I realized that was my chance, and I took it. I kicked him on his shin, yanked the rope out of his hands, and tried to make my escape, but Oblek hardly felt it; he quickly caught the end of the rope that he had tied around my hands and pulled on it hard, which made me spin around and fall forward onto my hands and knees.

Oblek sneered at me lying in the mud and held out his huge beefy right hand, curling his fingers as if he was catching something in the air in front of him. Suddenly I felt an invisible hand grab my throat. I choked and gagged as Oblek slowly cut off my air supply, clawing at the invisible hand and trying to wrench myself free. It was no use; he was using his magic again. The invisible hand was pulling me to my feet, lifting me up by my throat. I was terrified and tried to scream, but only choking sobs escaped my parched lips. I was feeling dizzy as I gasped for air, the world swimming before my eyes, and I was sure I was about to die.

Finally, after moments that felt like hours, he loosened his invisible grip on my neck. I landed on my knees, and, with a flick of his hand, Oblek pushed me backwards. I fell on my back and clutched at my neck as I gasped for air.

He had tried to kill me. This guy was truly a monster, a real thug. What the hell had I got myself mixed up in?

"That was only a warning, you foolish girl," said the evil Oblek. "The next time you try to escape, you will not be so lucky. The queen may want you alive, but she never specified your condition. I am quite sure she will not mind if you are missing a few body parts."

I started trembling. This guy was serious, and he was really going to hurt me if I didn't comply. I had no choice as he started pulling on the rope; I had to get up or risk being dragged along behind him all the way. I tried to calm my galloping heart and concentrated on just putting one foot in front of the other.

After a while, I had already fallen countless times, and my hands and knees were bleeding. Aching all over, I struggled to keep up. If I didn't or if I tried to get away, there was no telling what Oblek might do to me. Tears were streaming down my face as I ran behind him. Shaking and sobbing, I tried to stem the flow and pull myself together.

I followed Oblek down the hill and into the valley. I could see well enough because of the full moon, but the shrubs and bushes snagged and tore at my clothes as he led me along a muddy path that skirted the edge of the woods.

"Please, can't you at least tell me where we're going?" I pleaded again.

To my surprise, Oblek replied.

"Tonight we will stop at my castle," he said, "and at daybreak tomorrow we will ride for Nerenor. The queen will be eager to see you." He turned and grinned maliciously at me. I noticed through all the confusion in my mind that some of his rotting teeth were missing.

"Will we be riding . . . horses?" I asked, understanding slowly dawning.

"Yes, of course," he said, looking momentarily bewildered. "Why would you ask such a stupid question? Ah yes, in your world you have, what do you call them . . . " He snapped his fingers as if trying to remember. " . . . Those funny carriages you call cars to get around."

He yanked the rope and pulled me along again.

"Never really liked your world," he continued. "And I seldom go there; that's why I get people like your uncle to do my work for me."

I looked at him, astonished, as the bitter realities started seeping into my sleep-deprived brain. This world had no cars, probably had no electricity or running water, and was ruled by a queen who sounded like an evil tyrant. It looked like I had been wrenched into the dark ages.

How would I survive here, even if I did manage to get away from Oblek?

We walked the rest of the way in silence. I was exhausted and had abandoned my wet, muddy slippers somewhere along the way. My feet were cut all over and bleeding. I couldn't help it as big fat tears rolled down my face, but Oblek didn't care. He just pulled me along like a dog on a leash.

It was still dark when we finally reached his castle. It was nothing like Redstone Manor or the surrounding countryside that I had seen when I came into this world through the tapestry. The castle was bleak and sinister, and it stood out like a charred, ash-covered rock amidst a green, flowering valley.

At first glance I could tell it was an incredibly ugly structure. High stone walls surrounded the main tower, and a dirty, moss-covered moat encircled the castle on all sides. The keep was flat, squat, and covered in blackened vines and creepers. I shuddered as he led me towards the terrible place. A thick, gnarled forest stretched out behind it, and numerous guards were posted on the battlements.

I wasn't sure what to expect now. I wiped my face with my sleeve as best I could. My feet were burning, and I was not sure how much more of this treatment I could take. I wished for a warm bed and some food, but was not sure if I would get either.

A big wooden drawbridge swung down in front of us. The guards, recognizing their liege lord, had signaled the gate-keeper to lower the bridge. We entered a walled courtyard, and I stumbled to a stop behind Oblek.

I gingerly looked around. A big stone fountain of a goat-like creature spouting water dominated the central space. Looking up, I could see people peering out of the windows that surrounded the courtyard. I wondered if there was any-one there I could ask for help, but I doubted it.

"Guards!" commanded Oblek, without looking at me. "Take her to the dungeons. No one is to speak to this pris-oner, or it will cost them their head. Is that understood?"

The guards nodded and scurried to catch hold of my arms, one on each side. There was no use struggling—even if I did get free, where could I go?

"The pit has other prisoners, milord," said one scrawny guard with long, matted black hair, whose filthy hand was wrapped around my arm. "And all the other cells are full."

"Just put her in the pit," said Oblek. "The prisoners down there are to be executed at dawn, so anything she says will go with them to their grave."

The guards took me down the grey stone corridors and dark steps that led to the dungeons. They shoved and pushed me the whole way, even though I wasn't resisting. I had start-ed crying again and tried to cover my sobs, but the guards heard me, and they sneered and laughed as they thrust me down the stairs into the depths of the stone castle.

It was damp and dark down in the dungeons, where the air reeked of rotting food and other horrible things that I didn't even want to know about. I could hear moans and strange screeching noises coming from some of the other cells. I tried to ignore the sounds as the guards unlocked another door, which led deeper underground.

As I walked past the iron-barred dungeon cells, a thin, wrinkled hand shot out from between one of the bars and grabbed me. Shooting pain lanced through my arm as the hand clutched at me, digging long, dirty black fingernails into my skin.

A shriek of laughter made me look up. The weathered hand belonged to a gnarled, white-haired woman. Her face was brown and wrinkled like old leather, and her eyes were completely white. Was she blind?

"Finally she has come!" she shrieked.

"Shut up, old woman," said a guard angrily. He leaned over and pried her fingers off me. I was stunned and shaken as I was dragged to my doom.

The old woman didn't stop; she went on screaming, "She has come, she has come!"

Shrieks of cackling laughter followed me as I was led deeper down into the pit, the lowest and most horrible part of the dungeons. Obviously the old woman was mad. She couldn't even see me, but still, I was shaking.

The guards looked at me suspiciously as they shoved me

roughly into a cold, dark cell. The guards left, their booted feet thumping on the stone floor. I heard the wooden dungeon door creak and slam shut. Even the cackling laughter of the old woman dissipated, then . . . silence.

4
THE BLACK WOLF

I WAS SCARED and alone in a dark dungeon cell, and I didn't have any idea where exactly I was. There was no one to call, no one to help me or pronounce me missing. I sat down on the hard stone floor, huddled in the corner, and cried silently.

But I was not really alone.

I heard some scuffling.

Who else was in here with me? I started to panic all over again.

I looked around, my eyes adjusting to the darkness. Moonlight streamed in through a small barred window, which was high up on one wall of the dungeon cell.

"Who's there?" I asked tentatively. It seemed like the smart thing to do, but who knew what kinds of criminals were locked in here with me?

A young boy about my age stepped out from the shadows. At least he seemed to be about my age. He was tall and lanky, with blond hair that was more silver than gold and that reached past his shoulders.

"Good eve to you, my lady," said the boy.

Another person with dark hair stood motionless, leaning against a wall and hidden in shadows; I couldn't see his face clearly.

"We mean you no harm," said the first boy. "I am Kalen, and the quiet one over there is my friend, Finn. Don't worry about him, he's just upset at being caught." He stopped to take a breath and, before I could say anything, he started talking again. "Not to say that I am not upset too, but Mother always says there is no use worrying about something you have no control over. What is going to happen, will happen."

"Do you have to be so cheerful all the time, Kalen? We are in Oblek's dungeon. You know no one gets out of here alive," said Finn from the shadows.

Kalen looked hurt.

I wiped my own tears and got up from my corner, slowly moving closer to Kalen. Finn looked a little sheepish and stepped back into the shadows.

I instinctively liked Kalen. He talked strangely and extremely fast, but I could tell immediately he was a sincere person. I looked closely at him and his friend. When the moon shone through the window, they looked alike. Sleek, silvery-gold hair, bright violet eyes, and . . . oh! Kalen's eyes had just changed color, from violet to silver and back, while he was talking to me. And I wasn't sure if I was just imagining it, but I could swear that his ears were slightly pointed.

I shook my head dumbly. Was I seeing things?

"What exactly are you?" I asked quietly.

Kalen grinned. "Never seen one of the fae before, have you?" he asked gently.

"Fae?" I repeated.

"Yes, fae," he said, smiling again. "In the seven kingdoms we are sometimes referred to as fairies."

My eyes grew wide. Fairies. Was he serious? He couldn't be. I knew it wasn't possible—fairies don't exist. But I thought magical worlds didn't exist too, and look how wrong I turned out to be there.

Why had Oblek locked them up in the dungeons? He had even said that they were to be executed at dawn. Were they dangerous? I had no idea who to trust, but, if Oblek wanted them dead, then at least I knew they were not on Morgana's side.

Kalen started talking again. "You don't seem to be from around these parts," he said, looking at me more closely.

I shook my head, what could I say? That until tonight I never knew that this strange land existed? Could I trust them? I decided that maybe I could trust Kalen, but the other fae boy, Finn, looked like he would be a problem.

"So, um, you are both fairies?" I said, glancing at Finn.

"Yes, although most of us prefer to be called fae," said Kalen proudly, sticking out his puny chest. "Where are you from?" he continued, but obviously became tired of waiting for an answer and proceeded to answer his own question. "Probably from Andrysia or Kelliandria. Or maybe you are a tribal princess captured from Rohron? Although I thought the people from Rohron had dark skin."

I just nodded, intentionally silent. Where the hell was I? I wished I had a map of this world.

"Do you live nearby?" I asked, trying to move the conversation away from myself.

"Yes, and we are some of the last few left in Illiador. Most of the fae live in Elfi now," said Kalen.

"Elfi?" I repeated after him, sounding very silly, even to myself.

"Surely you have heard of the land of Elfi, the kingdom of the fae that lies to the south?" said Kalen.

"Oh, that Elfi," I said, trying to cover my lack of knowledge. "Yes, yes, of course I know Elfi, kingdom of the fae." I was talking quickly—too quickly—and the other boy, or fae or whatever, was looking at me with an unfriendly glare.

"Ever since Morgana became queen, our kind have been tortured, brutalized, and killed. We've been run out of our homes, had our festivals banned, and had our houses burned. Some say that Morgana is trying to run all the fae out of Illiador, since so many have left these lands and gone back to our homeland. Our village is the last one left."

"That's enough," said Finn. "Kalen, you can't tell her everything; she may be one of them. Who knows why they have put her in here?"

Again Kalen looked worried and his eyes turned silver. I felt sorry for him. It wasn't his fault, he just talked too much, and his tongue had obviously run away from him countless times before. I decided I needed to trust someone. I had no idea where I was or why I was sitting in a dungeon.

"Isn't there any way we can escape from here?" I asked Kalen finally, in a whisper.

He stared at me as if I had grown horns.

"Do you have magic?" he asked. "Are you a mage?"

My eyes widened. "Magic?" I repeated.

What was a mage? I had read about magicians—was this the same? Was Oblek a mage? He had some sort of magic—I had seen him use it on Christopher, and I had felt it when he tried to choke the life out of me.

"I am not a mage," I said quickly, trying to cover up my dumbfounded look. "I am just an ordinary girl, and I need to get away from Lord Oblek, or he is going to take me to Queen Morgana." I hoped that using their hatred for Morgana would spur them to help me.

"Why, what did you do?" Kalen asked, his eyes wide.

"I didn't do anything. It's because of my family," I said, not wanting to say too much. Not that I knew much to begin with. I still wasn't sure whom I could trust here, but these fae definitely seemed like a safer bet than that horrible Oblek.

"So who is your family?" asked, Finn moving out of the shadows. "Oblek would not have abducted just any girl. If we manage to escape, and you are with us, Oblek will have guards everywhere looking for you, so you will not get far. He must be planning to ransom you, not kill you. Just wait for your family to pay him and you will be able to go home.

We, on the other hand, are to be executed at dawn." There was an edge to his voice.

"No, you don't understand," I said desperately. "He said very clearly that he will take me to Morgana. Please, there must be a way out of this place."

"No one leaves Oblek's dungeons alive. There is no way out," said Finn, glaring at me.

"Don't scare her, Finn," said Kalen in my defense, moving in front of me, as if to shield me from him.

I couldn't understand what I had done to make Finn dislike me, but I was more concerned with how we were going to get out of that dungeon. I turned to Kalen. "Don't you want to find a way out? You said yourself that you are to be executed at dawn," I said. "Don't any of you have magic? I thought all fairies—sorry, fae—would have magic?"

Kalen looked at me intently. "It's a little more complicated than that. Not all fae have the same sort of magic. And we are still young—babies, really—in the fae world. Our magic may not emerge for many years to come."

I hung my head. We had no plan and no weapons, and Kalen and Finn didn't look like they were old enough to fight the guards. We were doomed. I sat down on the cold stone floor, hugging my legs. I clasped my medallion in my palm for comfort. I couldn't help a few tears from escaping again, and I brushed them away with the back of my hand, irritated at myself for being so utterly useless.

Kalen came up and patted me on my back awkwardly.

"Please, my lady, don't cry. I am sorry we can't help you, but we are in the same predicament. Our best chance now is to pray to the goddess, Dana. Only she can help us now."

Suddenly, there was a scraping noise at the dungeon door. I looked up through watery eyes.

"Shh," said Kalen.

I stopped crying, wiped my tears with my fingers, and tried not to sniffle. The other two were silent, too. I held my breath. Terror welled up inside my chest. Had they come for me? Or were they going to take one of the others? My hands had gone clammy, and I clutched them together to stop them from shaking.

We waited as the grating noise went on. After what seemed like hours but was really only a few seconds, the thick and battered wooden door to the cell opened slowly.

A young man in a billowing black cloak, with the hood over his head, stepped inside. He removed his cowl and turned towards me, just as a shaft of moonlight streamed in through the tiny barred window, illuminating the stranger. I stared up at him through my tear-soaked lashes. He wore a black mask over his glittering eyes. His dark, untidy hair fell in soft waves that framed his finely chiseled features, but his grey eyes looked like storm clouds as he scanned the room in one quick sweep.

He was over six feet tall, I thought absently, completely forgetting for the moment to wonder why he was here. He was lean, muscular, and dressed in a loose white shirt worn over fitted brown leather trousers. A dark leather belt round his waist had a whole arsenal of weapons tucked into it, including a sleek sword and a small knife. I also noticed another knife strapped to his thigh and an additional pair tucked into his high brown boots.

Who was he? Was he one of Oblek's men?

I looked down at the floor, trying to wipe my tear-stained face, then stood up. I smoothed my hair and tucked stray strands behind my ears. I must have looked a sight.

"Well, well, if it isn't the infamous Black Wolf," said Finn in a whispered sneer, coming out of the shadows. "Come to save the day again, have you? And how do you propose to do that this time? Oblek has doubled the guard, and there is a price on your head. Morgana's men have been given instructions to kill you on sight."

The mysterious stranger just turned and smiled at Finn. He didn't look perturbed in the least.

"Rafe, you came," said Kalen softly.

Rafe nodded as he shut the heavy wooden door quietly. "Did you doubt that I would?"

"Finn said you didn't have time to come get a useless pair of fae like us and that you were going to let them kill us," said Kalen. "But I told him that I knew you would find a way to save us," he added with a smug glance at Finn.

"Ah yes, Finn . . . quite the pessimist, isn't he?" said Rafe, looking Finn straight in the eyes.

Finn, quite surprisingly, appeared embarrassed and decided to keep quiet.

"Well, we're not out of danger yet," Rafe said, turning to Kalen.

"You shouldn't have come, Rafe," said Kalen seriously. "Your life is in enough danger as it is. We could have escaped on our own, you know."

Rafe smiled and patted Kalen on the back. "You know I would never let down my friends, Kalen, no matter the dangers. And I don't think your mother would have ever forgiven me if I let anything happen to you."

Kalen beamed at Rafe.

I glanced over at Finn, who looked very angry. I couldn't understand why. Wasn't he happy that Rafe or the Black Wolf or whoever he was had come to save us?

"And who is this?" Rafe asked Kalen, as if suddenly remembering I was there. He glanced over at me with an amused expression on his face.

"Another prisoner," answered Kalen quickly, and proceeded to give Rafe a quick summary of who I was and why I was here.

"So you see," he was saying to Rafe, "if we don't take her with us, she will surely die." Kalen was being quite dramatic, but I think it worked.

Rafe looked serious, obviously weighing the options of whether to help me or not.

"She comes with us," he said, after a moment of hesitation.

Finn didn't argue as we followed Rafe out of the dungeon.

"Who are you?" I asked as we moved quietly and swiftly in a line up the stairs.

"A friend," Rafe said simply, glancing back for a moment to smile at me. And I have to say it was the cutest smile I had ever seen. I didn't even know him, but whoever he was, I was intrigued to say the least.

Somehow he had managed to get the lower dungeon door open, and he stepped out first.

"Wait here," he whispered to us.

I heard a scuffle, and, sooner than expected, Rafe was back.

"All clear," he said in a jovial tone, as if he was enjoying this. Rafe seemed very confident, as though it was a hobby of his to break in and out of castles.

We gingerly stepped over two dazed guards, and Rafe took us through a narrow stone tunnel, which was a different path to the one where I had entered the dungeons. The stone tunnel was dark and damp as we silently followed Rafe. The only glow was from Rafe's hand, which illuminated the tunnel with a ball of light.

I gaped at him. Was he one of the mages Kalen had talked about? I was fascinated to see real magic at work once again, as long as it wasn't directed at me.

The tunnel opened into a small, shadowy alcove in the main castle. The corridors were deserted at this time of night, and we ran as quietly as we could through the dark passages of the eerie castle. Rafe seemed to know exactly where he was going, and the others followed him without question. As we entered the courtyard, we had to keep to the shadows, crouching at times and flattening ourselves against the dark stone walls as we moved.

"How did you get into the castle?" I asked, following Rafe.

"It wasn't difficult," he said, with a faint smile. "Oblek's guards are not very well trained. The eastern gate is poorly guarded, and half of them are drunk or passed out at this time of night. The hour before dawn is the best time for an escape."

"Or a robbery," I added, glancing at him from the corner of my eye. I guessed he was some sort of thief or outlaw from the way Finn spoke earlier.

He seemed to find that funny and chuckled. "True," he agreed.

"How do I know if I can trust you?" I asked. After all, I knew absolutely nothing about him except that he was a wanted man.

"I don't think you really have a choice right now, my lady," said Rafe, stopping abruptly and turning towards me.

I looked down. He was right; I didn't have a choice. He was my escape route, and I had to trust him, for now at least.

"We go to the stables," said Rafe softly, signaling Kalen and Finn to follow.

I glanced back. Finn was still scowling, but he didn't dare question Rafe.

There were three guards in the stables. They drew their weapons when they saw us, but were too surprised to cry out immediately for help. They just stood there, gaping at us.

Rafe raised his right hand and shot two bolts of white light from his palm. Both guards crumpled to the ground, just as Christopher had when Oblek's bolt had stuck him. The third guard tried to shout for assistance, but when he opened his mouth nothing came out. Rafe had done something with his magic, rendering the guard unable to speak.

Frustrated, the guard rushed towards us, his sword raised. Rafe already had his sword in his hand. He blocked a blow to the head from the remaining guard and pushed him backward, slicing him cleanly on the back of his knees, then hit him in the face with the hilt of his sword. The guard went down just as fast as the other two.

I watched Rafe, mesmerized.

"Come on everyone," said Rafe, quite casually, in spite of the situation. "We should leave now. It will be dawn soon."

I nodded. Was he for real?

Kalen grinned. "Whatever you say, Rafe," he said.

"Get the horses," Rafe ordered Kalen and Finn.

They untied and led three horses quietly out of the stable. I followed Rafe, but I was still nervous. I hoped that I wasn't making a mistake trusting him, but he was my only escape route, even though he could just as easily betray me to Morgana.

Suddenly a shout snapped me out of my silent

contemplation.

"The prisoners are escaping," a guard yelled, spotting us.

"Kalen, we will regroup at the meeting place," Rafe said quietly, so Finn couldn't hear. The two fae mounted up. "You," he then said to me, and held out his hand.

I faltered.

"Come with me," he urged.

Before I could respond, he jumped up onto the horse in one fluid stroke, clasped my hand in his, and swung me up behind him. I held onto his waist for dear life, as Rafe gathered up the reins and rode out of the stable.

Dawn was upon us.

The gates had just been opened to let traders and farmers into the castle, and our three horses galloped across the courtyard towards the drawbridge.

Shouts of, "Close the gates, close the gates," rang in my ears.

My heart was hammering in my chest. Everything was happening so fast. We were nearing the drawbridge, which was being slowly pulled up by creaking iron chains. Rafe let Finn and Kalen's horses go first. He held out his hand and shot jets of white light like before, and made a path for us through the guards. Kalen and Finn cleared the drawbridge. They galloped ahead, already out of harm's way.

A few of the guards had now pulled themselves together and started shooting arrows at us.

"It's the Black Wolf," shouted one guard.

"Get him," shouted another. "The queen is offering a fortune for his head."

A frenzy of chattering broke out as the word spread. More guards hastened to help their comrades. An arrow whizzed past my head, and I was suddenly terrified. If we were caught now, they would definitely kill us. What if an arrow hit our horse? What if an arrow hit me? Various scenarios started playing out in my head, all of them ending in a gruesome death. I was petrified, but I clung on to Rafe, determined not to fall off the horse.

Our mount galloped furiously towards the drawbridge, which was now at an angle, chains creaking as guards tried desperately to raise it. We had neared the gate, and Rafe spurred the horse faster and faster. The drawbridge was now a steep slope. The horse slipped once, and I nearly fell off; I screamed, but we were still thundering on.

I closed my eyes and prayed.

Finally, I felt the horse jump, and my heart jumped with it. I had never been so scared in my life. I could hear arrows whizzing past my head and the guards shouting. I felt a jarring impact as we hit the ground, but miraculously we were still on the horse.

When I finally opened my eyes, I realized that we had cleared the moat and were now heading towards the forest that lay in wait behind Oblek's dark castle.

5

AVALONIA

I COULD SEE Kalen and Finn in the distance; they were galloping towards the forest and away from Morgana's minions.

The guards chased us, but we had a considerable lead, and Rafe was a magnificent horseman, so we managed to shake them off. We lost them as soon as we entered the gnarled forest. For some reason, they didn't seem to want to follow us there. I had no idea where Kalen and Finn were; we had split up, and I was all alone with Rafe.

"Are you all right?" Rafe asked as he slowed the chestnut horse deftly to a walk.

"Yes, thank you," I said.

He craned his neck to look back at me and grinned, his smile dazzling. "It was a pleasure," he said, as if I had just thanked him for tea. I wished he would take off the silly mask that hid the rest of his face from me.

The forest seemed different once we were safely within its boundaries. From the outside it looked like a dark and shadowy place, but from the inside it was bright and cheerful, with sunlit groves, beautiful tall cedars, oaks, and sparkling waterfalls, which plunged effortlessly into shimmering ponds. Birds happily chirped their morning tunes, and the wildflowers were fragrant and bright. Dewdrops clung to the foliage, sparkling like fairy dust in the light of first dawn.

We rode along a small, winding path through the trees. Rafe seemed to know where he was going, but I had to figure out what to do next, and I was still trying to decide whether I should trust him. Morgana's guards also wanted him, so being with Rafe was probably the safest place for me to be right now.

"Where will you go now?" Rafe said, breaking the silence.

"I'm not really sure," I said truthfully. I couldn't decide what I should tell him.

"Oblek will not stop looking for you," said Rafe. "If he indeed intended to hold you for ransom, he will come after you." He paused. "Who are you and what is your name?"

I hung my head. I had to tell someone. Maybe he would know what to do, or maybe he knew who my real parents were. I had to take a chance.

"My name is Aurora," I said and proceeded to tell him everything that had happened to me since I arrived at Redstone Manor. I told him about my uncle and how he sold me to Oblek, about the strange tapestry, and even what they said about me and my family.

I didn't tell him about the dreams though; somehow I felt it was too private to mention. But it did feel good to finally have someone to talk to about all this, and strangely enough

I felt comfortable with Rafe.

Rafe stopped the horse, jumped down quickly, and turned to stare at me. His eyes had gone wide, and he was looking at me as if he had just seen a ghost.

"So," I said, trying again. "Do you have any idea why Oblek kidnapped me?"

Rafe nodded solemnly. "I have a pretty good idea, yes."

"And?" I prompted. At least here was someone who had some answers.

"And," he said, staring at me as if I had suddenly grown two heads, "I think you and I need to have a little talk."

I huffed. Rafe held his arms up to me to help me off the horse. I put my hands on his shoulders, and he lifted me easily. For a second that went by too fast, he held me close, and then he put me down. Being so close to him was muddling my brain, I couldn't think straight.

He turned and tied the horse to a nearby tree and scanned our surroundings once before he came back to me.

"Come," he said, holding out his hand.

I took it cautiously.

He led me through the forest, down a slightly worn path, deeper into the trees. I tried to keep up; my legs and back were aching from the vigorous ride. And I was quite sure that tomorrow I wouldn't even be able to sit down on my terribly sore backside. My hands and feet were cut and bleeding, and I was a complete mess.

We came to a little clearing, where the morning sun

danced and played on the surface of a pond. Wildflowers grew in patches near the water, and Rafe sat me down on a large moss-covered stone overlooking the shimmering pool. I dipped my cut and bleeding feet in the cool water and sighed as it immediately relieved the stinging pain. I washed my hands and bruised face, feeling a little better.

Rafe sat on a similar rock near me, took off his mask and ran his fingers through his dark, wavy hair. I didn't want to stare, so I pretended to wash my feet and peeked at him from under my eyelashes.

He was magnificent. I knew he was handsome even with the mask on, but without it he looked younger than I imagined. He seemed not that much older than myself, maybe just three or four years. He smiled at me, and I shifted uncomfortably on the rock. Somehow he made me feel like he knew exactly what I was thinking.

"You said you know why this queen wants to see me?" I asked.

Rafe nodded. "If you really are who you say you are, then you are not safe here in Illiador. Morgana will stop at nothing to get to you."

"Why?" I asked, horrified.

"Shhh," he said, quickly putting his finger to his lips.

I immediately shut up and looked around. I could see nothing, but I could hear a faint rustling in the bushes and I turned towards it. Rafe already had his sword out and had moved slowly in front of me, protecting me.

Suddenly the foliage in front of us parted, and a disheveled Kalen appeared in the clearing. "There you are," he said, completely oblivious to the fact that Rafe had nearly run him through with sharp steel.

"I don't know why you made this the meeting place," Kalen said to Rafe, "it's nearly impossible to find."

"That's the point," said Rafe, giving Kalen a half smile as he put away his sword.

Kalen came and sat down next to me. "Have you figured out a way for you to get back to wherever your home is, my lady?" said Kalen politely.

I shook my head. "No, not exactly," I said, looking over at Rafe, who was now leaning against a tree with his arms crossed in front of him, watching me.

I looked away quickly, and I was sure my embarrassment showed.

"Kalen," said Rafe, "can you keep a secret? We are going to need your help."

Kalen nodded his head vigorously. "Of course I can," he said, grinning from ear to ear.

Rafe rolled his eyes, but he quickly related my story to Kalen, whose eyes went wide at the mention of Elayna and Azaren. He listened quietly, which seemed like a first for him.

"So you see why it is not safe for her in Illiador," said Rafe to Kalen. "We must get her over the border to Eldoren."

Kalen nodded, still staring at me in disbelief.

I felt a chill go up my spine. "Why?" I asked. "Why won't I be safe here?"

"Because if Morgana or Lucian find you, they will kill you," said Rafe plainly.

I stood up abruptly. "Kill me!" I exclaimed. "Why would they want to kill me? I don't even know them. And who is Lucian anyway?"

Kalen's eyes went wide. "You don't know who Lucian is?"

"Obviously not," I said, becoming irritated at Kalen's disbelief. I was the one who had just found out that some crazy queen I'd never met wanted to kill me. I should be the one asking the questions.

"Lucian is the Archmage of Illiador, and Queen Morgana's right-hand man," said Kalen, with a tinge of awe.

"The arch what?" I asked incredulously. Did he just say archmage?

"The archmage," repeated Kalen.

Rafe laughed as he pushed himself away from the tree and came to sit beside me. "I think she heard you the first time, Kalen."

Kalen was looking thoroughly confused.

"I am sorry, my lady," said Rafe gently. "I think Kalen forgot that you have not lived in this world for long. I will try and explain as best I can. Morgana calls herself Queen of Illiador, although she is nothing but a deceitful usurper."

"Why?" I asked. "Whose kingdom did she usurp?"

He paused and looked at me, his grey eyes intense and his

lips turned up in a half smile. "Well, if I'm correct," he said finally, "yours."

I was shocked. Surely he couldn't have meant what I think he just said?

"Your father was the king of Illiador, and you were heir to the throne," said Rafe. "But before your second birthday, Morgana took her chance. She betrayed your father, Azaren, and, with the help of Lucian, killed your family and took the throne of Illiador."

"How could she do that?" I asked stupidly. "Why would she?"

"She was your father's half-sister," said Rafe, a trace of disgust in his voice. "He trusted her."

"His sister!"

"Half-sister," Rafe specified.

I was appalled. I looked at him, wide-eyed. He couldn't be serious; did he really mean that my own aunt would kill me in cold blood, just because I was her brother's daughter? My mind flashed back to the recurring dream of the woman called Morgana, with the gleaming dagger in her hand. A wave of panic rushed over me. If what Rafe said was true, and this Morgana was the same one from my dream, then I was in serious trouble.

"Why?" I asked, feeling sudden fear. "I don't want to be heir to anything. Why doesn't she just leave me alone? I'm not a threat to her."

"Just knowing you're alive is a threat to Morgana. She will

not rest until all of Azaren's bloodline has been removed. You are the only obstacle to her complete right to the throne of Illiador," said Rafe.

I hung my head. What was I going to do? Suddenly this world seemed extremely scary, and even more complicated than I had ever imagined.

My shoulders drooped. He had said that my parents were dead. For so many years I had hoped that my birth parents would come and find me, that they would regret giving me up, and when no one ever came to claim me, I was convinced that they had abandoned me. Now it looked like both my parents were gone forever and I was completely alone.

"Do you know how I escaped?" I asked.

Rafe shook his head. "I have no idea," he said. "But I know this: whatever saved you that day was extremely powerful magic."

"But how? Did my parents have magic?"

"Of course," said Kalen, interrupting. "All the nobility are from magical stock. It has always been like that since the kings of old, since Auraken Firedrake walked the world and was high king over all the known lands."

"Does this mean I can also do magic?" I had never felt or done anything that was unusual.

Rafe stared at me with a strange expression in his eyes. "Not everyone is born with the gift of magic. Sometimes it skips a generation or a sibling, and even those who have the gift may never truly learn to master it. We will just have to wait and see if you have the potential."

That was not the answer I was looking for, but it was a start.

We left the little clearing and Rafe led us deep into the forest on foot along a small, winding path. He had put on his mask again, and his black cloak rippled around him as he moved surely and effortlessly through the trees as if he knew this forest like the back of his hand.

"Where are we going?" I asked finally.

"Tonight you will stay with Kalen's mother in their village. She is a gifted healer and will tend to your wounds," said Rafe. "I have some important errands I have to take care of. Tomorrow I will come and fetch you and take you to Duke Silverthorne."

"Who?" I asked.

"Duke Gabriel Silverthorne, your granduncle," said Rafe. "If you really are who Oblek says you are, then the duke is the only one who will be able to tell us for sure."

"Do you know him well?" I asked. Dried leaves crunched beneath my feet as I walked beside him along a small, muddy path through the trees.

"Very," said Rafe. "I've known him since I was a child."

"But then you must have known my family too," I said, eager to know more.

Rafe nodded. "I have never had the pleasure of meeting your mother, Queen Elayna, as she died when I was very young. But I did know your father. He was an exceptional mage and king. One who genuinely cared for the common people, and they loved and revered him for it. He was also a fearless warrior, and his courage was the stuff of legends."

"Tell me more about him, please." I wanted to know all I could about my father.

Rafe smiled. "Once, when I was very young and living in Neris, your father was on an official visit to the city. I was standing in the crowd, but I was too close to the cliffs. I slipped, hitting my head on a rock and fell into the sea. Azaren saw me fall and jumped in after me. If it weren't for him, I would now be resting in a watery grave. Finally I get the chance to repay my debt by helping his daughter."

I nodded. My father sounded like a wonderful man, and I wished that I could have met him, even once.

I was not too happy, though, to hear that Rafe was just helping me out of some sense of duty to my father. I was grateful for his assistance, and his story explained why he wanted to help me. I had hoped that it was something more, that he was inexplicably drawn to me for reasons he couldn't understand. But the truth was, I was just a debt he had to repay. I frowned at my own foolishness; I had to stop reading so many romance novels. I hung my head in embarrassment and continued following silently.

I was apprehensive about meeting the duke. What if this was all a mistake? What if I was the wrong girl, where would I go then? I had nothing left in the world I grew up in except disappointment and heartache. It was going to be harder here, I could tell, but at least I had family, real family. I wanted to meet my granduncle, I wanted to learn about my real parents, and for once in my life I wanted to know who I really was.

"You will be safe here in Pixie Bush," said Kalen encouragingly, breaking my anxious reverie. "And my mother can find you some suitable clothes to wear."

I looked down at myself. I was mortified. In all the confusion I hadn't realized that I was still wearing floral pajamas and a pink woolen dressing gown, and I was walking around barefoot. I had forgotten that I had changed into my nightclothes before I had gone looking for the library in Redstone Manor. It was just last night, but so much had happened since then.

I looked over at Rafe. He was chuckling to himself.

Finally we stopped walking.

Rafe turned. "This is where I will take your leave, Aurora," he said.

"Thank you," I said to him. What more could I say?

"As I said before, it was a pleasure," said Rafe, his full lips curved in a dashing smile. "Until tomorrow, my lady." He bowed briefly, then disappeared into the trees.

I turned to look back at Kalen. "Now where?" I asked, eager to change and eat something. I was famished and exhausted, and I hadn't slept the whole night. I hoped Kalen's home was not too far from where we were, because I was too tired to walk any more.

Kalen grinned. "Now we go home, to Pixie Bush."

6
THE FAE

As WE MOVED further into the sunlit wood and passed the magical boundaries, I could feel a palpable change in the atmosphere. The leaves rustled gently in the breeze, and sunlight shone through the huge trees. Soon we reached a little wooden gate.

"Are you sure the guards won't follow us here?" I asked Kalen.

"Pixie Bush is protected by magical boundaries. If you don't know exactly where you are going, you can get lost in the deeper parts of the forest and wander for days without ever finding the village. Those who are not welcome, or have not been invited in, can never enter," he grinned. "Keeps Oblek's Guards out at least."

As we entered the boundaries of the little village in the forest, I saw a small wooden sign attached to a stick. It said: "Pixie Bush, Goldleaf Forest, Illiador."

The rays of the midday sun shone on the forest floor, creating dappled specks of gold that danced about our feet as we walked. I was completely entranced. It was as if I had entered yet another world. This was not the bleak, crowded stone castle of Lord Oblek. This was a fairy village, a magical place in the forest.

It was more fantastic than I could ever have imagined it might be. Tiny wooden cottages with thatched roofs covered in vines, and half hidden by foliage, nestled at regular intervals in the very heart of the woods, and small flower-lined paths connected the cottages. It looked like a picture out of a storybook.

I looked up. I could barely see the tops of the massive trees; some of them seemed to be reaching all the way to the clouds. The forest somehow looked larger from the inside than it did from Oblek's castle. Small specks of sunlight filtered in through the leaves and led the way as we walked through the little streets of the fae village.

Kalen seemed right at home.

"Where's Finn?" I asked.

"Finn must have gone straight home. Rafe doesn't trust him with his identity, so he didn't tell him about the meeting place."

"But Rafe trusts you?"

Kalen beamed, his smile lighting up his face. "Yes, he does," he said, puffing out his chest a little more. "Mother would have been worried after we were captured. It was she who told Rafe where to find us. He is a friend to the fae and is welcome in Pixie Bush whenever he wants. Even though he is a mage, he is a good person, quite unlike Archmage Lucian and the other mages of Nerenor."

"Then why didn't he come with us? Where does he live?" I asked, trying not to sound too eager.

Somehow I wanted to know everything there was to know about Rafe. And Kalen was the perfect person for it, since he loved to talk and seemed inclined to inadvertently say more than he should. In this case, though, it was a good thing. I could drill Kalen for information about Rafe, because I couldn't stop thinking about him.

"Rafe didn't tell you who he is?" asked Kalen, looking surprised.

I shook my head. "No."

"Then it is really not my place to say, my lady," said Kalen, quite to my surprise. "You should ask Rafe yourself when you see him."

"Is Rafe even his real name?" I asked. Somehow that seemed important.

Kalen hesitated momentarily. "It is the name he prefers to use, yes," he said finally.

Why was Kalen being so mysterious? What secrets did Rafe have to hide?

We walked quickly along the main street of the little forest village. It was a busy day, and all the little paths were bustling. I was relieved and relaxed a little. I felt safe here. Pixie Bush was lovely and bright and full of nice people—well, fae. Most of them looked quite ordinary except for the slightly pointed ears, but others were just too different to ignore.

Two small men with long beards and big ears stopped to say hello to Kalen. I tried to act like I did not find anything different about their appearance, but I soon realized that I couldn't help staring at their huge elephant-like ears and massive, hairy feet.

"Who were those two?" I asked Kalen after the little men had walked away.

"Oh, I forgot you don't know much about our people," Kalen said quietly.

"I don't know anything about your people," I whispered. "Until last night I didn't even believe that fairies exist."

Kalen nodded his understanding.

"The ones we just met are brownies, they are very good housekeepers," he said, pausing and looking around. "And those two, they are naiads—the fae of the rivers. They don't live here." He pointed at two tall ladies with green hair and milk-white skin, dressed in a thin and flimsy blue fabric. "Must be visiting for the market," he added.

"What market?" I asked, intrigued.

"Oh, didn't I tell you?" said Kalen, his big almond-shaped eyes lighting up. "Every year, the fae and other magical beings come together in Goldleaf Forest for the annual spring market. Normally, it is held in the daylight, but, because of the guards and the new rules that have banned fae gatherings, we are having the market tonight." Kalen stopped to take a breath. He spoke so fast, like a runaway train. "Would you like to come with me tonight? I mean, you don't have to if you don't want to. I can understand if you are tired after your terrible ordeal."

I grinned. "I would love to go," I said, meaning every word.

"Wonderful!" said Kalen. "First we will go home, and then tonight we can go together to the spring market."

I was elated. A midnight market in the heart of the forest! I would get to see all the different magical beings that lived in Avalonia, and I would worry about Morgana tomorrow. Tonight I was safe. Kalen had said the village was protected; Morgana couldn't get to me here.

I fiddled with my medallion, which I still wore round my neck, hidden under my clothes, as we walked quickly through the village of Pixie Bush. I was famished, and Kalen bought me an apple from a fae vendor's cart. I hungrily polished it off, as I followed Kalen to an ancient oak tree.

It was the most massive tree I had ever seen. The branches and leaves were spread so thickly that you could not see past the first few boughs. There were other oaks like this interspersed throughout the village between the tiny cottages, but this one was by far the tallest and largest. The width of the trunk was the size of a whole room.

At the base was a small opening. Kalen climbed inside and gestured for me to follow. I caught a glimpse of the inner recesses. It was hollow and lit up with a faint light. I followed Kalen into the trunk of the enormous tree. The inside of the oak was absolutely massive. A steep spiral staircase ran all the way up through it, carved from within the trunk.

As we climbed the steep stairs, it was not dark and gloomy, as I had first expected it to be. It was dimly lit with tiny lamps that glowed and flickered at regular intervals. I looked at one closely. It was a small glass ball, attached to the inside of the tree, and little lights were moving around inside. I stopped to investigate one of the lights.

"Wow!" I said. "These look like fireflies."

"Not fireflies," said Kalen, "fire-pixies."

I stared at the tiny pixies buzzing around inside the ball of light.

"Don't worry," said Kalen. "They are not trapped, they can leave whenever they want. It's just a job."

I smiled to myself; this world was slowly becoming much more interesting and not all that bad.

We climbed higher and higher and finally came to an opening in the side of the tree trunk, leading out onto one of the branches. I was about to walk through it when Kalen stopped me.

"No, princess, not yet. My mother's house is on the top-most branch," he said, with a hint of pride in his voice. "It has the best view, you know."

"Please call me Aurora," I said absentmindedly. "All this 'my princess' stuff sounds silly."

Kalen smiled. "All right, Aurora," he said.

I was still curious, and I decided to have a peep out onto the branch just the same. I peered through the opening. In the middle of the bough where the branches spanned out wider, balancing precariously between two broad branches on a wooden platform, was a small cottage with a little thatched roof and creepers covering the walls, like the cottages on the floor of the wood. I was spellbound. It was a life-sized tree house.

"Who lives here?" I asked, entranced.

"The Bettlebirds—they are not a very nice family. Mother has been trying to get them out of this tree for years," he said, continuing up the spiral staircase, with me in tow.

We passed another few openings leading out onto the branches. I peeped out quickly once or twice. All the branches had a little cottage built between the leaves, spaced out at regular intervals.

When we reached the topmost branch, we stepped out of the little door onto an extremely wide branch of the massive tree. There the sun shone brighter, and the tiny cottage looked absolutely magical.

The bough served as a small pathway that lead to the treehouse, which looked like the others except that the roof was bright green and made of leaves. It blended into the foliage surrounding it perfectly. Vines crept haphazardly up the walls and onto the roof. The windows revealed a cake and some freshly baked bread cooling on the windowsill. The smell was heavenly, and I was famished.

"Here we are," said Kalen. "This is my mother's house."

He went up to the door and knocked once.

It opened almost immediately, and a pleasant-looking woman with curly gold ringlets, a round face, and dancing blue eyes hugged Kalen fiercely and ushered us in. I looked around the little cottage in the trees. It was the cutest thing I had ever seen—quite large from the inside, sparsely furnished with a fluffy green sofa and a cream-colored rug that covered the wooden floor. It was homely and cozy, and a lazy fire was struggling to stay alight in the small fireplace, where a little pot was hanging, bubbling away.

After the initial happiness of seeing Kalen alive wore off, his mother began shouting at him. She looked very angry.

"What did I tell you about leaving the forest? Without the magical boundaries, it is not difficult for the guards to capture you. How could you, Kalen, how could you? What if something had happened to you? What if the Black Wolf had not managed to get there in time?" She paused for a moment. "A lovely boy, that Rafe," she sniffed.

I suppressed a giggle; at least now I knew where Kalen inherited his fast talking skills. I smiled at the plump fae lady, who suddenly looked surprised to see me, as though she had forgotten I was there.

"Oh!" said Kalen's mother. "Who is this little one?"

I smiled because the fae lady came up to my shoulders and had to look up to talk to me.

"This is my friend, Mother—the Lady Aurora. She was also in the dungeons at Lord Oblek's castle. Rafe rescued her as well," said Kalen, turning to me. "Aurora, this is my mother, Penelope Plumpleberry."

I smiled. The name suited her.

"Very pleased to meet you, Mrs. Plumpleberry," I said politely.

"Oh, you can call me Penelope. Everybody does."

"Mother, I promised Aurora she could stay with us for a night," said Kalen.

"Of course," said Penelope, bustling around the little cottage, making tea and cutting up the cake. "Will you have some, Aurora?" she asked.

I nodded. "Yes, please," I answered eagerly. My tummy was grumbling, and I was so hungry.

"Finn has gone out to attend to some errands. Come and sit here, and we can talk freely," Penelope said, patting the cushion next to her. "Kalen, bring the tea and cake."

I sat down on the proffered cushion.

"Yes, Mother," said Kalen, bringing over a little tray and setting it down in front of me.

"Now tell me, my dear . . . what exactly happened to you? Maybe I can be of some help," said Mrs. Plumpleberry, turning to give me her full attention.

I sipped on my delicate cup of violet tea, which happened to taste rather nice, gathered my thoughts and prepared to start my story once again.

"Well . . . " said Kalen. He obviously couldn't resist being the one to talk, so he proceeded to tell his mother everything: who I was, where he met me, and the fact that Rafe was taking me to see my granduncle, the Duke of Silverthorne.

"So you see, Oblek thinks I am the lost princess, and Queen Morgana now knows I am alive and wants to get me out of the way permanently," I finished.

Penelope looked stunned, much like Rafe had in the woods earlier, when I told him who I really was.

"Please say something," I urged, leaning forward a little.

She looked at me, her eyes bright and questioning.

"It was thought that all three of you died that day," said Penelope slowly, "but obviously your parents found a way to save you."

"How? How could they have saved me if they both died?"

"I don't know, my dear," said Penelope. "What I do know is that the whole west wing of the castle of Nerenor burned to the ground. Your parents disappeared, and Morgana assumed the throne of Illiador."

"Disappeared? You mean, died?"

Penelope looked away. "Yes," she said slowly. "Yes, although their bodies were never found."

A spark of hope leapt in my heart.

"But if I'm still alive, isn't it possible that they could be, too?"

Penelope shook her head. "I am sorry, my dear, I don't want you to get the wrong impression. Your parents must be dead. If they were not, they would have returned by now, or someone would have seen or heard something. No one has even whispered that Elayna or Azaren could be alive."

I hung my head, the memories of my dream fresh in my mind. I could see Morgana coming at my mother to stab her. I didn't want to say anything about the dream to Penelope and Kalen. Somehow it seemed too private to talk about. At least now I knew I hadn't made it all up, and I wasn't crazy. But why had the dream begun occurring only recently?

"How did Morgana know I was alive?" I asked.

Penelope shook her head. "I don't know, my dear," she said, putting her hand on my arm.

"Do you also think Morgana will kill me if she finds me?" I asked finally, although I think I already knew the answer.

"Yes, that much is certain," said Penelope. "If Morgana knows who you really are, then she will not stop coming after you. You need to get out of Illiador before she does."

Suddenly I didn't feel so grown up. I stupidly wished that I could go home again, to my mother. But that was not possible anymore. My parents were dead, my real ones and my adoptive ones. I looked down at my feet as tears welled up in my eyes. A few stray droplets ran down my cheek, but I wiped them away, sniffing a little.

Penelope must have felt sorry for me because she leaned over and gave me a hug. I hugged her back, eager for a little maternal warmth.

"If you want to find out more, then you must travel to Eldoren with Rafe. He is right, Silverthorne will know what to do," said Penelope finally.

"But can you please tell me a little more about my family

before I go?" I asked. "I'm still confused how I am related to the duke."

Penelope nodded and proceeded to tell me what she knew.

"You are part of one of the most powerful families in the whole of Avalonia. King Ereneth, your grandfather, is a descendant of the Firedrake dynasty, the first and longest reigning dynasty, which began with the first king of these lands, Auraken Firedrake. Ereneth married Fiona Silverthorne, your father's mother, who was the sister of the Duke of Silverthorne, one of the most formidable families in Eldoren."

"So who was my mother?" I asked, wide-eyed.

"Elayna was a daughter of the royal house of Gwenfarith-Aran of the fae," said Penelope, slowly.

"Fae," I whispered. "My mother was fae?"

Now I was really shocked. I had presumed that my mother was a mage like my father or just an ordinary person. But fae! Who'd have thought?

Penelope nodded. "And not just any ordinary fae, your mother was one of the Immortals."

"Immortals," I squeaked. "If she was immortal, how could she have died?"

Penelope smiled. "Most of the fae have very long lives, spanning centuries, and those of the royal house of Gwenfarith-Aran are immortal. But even immortal fae can be killed using the right weapon."

I nodded, thinking back to my dream where Morgana

stabbed my mother with the dagger.

"So, if a child is born of a fae and a mage, what do they become?" I asked, intrigued.

"Well," said Penelope thoughtfully. "They take on either trait or power, or the magic can skip the generation completely. If you do have the potential for fae magic, I should be able to sense it."

My eyes widened. "So," I said, "can you sense anything?"

Penelope held my hand in hers and closed her eyes. I could feel a sort of tingling sensation in my hands when she touched them.

Finally she looked at me and shook her head. "No, nothing," she said, hesitating. "But do not be distressed, Aurora dear, you've probably taken on your father's magic. The magic of the mages is different from that of the fae. The Duke of Silverthorne is a very powerful and experienced mage, and he will be able to sense that."

Kalen nodded. "Yes, the duke is very influential in Eldoren and is chief advisor to the king. Silverthorne Castle is the only place where you will be safe."

"This is true," said Penelope. "If Oblek tells Morgana you have escaped, it is only a matter of time before she sends the Shadow Guard to hunt you down."

"Who are the Shadow Guard?" I asked. A twinge of fear ran down my spine. I didn't like the sound of anything hunting me, especially something with a name that began with shadow.

"They are the scourge of Illiador; Morgana's personal guard, loyal only to the queen and the archmage. They are not only mages, but also hardened warriors, enhanced by a powerful magic. They're trained by Lucian himself. We need to get you over the border to Eldoren as soon as possible," said Kalen.

"But I want to see the night market." I knew I was being childish, but I really wanted to visit the magical fairy market. I didn't think I would ever get a chance like this again.

"Please," I pleaded, looking at Penelope, and back at Kalen.

Kalen must have felt sorry for me, since he seemed to agree. He turned to his mother. "Yes, Mother, maybe we can see the market tonight and tomorrow morning we can head off to Eldoren."

"Is it far?" I asked. I was not too keen on riding for hours, to who knew where.

"No, not really, it's just on the other side of the Cascade Mountains," said Kalen. As if popping over the mountains was a simple feat.

I was horrified.

"You want me to travel over a mountain? On what, horseback?" I squeaked.

Kalen grinned. "Not used to riding, eh?"

"I know how to ride, but how many days will it take?" I asked, hesitantly.

"It's not too far. We are right on the border," said Kalen.

"About five to seven nights, depending on the weather."

"What! Seven days? Where will we sleep?" I asked, horrified at the prospect of traveling over mountains on horseback for a week.

Kalen looked confused. "We sleep outside. We will have to make camp. Don't worry, I know how to light a fire to keep away the wild creatures."

"Wild creatures," I repeated. "Camping outside!" This was not my idea of safe at all.

"And we must get you some suitable clothes," said Mrs. Plumpleberry, eyeing me up and down. "I think I have something that may fit you. My eldest daughter, Dewdrop, left some of her things here when she moved away after her marriage."

Kalen grinned again. "Try and get some rest, Aurora, tonight we will go to the night market."

7
THE MIDNIGHT MARKET

LATER THAT NIGHT, after I had eaten well and rested, we set out for the midnight market. I followed Kalen along the small path, from Pixie Bush into the very heart of Goldleaf Forest. The full moon shone brightly through the rustling leaves, and the forest path was dappled with dancing specks of silver that flitted ahead of us, guiding the way. It was strange how the whole forest seemed to be awake for the market. Birds chirped high above us, and little forest animals poked their heads out of the bushes just in time for me to see them before they disappeared again into the dense undergrowth.

Mrs. Plumpleberry had healed my hands and my feet with a magical ointment she made herself. I had changed into a pretty linen dress, dyed a lovely emerald green, with wide bell sleeves. It was bound at the waist with a green-and-gold-trimmed sash and flowed down to my ankles. My feet were wrapped in soft muslin bandages, and I wore supple leather boots, which belonged to Kalen's older sister. When I looked in the mirror after getting dressed, I was stunned at the transformation. In my normal jeans or tracks I looked like a gawky teenager, but in this dress I felt like a grown-up.

The night air was chilly in the forest, and Penelope had very generously given me a brown woolen cloak to keep myself warm. I was grateful for her kindness and sound advice, and I hoped I would be able to pay her back someday.

"Your mom is very sweet," I said to Kalen, as we walked quickly down the forest path. "She seems to know a lot."

"Oh, Mother knows everything," said Kalen, picking up a pebble. "She is a very old fae, after all."

"Is she? She doesn't look very old to me," I said, confused.

"Mother is three hundred and ninety-three summers old," said Kalen.

"Three hundred and ninety-three years old," I repeated, aghast. Penelope didn't look a day over forty.

Kalen nodded. "Our race ages very slowly. She will only start looking old when she has completed a thousand summers," he said. "She is one of the elders of the village—but her magic is still strong and she is a gifted healer. Many have come to her for help over the years. Once she even helped your granduncle, when he was injured in the woods not far from here."

It seemed to me that we had been walking for quite a while when I could suddenly hear voices and noises quite clearly in the quiet forest. We came to a large clearing, and the delightful sight left me spellbound. The forest was alive, radiant and subtly lit by pretty, different-colored lanterns hanging from the towering trees. Beautifully decorated stalls

81

and multicolored tents had sprung up all over the place. Some were nestled between the tall trees, and some were haphazardly placed around the edge of the clearing, forming a slightly wonky circle. Fae of all sizes, shapes and colors wandered around, having a marvelous time. There were dryads, naiads, brownies, and little pixies with wings who flitted about the place in groups, laughing and eating at the food stalls.

We came to a stall, which was manned by a small, funny-looking fae with a pointy nose and long ears. Kalen identified him as a gnome. He was selling some strangely colored liquid in glass bottles and was haggling unashamedly about prices with two old ladies, whom I thought were very sweet.

As we walked through the market, Kalen chattered on.

"Although some of the larger towns have shops that sell magical ingredients for potions," Kalen was saying, "this is the only place you can find some of the really rare items."

I followed Kalen, who was entering a green tent, where the sign outside read: "Buy a plant for your home and garden." That sounded quite interesting. Maybe I could buy a plant for Kalen's mom—she had really helped me, after all—but I remembered I didn't have any money.

The tent was not what I expected at all. The inside was bewitched to look like a large greenhouse; like the forest, it was much larger inside than it appeared from the outside. The moonlight shone through the glass ceiling, and rows of plants and flowers lined the sides of the tent. We decided to explore.

I walked through the rows of plants, looking at the labels that were written next to them. There were strawberry plants in a small tray, growing wonderful, juicy strawberries, each one of which had a dollop of cream on the top. The sign near it said: "Grow your own strawberries and cream."

"Try one," said Kalen. "No one is watching."

I couldn't resist; I loved strawberries and cream. I popped the whole strawberry into my mouth. It was delicious and the cream was thick, fresh, and sweet. It was wonderful.

"Lovely, yes?" said Kalen.

I nodded, since my mouth was full.

"Ms. Herbchild is wonderful at growing things. These strawberry plants with cream are one of her new inventions, but you can only grow them on trays inside the house, or the gnomes lick off all the cream."

I made a face at the thought of eating a strawberry that had been licked by a gnome.

A small lady with mousy brown hair and fae ears came over. "I see you like my new plants," she said, giving Kalen a pat on his back. "Kalen, it's marvelous to see you again."

Kalen grinned at the fae lady. "Good to see you too, Ms. Herbchild."

I was impressed; he seemed to know everybody here in the market.

"Feel free to sample some of the new fruits," Ms. Herbchild said, as she walked off to attend to another customer.

We thanked Ms. Herbchild, since she didn't take any money from us, and walked out of the tent and over to another stall. It was all so exciting. I hoped we would have enough time to see everything before we had to go back.

A small, colorful stall, draped in light green and yellow muslin, was selling charm bracelets. I went over to have a better look. The lady selling the bracelets was thin and tall, with olive skin and glossy black hair. She wore a plain white cotton dress and had covered her shoulders with a brown shawl. Her skin was heavily tattooed with strange symbols that ran down her arm and the side of her neck. I wondered what they were as I inspected all the things she was selling.

"Would you like a charm, my little one?" said the lady, after I had a chance to look around.

I shook my head. I knew I had no money, but still I was very intrigued. They sounded quite fascinating.

"Come, come, my dear, you will never find something like this in this part of Avalonia. I can give you a wonderful five-charm bracelet for only one gold damarin and two silver trilts," said the lady, picking it up and showing me the bracelet more closely.

It was an intricate piece of work. The bracelet was finely crafted, and the tiny charms that hung from it were made in different colors and shaped in curious-looking designs.

I was fascinated; maybe Kalen could lend me the money to buy it and explain how to use it. I looked around for him and waved him over. When he saw me he came over quickly and pulled me away from the stall.

"Stay away from her," he said seriously.

The lady made a face as she turned to her next customer, her multiple bracelets jingling as she moved.

"You never know what these witches put in those charm bracelets. Many things can go wrong. They are not really safe," said Kalen quietly to me.

"She was a witch?" I asked, looking back at her.

Kalen nodded, pulling me towards another red-and-white tent. "Come in here, I want to show you something."

Outside the tent was a sign: "Magical Creatures, Familiars, and Companions." I wondered what he wanted me to see. I couldn't handle a pet right now; I was having a hard enough time looking after myself as it was.

The inside of the tent was built like a stable, and, like the plant tent, it was larger inside than it looked on the outside. Kalen had tried to explain to me about fae glamour, but it was very different actually seeing it work.

This was not a place for puppies and kittens; the tent was filled with strange-looking creatures. Most of them were in cages, and some of the others were tied up. There were birds, mice, snakes, and other beasts that I could not identify. A lizard with the head of a frog peered at me from a small cage, and a birdlike creature with the face of a cat hissed as I walked past. I tried to keep as far away from the cages as I could—the animals didn't look very friendly.

At the back of the tent in the last stall was a white horse, and I couldn't keep my eyes off it. As we got closer, I could see what it was that had gotten Kalen so excited. The strange white horse had beautiful, iridescent wings. It stood in its stall watching me, head held high and stamping one massive hoof. Its coat was the color of fresh snow, and its magnificent mane fell in thick cascades down its powerful neck.

I stared at the mythical winged horse in wonder. Avalonia was truly an amazing place.

"That's a pegasus," said Kalen, now whispering. "They are very rare outside of Elfi. I wonder how it even got here?"

We went over to look at the pegasus more closely. Before I could ask Kalen any more about it, a tall man with slick black hair ran up to us.

"Interested in this pegasus, eh?" he said, standing a little way from the horse. "Got this one at a real steal, I did. She was bruised, hurt, and caught hard by a band of goblins in the Cascade Mountains, she was." The slimy looking man looked around suspiciously, as if someone was going to pounce on him any moment. "I can give you a good price for her, I can."

All of a sudden, there were disturbing noises from outside the tent. People were screaming, and the pegasus-seller ran out to have a look. I looked at Kalen, but he seemed as confused as I was.

"The Shadow Guard," shouted the pegasus seller, running back into the tent.

"What?" said Kalen. "In the forest? We must get out of

here, and fast." He took my hand and we ran.

My heart was racing, and I was suddenly afraid. How did the Shadow Guard know about the midnight market? Kalen had said I would be safe here. I was terrified at what Lord Oblek would do to me for escaping his dungeons if he caught me again.

As we came out of the tent, the happy, peaceful clearing was now a mess, with upturned stalls and tents that had been ripped and destroyed. Lanterns lay burning on the mossy floor, and everyone was running helter-skelter into the forest. Kalen went to help two dryad children who had fallen down.

Then I saw the reason for the screaming and confusion: the Shadow Guard.

Moving about the clearing like dark, menacing shadows, there were two of them, and their very presence sent shivers down my spine. They had pale white skin, and their hands were skeletal, with sharp, clawlike fingernails. I couldn't see their faces, which were hidden under black hooded cloaks.

There were other guards with them, human guards in uniforms, and they were rounding up groups of fae. A small group of gnomes sat in a little heap, all tied up, and they looked absolutely terrified. Some of the older fae had engaged in a fight with a couple of the guards. Two were struck down by Shadow Guard magic and lay motionless on the floor.

I was aghast. They were killing people, and it was my fault;

they were here for me. I didn't know what to do. Should I give myself up? What if they kept killing these poor fae folk? They had done nothing wrong except allow me to stay.

Suddenly, sharp hands closed about me from behind. I tried to struggle, but it was useless. Whoever was holding me was too strong for me to move. I kicked and screamed, but nothing helped.

"Is she the girl?" I heard the guard who held me ask someone. I craned my head to see Oblek walking towards us. He looked at me with so much malice in his eyes that I had to look away.

"Yes, that's her," said Oblek, stopping in front of me. "You thought you could escape me, little girl. I told you the next time you tried, you would be sorry."

"How did you find me?" I managed to say through the panic.

He looked over to the trees, and I saw Finn walking towards us. I couldn't believe Finn had given me up to Oblek. I knew he didn't like me, but why did he hate me so much and do something that caused so much destruction to his own kind?

"Tie her up," said Oblek, grabbing me by my arm. "We take her to the queen." He turned to Finn. "You will be well rewarded, Fae."

I trembled. He was going to take me straight to Morgana. How would I escape now? What should I do?

Suddenly, there was a flash of white light. It shot past me

and hit Oblek, who collapsed on the ground beside me. I was free. I looked around, but where should I go? And where did the light come from? My eyes darted across the forest, to the other side of the clearing. That's when I saw him—the Black Wolf.

With his dark, tousled hair, shining grey eyes, and ebony cloak rippling about him as he walked carefully and purposefully towards the guards, he looked like a sleek black panther ready to pounce on its prey.

Rafe held out his hands, and jets of white light shot out of his palms. The human guards crumpled like toy soldiers. But he now had the undivided attention of the Shadow Guard, and they slowly and confidently started closing in about him. For a split second, he looked over at me, his grey eyes shimmering with concentration. His eyes were hard set and brimming with anger.

"Run!" he said simply. His voice was powerful, strong, and one that you immediately obeyed, even if you didn't want to.

"Run, Aurora, now!" he said again.

His sword glistened in the moonlight as he drew it from its sheath and prepared to meet the Shadow Guard. I was about to turn and run, but I couldn't help watching him for a few seconds more. He was now battling both the Shadow Guards with his sword. It flashed and swirled like it had a mind of its own. I thought I saw a light surrounding him, and it flickered lightly with a faint blue hue.

I was entranced; I had never seen anyone fight with a sword like that before. He was like a young Sir Lancelot, or more like Zorro with magic. I couldn't keep my eyes off him. He was magnificent, and he had come back for me.

Just then I heard Kalen shout out, "My lady, over here."

I turned towards his voice. He was standing amongst the trees on the other side of the clearing, holding the pegasus who looked like it was about to bolt at any minute.

I ran towards Kalen, my heart pounding in my chest. I glanced back just for a second to see Rafe now surrounded by the Shadow Guard. They had advanced in an attack and were shooting bolts of red fire at his shield. Kalen had started muttering a running commentary in my ear as soon as I reached him.

"Look at him move. Do you have any idea how much concentration it takes to hold a magical shield like that and fight at the same time?" Kalen was saying. "And this is not just any fight, he is battling the Shadow Guard."

The pegasus had started putting up a fight; it obviously wanted to bolt away from the loud sounds. The other fae and Finn, had disappeared into the trees. Oblek had managed to revive himself and stood up unsteadily. The human guards were on the floor, and there was just Rafe and the two of us against Oblek and two Shadow Guards.

Rafe's invisible shield was still holding, but his sword had fallen, and now red and white jets of light shot back and forth between him and the Shadow Guard. How long could he keep this up? I had to do something, help him, or he could die.

"Try and get on," said Kalen, holding the pegasus. "She will not let me ride her, but maybe she will take you. If you are of the royal house of Elfi, the pegasus will carry you."

The pegasus still showed no signs of calming down, and it was taking all of Kalen's strength, such as it was, to hold her. She seemed to want to run free, but she was pulling in the direction of the fight instead of the other way around. I tried to calm her down and put my hand on her neck. My palm tingled faintly. Suddenly the pegasus stopped and was completely still. And then something extremely strange happened. I heard a soft musical voice in my head.

"Climb on, and I shall carry you, Princess," said the voice.

I looked around, and back at the pegasus. Did she just speak to me in my head? No! That was impossible! But supposedly, so was magic.

"Yes, it's me," the voice said, "and we don't have much time. Do you want to help your friend there or not? I'll explain later."

"Okay," I said in my mind, tentatively pushing the thought out at the pegasus. I hesitated for a brief second. Kalen gave me a boost, and I jumped onto the pegasus's back. Kalen looked at me with his mouth open wide. I guess I was of the royal line of Elfi, after all.

"Go," said Kalen. "Get to Eldoren, and go straight to Silverthorne Castle. Tell your granduncle everything that has happened. The duke will know what to do."

"We must help him," I said out loud, looking over at Rafe.

"Do not worry, my lady," said Kalen. "Rafe can take care of himself. You just get out of Illiador as fast as you can. He will meet you there."

I nodded, as the pegasus reared once and cantered towards the clearing. I held on tight and concentrated on staying on. Suddenly I realized the pegasus was running straight towards the Shadow Guard.

Kalen was shouting, "You're going the wrong way! You need to get away from this forest fast."

"I hope you know how to create a shield," said the voice in my head. "You're going to need it now."

"I can't," I gasped out loud. "I have no magic."

"You may not know how to use your magic, but you do have it, or you would not be able to speak to me with your mind," said the pegasus. "For now, I will shield you. Don't worry, I know what I'm doing."

"You have magic?" I asked.

"I am a pegasus, protected by the old magic of the fae. The magic of the Shadow Guard cannot harm me," said the pegasus. "And my magic protects those of the royal house of Elfi."

This mind-talking was weird, but I was quickly getting used to it.

"It's you they want," said the pegasus. "I will draw their

fire away from the Black Wolf to give him enough time to escape. But you must hold on tight. Whatever happens, do not let go."

We were nearing the fight. I could see Rafe's shield wavering as the pegasus increased her speed into a gallop in one fluid motion. It was like riding on air, and soon we really were—we were flying. The pegasus spread her powerful wings and shot into the sky like a hawk, flying directly over the clearing.

The Shadow Guards looked up, and their shields faltered. Rafe hit both of them squarely in the chest with powerful bolts of white light. They fell to the ground, but Oblek raised his hand, a ball of red fire growing in his palm.

"Now," said the voice in my head. "Hold on."

I closed my eyes and held on tightly to the pegasus's neck. I was scared, but I knew I had no choice.

Just then I heard Rafe shout, "No!"

I looked down for a second, in time to see a jet of red flames shooting towards me.

"Be calm," said the voice in my mind.

I felt a jolt hit my back, but there was no pain. I was still on the pegasus's back, flying out of the forest. I vaguely made out Rafe's dark shadow disappearing into the trees. I had done it. I had escaped, and most importantly, Rafe was safe.

8
SNOW

I CLUNG ON tightly to the pegasus's neck as we rose up over the trees of Goldleaf Forest and flew towards the Cascade Mountains.

"That was very well done, Princess," said the pegasus, a calm voice in my head.

I smiled. I had only just caught my breath, and my heart was still racing. I never imagined that pegasi could talk.

"How did you know who I was?" I asked the pegasus, pushing the thought out to her.

The pegasus answered in my mind. "When you touched me, I felt your power. You are unmistakably of the royal line of Gwenfar-Ith-Aran of the fae. We pegasi have our own magic; I could see who you were, just the same as if you were telling me."

"Can you talk to everyone like this?" I asked.

"Only to the royal fae," she said simply.

It was an amazing and exhilarating feeling, racing through the sky on the back of a magical winged horse. The pegasus's powerful wings soared through the air. Soon we had cleared the forest and were flying higher and higher towards the

Cascade Mountains.

"Where do you want to go, Princess?" said the pegasus, "I can take you anywhere you wish after we rest."

"I need to go back and see if my friend Kalen is okay," I said, "and Rafe as well."

"That I cannot do, Princess," said the pegasus in my mind. "Illiador is not safe for you now. The Shadow Guard were all over the place. Pixie Bush is where they will search first."

"But I need to know my friends are all right," I said, a little worried. Right now the pegasus was the only one who knew where we were. Without her I would be lost.

"Your friend, the little fae, will be fine. Do not fret, dear one. And the Black Wolf can take care of himself as well as the others. He will see to it that the fae are safe. I know of him; he may be a mage, but he is a friend of the fae."

I resigned myself to the fact that I wasn't going to be taken back to Pixie Bush. My only choice was to go to Silverthorne Castle and meet my granduncle, the duke.

"I need to go to Silverthorne Castle in Eldoren," I said politely. "Do you know how to get there?"

"Yes, of course," said the pegasus. "But why do you need to go to Silverthorne Castle? Better yet, just show me why. It's quicker that way."

"What do you mean?" I asked. "How can I show you?"

"This is fae magic. Just put your palm on my neck and think about the events as they happened, and I will see it, too," said the pegasus.

I closed my eyes, and put my left palm on the pegasus's neck and thought about Redstone Manor, my adoptive parents, Christopher, Cornelia, Count Oblek, the tapestry, meeting Kalen and Rafe in the dungeons, Finn's treachery, our escape to Pixie Bush, and Mrs. Plumpleberry's healing salve and sound advice.

"That is quite enough," the pegasus said. "I will take you to Silverthorne Castle. But I must rest a while; the magic I used to protect us from the Shadow Guards magic has weakened me."

"Okay," I said, relieved that at least I didn't have to ride through the mountains for days with Kalen. I would have had to travel with Rafe too, though, and it would have been interesting to spend more time with him. I guess it was not to be. I was still a little apprehensive about where we would sleep that night, because the pegasus needed to rest. Some people may like camping under the stars, with wild animals around, but I did not. It was not really my idea of a good time. Flying to the castle on the back of the pegasus was absolutely the best thing that could have happened.

"Can I ask you something?" I asked hesitantly.

"Of course."

"What do I call you?"

The pegasus laughed, more like a neigh, but I could feel her emotions. It was amazing.

"My name is Gwyneira, which means, 'white as snow' in

the old language of the fae," she said.

"May I call you Snow?" I asked. It sounded like a wonderful name for a pegasus.

The pegasus laughed. "Yes that is acceptable," she said. "I like the name Snow."

I smiled. "Perfect!"

We were now flying higher and higher over the Cascade Mountains. The wind whipped around my face and hair, but I didn't care. The moon was full and bathed the mountains in its silvery light. Riding on the back of a pegasus gave me the most wonderful feeling of freedom. After about an hour, we descended through the low-lying clouds and Snow carefully flew through the trees and into a clearing in a forested area of the mountains.

I slid off Snow and cautiously looked around.

The moonlight lit the little clearing, and Snow led me to some bushes, which she told me to push apart. I struggled a little with the dense foliage but finally found a small opening to a dark cave. I peered inside; there was no light, and I quickly backed away.

"There is no way I am going in there," I said to Snow out loud.

"Would you prefer to sleep outdoors?" asked Snow, sounding a little confused. "I'm afraid I have no idea how to light a fire, and it will get cold. If you knew how to use your magic, you could have done it, but since you cannot, we will have to make do with the cave."

I nodded, feeling upset that I had no magic and a little nervous. I had no idea what was inside that cave, and I was not going in there to find out. I would much rather sleep outside.

"Fine," I said abruptly, "I'll just sleep against a tree or something."

I looked around for a suitable spot. I located an old oak that looked quite comfortable, relatively speaking. It was a massive, ancient-looking tree, and the thick trunk had a small hollow in it, big enough for a person to fit into. I maneuvered myself inside and slid down against the inside of the mossy trunk, hugging my knees together and resting my head on them. I was cold and tired, so I wrapped my woolen cloak tightly around me as best I could, and, despite the circumstances, I immediately started nodding off.

Snow stood next to me. "I will be here to watch over you, Princess. Do not worry. I just need a little rest, and as soon as dawn approaches we shall be on our way."

"Okay," I said in my mind, already half asleep. The cool fresh air of the mountains was making me really drowsy. The leaves rustled gently, lulling me into a fitful sleep.

I hardly felt like I had had any sleep at all when I heard Snow's voice urgently calling to me in my mind. My eyes snapped open and I looked up, but it took me a minute to get my sleep-befuddled brain together. I scanned my surroundings quickly and got up from my place on the forest floor, using the big oak for support.

Two guards were holding Snow by her mane, and she was struggling to get free. The men who were holding her were wearing rusty armor and equally tarnished shields that bore the crest of a black rose.

"Morgana's guards," said Snow quickly. "Run, Princess; these look like scouts, so the Shadow Guard will not be far away. You must get out of here, now."

I whirled around in a complete panic. What was I supposed to do? I couldn't just leave Snow to the guards. What if they killed her?

"Leave me," Snow said. "Your life is far more important."

Terror welled up in my chest, and I turned to run, but two more guards were coming out of the trees behind me.

I was surrounded.

"There is no use trying to run, milady," said the gruff voice of one black-toothed guard. He was grinning manically at me.

I took a step back and felt something sharp prick my back.

"Don't move," said another guard from behind me. I couldn't see his face, but they all seemed to look the same to me. Dirty, filthy, matted hair, black grins and rusty armor.

From the corner of my eye, I could see the bushes rustling. What else was out there?

I heard a low growl, and, before I realized what was happening, a massive lion-like creature with a mane of burnished gold and powerful red wings came leaping out of the darkness of the forest, its sharp teeth flashing in the moonlight. It had a jagged, spiked tail and the face of a man. I recognized the mythological creature from a picture I had seen on the Internet.

I froze in my tracks: a manticore!

It snarled, showing multiple rows of razor-sharp fangs, and pounced on the guard who had a sword to my back.

I heard more growls and screaming, but I didn't want to look back. I ran towards the trees, and I saw Snow moving towards me, free. The other two guards who had been holding her now had their swords out and were advancing on me. I tripped over a fallen tree limb and hit my shin. The pain didn't register as I got up and tried to reach Snow.

I needn't have moved at all, as the manticore flew over me and attacked the two guards, ripping out the throat of one and pouncing on the other, slashing his arms and legs with his deadly tail. I looked on in dismay as the guard screamed and tried to get away, but the creature just tore out his throat. The rest of the guards lay unconscious or dead on the ground around us.

I was trembling and rooted to the spot. Would the manticore turn on me now? I had no idea why it was here.

"Do not be afraid, little one," said Snow calmly in my head. "You have nothing to fear from this creature. He is a friend and a protector; he came only because you were in trouble. All the creatures of the fae are loyal to your family."

I looked over carefully at the manticore. He was sitting on his haunches and did not move, looking straight at me with startling gold eyes, full of intelligence. His fangs were still dripping blood, much to my dismay, but his eyes looked kind and full of anguish.

I looked at the dead bodies strewn about the forest clearing, and I started to feel sick. I moved towards a tree and retched, but as I hadn't eaten anything, there was nothing much to throw up. I wiped my mouth as best I could with the sleeve of my dress; it was disgusting, but I couldn't help it. I was surprised at myself. In a situation like this, I really expected to have fainted, but I didn't, and I was pleased with my fortitude.

I turned to see the majestic creature still watching me. There was something about him that was comforting, and I moved forward. The manticore must have been startled, because he stood up and started walking away. I watched his furry, gold body move slowly towards the darkness of the trees, his lethal tail swishing behind him. He stopped once and turned to look at me before spreading his great leathery wings and flying off into the shadows of the vast mountain range.

I let out a deep breath I hadn't even realized I was holding. "Where did that creature come from?" I asked Snow as I got onto her back, this time with the help of a rock that I used as a mounting block. For the first time, I realized how inconvenient it was riding in a dress, as my legs were exposed, but I figured it was really not the time or the place for modesty and settled myself on Snow's back.

"The manticore is an ancient fae creature," said Snow. "There are not many left, especially in these parts, but they have been seen in these mountains before. They are born of magic, so it could sense who you were and came to help."

I wondered what other creatures lived in these mountains, but I didn't want to stick around and find out. I concentrated on holding on as Snow cantered across the open space, spread out her massive wings, and soared into the air again. We flew over the Cascade Mountains towards Eldoren and Silverthorne Castle.

I could not believe what I was doing: riding a magical winged horse, running from the mysterious Shadow Guard, becoming friends with the fae, meeting manticores in the forest and heading towards a family I had never met before. I had to admit I was apprehensive. What if they didn't like me? What if they didn't want to help me? What if . . . ?

My thoughts were cut short as the sun rose over the mountains to the east. I forgot about everything else as I watched the magical land of Avalonia stretch out before me as far as the eye could see. We glided over the Cascade Mountains, which marked the boundary between the kingdoms of Illiador and Eldoren, and I was immediately mesmerized.

The land ahead was covered in wild, green grass. Sprays of pinks, purples, yellows, and reds undulated down into the waiting meadows of the flower-filled valley beyond. It was the most wonderful sight I had ever seen. Rolling hills, colorful fields, green pastures, working farms, massive estates and small villages speckled the countryside. To the right was an emerald-green wood, which stretched out to the hills beyond.

In the center of the valley was what looked like a little hill. At the very top was a magnificent castle, its tall towers glistening in the sunlight as they stretched effortlessly towards the sky. Pristine white flags, each decorated with a single bluebell, fluttered from the castle turrets. Around it, a huge walled town sloped down the hill in concentric circles and spread out into the valley below. Sunlight glinted off the tops of the tallest trees of the forest, and the whole valley was bathed in its warm blanket. It was like nothing I had ever seen before, but it was also everything that I had imagined since I was a little girl.

"That is Fairlone," said Snow in my mind as we flew over the large town. "This whole valley belongs to the Duke of Silverthorne."

Fairlone was a huge bustling town, with broad cobbled streets and paved paths. A great wall surrounded the town, with four massive wooden gates and armed gate towers.

We circled the castle and the town once, and no one looked up, which was a relief, since I was quite sure that, even here, a pegasus was a rare creature. We flew over the outer section of the town, and I looked around; the houses here were closely packed and looked quite run down. The people were dressed in dull, patched clothes, as they were in Lord Oblek's castle in Illiador. Snow explained that this was the poorer part of the town. As we flew closer to the magnificent castle on the top of the hill, I could see a change. The inner town was highly protected by another wall that ran in a circle around the castle.

Wide stone archways, whitewashed buildings, and large, well-kept houses lined the cobblestone streets. Elegant shops and colorful street sellers brightened the main avenue. The buildings were bigger and more ornate, with tiled roofs and brightly colored walls. It was morning, and well-dressed people were bustling round fancy shops and going about their everyday errands.

The men were smartly attired in well-tailored doublets and hose, wearing richly bordered, thick cloaks that swirled about them as they walked. Many wore swords on their belts and some rode on prancing horses. The women were dressed in beautiful silks and velvet, richly embroidered dresses, hooded mantles, and luxurious cloaks. Some were driven about in small, one-horse open carriages.

Finally, we flew out of the sky and descended into the stone courtyard of Silverthorne Castle. I was mesmerized and a little disoriented after my long flight on Snow's back. I looked around. The castle was massive and full of activity.

Guards had just realized that we had landed in the center of their castle courtyard and sounded the alarm. Within sec-

onds, numerous soldiers had surrounded us and were pointing nasty-looking spears in my face.

9

THE DUKE

I LOOKED AROUND. Archers had posted themselves at regular intervals on the castle walls, and all the arrows were pointing right at me.

"I want to meet the Duke of Silverthorne," I said, trying to sound like I knew what I was doing.

"So does half the kingdom," said a guard with curly red hair.

"And the other half is plotting his downfall," said another.

"What's your business here?" the first guard growled, still pointing his spear at me.

"Um, tell him . . . tell him that his niece is here," I said hesitantly.

What else could I say? How was I supposed to explain myself?

"He doesn't have a niece," said the red-haired guard, not believing my story for a second.

"What is all this commotion about?" came a large booming voice.

The guards jumped but held their spears in place.

"Who is this?" said a big, burly man with salt-and-pepper

hair, his voluminous cerulean cloak billowing in the wind as he came striding down the broad stone steps into the castle courtyard. He was wearing a silver breastplate and a massive sword strapped to his hip. I wondered if this was my grand-uncle, the duke.

"She just arrived, Captain," said the red-haired guard, standing up straighter. "She says she wants to see the duke, says she's his niece."

"Does she now?" said the captain of the guard, walking closer to me. Snow stamped her hoof and snorted, but he did not even flinch. Finally he stretched out his hand to help me off the pegasus. "Declan Raingate, captain of the duke's guard, at your service, my lady."

He seemed a gentleman, and his brown eyes were kind, so I took his hand and jumped off Snow. "Thank you," I said, straightening my skirt and smoothing my hair, which resembled a bird's nest after all that flying.

"See that the pegasus is well housed in the main stables," said the captain to one of the guards. I liked him already.

"Right away, sir," said the red-haired guard, scurrying to do the captain's bidding.

"Follow me," Declan said, turning to walk up the steps to the castle. "I will take you to the duke."

The guards all straightened their spears and retreated to their posts. The archers put away their bows and returned to their jobs on the battlements. I was relieved. Silverthorne Castle was a fortress; Oblek and Morgana would have a hard time getting to me here. I already felt much safer.

I followed Captain Declan up the great white stone steps, through the big wooden doors, into the castle. We walked down drafty stone corridors and up a wide spiral staircase in one of the towers. Declan knocked once on a stout oak door and opened it without waiting for a reply.

"Can't a man get any work done around here? There is always something that needs my attention," said an old and distinguished-looking man with white, shaggy hair and a clipped white beard, looking up from his desk and putting down his quill. He was wearing a midnight-blue velvet dress-ing gown lined with intricate silverwork.

I figured that this must be my granduncle, the duke.

"My apologies for disturbing you at this time of the morn-ing, Your Grace. But the matter is of some importance," said the captain of the guard, walking into the brightly lit room.

The duke finally noticed me, and I thought I saw a flicker of recognition in his eyes; then, just as quickly, it was gone.

"And you are?" asked the Duke, looking straight at me.

"My name is Aurora, and I think you are my unc—" I said quickly, but the duke suddenly interrupted me.

"Thank you, Declan, but I will speak with this one alone," said Duke Silverthorne.

The captain of the guard bowed once and left the room.

I looked around; this appeared to be the duke's study. It was a large, high-ceilinged room lined with oak beams but it was bright and airy, with immense windows, which were hung with rich crimson and gold velvet curtains. Big comfortable armchairs were placed about the room. A mahogany desk and an extra-large chair stood behind it. Exotic rugs covered the cold stone floors, and beautiful but slightly faded tapestries lined the walls, all depicting scenes with different fae creatures—unicorns, dragons, pixies, flower fairies, and beautiful lush green forests.

The duke gestured for me to sit down opposite him.

"Now, what is all this really about?" said Duke Silverthorne sternly. His blue eyes shone questioningly, as if he was trying to piece together a puzzle.

"Well," I said hesitantly, sitting down on the offered chair.

I wasn't exactly sure what I should say. I decided to keep it short.

"It turns out that you are my granduncle, and my aunt, Queen Morgana, wants me dead. Oh! And I have nowhere to go and no way to get back home, not that I really have a home anymore," I said. "That's about the gist of it."

The duke studied me carefully and narrowed his eyes. "I think you'd better start again, from the beginning," he said, peering at me from under his big, bushy eyebrows as if he knew exactly what I was talking about. He didn't seem surprised.

I proceeded to recount the full story. When I finished, the duke was quiet, and he was still looking at me very sternly.

"You do look a lot like Azaren," he said finally, his eyes going slightly misty. "But we can never be too careful. I have on occasion heard stories that Elayna and Azaren's child had somehow escaped the massacre at the Star Palace, and once there was even a rumor that the princess had been found in Brandor." He paused, assessing me again. "Of course, she was brought to me."

"And?" I said, urging him to go on.

"And she was an imposter, of course."

"How could you tell?" I asked, now sitting on the edge of my seat and wiping my sweating hands on my skirt.

"You will find out all you need to know in good time," said the duke, "but first, we need to test you, to see if it's true that you are the child of Azaren and Elayna, and not some shapeshifter sent by Lucian to deceive us."

"Shapeshifter!" I said, jumping up from my chair. "You think I am a shapeshifter? This is getting more and more absurd every minute."

I was really upset now. The last two days had taken their toll on me, and I had hardly slept since this all began. Now, when I was just starting to believe all this nonsense myself, my granduncle, who seemed to be the only one who could help me, thought I was an imposter.

I couldn't help myself as the words tumbled out of my mouth.

"I was taken from my home and my world in the middle of the night, thrown in a dungeon, barely escaped with my life, and fought the Shadow Guard, who want to take me to Morgana." I was pacing and waving my hands around as I spoke. "Just two days ago my biggest problem was trying to stay away from my horrid cousin Cornelia, who suddenly doesn't seem so horrid after all, especially after I found out about my aunt who wants me dead."

I took a deep breath and went on. "I just want to go home, but I don't have anywhere to go. My adoptive parents are dead and so are my real ones. I have no family, no friends, and no one cares what happens to me."

I sat back down in my chair and bent over, holding my head in my hands. I had come to the end of the road. I had never felt so alone, so helpless and at a loss as to what to do next. Suddenly, all the loneliness and despair of my life that I had bottled up for all these years came rushing back. This was worse than the hollow feeling in my chest when I realized I was adopted and thought that my real parents never wanted me. It brought back a flood of memories. The years of waiting for the day when my parents would return and sweep me away to a beautiful, loving home surrounded by my real family. And the day I finally realized that they were never coming back. I couldn't help releasing the tears that splashed down my face. Wrenching sobs racked my body. I couldn't stop crying, and I wept for what seemed like hours.

When I finally lifted my head and pulled myself together, I saw that the duke was smiling. I dried my eyes with the handkerchief the duke very politely handed to me.

"Thank you," I said, embarrassed at my watery outburst. The duke must think I was nothing more than a scared child who cried every time life seemed too hard.

"Everything happens for a reason, and nothing is an accident. It is all part of a much larger divine plan," Duke Silverthorne said gravely, but in a surprisingly kind voice. "When difficulties come, we must see them as what they are—opportunities and a new path to discover your potential. How will you ever know the magnitude of courage you are capable of if you have never experienced the hopelessness of fear?"

I nodded and tried to act like I understood, but adults always said these philosophical things to make you feel better, and frankly, at the moment, it wasn't helping.

"Now, about the test," the duke said, smiling again after I had finally composed myself. "It's only a simple one. Every mage has a specific magical essence, and I can touch your mind and read yours."

What would he discover in my mind? I must have looked as alarmed as I felt, because the duke quickly tried to reassure me.

"Now, my dear, you must not be worried, I would never delve into your private thoughts. That would be considered the height of rudeness in our world, since a lot of us can talk by mind contact."

"We have phones for that," I said absentmindedly.

The duke laughed. "Yes, it is quite a mystery how you came to be brought up in a different world. I have traveled there on occasion myself for some work. Didn't like it much, though," he said, chuckling to himself.

I smiled at that. I wondered what he had been doing, wandering round in other worlds. Were there more gateways like the one I came through?

Finally he stopped laughing and leaned back in his chair. "I do believe you have traveled here from a different world, and the tapestry you have described is the last of its kind, although there are many other ways to travel to your world. But whether you really are the child of Elayna and Azaren remains to be seen."

I nodded, clasped my hands together in my lap, and tried to behave in a more grown-up fashion.

"Right, the test," he said. "If you are truly of Azaren's bloodline I will know. But you must not fight me. I would not want to hurt your mind in any way."

"Hurt my mind!" I didn't particularly like the thought of someone poking around in there. "What are you going to do to me?"

"Don't worry, just calm your mind and let me look into it. It is quite a simple test we do when the paternity of a child is in question." He coughed, looking embarrassed. "We perform this on babies, but their minds are so free that it's easier."

"Oh, like a magical DNA test," I said, feeling a little relieved. That made sense.

The duke laughed again. "Yes! I am sure that in your world you can ascertain these things by way of what I believe the human race calls science."

I nodded. "Yup, that's it! Science. Not much use 'round here though, since you guys have magic and all."

The duke smiled. He seemed to find me amusing for some reason.

"You're correct. Magic and science have never done well together, one of the main reasons for Avalonia growing apart from the human world—science and magic were clashing," he said.

"Okay, let's get this over with," I said, sounding braver than I felt.

"Please come and sit in front of me," said the duke, gesturing to a high-backed, velvet-upholstered chair. I went over and sat down opposite him.

"Now, my dear, just concentrate," he began. "Make your mind blank. Try to rid yourself of all thoughts, so I can see clearly who and what you are. Your essence will also tell me if you have the potential to be a mage, or if you have taken on the traits of your mother's race."

"I'm ready," I said, closing my eyes.

The duke placed his fingertips lightly on my temples, and I tried to shut out my wayward thoughts, but they were flitting in and out of my head like mischievous butterflies. It was difficult to make my mind go completely blank. I opened my eyes to peek a little. The duke was frowning.

"What's wrong?" I asked.

"I don't know," said Duke Silverthorne, removing his hands from my temples. "I should be able to sense your magic, but somehow there is nothing. I can't sense a thing."

"That's what Penelope said."

"Penelope could not sense your magic either?" the duke asked, looking even more perturbed.

I shook my head. "No, she said I must have mage magic and that's why she couldn't sense it."

"I don't understand," said the duke. "Even if you were ordinary, just a human, I would be able to ascertain that, but your mind is a mystery, a complete blank."

The duke was staring at me as if he was trying to piece together a very irritating puzzle.

"This is very peculiar," said the duke. "Even when I met you, I felt no magic. Usually a fully trained mage like myself is able to sense the magical essence of another person, mage or fae. I sensed nothing, and I can't get into your mind."

"So, what does this mean?" I asked. "If I have no magic, I can't be Azaren and Elayna's daughter?"

"Not necessarily," said the duke, pausing to think. "Normally I would have dismissed you by now, but there is something about you that I can't put my finger on. You did speak to the pegasus with your mind, did you not?"

I nodded. "Yes."

"That is strange," said the duke. "For a pegasus to talk to you, you have to be of royal fae blood. But if you have no fae magic that Penelope could sense, how did you do it?"

I shrugged. What could I say? I had absolutely no idea how I had done it myself.

"The pegasi are an ancient race of magical beings," said the duke, "and they possess the old magic of the fae. It is very rare for a pegasus to make such a mistake. That is why I am not really sure how to proceed with you."

I was disappointed; having magic was one of the best things about this place. But, on the other hand, if Morgana knew that I wasn't a threat to her, she just might leave me alone. Where would I go now? If the duke did not believe me, I would be shoved out into a world where I had no idea how to survive on my own. Maybe Snow would be able to take me back to Pixie Bush.

The duke sat back in his chair, resting his elbows on the arms of the chair. He folded his hands together and stared at me. I suddenly felt very uncomfortable at the way he was looking at me. I wasn't sure what to expect now, and I fidgeted in my chair. I nervously started fiddling with the gold medallion that rested round my neck, as I always did when I was feeling uneasy.

"What is that?" said the duke sharply, suddenly springing up from his chair.

"What?" I asked, looking around. Everything looked the same to me.

He came over to me and pulled out my necklace.

"Hey!" I said. "It's mine! It's the only thing I had with me when I was found as a child."

The duke just stared at it. It was a small gold disc with strange etchings on it, which I could never figure out, but the duke obviously knew what it said, because he was reading it.

"I don't believe it," he said falling back into his chair after he had inspected it thoroughly. "I really cannot believe it." He kept saying it again and again and staring at me. "This is impossible—it is a myth, a legend, it doesn't exist, and neither should you."

Not exist! What was this guy talking about? I needed some answers and soon.

The duke leaned forward in his chair and looked at me more closely, his bushy white eyebrows joining together as he scrunched his forehead. "There is a reason I could not sense your magic, and I finally know what it is."

"So, you mean you believe me?"

"Yes, Aurora, I do believe you," said the duke, using my name for the first time. "That medallion you wear around your neck is no ordinary piece of jewelry. It is a very powerful magical artifact that was thought to be lost long ago and has faded into the realms of legend. Your father or mother must have found it somehow and made you wear it."

"Why?" I asked, my eyes wide. What the hell was I wearing round my neck? "Why would they do that?"

"They did it to protect you, of course, Aurora," said the duke calmly. "When a mage and a fae marry and have children, the child is born with either trait, mage powers or fae magic."

I nodded. "Yes, I know that. Mrs. Plumpleberry told me."

"What she didn't tell you is that, on extremely rare occasions, the child born takes on both the parents' magical powers."

I gasped. "But is that even possible?"

"From the beginning of this world, there have been only six known fae-mages in Avalonia. You, my dear, are the seventh," said my granduncle.

I just gaped at him with my mouth open. "What is a fae-mage?"

"Exactly what it sounds like," he said, shaking his head. "And unless I am sorely mistaken, not only do you have mage powers within you, which are exceptionally strong I may add, because of your bloodline, but you also have fae magic. And not any ordinary fae magic, but probably immortal fae powers, since your mother was one of the immortal fae."

"What?" I said, disbelief clouding my senses. "But you just said you couldn't sense anything. You said that I have no magic."

"I was wrong," said the duke. "The reason neither Penelope nor I could sense your powers is because you are wearing the Amulet of Auraken."

"The what?" I said, looking down at the small gold medallion that I had worn around my neck for as long as I could remember. Was he serious? First he didn't believe me, now he thought I was some legendary fae-mage.

"I will tell you everything you need to know, but we have one more thing to do before we begin," said the duke. "Take off your amulet for just a moment, although not for long, because it's what keeps Morgana from finding you with magic."

"Are you sure?" I asked skeptically. "And what if I take it off and Morgana finds me here?"

"It doesn't work that fast. You have to have it off for a certain amount of time for Morgana to find you, and even then she has to be looking at exactly that moment."

I hesitated. I had never taken the amulet off before; somehow I never felt the need to. I even kept it on while I slept. It was all that connected me to my birth parents. They had given it to me for my protection, and it had kept me safe from Morgana for all these years.

"Don't be afraid, Aurora," said the duke kindly. "I only want to test the intensity of your powers, so we know what we are dealing with. Just the presence of that amulet around your neck tells me that you are indeed telling the truth."

I hesitated, but I removed the amulet and put it down on the table in front of me. I glanced down at my hands. They had started tingling, and then slowly a strange light started seeping out of my palms. It was as if I was lighting up from the inside. Soon my whole right hand had started glowing with an iridescent, blue-white light. I was stunned. I really did have magic.

"That, my dear, is truly a remarkable sight to behold," was all the duke said, as he stared at me. "Please, put the amulet back on now, Aurora, that is more than enough."

I slipped the chain round my neck. The amulet rested

THE LAST OF THE FIREDRAKES

heavy against my chest, and the light that had infused my body went out.

"Like I said before," said the duke, "there have been instances when a child has taken on both powers. It is very rare, and you are the only fae-mage to have been born in over a thousand years."

"A thousand years! Are you serious?" I blurted out.

The duke looked amused. "Yes, I am very serious, Aurora. Your powers are probably unsurpassable, but you will have to learn how to use them, or it could lead to disaster. A fae-mage who cannot control both her mage and fae powers is a threat to herself and to the world around her. For now, tell no one what we have discovered here. I will let you get settled in and then we will begin lessons to help you learn to wield your magic."

He suddenly got up from his chair and came over with his arms outstretched. I stood up awkwardly as the duke enveloped me in a big bear hug. Unexpected, happy tears pooled in my eyes as I hugged him back.

"Welcome back, Aurora," said the duke, stepping back, but still holding on to both my arms and looking at me, as if he was seeing me for the first time.

"Thank you, um . . . Duke," I said, a little embarrassed at the sudden affection. Ever since my adoptive parents died, I had forgotten what it was like to have someone actually care about me.

The duke laughed, a happy, deep rumble. "Call me Uncle

120

Gabriel from now on, Aurora—after all, we are family."

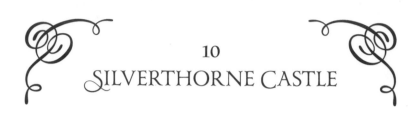

10
SILVERTHORNE CASTLE

UNCLE GABRIEL summoned a plump maid who was to show me to my room.

"Now you must rest," he said. "It's been a long ordeal for you, and I am sure you will be glad to have a decent bed to sleep in. Tomorrow my daughter, Serena, and my grandson, Erien, will be visiting for a while. It is fortuitous, as now you can meet the rest of your family. Herring here will show you to your room."

I thanked my granduncle and followed Herring. She led me down many long corridors. Some were small and draughty, with dark stone walls and slits for windows, and some were brighter and wider with high ceilings, where large open arches lined the corridors and the walls were covered from ceiling to floor with beautiful tapestries. We crossed small, enclosed courtyards, and long, open walkways, through huge echoing halls, and up the main stairs to the second floor of the east wing of Silverthorne Castle.

I tried to remember how I got there. It would be quite a task getting around a castle this huge. I was sure I would get lost before I could manage to find my way around without effort.

I was just too tired to take in the rest of my surroundings. When I reached my room, I wobbled over to the bed and fell asleep almost immediately, without changing my clothes.

When I woke up, I was disoriented. I had no idea what the time was, and for a moment I couldn't even remember where I was. This was the first time I had slept so soundly. The dream had not returned, and I hoped it never would again.

I looked over to see the same young maid bustling about the huge room quietly, doing some chores. Then I remembered the mages, the fae, the dungeon, and Silverthorne Castle. Oh no! It hadn't been a dream. I really was in a strange magical land where nothing made sense, and now was the time to face reality. I racked my sleepy brain for the girl's name.

"What time is it, Herring?" I asked politely as I sat up in my massive four-poster bed.

"Oh you're up, my lady," said Herring, coming over to the bed. "It is now evening and time for supper."

I looked around. Herring had opened the heavy velvet curtains surrounding the bed, and muted sunlight streamed in through a large open window. Sumptuous rugs covered the white stone floors, brightening the enormous room. Ornate mahogany dressers and a few luxurious chairs were scattered about, completing the space. I was shocked; I had slept the whole day! And now I had no idea what I was supposed to do.

"Would you like me to run you a bath?" said Herring.

I got out of my bed and followed her over to a curtained doorway.

The bathroom was a cavernous room, with beautiful arched windows adorned with thick green velvet curtains with a gold trim. A huge marble bath with a silver fountain shaped like a water sprite with a jug lay proudly in the center of the room. A green silk daybed strewn with comfortable, colorful cushions lay along one wall. There was an alcove, which expertly hid the garderobe, a medieval-style toilet.

I hadn't really thought of all the bitter realities, and now this was one of them. The garderobe was in the shape of a huge high-backed chair; I had read about them in history class. It was not as rustic as a real medieval privy. It was very clean, and it didn't smell at all. In fact, it was quite comfortable. And I knew most people didn't have the luxury of privacy, as typically medieval toilets were communal. At least it looked like the castle had some sort of drainage system.

Next to it was another room. As I pulled back the heavy, emerald-green curtains that separated the rooms, I gasped. The room beside the bathroom was just as large and filled from top to bottom with some of the most beautiful clothes, slippers, and boots that I had ever seen. I looked up and down at the endless rows of clothes. They were just too beautiful and all my size. There were gorgeous silk dresses, exquisitely adorned with flowers, butterflies and vines and stunning pale chiffon dresses, which were worn with long fitted coats that were buttoned down the front but slit open from the waist, so that the swirling chiffon could be seen.

I ventured further into the vast closet, touching all the clothes with the tips of my fingers as I admired the wonders I had just discovered. I had never seen such wonderfully crafted, soft leather boots. Some were for riding and others were daintier and could be worn under dresses. There were also riding clothes, breeches, and long-sleeved doublets specially made for women. Plainly put, it was everything that I could ever need if I lived here.

"The duke will be expecting you in the great hall soon, milady," said Herring.

I was so taken aback by everything that I didn't have time to process all that had happened. It was only when I soaked my tired body in the huge bathtub that I thought about what this all meant.

Everything had changed. This wasn't like going off to boarding school or to college. There were no rules to follow, no way to know if what I was doing was right. Who to trust? Who should I stay away from? My granduncle seemed nice enough, and later that night I would be meeting other members of my father's family, my aunt Serena and young cousin Erien.

I wondered if they would they like me. Was Uncle Gabriel going to tell them I was a fae-mage?

There were just too many things to think about, so I quickly got out of the tub, dried myself off with a thick and extremely soft muslin cloth that Herring had given me as a towel, and hurriedly dressed myself in a simple, rose-pink silk gown. It was the most beautiful thing I had ever owned.

Avalonia didn't seem so bad after all, I thought, as I studied myself in the mirror. I had let Herring have her way with my hair since she insisted on doing it up for me. She had seemed distraught that I wanted to do my own hair and dress myself. I was pleased that I had let her do it in the end; it made a real difference to my appearance.

The rose-pink dress fit me perfectly, and it was bound about my waist with a thick gold sash weighted on the ends with real rubies. My dark hair, usually straggly and tied roughly in a ponytail, was washed and combed and held back from my face with elegant pins, and small, white flowers had been artfully woven into it.

I could hardly recognize myself.

Aunt Serena came to see me in my room. She was tall and beautiful with warm blue eyes and long hair the color of fresh honey. She immediately came up to me and hugged me fiercely, then looked me up and down and hugged me again. I have to say I was secretly happy with all the attention.

"I'm so glad that the clothes fit you," she said warmly. "My father kept my whole room and wardrobe intact when I got married. None of it fits me now, so I'm happy someone can make use of it."

"Thank you, Aunt Serena," I said. "The clothes are really beautiful. Are you sure you don't mind?"

"Not at all, my dear," she said, giving me a big hug. "That's what family is for."

I was touched. She had only known me for a few minutes, but Aunt Serena treated me so kindly.

"My father told me what happened to you," said Aunt Serena in a softer voice, after she had dismissed Herring. She looked at me in wonder. "I can't believe it, Azaren and Elayna's daughter, and a fae-mage on top of it all. My father was right, you do look a lot like Azaren."

I smiled at that. Aunt Serena was cheery and warm. She seemed a wonderful person, and I already felt quite at home.

"Well, it appears that you have been a busy little lady since you got here," said Aunt Serena, smiling and putting her arm around my shoulders. "Father says your story is very intriguing. You can tell me all about it while we go down for supper."

I nodded and accompanied Aunt Serena down the castle corridors to the main hall where a feast was being held.

The great hall was massive and filled with people. Long wooden tables and benches lay interspaced across the room. The hall was packed to bursting point, and raucous laughter and the clink and tinkle of plates and mugs filled the air. There were people eating and talking, and a scruffy looking group of musicians were playing a lively melody in one corner of the vast room.

I followed Aunt Serena to the other end of the hall, where a wooden dais stood. Uncle Gabriel was already there. Sitting next to him, on his left, were two men I had never seen before, and the duke introduced them to me.

First, I met Lord Larney, the thin one who looked like a crow. He had oily, black hair, which was thinning at the temples, and his nose was pointy and reminded me of a beak. The second man, who had not looked up from his food, was Sir Gothero, and I thought he looked like a fat, angry toad. His face was red and splotchy, and he ate his food with his hands, oblivious to the droplets of sauce dribbling down his massive double chin.

I disliked them both at first sight.

Uncle Gabriel introduced me as his ward, who had come to visit from another kingdom. He had explained to me earlier that no one must know who I really was. The two men got up and bowed, first to Aunt Serena.

"My lady," said the one who looked like a crow, in a slick voice. The fat, toad-like fellow mumbled something incoherent and planted a sloppy kiss on Aunt Serena's hand. She had to discreetly wipe it on her skirt. Aunt Serena nodded at them and sat down on her father's right, with me seated next to her.

I smiled and nodded at the two already drunk men. They didn't seem to be too interested in me, and I was thankful for that.

I glanced at Uncle Gabriel. He had given up listening to

the ramblings of the insipid Lord Larney, and was busy eating his food, spearing the contents of his plate with a small, sharp dagger.

I looked down at my plate. I was famished, and Aunt Serena had piled my plate with everything that the blue-and-gold-liveried pages were serving. It included small game pies with golden crusts, fresh breads, sliced meat, and cheeses that were quite different from those I had eaten before, but nonetheless quite delicious. There was a fish dish in a citrus sauce, roast duck and venison with some delicious looking vegetables, and a whole roast boar, which was carried through the hall by four plate bearers. I wondered how I was possibly going to eat so much food, but I was quite happy to give it my best shot.

Suddenly, a handsome young boy, slightly older than me, arrived huffing and puffing. His fine, blond hair kept flopping onto his face as he pushed it away irritably only to have it fall back into his heavy lashed, blue eyes all over again.

"Sorry I'm late, Mother," he said and sat down next to me.

Aunt Serena gave him a fierce look. "And where have you been, young man?"

My blond cousin laughed jovially. "Oh, just catching up with some old friends," he said, as he started eating immediately.

"Can you at least have the decency to greet our guest before you stuff your face?" said Aunt Serena, softly but sternly to Erien.

He turned, embarrassed. "Greetings. Pleasure to make your acquaintance, my lady," said Erien formally, suddenly remembering his manners.

So this was my cousin Erien? He was tall and lanky, but he ate like a big, burly man. I smiled back at him. I was not sure if Aunt Serena had told him who I was, so I didn't say much.

Aunt Serena just shot him a withering look. Erien probably thought the admonishment was over, but I had seen that look before. That was the same look my adoptive mother gave me when she was in company and couldn't shout at me. Poor Erien was going to get an earful after dinner, I was sure of that.

It was a dark night, and storm clouds thundered above the castle as I hurried down long stone hallways after dinner, searching for my room. I wished I had asked someone to show me the way instead of wandering aimlessly through the corridors for an hour, trying to find it myself.

I made a few turns that turned out to be dead ends or locked doors, when I noticed a figure crouching near one of the doors at the end of the corridor. The door was ajar, and the figure was obviously spying on someone.

My heart started hammering in my chest, and I inched closer to try and glimpse who it was. Suddenly, the figure turned just as lightning flashed outside. I breathed a sigh of relief; it was Erien. But what was he doing listening at open doors?

He waved me over and put his finger to his lips. I moved closer and crouched beside him, listening.

"I told you, Gothero, we must inform the duke," a voice I didn't recognize said.

"He will throw us in the dungeon as soon as he knows," said Gothero, his deep voice distinctive. "We cannot defy Morgana; Lucian will hunt us down. It's better we do what she wants. Silverthorne will forgive us eventually."

"Dead men don't forgive."

"I was joking," said Gothero.

"Well, it's not funny," the other man said.

I moved closer to Erien and the door. Candlelight flickered and I could see into part of the room. Gothero was sitting at a table holding what looked like a small green bottle, and Lord Larney was pacing up and down the room, quite visibly upset at the whole situation.

"Morgana is paying us very well," said Gothero, putting the green bottle down on the table in front of him. "All we have to do is make sure the duke drinks this. He will be dead by morning, and we will live in comfort for the rest of our lives."

Erien slid his sword out of its sheath, and I tried to grab his hand to prevent him from doing something stupid, but he jumped up before I could stop him.

"Erien, no," I whispered, in my last attempt to hold him back.

"Traitors," shouted Erien as he rushed into the room, brandishing his sword at the two startled men.

I ran into the room after him. "Erien, please be sensible," I said, trying to calm the situation. What was he thinking? He should have called someone instead of rushing into the room like that. If these men were contemplating killing the duke, they must be very dangerous, and there was no telling what they might do.

Gothero laughed and got up from his chair. "What are you going to do about it, boy?" he said, unsheathing his sword as he moved—which was surprisingly fast for a man of his size.

Erien stopped and prepared to defend himself. The other man, Lord Larney, was inching towards me on the other side, his sword already in hand. I looked around, frantically searching for some sort of weapon I could use to defend myself.

"I will make sure you hang for this," said Erien to the traitors.

"You and whose army?" Gothero sneered, inching closer towards us.

"I don't really think they need one," said a familiar voice behind me.

Larney's and Gothero's eyes widened at the sight of the person behind us. I didn't turn; I didn't need to. I knew exactly who it was.

"The Black Wolf, here! In the castle?" said Larney, recognizing him. "How? Where are the guards?"

Erien laughed when he saw Rafe. "Looks like you two might as well give yourselves up now," he said to the traitors.

"Put down your swords," said Rafe, coming up to stand beside me, "and you might get a fair trial."

"You can't do anything to us," said Lord Larney, slowly moving backwards. "You're an outlaw, wanted by the queen."

"She's not my queen," said Rafe, inching closer and repositioning himself slightly to shield me from them.

"Catch him. Morgana will reward us well for capturing the Black Wolf," said Gothero, glancing at his companion.

But before they could decide what to do, Rafe raised both his hands in front of him. Two bolts of white light shot out of his palms and hit the traitors in the chest. They collapsed on the white stone floor, in disheveled heaps.

"Are they . . . ?" I said, hesitant to finish my sentence.

"Dead? No," said Rafe, walking further into the room and bending down to bind the wrists of the fallen man. "They are merely stunned."

"So will they be all right?" I asked.

"Well, enough to stand trial, that's for sure," Erien answered, walking up to Rafe and helping him. Rafe finished tying up the men, got up, and clasped Erien's forearm in greeting.

"It's good to have you back in Silverthorne Castle, my friend. What brings you to these parts?" said Erien with a genuine smile on his face.

"I came by to see if the young lady got here safely," said Rafe, glancing at me.

"Ah, yes, Mother mentioned that you found her and sent her to us," said Erien. "You must tell me all about your adventures while you're here."

"I'm afraid I can't stay long," said Rafe. "People will recognize me soon enough. I'm sure the Lady Aurora will regale you with stories of our daring escape." He smiled at me, and I knew I was blushing.

Erien laughed. "I look forward to it. But right now I'll go and get Captain Declan to remove these men to the dungeons until my grandfather decides what to do with them."

"I should leave before he gets here," said Rafe with a grin. "I don't think the captain of the guard likes me very much."

"Probably a good idea," said Erien, chuckling and running off to summon the guards.

Rafe came over to stand in front of me. "We should get out of here before the guards come to take away the prisoners."

I nodded. "Thank you for saving me once again," I said, smiling up at him.

"It seems to have become a new job of mine," Rafe said, his lips quirking up in a suppressed smile.

I laughed at that. "Sorry," I said.

"Don't be. I'm not complaining," said Rafe, winking at me and walking out of the room where the two stunned men were tied up.

I smiled and followed him into the shadowy corridor

where half-burned torches lined the white stone walls. The thunder had abated, and shafts of muted moonlight sauntered in through the massive windows.

"Come," said Rafe, "I will escort you to your room."

"But I don't know where it is," I said, biting my lip and feeling very silly as I said it.

He stopped walking. "So how were you planning to get to your room tonight?" he asked, his eyes narrowing.

"I just thought I would find someone who would be able to tell me where it is," I said, trying to explain my apparent stupidity but failing miserably. "But then I got lost and saw Erien spying on those men, and, well, you know the rest."

Rafe started laughing, a deep, warm sound. "You really are very amusing, Aurora. I don't think I've ever had so much fun as I have since I was fortunate enough to stumble across you in Oblek's dungeon."

"Fun!" I said. "Are you mad? I've been almost killed three times since yesterday, and you think it's fun?"

Rafe nodded. "Except for the Shadow Guard in the forest, you weren't really in much danger. Oblek's guards are useless, and Larney and Gothero are fools. I wouldn't have let anything happen to you, Aurora," he said, more seriously. "I really wish you would trust me."

"I do trust you, Rafe," I said. "It's just that there is so much that has happened, I really don't know where to start."

"I met with your granduncle when I got here," said Rafe as we resumed walking, "and he told me what he discovered about you."

"He did?" I said.

Rafe nodded. "Your granduncle knows that your secret is safe with me."

I was surprised. Uncle Gabriel had expressly told me not to tell anyone who I was. Secretly I was relieved that I didn't have to lie to him.

"What will happen to Larney and Gothero?" I asked.

"It depends on your granduncle," said Rafe, "but I suspect they will be made examples of and hanged as traitors."

"Hanged!" I was horrified. "But they didn't actually kill him, they were only planning to."

"Yes," said Rafe, "but what if they had succeeded? This way it will deter anyone from trying to plot against the duke again."

I was unsettled. The justice system here was swift and cruel. One mistake, and you could be hanged the next day. Not that I didn't think what they did was wrong, and they should be locked up and made to pay for their crimes. But hanging? I thought it was a bit harsh.

Rafe stopped outside a stout oak door. "The kitchen is through here," said Rafe. "I'm sure you will manage to find someone to show you where your room is."

"Thank you," I said, relieved.

"I will take your leave now, Aurora," said Rafe.

"You're going right now?" I asked tentatively.

Rafe nodded. "I cannot take the risk of anyone seeing

me. Although most here are loyal to the Duke, there are also those who would sell me out to Morgana in a heartbeat."

"Who are you really?" I asked, my curiosity getting the better of me.

Rafe grinned. "It's better that you don't know for now," he said.

"Better for whom?" I asked, crossing my arms across my chest. He was really good at evading questions about himself. He now knew everything about me, who I was, and that I was a fae-mage, but I knew absolutely nothing about him. "How come you're always in the right place at the right time?"

He shrugged his shoulders. "Just luck, I guess," he said nonchalantly, but his eyes held a trace of humor.

He still hadn't answered any of my questions, and my mind started wandering.

"How did you get here so fast?" I asked. "I just got here this morning, and I was traveling on a flying horse. Kalen said it would take five to seven days to travel over the mountains."

"There are shortcuts through the mountains if you know where to look," said Rafe, smiling mysteriously.

"What do you mean?" I asked.

"Over the years, the fae created magical gateways, passages of sorts that are strewn all over the place," said Rafe.

"Like the one I came through from the other world?"

"Something like that," answered Rafe, smiling. "Some

gateways are just small stops, closer in range, and much easier to use. Some are further away and can also be just one way. I've used the one through the mountains countless times. There aren't that many left; some don't even work anymore. But it comes in handy in my line of work."

"So what is your line of work? Are you an outlaw, an assassin, or a sword-for-hire kind of guy?" I blurted out.

Rafe laughed. "You, my dear Aurora, ask too many questions."

I blushed. What had I said?

"No, I am not an assassin, nor do I sell my sword to the highest bidder," he said, pausing for a moment. "I am wanted by the Illiadorian Guard for helping those who cannot help themselves."

"So you're an outlaw then, just like Robin Hood?" I said, beaming. I knew he had some good qualities apart from being dangerous and devastatingly handsome.

Rafe looked confused. "Robin who?"

I stifled a laugh.

"Does it really matter who I am?" he said finally, shrugging.

"I guess not," I said, dropping the topic. I would just ask Uncle Gabriel about him later if he didn't want to tell me right now.

"I really have to leave now, Aurora," Rafe said. "I just wanted to make sure you were all right and see you once before I went away."

"Will I see you again?" I said and started blushing as soon as the words left my mouth.

"I certainly hope so," Rafe said, smiling. "Don't get into any more trouble until I get back."

I grinned. "I will definitely give it my best shot," I retorted. "But I can't make any promises."

Rafe smiled, his eyes crinkling slightly in the corners. "I would expect nothing less," he said, bowing low and kissing my hand. "Good-bye, Aurora."

"Bye," I said weakly.

He turned and walked away, his black cloak billowing behind him like a second shadow.

The kitchen was an enormous room with a high ceiling held up by massive beams and dominated by a long wooden workbench and table. Pots and pans were washed, stacked, and hung on neat display, and the fireplace had a big iron pot bubbling away in the corner. The castle cook, a sweet little middle-aged woman, was still awake, having a cup of something hot with two of the kitchen maids. They jumped up when they saw me.

"Sorry to bother you," I said, "but could someone please help me find my room? I seem to have forgotten how to get there."

"Of course, my lady," said the cook. "Would you like a cup of snowberry milk? It does wonders for soothing the nerves and helps you sleep."

I nodded. "That would be lovely, thank you."

I followed one of the maids who showed me to my room. This time I made sure I paid more attention to where I was going. I had my snowberry milk and lay down on my comfortable four-poster bed, my thoughts in a mess. As if I didn't have enough to think about, now I couldn't get Rafe out of my mind. I hardly knew anything about him, except that he was an outlaw and dangerous.

I had no time for this; I had to forget about Rafe. I had to concentrate on the real reason I was here: to learn to use my magical powers before Morgana found me. That's what I kept telling myself again and again. And although my head was saying I was an idiot, my traitorous heart waited for Rafe's return in silent anticipation.

11
LESSONS IN MAGIC

IT WAS A BRIGHT spring morning, and the sun streamed in through the large windows, warming the plush carpets that lay on the cold stone floors. I got out of bed, went over to the window, and looked out at the grounds beyond. Birds were chirping high in the trees, and the gardens were awash with beautiful flowers lining the shaded groves and walkways surrounding Silverthorne Castle.

The rest of the castle was already busy with their morning chores. Uncle Gabriel had sent a message to meet him in his solar after breakfast. Herring brought a tray to my room, and the delicious aromas of freshly baked bread and chocolate made me realize just how hungry I really was. I wolfed down my cinnamon bread smothered with whipped strawberry butter and finished my huge cup of creamy hot chocolate. I wanted to go and see Snow first, but I didn't want to give a bad impression by being late. So I dressed quickly, pushed stray thoughts of Rafe from my head, and ran down to the stables as fast as I could.

Snow was waiting for me. "Good morning, little princess," said the pegasus. "I hope you got a good night's rest."

I put my hand on the pegasus's neck and stroked her beautiful mane. "I did, thank you, Snow," I said pushing my thoughts out to her. I was happy to see that she was comfortable and treated well. I told her everything that had happened using the magical bond between us. It was much easier and faster explaining things in this way.

"I'm glad you found what you were looking for, my dear," said Snow. "I think you should listen to your granduncle; he knows what he is doing and is also a powerful mage. He will teach you what you need to know."

I nodded. "I had better go for my lesson now," I said. "I'll be back to see you later," I called out as I ran out of the stables and back into the castle.

Uncle Gabriel's solar was his study: the same room he had taken me to before, which was where we were to conduct our lessons. My granduncle was seated behind the big mahogany desk, scribbling away on some parchment with a quill he kept dipping in an inkpot.

Oh great! No proper pens and paper . . . this was not going to be easy, getting used to the life here. No electricity, no cars, no phones—how was I going to learn how to survive in this world?

"Come in, come in," said Uncle Gabriel, in his usual brusque manner. Although I did see Uncle Gabriel last night at dinner, I had hardly spoken to him alone since I got to Silverthorne Castle. I smiled as he gestured for me to sit down on the chair opposite him.

"First," he said, sitting up straighter in his chair. "I wanted to thank you for catching those two traitors red-handed."

I blushed. "I really didn't do anything. It was Erien who found them," I said. "What will happen to them now?"

"They shall be exiled and sent to the slavers in Brandor," said the duke. "It will do them good to learn to serve others."

"Isn't that a bit harsh?" I said. Slavery was abhorrent, and I didn't think anyone deserved that.

My granduncle shook his head. "It is better than an execution, Aurora. They did try to kill me, after all."

I nodded and hung my head. I still didn't agree, but I kept my mouth shut.

"Today you will start lessons with me and learn to access your mage powers," said Uncle Gabriel. "There are a few training exercises I want to start with, which will help you to access and channel your magic. I want you to have an open mind, and follow my instructions very carefully."

I listened intently, breathlessly awaiting the secret I was so anxious to discover—how magic worked.

"You are still young and so far your powers have been diminished by the amulet, but if you have tapped into your fae magic already by mind bonding with the pegasus, that means that your powers are already manifesting," Uncle Gabriel said.

He lit a candle and put it in front of me on the table.

"Now, our first lesson is going to be on concentration," said Uncle Gabriel. "I want you to focus on this candle. Remove all other thoughts from your mind."

I stared at the candle, my thoughts drifting in and out. Uncle Gabriel had said he was going to teach me to do magic. This was not magic; this was torture. My thoughts flickered back and forth like the flame on the tip of the candle. Finally I looked up.

"This is silly. Nothing is happening," I said, getting frustrated.

"You are not concentrating," Uncle Gabriel said, glancing up briefly up from his work. "Block out all other thoughts. If they come, push them away and keep focusing on the candle. Nothing else is of importance; your whole mind and concentration is on that candle."

I tried again, but my thoughts wouldn't leave me alone. Every time I looked up, Uncle Gabriel made me try again. He even changed the object of my concentration, from the candle to a smoothly polished stone, to a vase and back. I tried again and again, and every time it was the same, my thoughts came and went, flitting about in my mind, and my concentration was broken.

"Same time tomorrow, Aurora, and please practice. I expect you to concentrate on an object for measurably longer. Holding your concentration is one of the key aspects to working with your magic. You have to learn to channel your powers properly. If you can't control your mind and will, then when you release your powers, they will be all over the place, and we don't want that," he said seriously.

He returned to the chair behind his desk and continued with his paperwork. I left Uncle Gabriel's study, confused. What was that? What had I learned today? Nothing!

I walked through the gardens, meandering on shaded paths, and went over everything he had said. I thought magic was going to be wonderful and exciting, but it looked like all it was going to be was hard work. And doing all this without taking off my amulet was going to be harder still and very frustrating. Even though I had all this incredible magic, I was not allowed to use any of it fully. I hoped I learned to control my powers soon—Morgana was still looking for me, and when she finally did find me, I'd better be ready.

The next day was rainy and gloomy, and I remained indoors, reading some handwritten books that I had found in the library.

They were quite interesting, and I enjoyed them because some had my father's and mother's names in them. A Concise History of the Illiadorian Royal Family and The Making of the Treaty: Life in the New Kingdoms were both particularly engrossing. I plowed through the books. Now I knew the whole history of my family, or at least the more recent part of it.

The books also said that, when Azaren died, Morgana was named heir to the throne, but there were some who rebelled against her claim openly. The rebellion was squashed, and now Morgana and Lucian had unrivaled power in Illiador. The other kingdoms formed an alliance and accepted her as a ruler, as long as she adhered to the treaty. So for now I was safe, as the treaty stated that all seven kingdoms would live peacefully together. Morgana couldn't get to me in Eldoren. Or could she?

What I read didn't sound right, however. Uncle Gabriel had said that Morgana betrayed Azaren and usurped the throne, but the books gave quite a different picture. I had never met her, but she scared me. She seemed merciless and thoroughly evil. How could she betray her own brother and try to kill her own niece?

While I was daydreaming, Erien came into the library.

"I've been looking for you everywhere," he said as he sat down with a thump on the window seat beside me. He took the book from my hand. "What are you reading? Has my grandfather been trying to get you to study already?"

I smiled. It was nice to have a cousin who actually liked me. "No, these are just some books I found here," I replied. "I was reading about Morgana."

Erien's face hardened. "And?"

"I was wondering . . . the book said that there was a rebellion, but she stopped it, and now she rules with the blessing of the people."

"Is that what the book says?" said Erien angrily. "Aurora, you should know better than to believe what is written in books." He picked up one of them and looked at it. "Pfft, written by Adrian Longslade, I should have known. I wonder how this even got in here."

"Who is he?" I asked.

"He's a lackey of the archmage, and a lying scoundrel. All his work is adapted to suit Morgana."

"What really happened?" I asked.

"Morgana," he answered softly, "massacred thousands of families just to make an example of them—men, women, children, everyone. Whole villages were scorched to the ground until the other kingdoms threatened to wage war on Illiador." He paused, staring out the window before he went on. "She is ruthless, Aurora, truly evil." He was whispering now. "Some say that Archmage Lucian is not just a mage, but also secretly a dark sorcerer, a user of black magic."

"But he's the archmage!" I said, astonished.

"Yes, and Morgana trusts him implicitly. He has some hold over her. No one knows why his magic is so powerful. Everyone fears him, even the Mage Guild. No one will go against him openly; to do so would be certain death."

I listened with my mouth open. A dark sorcerer—what was I getting myself into? Lucian sounded worse than Morgana, and she massacred women and children.

I shook my head then suddenly jumped up.

"Oh no! I'm late for my lesson with Uncle Gabriel! Bye Erien, see you later," I said, as I rushed out of the library.

I ran down long stone corridors and flowering, open walkways until I reached Uncle Gabriel's solar.

"You're late," my granduncle said when I finally reached his study, huffing and puffing. "Today we are going to try something different."

I hoped I would finally learn some real magic. All I had learned so far was to stare at a candle without blinking. He made me sit down comfortably in the chair opposite him.

"Now close your eyes, and push away stray thoughts. Make your mind blank," he said.

I did as I was told. The concentration lessons had helped; I was getting much better at it.

"Concentrate inside yourself. There is a power within you that lies dormant. It needs to be controlled, and you can only do that if you identify it. You must separate your mage powers from the fae part. Your mage magic is like a ball of blue-tinged, white light that resides within you."

I tried to do what he said, but there was nothing: no white light, not even a flicker. I tried again. Still nothing. My concentration broke, and my thoughts were whirling around in my head like a runaway carousel.

"Maybe I should take off the amulet?" I asked.

Uncle Gabriel frowned. "No," he said. "I believe you can do this with your amulet on. Your powers are not bound, they are only diminished in intensity. Later, when you know how to control it at will, then you may take off the amulet. Let's try it again, shall we?"

Uncle Gabriel made me try it again, and again, and again, but there was still no sign of any magic. I was getting frustrated; nothing was happening.

"Don't have any doubts," he said, as if reading my mind.

"You do have the power within you. Your heritage is one of the greatest in magical history. You have the gift. I'm quite sure of that."

I tried again. Stray thoughts were still buzzing away in my mind, and I tried to brush them away like bothersome flies. What if it took years to learn magic? I finally managed to push away the doubts and tried again. I concentrated hard inside myself, where Uncle Gabriel had said the source of my power lay dormant, waiting.

I looked inside, quiet in the darkness, silent.

Then, suddenly, there it was. I could see it in my mind's eye, a tiny blue-white light; it was small, but it was there, and it was steadily growing brighter. I could feel a tingling in my body, as if the light was coursing through my veins. I was amazed; I could feel the power moving within me. I felt strong, full of energy, and full of hope, as if anything was possible.

I opened my eyes, and a tiny bluish-white flame ignited on my fingertip, flickered slightly for a moment, and fizzled out. It was but an instant, a glimpse, a touch. But it was real; it was there.

"Very good," said Uncle Gabriel, smiling broadly. "Very good, Aurora!"

"What was that?" was all I could say. I was shocked and elated at the same time. I had definitely done something, and this time it was without removing my amulet.

"That was your power source," said Uncle Gabriel. "All

mages have it. But our powers are not limitless. When you use your power, skill, or gift—whatever you want to call it—you deplete your power source, and it takes a while to rejuvenate itself. That is why you must remember to be very careful. If you try to do something that will take more power than you can generate, your body will not be able to handle the pressure and you could die."

"Die!" I said, wide-eyed. "You can't be serious?"

"I am very serious," said Uncle Gabriel, "and you should be too. The power that you have is not something to be used for mere play and tricks or mundane things that you are too lazy to do the hard way."

He looked very serious, so I hung on his every word. I didn't want to make a silly mistake and kill myself just because I didn't know what I was doing.

"I want you to practice being in touch with the power source within yourself. Then tomorrow we can begin using it. I think we will start with shielding. Learning to defend yourself is now your first priority."

I grinned at my granduncle. Finally, I would learn to use magic!

The next day Uncle Gabriel had a new lesson plan. Learning shielding was not as difficult as I imagined it would be, but it was definitely not pleasant.

"We will start with small, non-magical attacks first," said

Uncle Gabriel. "It's far easier to shield yourself from any-thing nonmagical than it is to shield yourself against a magi-cal strike. Remember, a shield can only protect you from magical strikes and flying weapons, like arrows, but it will not protect you from a person." He paused. "For instance, if someone came to hit you or strike you with a sword, a magi-cal shield would not help. You also have to learn to defend yourself the ordinary way."

I didn't like the sound of that. I was tall at sixteen, but I was thin and not very good in a fight. I considered learn-ing how to use a bow and arrow. It sounded more me than whirling around with a huge sword that I probably couldn't even pick up.

"What's a magical strike?" I asked, intrigued. "Is that what you call the bolts of light mages shoot from their hands?"

Uncle Gabriel nodded. "Yes. You will learn how to per-form magical strikes soon enough. But first you must get used to putting up a shield. It should come as second nature to you."

Before he finished talking, he started throwing nuts at me, one at a time.

"Hey!" I said as the nuts bounced off my head, my chin, my cheeks. I put my arms up to shield my face.

He smiled. "Getting angry won't solve your problem, Au-rora," he said, as he continued to throw nuts at me. "Be calm, and control your thoughts, concentrate and touch your power source. Anger only slows the process; it weakens the shield."

I tried to concentrate on what he was telling me to do, but the nuts kept hitting me and breaking my concentration. Although the nuts were small, they stung when they hit, and it was becoming impossible to concentrate.

But I knew I must; it was the only way for the irritating nuts to stop reaching me. I looked at Uncle Gabriel. He was leaning nonchalantly on his desk and was systematically throwing nuts at me. His lips were curved in a smile. He was enjoying this, I realized, which made me more determined to show him that I was more than capable.

I knew what I had to do. I closed my eyes and silenced my mind, just like I had in my concentration lessons. I looked deep inside; there in the silence I could feel it. The white-blue light pulsated; it had grown since the last time I saw it, and this time it was easier to reach it.

"Now concentrate, and imagine a shield growing around you, a shield of light. Nothing can penetrate the shield unless you let it," said Uncle Gabriel.

I did as I was told. Imagining the shield, I could feel the white light coursing through my body; I drew it around myself like a cloak. Suddenly the barrage of nuts stopped. I opened my eyes, all the while conscious of what I was still doing. The nuts hadn't really stopped, Uncle Gabriel was still throwing them at me at regular intervals, but somehow they bounced off an invisible shield that I had created. Just as I was patting myself on the back for creating the shield,

I could feel it wavering. My concentration broke, and a nut hit me on the head.

"Ouch!" was all I could say as I stood in front of Uncle Gabriel, rubbing my forehead.

"That was very good," said Uncle Gabriel, laughing. "I knew you could do it, even with your amulet on."

I tried a half-smile. Although I was inwardly pleased with myself for managing a shield on my first try, I didn't appreciate being pelted with nuts, but Uncle Gabriel seemed to think it was very funny.

"I can try again," I said, determined to show him that I was stronger than I looked.

"That will be all for today, Aurora," said my granduncle, sitting back down at his desk. "I have work to do and you must be tired after using your powers for the first time."

"No, not really," I said, shrugging. I didn't feel like I had put in much effort, and I wasn't tired at all. "Should I be?"

"Well, ordinarily, yes," said my granduncle. "But it seems your powers are different to what I expected. A shield attempt by a novice should have tired you out to some extent, at least."

I shook my head. "I don't feel any different."

"That's good, very good," said Uncle Gabriel. "But that doesn't mean that you mustn't be careful. Magic requires a lot of strength of will and character. Just having powerful magic does not necessarily make you a great mage. You have to think before you act, because magic always comes with a price."

I nodded. Uncle Gabriel's philosophical statements always went a bit over my head. What did this mean? How different were my powers really?

"I also want you to keep in mind that the amulet you wear around your neck, although keeping you safe from Morgana, diminishes your powers to that of an ordinary mage."

"I understand that it keeps Morgana from finding me with magic," I said. "But why does it diminish my powers?"

"Well," said Uncle Gabriel, leaning back in his chair and stroking his beard. "The amulet you wear around your neck was created thousands of years ago by the first fae-mage, Auraken Firedrake. He was high king over the seven kingdoms and Avalonia flourished under his rule. But one of the king's advisors, Haldred, a powerful mage, turned to dark magic. He rebelled against the high king and led an army of dark sorcerers into Illiador. Auraken rode out to meet Haldred in battle. He defeated him and his army of evil creatures: dark fae, demons, and hideous abominations from the depths of the underworld. The survivors fled north, beyond the Silverspike Mountains and into the land that is now known as Maradaar, or the Darklands."

"And the amulet?" I prompted. Uncle Gabriel had started rambling, and I didn't want to go into a full-fledged history lesson at this moment.

"Ah yes," he said. "Auraken made the amulet after many attempts on his life, to mask his own powers so that he could move about the land undetected. But the amulet is infused with powerful magic, and as I just told you, all powerful magic has a price. The amulet, when worn, diminishes a fae-mage's powers to that of an ordinary mage. That is the price you must pay for its protection."

I sort of understood what he was saying.

"But if I take it off, won't I learn faster?" I asked.

"That is a very good question," he said. "One of the main advantages of wearing the amulet, other than its protection, is its ability to control the intensity of a fae-mage's powers."

"I don't understand."

"A fae-mage is a very rare and very powerful being with almost limitless, but wild magic," said Uncle Gabriel. "The magic you possess is almost impossible to control without the right training."

"What do you mean?"

"Sometimes in times of great stress or need, your powers can come forward like a defense mechanism," said Uncle Gabriel. "Fae-mages have been known to destroy whole villages before they were found and taught magical discipline. You must learn to call your powers at will and then learn to control them, because control is the most important element in the use of magic. Without it, magical powers can do a lot of damage to yourself and those in your vicinity."

"Oh!"

"That is why you must be very careful. No one must know that you are a fae-mage. The time will come when you will be able to reveal yourself to the world. For now your life is in danger. If Morgana found out what a threat you really are, she would stop at nothing to find you."

"But you told Aunt Serena and Erien?" I said.

"That's because Serena and Erien are family. They would never betray you."

"And Rafe?" I had to ask. "Why did you tell him?"

"Ah, yes, Rafe," Uncle Gabriel said, with an indulgent smile. "I trust him completely, and I need his help from time to time with things that I cannot trust anyone else with."

"So who is he really?" I asked, trying to sound casual.

"It's better you don't know, my dear," said Uncle Gabriel, trying to look serious, but I could make out that he was suppressing a smile.

Why would no one tell me anything about Rafe? It was so frustrating.

"I hope I won't need to tell you again that you must keep the amulet on at all times," said Uncle Gabriel. "For now, you will let your fae magic remain dormant until such a time that we can acquire a teacher for you."

He got up and went over to the other side of the huge desk, rummaging through parchments, muttering to himself again and shaking his head. "Never in all my years . . . wonderful, wonderful . . . very strong and immortal fae too." He turned to look at me. "In fact, you are the only fae-mage besides Auraken Firedrake ever to be an immortal fae."

"What?" I said, completely forgetting my manners for the

hundredth time.

Uncle Gabriel looked at me sharply. "What I mean, my young Aurora, is that of all the seven fae-mages ever to have lived, you and Auraken Firedrake are the only ones born to an immortal fae. All the others were born to ordinary fae beings."

I let the words sink in. Was this guy kidding me? First I found out I was actually from another world, then I found out I was the daughter of a king and I wasn't even completely human, then I discovered that I had two kinds of powers even though it was unheard of. Come to think of it, I wasn't even normal here in Avalonia, where everyone had magic and different powers. I was a strange being that no one had seen in over a thousand years. And apparently I was going to live for a very long time.

"What exactly is the difference between immortal fae powers and ordinary ones?" I asked.

"You will learn about your fae heritage another time," he said. "We have to do this in steps. First we concentrate on your mage powers. Learn to control that, and then we will see about your fae magic."

I nodded. I was still utterly confused, but somehow I felt a little relieved. At least I finally knew who I really was.

"I have some important people coming to meet with me later today," said Uncle Gabriel, rummaging through his papers. "We will continue this lesson tomorrow, I have a lot of work to do."

12
SHIELD

AFTER MY CLASS with Uncle Gabriel, I ran down the endless steps and long stone corridors into the courtyard. Finally I caught up with Erien. He was just going out for his daily ride.

"Hey Erien," I called out.

He stopped and turned around. "Good afternoon, cousin, did you have a good lesson with grandfather?"

"Oh yes," I said. "I learned to create a shield."

"Oh good, a magical shield is really helpful," he grinned. "Got me out of many scrapes in school."

I smiled at his nonchalant attitude towards magic.

"So do you go to some sort of school for magic then?" I asked.

Erien nodded. "I'm in my second year at the Academy of Magic at Evolon," he said. "Your father went there too."

"He did?"

Erien nodded. "Azaren was a legend there; all the teachers loved him, not because he was a prince, but because his powers were truly exceptional. Now Evolon is run by one of the most brilliant minds of our times, the Mastermage Elial Dekela. He changed the laws completely, allowing mages from classes other than the nobility who have the gift to study at Evolon."

"What do you mean?"

"Well, in the old days, only those from noble families used to be accepted to study at Evolon and Nerenor."

"What's Nerenor?"

"The Academy of Magic at Nerenor is the rival school to Evolon," said Erien. "It is situated in the north of Illiador, in the city of Nerenor itself."

"I was wondering, can I come with you for a ride?" I asked. "I would really like to hear more about Avalonia."

Erien looked perturbed. "I am not really supposed to be taking you out of the castle. My grandfather said you were to travel only with guards."

"What about you? Why are you allowed to go without guards?"

"I'm not really allowed to go," said Erien, looking a bit sheepish. "I was just seeing if I could sneak off for a while. I know a back way out of the castle. The gatekeeper at the eastern gate is a friend of mine. He often lets me go for rides alone."

"But isn't that dangerous?" I said.

"No, not really," said Erien, shrugging his shoulders. "I don't go far, and Grandfather's troops manage to keep the woods relatively safe. It's just that I hate having someone fol-lowing me all the time. Being from the nobility can get very suffocating. Sometimes I just need to get away on my own and clear my head."

My eyes lit up. "Then let me come with you," I pleaded. "You said yourself that it's safe in these woods. We can go for a ride and be back before anyone even knew we were gone. And I can shield myself now. What could go wrong?"

Erien finally agreed begrudgingly to my request and found me a pleasant-tempered chestnut mare to ride. I ran over to meet Snow and check on her, explaining that I couldn't ride her since we would be too conspicuous and I had to blend in. I got on my horse and followed Erien through the eastern gate, through the town of Fairlone and into the valley beyond.

Riding along the little paths in the countryside was pleasant and uneventful. We crossed green meadows strewn with carpets of wildflowers and passed isolated farmhouses. The little valley was awash with a myriad of colors.

After ambling through the woods for a while, a pleasantly shaded thicket of old beech provided a nice resting place for us. We ate our meager meal of bread and cheese with a few salted pieces of roasted meat that Erien had taken from the kitchens before we left. It was quite good, and the stream water was fresh and clear. I had never tasted water so sweet and refreshing.

"We should return to the castle soon," said Erien, getting back onto his horse. "An emissary from Brandor arrived today, and Mother will be expecting us at dinner tonight."

"Where is Brandor?" I asked as I struggled to mount the chestnut mare, who insisted on shifting every time I tried to get on.

"Brandor is a neighboring kingdom and lies east of Illiador and Eldoren. It stretches all the way to the Sea of Shadows and is ruled by the Council of Five."

"Don't they have a king or queen?" I asked, finally settling the horse and getting on.

"No, they don't actually, because many years ago there was great internal strife in the land, and the nobility overthrew the king. But they could not decide which family would take the throne, and so the council of five was born," he explained.

"Who are they?" I asked.

"The Council of Brandor consists of five powerful mages, each one from a noble house, and the heads of each family sit on the council."

"So there are mages everywhere, in all the kingdoms?" I asked. I really wished I had a map. This world seemed to be so vast.

"Yes," said Erien, "there are mages in all the seven kingdoms, but Illiador and Eldoren have the highest population of mages in Avalonia. It's only in Elfi that mages are few and rarely seen."

"Elfi is the kingdom of the fae, right?" I asked, trying to create my own map in my head.

"Yes," said Erien, "and your grandmother, Izadora, is

queen of the fae."

I was taken aback at this. I never stopped to consider my mother's fae family. I had a grandmother. Did I have more uncles, aunts, and cousins?

"What is my grandmother like?" I asked.

"I have never met her personally," said Erien, "but my grandfather has. She is said to be a wise and just queen and very powerful. It was said that Izadora was distraught when she learned what happened to her daughter. She would be so happy if she knew you were alive."

"When will I be able to see her?" I asked.

"For now, Grandfather will decide," said Erien. "You still have to learn to use your powers before you can undertake such a long and dangerous journey."

I nodded while I ambled beside him on my horse, and the cool forest breeze brushed my face as we rode. It had rained the night before, and the forest smelled fresh and new. Tiny droplets of water glistened on emerald leaves, which rustled in the summer breeze and fell to the ground creating little pools on the forest floor.

I tried to concentrate on keeping my horse from wandering off to eat some foliage. It was starting to get dark, and the orange-pink sky was steadily growing dim as we rode along a long worn-out path, back to Silverthorne Castle.

I was plodding along behind Erien when he suddenly stopped.

"Wait!" he said softly, but his voice was tense.

Just then, Erien turned his horse and unsheathed his sword. I whipped my head around, fear rising in my chest. Had Oblek found me again? Were the Shadow Guard here?

A group of men was circling around us, coming out from their hiding places behind the trees. I didn't even hear them approaching. I guessed learning shielding was not going to help me at that particular moment.

"Get behind me," Erien said, with an authority in his voice that that I had never heard before.

I moved my horse, but the men were closing in. They were dressed in filthy, brown rags and most had bandanas tied on their faces, obscuring their identities.

"Bandits," hissed Erien, and jumped off his horse, scowling. "Won't be much of a fight."

One of them caught my horse's bridle. I tried to wrench it away, but he held on tight. Another man caught my leg, and his companion pushed me from the other side, causing me to fall off the horse with a thud and bang my head on the forest floor. I was stunned for a moment as I tried to get up. Rough hands caught hold of me, and I couldn't get free; there was nowhere to run.

I started to panic. Erien had said these woods were safe, but it wasn't looking that safe to me right now. The men were now coming at us from all sides. They had surrounded us, and they were still quietly moving forward.

Then the man at the front spoke. "What do we 'ave 'ere?" he said, in a strange guttural voice. He had dark matted hair and black, rotten teeth and was the only one who didn't cover his face. "You look very much like the girl the Shadow Guard are offering a huge reward to capture."

Erien glanced at me for a second. "You have the wrong girl," he said, taking a step forward.

The leader just laughed at Erien. "No, in fact, I think I have exactly the right one," he said as he advanced, with a nasty looking, rusted sword in his hands.

One bandit with filthy, rough hands was still holding on to my arm. They all looked pretty dangerous to me, but Erien didn't think so. He was going to take them on on his own. What was he thinking? Was he mad?

"Let me go! Let me go!" I screamed and kicked, struggling to get free.

I managed to squirm away from the clawing hands but fell backwards rather painfully on my behind. The bandits had started circling, and my hesitation cut off our escape route. Most of the bandits carried knives and iron implements that served as weapons, although only the leader had a sword.

Suddenly a voice in my head spoke, "Do not worry, little one, I am here."

I looked up to see Snow flying down towards us, her huge wings spanning out and covering the sky. On her back, looking furious, was Uncle Gabriel, brandishing his flashing sword in his hand.

"Erien!" he barked, as the pegasus landed in the middle of

the circle of bandits. "Take Aurora and get back to the castle." He jumped easily off the pegasus. "I will handle them."

"He's a mage," said one of the men, taking a step back.

"So what? He's only one. We're ten of us. The young ones won't be much trouble. Capture the girl, hand her over to the Shadow Guard, and collect our money—simple," the bandit leader said, letting out a sick, twisted laugh.

I was terrified. Did Uncle Gabriel really think that he could fight so many of them?

"You dare to threaten a lord of Eldoren," said Uncle Gabriel, looking more menacing than I had ever seen him. "I have had reports of a group of bandits in these woods that have been terrorizing travelers. I think this is a perfect opportunity to get rid of you lot for good."

The bandit leader sneered, "You're just one old man. What can you do?"

Another bandit didn't look too convinced. "That's the Duke of Silverthorne himself," he hissed in the leader's ear. "I was in his dungeon for three years. Maybe we'd better get moving."

"He's got no guards," spat the leader. "We'll finish him off here in the woods and make an example. The nobility think that they can do whatever they want. But I will make them pay for it. I will make 'em think twice b'fore—"

His words were cut off as Uncle Gabriel swung his huge sword, cutting down the leader in one clean sweep. He fell to the ground in a mass of crimson while another two bandits dropped their weapons and ran for their lives.

"Who's next?" said Uncle Gabriel, whirling his sword in his hand with such dexterity that I could only look with wonder. I needed to learn to fight like that, I thought suddenly to myself.

The rest of the bandits were still closing in on us.

"They are just bandits; none have magic. I'll take care of them," said Uncle Gabriel. "Go! I will see you at the castle."

Twilight was upon us, and dark shadows moved about the forest floor like additional warriors in the fight. Uncle Gabriel took a step forward towards a group of three bandits, who were now looking very unsure of themselves.

"Create a shield, and get on Snow," said Uncle Gabriel to me quietly, so only I could hear.

I nodded, closed my eyes and concentrated hard. I infused myself with the white light and drew a magical shield around myself. Snow was struggling, as two bandits caught her mane. She could have flown off, but she was waiting for me.

"Shield yourself, and run towards me," said Snow's voice, calming my distressed mind.

I looked around; we were completely surrounded, and the bandits were still coming. They were now circling Uncle Gabriel and Erien. I got up from a sprawled heap, gathered my skirt, and ran towards Snow. It was hard, trying to concentrate and keep my shield around me at the same time.

Suddenly a knife came whizzing towards me and bounced

off my invisible shield just inches from my face. I whirled around to see Uncle Gabriel shoot bolts of white light from his fingertips, and two men crumpled before my eyes. There were four more bandits left, and they were advancing, with two more still holding on to Snow. How many of them were there? I couldn't even count. They kept materializing one by one, out from behind the trees.

"Run now!" Uncle Gabriel said urgently to me. "Erien! Go with her."

"But I want to fight," said Erien childishly.

Uncle Gabriel looked furious. "By the Gods, Erien, I said go now! Hold your shield until you are both out of harm's way."

Erien ran with me towards Snow.

I looked back for a second and saw that Uncle Gabriel was now battling the rest of the bandits with his sword. He whirled around and fought like a young man. I was amazed at his agility and strength. I ran as fast as I could and pulled myself up onto Snow's back with the help of her mane. Erien fought the men holding the pegasus, and I had to admit he was pretty fast and quite a good swordsman. The bandit's weapons were flung away as they ran from Erien's flashing sword. He jumped onto Snow behind me.

"Shouldn't we go back?" I said to Erien. "What if Uncle Gabriel needs help?"

Erien laughed, completely undaunted. "Oh, Grandfather can take care of himself," he said. "It's the bandits who you have to worry about. I just hope he doesn't hurt them too badly; the last lot couldn't stand trial for a month until they had healed." He laughed again, as if at some secret joke.

Snow cantered gracefully along the forest path, spread out her powerful white wings, and flew off into the sky towards Silverthorne Castle.

13
THE HEIR

BY NOW the whole of Silverthorne Castle was awake. Uncle Gabriel came striding into the courtyard with a thunderous look on his aging face.

"How did he get here before us?" I asked Erien. "The last time I saw him he was battling bandits in the woods, and now he's back here at the castle as if he never left."

"The forests around these parts have gateways that lead in and out of the castle," whispered Erien. "The fae have left them all over the place. We used to use this one very often when we played Princes and Dragons."

I nodded, understanding. Rafe had explained about the fae gateways.

Aunt Serena followed her father and appeared just as angry as him. Uncle Gabriel looked like he was going to burst a blood vessel. First, he called to some of his guards and gave them the precise location of the bandits.

"We really need to have a talk, young lady," said Uncle Gabriel, coming up to me. "Do you not understand the dangers that surround you, or do you openly want to defy authority? Tonight's performance has greatly disappointed me."

I hung my head in shame. I didn't want to be a disappointment, I just wanted to have some fun and learn about this world, so that I wouldn't be as ignorant about the dangers anymore.

"How could you sneak out of the castle without telling us?" Aunt Serena added. She also looked extremely upset. "I was almost eighteen summers before I was allowed out of the castle alone. You've only been here a few days and already you are sneaking out and getting caught by bandits in the woods. What if there was something else out there other than just bandits? You may not have been so lucky."

"And you," she said, turning to Erien, "have you no sense? Aurora has no way to defend herself yet. Do have any idea what losing her would mean to us, to the kingdom, to all the kingdoms? I cannot even begin to think what will happen if she . . . "

"Enough, Serena," said Uncle Gabriel sternly. "This is not the time or the place to talk about this. We shall retire for the night, and in the morning we can decide what has to be done."

"All right, let us go back inside," said Aunt Serena. "It's late and you must be very tired."

I nodded.

"And Erien, you are confined to your quarters until I say otherwise. Is that clear?" said his mother, looking at her son fiercely.

Erien just nodded, looking very sheepish.

"It wasn't his fault; I made him take me. I threatened him," I lied, trying to save my cousin from a seriously long grounding. I hated lying, but it would be just horrible if Erien were blamed because I begged him to take me.

"I highly doubt that," said Uncle Gabriel, "but, all the same, I will have to have a talk with you, young man. Now, I don't want any more arguments from you, Aurora. Get to your room immediately, and stay there."

I knew better than to argue when he was in this mood and nodded. I had expected the punishment to be worse. The note of finality in his voice was enough for me to know that there was no use arguing now.

"Sorry, Snow," I said to the pegasus in my mind. "I nearly got you captured again."

"I'm fine. Just get some rest, my dear," said Snow.

I half turned to see Snow being gently led away by one of the other grooms.

"Snow?" I said. "How come you let the Duke ride you? I thought only the royal fae can ride a pegasus."

"No, my dear one, a pegasus has a choice whom they allow to ride them," said Snow, still walking away. "Your uncle came to me, told me you may be in danger, and asked for my help to get him there in time."

"You can speak to others too?" I asked, genuinely surprised.

"Not exactly. I can understand what people say, although

I cannot reply," said Snow.

"Thank you," I said, meaning every word. What would I have done without her?

"No, no, my dear little princess. I am here to protect you. Call to me whenever you are in trouble. Wherever I am, I will come to you," said Snow as she walked gracefully away into the duke's magnificent stables, her beautiful wings shimmering white in the moonlight.

The next morning was awkward. Uncle Gabriel didn't speak to me at breakfast. I guessed he was still very angry about last night. The breakfast room was a light and airy place. Not exactly a room, but a lovely little gazebo, which was attached to the informal dining room of the castle, over-looking the vast gardens of Silverthorne Castle.

Aunt Serena made polite conversation, and Erien, com-pletely unaware of the tension in the room, was tucking away into his eggs and fried ham like it was his last meal. Everything was delicious, but I couldn't eat. I played with my boiled egg and nibbled on a slice of freshly baked bread filled with delicious dried fruits and nuts. I then washed it down with a cinnamon-infused honey and milk concoc-tion, which was apparently Erien's favorite and something the cook always made when he was residing in the castle.

I was supposed to go straight to my room after break-fast, but I meandered a little, strolling through the flowering courtyards and long corridors until I ended up, quite uncon-sciously, outside Uncle Gabriel's study.

I heard Aunt Serena mention my name, and I went closer to have a small peek, since the door wasn't completely shut. I knew it was wrong, but my curiosity got the better of me.

"She must go," Uncle Gabriel was saying.

"It will be difficult for her to stay hidden," said Aunt Serena.

The door opened suddenly, and Uncle Gabriel's stormy face came into view.

"Come in, Aurora," said Uncle Gabriel in an exasperated voice.

I rolled my eyes. How did he know I was eavesdropping? Aunt Serena smiled at me as I entered the room and shifted uncomfortably in her chair. What had they been talking about when I had very rudely interrupted them? I wondered.

"Well," said Uncle Gabriel curtly, rubbing his temples with his fingers. "Sit down, Aurora."

He sounded tired. I was getting a little worried about where the conversation was leading. I tried to fight the panic that had started accumulating in my chest. Would they throw me out just because I went into the woods? Would they punish me because I was eavesdropping? I had no idea what they were going to say or do. I sat down on the chair next to Aunt Serena.

"I was going to speak to you later today, but I guess this is as good a time as any," Uncle Gabriel went on. "After all that has happened, I think you should have a better idea as to what exactly we are doing."

"That would be nice," I muttered under my breath.

"Aurora, you must at least try to understand how important your safety really is," he paused. "I blame myself. I should not have kept you in the dark. After all, it's your life and your kingdom that we are fighting for."

"What do you mean?" I asked, looking at my aunt and uncle.

"Morgana is a tyrant," said Aunt Serena. "She must be stopped." She put her arm around my shoulders. "You are the heir of Azaren; you must be the one to take back your father's throne and end Morgana's rule forever."

"Take back the throne!" I said, aghast at her proposition. "Are you serious?"

Just because I was the daughter of the real king didn't make me fit to rule a kingdom. What did they expect from me? A girl of sixteen—with barely any magic—to capture a throne and then run a kingdom? I laughed to myself at the absurdity of that thought. What were these guys thinking? I was not comfortable with making decisions, especially when it might endanger people. Being anonymous suited me. I didn't want to be a queen, although being a princess or a duchess would have its perks. I wanted to enjoy my life, but now I realized that a comfortable, stress-free life was not going to be possible.

Uncle Gabriel nodded. "You don't seem to have any sense of responsibility, Aurora," he said. "You are who you are, nothing can change that."

I looked down at my hands. I wanted to live up to the expectations that they had in me, but I didn't think I could do this; I wasn't queen material.

"Morgana's attempt on my life was all part of Lucian's wayward plans for supremacy over the seven kingdoms," my granduncle went on. "The archmage wants to implement an old law, one that was done away with centuries ago."

"What is it?" I asked.

"He wants to break the treaty of the allied lands and invoke the old title of Illiador as the high kingdom, as it was in the days of old Avalonia, and," he paused, "name Morgana high queen of all the seven kingdoms."

I gasped. "Can he do that?" I asked, disturbed at this new turn of events.

Uncle Gabriel nodded. "As archmage, Lucian has a sway over both the council of thirteen in Illiador as well as the entire mage guild." He paused. "He has also, as we feared, allied himself with the Drakaar."

"The Drakaar! Who are they?"

"Rogue sorcerers, users of dark magic, and not ones we want to be associated with." He looked at me very seriously. "They are different from mages, Aurora. They don't follow the same magical restraints that we do."

"They are never to be trusted," said Aunt Serena seriously. "The seven kingdoms only remain safe from them because the mage guild has skilled and powerful warrior-mages who protect these lands."

"What your aunt says is true; the Drakaar are very power-ful and extremely treacherous. They have no rules or regula-tions to temper their magic," said Uncle Gabriel.

"Where are they from?" I asked.

"They live beyond the Silverspike Mountains in the land we call Maradaar, or the Darklands. They are not part of the seven kingdoms, and no one has ever traveled into the Dark-lands and returned."

"But why are the Drakaar helping Morgana?" I asked. "Don't they have their own king?"

My granduncle nodded. "They do—his name is Dragath. He is a powerful demon lord who ruled these lands in an age long before the seven kingdoms were founded."

"So where is Dragath now?" I asked, horrified at the thought of encountering a demon lord.

"He is long gone," said Uncle Gabriel. "But the Drakaar still worship him like a god."

"What happened?"

"Some say he's gone forever," Uncle Gabriel replied, "but it has also been said that he is still alive, trapped in his magi-cal prison for all eternity."

"Who trapped him?" I asked.

"Auraken Firedrake, the first fae-mage," he said. "No one knows for sure what really happened, but the legends say that Auraken defeated Dragath in an extraordinary magical battle that shook the foundations of our world."

Aunt Serena laughed at this. "Dragath is only a bedtime

story told to children around campfires at night to scare them, Father," she said.

"Maybe," said Uncle Gabriel. "But know this: Dragath may be gone, but the Drakaar are not, they practice a dark magic older than any known to us. Lucian and Morgana are using the threat of the Drakaar to strike fear into the hearts of any that oppose them. After what happened last time Morgana was opposed, everyone is too scared to go against her openly."

I remembered the horrific story Erien had told me about Morgana in the library, when she seized power after betraying my father, and the nobles opposed her rule. How Lucian, on Morgana's instruction, massacred thousands of families until they all accepted her as queen.

"All the other kingdoms in the treaty have been given a few months to recognize Illiador as the high kingdom and Morgana as high queen," said Aunt Serena.

"And if they don't?" I asked. I knew I wasn't going to like the answer.

"If they do not," said Uncle Gabriel, "Morgana and Lucian will wage war on all the other kingdoms, including Eldoren."

"And our kingdom will have to go to war after a hundred years of peace," added Aunt Serena softly, with pain showing clearly in her eyes.

"Right now, the immediate danger is that Maradaar has already joined Morgana's army," said the duke. "At the moment the northern kingdoms of Andrysia and Kelliandria are in the most peril, as they are located in between Maradaar and us. The Drakaar will attack there first, and unless the dwarves of Kelliandria come to their aid, Andrysia will not stand a chance. I must convince the dwarf king to come out of the mountains and take up arms against Morgana and the Drakaar."

"What about the fae, or the other kingdoms?" I asked helpfully.

Uncle Gabriel shook his head. "Brandor is weak; they barely have enough warrior-mages to protect their own kingdom. And Rohron has no real leader; they will not help."

"And the fae?" I prompted.

"The fae rarely interfere in the wars of the mages. Although they are part of the treaty, they are not bound to come to our aid," finished the duke.

I shook my head. I was so caught up in my own little world that I did not, could not, fathom the enormity of the situation.

How was I supposed to deal with Morgana and Lucian when I couldn't even deal with a few bandits? Everyone seemed to have such hopes pinned on me, and I had just demonstrated that I was not fit enough to be what they wanted me to be. What exactly that was, I wasn't really sure. They seemed to be planning to oust Morgana from the throne and make me queen. Was that why they wanted me to stay—to use me as a way to threaten Morgana's claim to the throne of Illiador?

The whole concept of being a princess who had to fight to regain my kingdom was so absurd. I was no hero. I was in a strange and unfamiliar world where I had absolutely no idea what was going on. And, although I supposedly had all these great powers, they were of no use until I learned to control them. At the rate I was going, that was going to take forever, and time wasn't exactly on my side right now.

"Now," said Uncle Gabriel, "I will have to travel to the northern kingdoms and speak to Queen Maya of Andrysia and make sure she doesn't accept Morgana as high queen."

"They will be scared, Father," said Aunt Serena.

"That is why I must go, and I will go alone. If I can assure them of our friendship and pledge my word that our ally, the dwarf king Ranthor, will join forces with them if they are attacked, then they may stand strong. But first, I will have to go and see Ranthor; he will not agree so readily. The dwarves have long since distanced themselves from the wars of men and mages, and Ranthor himself has not left his stone fortress in over twenty years. I will leave at first light. It is best that no one knows of my quest." Uncle Gabriel paused, and looked at us seriously.

I nodded affirmatively, and so did Aunt Serena.

"Good. Now that we understand each other," my grand-uncle said, "we come to the other problem."

"Which is?" I asked. Now what?

Uncle Gabriel turned towards me. "You cannot live in

Silverthorne Castle alone, and I think it will do you good to be around people your own age, mages like yourself. You need to learn to wield your magic, as I will be unavailable to teach you for a while."

"Where will I go?" I asked, suddenly afraid to go out into this world alone again. Here in Silverthorne Castle with my granduncle and Aunt Serena I was protected and felt safe. Out there, Morgana or Lucian would find me.

"Evolon," said Uncle Gabriel.

"Evolon!" I repeated. I hadn't expected that. "The best school for mages in the whole of Avalonia?"

Uncle Gabriel smiled. "Well, yes, I guess Erien has already told you all about it. He is very fond of his school," he said. "Evolon is the best, and you must go there if you want to truly learn to use your gifts and powers. There is only so much I can teach you here, and above all you need to learn some discipline, young lady."

"But what if someone tells Morgana I'm there? Won't she send Oblek or someone else to capture me, or try and kill me, again?" I asked.

Serena got up from her chair and came over and put her arm around me. "We will not let that happen," she said, "but it's better to be safe. That's why you will take up a new identity and a new name."

"What! Change my name? I don't want to," I said, mindful that I was sounding childish. It was for my own good, I knew that, but I still didn't want to do it.

180

Uncle Gabriel ignored my outburst. "You must blend in with the students in Evolon, Aurora. You will be a god-daughter of mine from Andrysia who has come to study at Evolon. No one will suspect anything, and, in any case, I have acquired the help of Penelope Plumpleberry who, as a great favor to me, has agreed to leave her home in Pixie Bush and come and teach as a professor of Healing and Ancient Studies at the academy. So you will have her watching out for you. She already knows part of your secret, and she is a powerful fae. Few will have the courage to cross her."

I smiled at that. I liked Penelope a lot, and I was glad that I would have someone to talk to, who knew whom I really was. I wished Kalen would come too; I missed his brisk chatter.

"Evolon is also a magically protected place. As long as you are within the walls of the academy, Morgana and the Shadow Guard will not be able to find you," added Uncle Gabriel. "Of course it goes without saying that you must keep your amulet on at all times. No matter what, do not take it off. No one will pay much attention to you, and they will just think that your magic is not strong enough for it to be sensed as yet."

I nodded. Evolon!

Maybe it wouldn't be that bad; after all, even Erien went to school there, and Penelope would be teaching as well. At least I would have someone to talk to, since I was apprehensive about making friends. But now I would have to lie to everyone about who I really was. I even had to change my name. It would take some time to get used to it.

The next day Aunt Serena woke me up early. My things were already packed, so we had a quick breakfast of hot chocolate and cinnamon-nut bread—with dollops of strawberry butter smeared all over—while we got ready to leave for Evolon. Snow would not be going with me. Uncle Gabriel had said that having her around would raise too many questions, and I was supposed to blend in. I went down to the stables to say good-bye. I really hoped I would be able to see her again soon.

Uncle Gabriel rode with us out of the town with an escort of castle guards. When we reached the edge of the woods, he held up his hand and ordered the guards to go no further. Uncle Gabriel led his horse further into the forest and gestured for us to follow while the guards stayed back, guarding the perimeter.

"Aren't the guards coming with us?" I asked. Was Uncle Gabriel sending me off with only Aunt Serena and Erien for protection? What if we came across bandits or Shadow Guards?

Uncle Gabriel stopped his horse and got down in a small clearing. I followed, as did Aunt Serena and Erien. He must have sensed my distress, because he lowered his voice and put an arm around my shoulder. "Do not worry so much, my dear," he said kindly. "The guards draw too much attention. But I would not send you on such a journey without adequate protection."

"You're coming with us?" I asked hopefully.

Uncle Gabriel shook his head. "No, my dear, I cannot this time, but I have sent for someone who is more than capable of protecting you all and seeing you safely to your destination."

"Who?" I asked confused, looking around.

I followed Uncle Gabriel's gaze to a tree at the edge of the clearing. My heart leapt in my chest, and I couldn't help the grin that spread across my face.

Rafe was leaning lazily against an old willow tree. His arms were crossed, and he was staring intently at me. He was wearing his signature black cloak and mask, but I had no doubt who it was. He smiled, and I was elated. I was so glad he was back; it was wonderful seeing him again. If Rafe was going with us, I was positive that I would be absolutely safe.

Rafe pushed himself away from the tree and walked over to us. "Gabriel," said Rafe, inclining his head to my granduncle.

"Rafe," said Uncle Gabriel, "thank you for your help. I hope I don't need to remind you to make sure no one finds out her true identity."

Rafe nodded. "I shall take care of it."

"Good," said Uncle Gabriel. "Then I think you should be on your way."

Aunt Serena hugged her father, as did Erien. Finally Uncle Gabriel turned to me.

"Remember what I've told you, Aurora," he said seriously, giving me a leg up onto my chestnut mare. "Keep a low profile in school, and keep your amulet on at all times. We do not want anyone sensing the extent of your powers."

I nodded.

"There is something else," he went on. "I have not informed Penelope Plumpleberry that you are a fae-mage. For now, let us keep it like that."

"Why? I thought you trusted her."

"I do," said Uncle Gabriel, "but powers like yours can scare even the most loyal of people. The fewer people who know of your special gift, the better."

"But Rafe knows?" I said.

Granduncle Gabriel nodded. "I explained this before," he said. "He knows because I trust him, and, as you can see, he helps me out once in a while."

"Tell me who he is, please?" I asked softly, bending down slightly off my horse, hopeful that he would give me some sort of answer.

Uncle Gabriel smiled mischievously. "Why, he's the Black Wolf, my dear," was all he said.

I huffed at his vague answer, but nodded nonetheless. It was obvious he was as close-lipped about Rafe's true identity as everyone else, and I figured Rafe was right, it didn't matter who he really was; what really mattered was that he was here, and I was going to spend the next few days with him.

Despite my situation, which had me running, hiding and afraid for my life, I grinned. I was happy. I was with Rafe, and that was all that mattered, for the moment at least.

"Take care of yourself, little one," Uncle Gabriel said, waving me off.

Rafe leaped up onto his black monster of a horse, and I had to struggle with the reins of my mare, who had decided that all she wanted to do was follow the big black stallion. I rolled my eyes and giggled to myself. Like rider, like horse.

I waved a final good-bye to Uncle Gabriel as we rode through the Willow Woods and onward into the world beyond.

14
JOURNEY TO EVOLON

WE RODE IN SILENCE through the forest, stopping only to rest the horses and fill our leather water flasks from small forest pools. Rafe seemed preoccupied and kept to himself most of the time. Erien and Aunt Serena didn't seem like they wanted to talk, so I just followed and wondered if I would get a bed to sleep on that night.

It turned out I was not going to get my wish. As the sun set behind the trees, the quiet woods became a menacing maze of dark shadows and hidden dangers. Rafe led us to a small clearing, which was sheltered by an overhanging rock. He and Erien set up camp while I helped Aunt Serena water the horses and tie them to a tree. Aunt Serena unpacked our food of bread and salted meat slices while we sat around a small fire that Rafe had lit. The castle cook had also packed some pigeon pies. I loved those, so I wolfed down a few, along with some sort of smelly cheese.

"Do you think we should put out the fire, Rafe?" said Aunt Serena.

"That will not be necessary. The forest gets cold at night.

I will keep watch," said Rafe, sitting himself down against a sprawling willow with his sword across his knees. "Get some rest. It will be a long ride tomorrow, and we have to make one stop before we reach the town of Greystone."

"Stop?" I asked. "Where?"

"You shall see," said Rafe with a half-smile.

I smiled back at him and lay down on the soft forest floor. I was so tired, and my thighs were aching terribly. We had to sleep on woolen blankets that we spread out on the ground. It was cold in the woods at night, and we slept close to the fire.

"Rafe," I said, turning towards him.

"Yes, Aurora."

"Thank you for everything you've done for me," I mumbled. "I really don't know what would have happened if you didn't save me from Oblek and the Shadow Guard."

"You don't need to keep thanking me, Aurora," said Rafe. "I'm glad to help. I owe your father a debt for saving my life. I'm just returning the favor. Now get some rest, because we still have a long journey ahead."

"Okay," I murmured, as I turned over on my blanket. "Good night."

"Good night, Aurora."

So it wasn't because he liked me that he kept coming back. It was part of some sense of duty he had. My heart sank as I gazed into the darkness of the woods, my eyes shutting. I had to face the fact that Rafe was not interested in me in any romantic sense. He was only doing what he thought was right. Exhaustion took over and I quickly fell into a fitful sleep.

Waking up in the forest, at the first light of dawn, was an amazing experience. Muted sunlight filtered in through the rustling leaves. Birds chirped away to their hearts' content, and dewdrops nestled like shimmering crystals on the foliage and even on my hair and clothes. I lay in my makeshift bed and stared at the brightening sky.

"Good morning Aurora," said Rafe. He was already packing things into the saddlebags. "Did you sleep well?"

I blushed and smoothed my hair. I must have looked a complete mess. But Rafe was smiling, and I couldn't help smiling back.

"Yes, thank you," I muttered, still sleepy.

"We must be on our way," he said.

Aunt Serena and Erien were also awake and packing up their belongings.

"Do you need to freshen up, my dear?" said Aunt Serena. "There's a small stream just behind those bushes."

I nodded and headed for the stream. I wanted to wash my face and brush my teeth with the mint-infused powder that Aunt Serena had given me. I had to use my fingers, because, apparently, they didn't have toothbrushes in Avalonia.

I tied my long, unruly hair with a ribbon as I returned to

my traveling companions, feeling somewhat brighter but still muggy from wearing the same clothes since the day before.

After we ate our adequate breakfast of bread and cheese, we got onto our horses and followed Rafe through the brightening woods. Along the way we passed travelers and riders, who didn't give us a second glance. Wagons loaded with goods traveled the forest road, and Rafe stopped to talk to a group of pilgrims who said that they were on their way to the temple of Karneth in eastern Eldoren.

When he got back onto his horse, Rafe looked troubled.

"What has happened?" asked Aunt Serena, riding up next to Rafe.

Rafe shook his head. "It may be nothing," he said, "but the pilgrims said that they saw what looked like a Shadow Guard not far from here in the woods."

"Shadow Guards!" exclaimed Aunt Serena. "Here, in Eldoren?"

"So it seems," said Rafe seriously. "We must keep to the inner paths. Follow me."

We rode through the Willow Woods for two days, sleeping under the stars and trying to evade the Shadow Guard. After the first night, Rafe refused to light a fire, even though the forest would get chilly. He did not want to take the chance of a Shadow Guard picking up our trail, and we had to wrap ourselves in our cloaks, huddled together most uncomfortably, to keep warm. On the fourth day of our journey, after a few hours of riding at a fast pace through the woods, Rafe stopped his horse and got off. We all followed, and he tied the horses to a nearby tree.

"There is someone we have to meet," Rafe said. "Your granduncle's orders."

Aunt Serena didn't argue, so Erien and I just followed. We had to push branches and leaves out of the way to get to a thickly shaded grove. In the middle, nestled between two massive trees and countless bushes, was a little wooden hut. It reminded me of the cottages in Pixie Bush, but this was more unkempt and wild, with creepers and branches encircling the hut as if it too was part of the forest.

I wondered who lived there. Who was Rafe taking us to see? And why?

Rafe knocked on the little rickety wooden door and slowly pushed it open. We all followed him inside the cottage.

An old lady was sitting on a chair near the fireplace. Her long, snowy hair fell past her waist, and her ears had the unmistakable point to them that I now recognized immediately.

She was fae.

The hut was warm and inviting, and calming smells of lavender and vanilla wafted towards us as we entered. The old fae lady looked up from her sewing.

"Ah! Rafe, my boy," said the old fae woman. "I have not seen you for many summers."

"Magdalene," said Rafe, bending down on one knee and clasping her wrinkled hands in his. "How have you been?"

"Terrible, I can tell you," said Magdalene, chuckling.

"My back hurts and my legs ache when I walk. It's not easy being over a thousand years old."

My eyes widened, a thousand years old? Was she kidding? Mrs. Plumpleberry was three hundred years old, and I thought she was old.

The old lady's eyes turned to me. They were violet, like Kalen's, but so full of wisdom that I was momentarily taken aback.

"Is she the one Silverthorne has been waiting for?" she said simply, looking back at Rafe.

Rafe nodded. "Yes, Maggie, it is she. I must say I am surprised you know about her."

"I know many things," she said cryptically. "But Silverthorne did send me a raven with the news. I have been expecting her." The old fae lady chuckled.

Rafe raised his eyebrows, quite obviously surprised.

"Serena, my child, come here," she said to my aunt.

Aunt Serena went over and hugged the old fae lady. "Maggie, it's good to see you," she said.

The old lady smiled. "How is your father?" she asked.

"The same," said Aunt Serena, smiling. "Grumpy as ever and running about the kingdoms as if he were still a young warrior-mage."

The old fae lady burst out in a fit of laughter that sounded like a hacking cough. Aunt Serena laughed with her, as if only they were privy to their private joke.

"Well then, all is right with the world for now," Maggie

said finally, her voice scratchy. "If Silverthorne is on top of things, I do not worry much."

"Come here, my child," she then said, turning her violet eyes on me and stretching out her hands. She held my hands in her old wrinkled ones and looked at my face. "Aye, it is she," said Magdalene after a perceptible pause. "Let me see the amulet."

I looked over at Aunt Serena, who nodded slightly. I pulled out the Amulet of Auraken. The old lady fingered it with her bony wrinkled fingers and mumbled a few words in a language I couldn't understand. She looked like she was reading the inscription.

Finally she looked up and gave me a toothy grin. "So, young princess, I'm glad that all my work was not in vain."

"What do you mean?" I asked, confused. How did she know me?

"Come, sit and I will tell you," she said. "Be a dear and bring over the stool from by the window please, pet."

I did as I was asked, and soon Aunt Serena and I were seated on small wooden stools. Erien sat on the floor, and Rafe lounged against a wall. It wasn't every day you met someone who had lived for a thousand years. The amount of knowledge that she had accumulated over the centuries must be immense, so I listened intently to what she had to say.

"When you were born, you were a little menace," Magdalene said, laughing to herself. "In your first month alone you stunned three of your nurses, and their memories had to be modified because of it. By the time you were a few months old, strange things had started happening all over the palace. Old dogs were turning back into puppies, and cats were turning into birds. Once when you were taken to the gardens for a walk, the stable grooms complained that all the horses in the stables had turned into pigs."

I burst out laughing at that one. "So it was me?" I asked. "I did all that?"

Magdalene nodded, her expression becoming more serious. "That and much more," she said. "Even as a baby your magic was stronger than most, and mages don't come into their powers until they turn sixteen. You were a nuisance in the palace. Your mother was forever being blamed for the mysterious fae magic that was alarming the people of Illiador. Many times she would take the blame for it, and, because everyone loved Elayna, they chalked it up to the mischievous streak of the fae. Your parents finally got so worried that your mother came to me for help. They were afraid that, once people found out that their child was a fae-mage, you would be killed before you could even grow up. It was I who gave them the amulet that you now wear around your neck. I had come across it in my travels through the Old Forest."

"Maggie," said Aunt Serena softly, "if you knew all these years that she was a fae-mage and wore the amulet, why didn't you tell any of us? We would have kept searching for her. We gave up hope because there was no magical trace left of her when she was sent to the other world."

The old fae woman looked straight into Aunt Serena's eyes. "It was not her destiny to be found by any of us," she said, her eyes turning the color of icy pools. "Her destiny was set long, long ago, before she was even born. There are powerful forces at work here, forces you cannot even begin to comprehend, forces that have shaped our world from before the dawn of time. Everything is not always exactly as it seems, and it is ultimately Aurora's choices and strength of character that will determine her fate and the fate of all of Avalonia."

"And what is my fate?" I said, too intrigued to remember my manners.

"There is a long road ahead, and soon you will find out where your true path lies. But not today," she answered, her eyes turning back to a calm shade of violet.

I nodded. As usual, I rarely got a straight answer in this world, but I was thankful that Magdalene shared that much with me. It was a glimpse into a life that I did not remember. And it made me realize that my parents must have loved and cared for me before my aunt cruelly murdered them.

I stared out of the window, thinking about my parents and what they must have been like. I could picture them in my mind now, since I had seen portraits of them at Silverthorne Castle. I did look a lot like my dad: jet-black hair, striking green eyes, with heavy lashes. But my heart-shaped face and wide full mouth was so much more like my mother. It was quite amazing to see the resemblance. It was a good thing I didn't inherit the fae ears, or I would have never been able to hide myself in plain sight.

Finally Rafe spoke. "Maggie," he said, "I need a small favor."

Magdalene chuckled. "Don't you always, young man?"

Rafe smiled, looking a little embarrassed.

"We need you to change Aurora's appearance," said Rafe.

"What?" I spluttered. "I'm not changing the way I look." I shook my head vigorously to emphasize the fact. "Aunt Serena, say something!"

"I'm sorry, my dear, but it has to be done," said Aunt Serena.

"But, but, no . . . " I said to no avail.

They both ignored me, and Rafe went on. "Something understated; she must blend in."

Magdalene nodded. "Absolutely," she said, as she leaned over to me.

Before I knew what she was doing, she ran her hands over my hair, and then one hand over my eyes and face.

"Done," she said.

"What's done?" I asked, bewildered. What had she done to me?

I looked around for a mirror, and Magdalene took a small silver one from a nearby shelf and handed it to me. I clasped the silver handle and brought it to my face. I was aghast; she had changed my beautiful black hair to a mousy brown color. Gone were my raven-black locks. I touched the back of my head and only felt a soft mop of short cropped hair. She had cut off my hair! And my eyes . . . instead of emerald-green, they were brown, and not a nice brown; it was a bit like the color of mud speckled with dirt. I hated this look. It was just not me.

I looked up at Magdalene. "Couldn't you have made me blonde and blue eyed?" I asked hopefully.

Magdalene chuckled. "We want you to blend in, not stick out like a sore thumb," she said.

Rafe nodded solemnly. "Yes, Magdalene. This is perfect."

"Now she looks nothing like Azaren or Elayna and looks quite unobtrusive, thank you," said Aunt Serena, inspecting me closely.

"Glad to be of service, my dears," said Magdalene, still chuckling to herself.

I looked over at Erien. He made a face but said nothing. I looked horrid and so plain that even if Rafe had any inclination towards me, he would not anymore.

"We must be on our way," said Aunt Serena, getting up. "It's a long way to Greystone, and I want to get there before nightfall. At least we will be able to sleep in a proper bed tonight."

I was glad to hear that. Camping under the stars was okay for a few nights, but I didn't want to make a habit of it.

"I am so glad that you brought this child to see me," said Magdalene. "I never thought I would ever get to see a fae-mage again." She stood up and turned to me, taking my face between her leathery hands. "You have a great destiny, little one. Choose your battles wisely, and do not let your pride get the better of you. A wise queen is a just and humble one."

We all thanked Magdalene and rode off through the forest, towards the town of Greystone, where we would be able to spend the night and pick up supplies.

Soon we reached the gates of the little town, which was surrounded by moderately high, but crumbling stone walls. It was situated on the banks of the Pinebrook River, which wound its way through the Dewberry Valley and into the Stardust Sea. A small castle rose up near the town walls. It looked run down and quite bleak, very different from Silverthorne Castle.

"Who lives in that castle?" I asked Rafe, as he rode up beside me.

"It belongs to the marquis of Greystone," said Rafe, "but he lives mainly at his townhouse in the city of Neris near the palace. His steward runs the estates and the town. Normally your aunt would stay at the castle, but this time I have made other arrangements in the town itself. It's better that no one knows we are here."

"What about you?" I asked. "Won't someone recognize you without your mask?"

"No one really knows me here. I will keep my hood on," said Rafe. "Don't worry. You are safe with me."

"I wasn't worried about myself," I said, embarrassed as soon as I said it.

Rafe smiled. "I know," he said and winked at me as he rode forward towards the town gates.

A guard was at his post, but he was asleep. Rafe did something with his hand, and the man woke up with a start. He looked down at us from his post on the gatehouse.

"Who goes there?" he said with a sleepy voice. "Don't you people know the gates don't open until morning? Go away and come back tomorrow. We don't open the gates to strangers and . . . "

Rafe held out some gleaming gold coins that shimmered in the moonlight. The guard's eyes widened, and he grinned at Rafe.

"I shall open the gate right away, milord," said the guard, scurrying to open a smaller gate. We led the horses through on foot.

The little town was asleep as we walked quickly through the deserted streets. A few lanterns were still burning, but most had lived out their lives. Two stray dogs ran by, and one tried to snap at the heels of my horse, but Rafe shooed them away. Tiny cobblestone paths crossed and intersected in a maze of streets. Badly constructed wooden houses with patched roofs were crammed together, the upper floors almost touching each other, creating a tunnel passage over the street below. This was not like the clean, whitewashed town of Fairlone. Greystone was much smaller, more like a village, and very dreary.

"That is the town hall," said Erien, pointing to a large,

rickety, two-storied house with a crumbling roof and battered walls.

"It looks so rundown," I said, looking around as we crossed the deserted town square.

"That's because many of the townspeople have left and moved south to Calos or Mirin or any of the other villages on the southern coast," explained Rafe.

"Why?" I asked, always interested to learn what I could about Avalonia.

"This was once quite a prosperous town, but Greystone is too close to the Illiadorian border," Rafe answered.

I nodded, understanding. Morgana's terror was slowly moving into Eldoren too.

As we walked through the quiet, sleeping town, I felt like someone or something was watching me, and I glanced back twice. It was as if some presence was boring into my back, but when I turned there was nothing there but shadows. Rafe did not seem to notice anything unusual, so I decided not to say anything. Maybe it was just my tired mind playing tricks on me.

We came at last to a large wooden house two stories high. Above the heavy wooden door was a sign: The Dancing Daisy Inn. Rafe knocked once and waited. A short, fat little man opened the door. He was wearing his nightclothes and looked very sleepy and angry to be woken at this hour. But when he saw Rafe, his eyes widened and he gave a short bow, silently ushering us in.

"I have your rooms ready," he said, as Erien, Aunt Serena and I followed him up the rickety wooden stairs. Rafe came up behind us.

The inn was a warm, cozy, well-kept place. It was basic, but better than what I expected from it. Four unpolished wooden doors lined the small pokey corridor on the first floor of the inn. The little man led us into the first one, unlocking the door and opening it ever so carefully, as if he were opening the door to a treasure chamber.

"Thank you, Bumbletree," said Rafe, jovially patting the man on the back, setting him at ease. The little man bowed again and continued bustling about the room, closing windows, and tidying up.

The innkeeper showed me to my room, which I was sharing with Aunt Serena. It was small but comfortable, sparsely decorated with a frayed crimson rug on the otherwise bare floor. Two wooden beds with fresh sheets lay by the wall under the window, and a desk and chair were placed next to it. Across the room, a small candle lantern, half-burnt, lay on the little dresser, and a comfortable armchair that was patched in many places stood beside it.

The room was relatively clean and tidy, and I was too tired to be fussy. I washed in the copper basin with the jug of water and rough cloth that was left in the room and lay down on the bed.

My body was aching all over from spending the whole day in the saddle. I loved riding, and when I was little my parents would take me riding in the country, but I was not used to being on top of a horse for more than an hour at a time. My thighs were in agony, and my hands were blistered. I wondered if I would even be able to walk the next day.

Aunt Serena was asleep before I knew it. But I lay in bed thinking about the days to come. My thoughts whirled around in my head. Names of people I had never met, places I had never seen, and my change of name and identity.

I rolled over in my hard bed, trying to get some sleep, but I was upset and a little frightened. Starting a new school was going to be a challenge. I was not a very outgoing person, and I wondered what the other students would be like. Would I find anyone to be friends with? Even if I did, I would have to lie about who I really was.

Nothing could be worse than what I suffered at my old school, I told myself. At least here I had a fresh start, without Cornelia to make my life hell. In fact, thinking about Cornelia didn't bother me anymore; Morgana was now definitely the one I had to watch out for. At least in Evolon, I would be safe for a while until I learned how to wield my magic.

I clutched the gold amulet around my neck and looked at it closely for the umpteenth time. Who knew that such a small thing could be so powerful? I slipped it back under my shirt. Finally I fell into a quiet sleep, without dreams of gleaming daggers or Morgana.

The next morning I woke quickly, got out of bed, and went over to the window. The sun was shining, and it was a crisp spring day. The sleepy, deserted town of last night was now a colorful, bustling place. I opened the wood-framed window, and, from my window seat, I could see everything that was happening in the streets below.

Different colored stalls and traveling vendors had parked their wares at various street corners, which led out from the town square. The main street was busy, noisy, and full of people haggling over prices and carefully choosing the best items.

Some of the men were dressed in dull, old clothes and looked like they were going about their daily work. There were women in dreary, homespun wool dresses and linen bonnets, who were chatting away at street corners with baskets filled with fruits and vegetables hanging on their arms. Children dressed in patched, ill-fitting clothes, many looking very poor and underfed, were running about in the crowded streets.

There were shops and multicolored outdoor stalls selling all kinds of delicious-looking fruits and vegetables, flowers, and even pots and pans. There was also a small group of entertainers who were putting on a show for the people in the town square.

I washed my face and dressed quickly. Aunt Serena had already left the room, and I wasn't really sure what I should do. Should I wait for her to come and call me? She hadn't said anything last night, so I decided to go check on Erien. Or at least I told myself that it was Erien I was searching for. He wasn't in his room either, and neither was Rafe. I warily went downstairs to ask the friendly innkeeper where everyone was. They were probably having breakfast. But why hadn't they woken me?

The main room of the inn was bustling with life and full of diverse people. A few long tables and benches were arranged round the room. No one took any notice of me, and I sat down at the nearest table. The smells of freshly baked bread filled my nostrils, and I realized that I was absolutely famished.

Over by the window, three extremely loud men were drinking something green and frothy from big wooden mugs, which they flailed around in the air while talking. A middle-aged woman with two children was sitting on the bench next to them, and she seemed to be having a very hard time trying to get her wailing offspring to eat. A few others still wearing their cloaks had sat down and were quietly eating breakfast, but Aunt Serena and Erien were not there.

The innkeeper saw me and hurried over. "Apologies, my lady; the others didn't want to wake you, and the countess said she would be back soon. Would you like something to eat?"

I nodded. My heart started beating faster. Where had Aunt Serena gone? Surely she wouldn't leave me stranded and ride off? I shook my head and laughed at myself for being silly.

The innkeeper brought over a basket of fresh bread with a bowl of freshly churned white butter, a whole honeycomb on a wooden plate, and a small pot of a red berry jam, which was delicious. He also produced a big bowl of freshly picked strawberries and with it a jug of thick yellow cream. I ate furiously; everything was delicious, and who knew when I would get my next meal?

I was just finishing my third helping of strawberries and cream when Aunt Serena and Rafe came back to the inn. A few of the people in the inn looked over at us, but quickly resumed their own business. Aunt Serena sat down next to me, but Rafe stood. He didn't take off his cloak, and he still had his hood on.

"Did you have a good rest?" he asked me nonchalantly. He looked like his mind was somewhere else.

I nodded. My mouth was still full.

"Have you finished your breakfast?" Aunt Serena asked me. "We should get going. It's still a long way to Evolon."

"Where's Erien?"

"Seeing to the horses," said Aunt Serena.

I nodded again, took a piece of buttered bread, and got up.

Rafe turned to the innkeeper. "I have something I want you to do for me, Bumbletree," he said softly.

"I am always at your service, milord," he said.

Rafe nodded and gave him a sealed scroll. "See that it is

delivered to our mutual friend," he said simply.

The little man nodded back and tucked the scroll into his apron pocket.

I was curious. Mutual friend? Who was this mutual friend, and what was in that scroll? I decided to ask him later, when he was in a better mood. At the moment both Rafe and Aunt Serena looked very preoccupied.

"I would advise you to take the old road," said the little man to Rafe quietly, as I put on my cloak. "The king's road has blue cloaks patrolling all the way south."

"Blue cloaks?" I asked, turning to Rafe.

Rafe nodded. "The King of Eldoren's elite guard," he said. "We will keep to the inner roads."

Aunt Serena nodded, agreeing with him. "But why are the blue cloaks here? The king is in Neris," she said.

The little man lowered his head and nodded. "Yes, he is, my lady. But there is something else you should know." He paused, looked around and said, "The Shadow Guard have been seen prowling about these parts. There were six of them seen just north of here last moon tide."

"Six!" hissed Aunt Serena, horrified.

The little man nodded. "They say that the Shadow Guard have been roaming the southern lands more frequently now. They have even been seen as far south as the villages in the valley. They seem to be searching for someone, a girl. Supposedly with long, jet-black hair and eyes like a cat," he added and looked at me for a second before he turned back to Aunt Serena. "That's why the blue cloaks are out in full force; the Shadow Guard have to be kept in check."

Rafe was quiet. "I will send a raven to Silverthorne to keep a watch," he said finally. "Thank you for warning us."

Aunt Serena thanked the innkeeper while Rafe paid him, and I popped a few blueberries into my mouth. I followed Aunt Serena and Rafe to the stables, which were situated at the back of the inn. Erien had already saddled the horses, and they were ready and waiting when we arrived there.

We rode through the crowded morning market. The tiny streets were paved with cobblestones, and some were simple, rough mud paths, which were now littered with people and livestock. I saw some pigs wallowing in the mud outside a small house that looked like it would fall down with a sudden gust of wind.

We passed through the town gates, which were now open. Oxen-driven carts, filled with fruits, vegetables, and bags of what looked like grain, were rolling in at a leisurely pace, driven by farmers who had come a long way to the town to sell their goods. Numerous people, chickens, and dogs rushed about the horses' legs, and I had to struggle to keep my horse from being startled.

They had a ship waiting for us on the river. It looked a bit like a pirate galleon, but smaller and better suited for river travel. We got off our horses, and Aunt Serena's guards led them onboard and below deck where the horses were stowed. The crew started scurrying around the deck, getting ready to raise the anchor and unfurl the sails.

"This is where I take your leave," said Rafe.

"But I thought you were supposed to escort us all the way to Evolon," I blurted out without thinking, as usual.

Rafe smiled, his lips curving slightly. "I have done what your uncle wanted. You will not be recognized now," he said. "Your Aunt Serena's guards will escort you from here. I assure you, you shall be quite safe."

"Why did you tell the innkeeper that we would be traveling by the old road?" I asked.

"Always helps to be careful," he said, "just in case anyone recognized me."

I nodded. What else was there to say?

"Till we meet again," said Rafe, spurring his black monster of a horse into an easy canter and riding away towards the forest from which we came.

15
THE ACADEMY OF MAGIC

AUNT SERENA and I had a comfortable cabin aboard
the riverboat, with two beds that were attached to the walls
on opposite sides of the room. In the center lay a rough
wooden table and large, unwashed windows lined one side
of the cabin. It took us three days of peaceful sailing down
the vast Pinebrook River to reach Neris, the capital city of
Eldoren, which was situated on the coast of the Stardust Sea.
The whole journey, I sat in my cabin, brooding about Rafe.
Why didn't he come with us? I was also upset that he didn't
say a proper good-bye. What if I never saw him again?

We got off near the northern gate and rode our horses
into the sprawling city. I was getting more used to sitting
on a horse for longer journeys, and my legs and arms had
stopped hurting so much, although my butt was still a bit
sore from the rough leather saddle.

Neris was completely different than Greystone. It was not
a small town or a village; it was a huge, walled, bustling city.
It was situated in a comfortable bay with hills and woods
flanking two sides. The Pinebrook River ran through the
center of Neris, and numerous narrow stone bridges con-

nected the two divided parts of the city.

At the edge of Neris at one end, beyond the city walls, mounted on a pristine white cliff like a crown to the magnificence of the seaside city, lay the towering white walls of the Academy of Evolon.

Far in the distance, right on the other side of the city—its walls glistening in the midday sun—lay the impressive Summer Palace, the seat of the kings of Eldoren. It overlooked the azure sea of the Bay of Pearls, with the hills to one side and the splendor of the city to the other.

As we rode through the city, I was amazed at what lay before me. I noticed that there were more merchants and traders here than in Fairlone. Shops and street-sellers were everywhere, selling an assortment of items. There were jewelry shops, dressmakers, candle makers, glove shops, booksellers, locksmiths, bakeries, tanners and rope makers, comfortable inns, and whitewashed taverns.

Large stone houses were connected by a network of streets and broad avenues. Some were enormous and two and three stories high. Elegant shops and spacious inns lined the crowded streets. The town square was full, and the docks and warehouses were bustling with people. Sandy, white beaches with splendid towering white cliffs adorned the seaside city of Neris. Erien explained that on this side of the river were the mansions of the nobility, and the inside of the houses were massive, extravagantly done up, with beautifully manicured enclosed gardens and courtyards.

We rode through the wide streets and over one of the narrow bridges to the other side of the city. Here the houses were made of wood, smaller and more cramped together, with small cobblestone paths, which crisscrossed into alleyways that led to run-down houses. Parts of this side of the river were still respectable, where the merchants, traders, and shopkeepers lived. The shops here were more down-market, I noted. There were blacksmiths hammering at their anvils, taverns, and brothels with prostitutes selling themselves on dirty, deserted street corners. Here most of the streets led down into darker alleyways where drunks languished and the garbage was not swept up.

Erien explained that this was the old town of Neris. Many years ago the city was just a small fishing village, and slowly it grew into an unplanned town, but always on this side of the river. Then the mages came and built the Academy of Evolon, and soon the little town became a sprawling city. The king of that time, Dorian the third, built the Summer Palace here, as he wanted a home by the sea.

"You see," Erien was saying, as I slumped on my ambling horse, "the original king's palace is Caeleron Castle, situated north of here in the hills. The court moves there during the winter and returns to the city for the summer. It is the height of the season in Neris, and there are balls and parties held by all the nobility during summer and the harvest season. In the winter, most of the nobility leave Neris and return to their country estates, which are situated all over Eldoren."

I nodded. The life of the Eldorean nobility sounded very exciting and glamorous.

"So, do you have a house here in the city?" I asked Erien.

"Yes, of course. Elmsdale House is all the way on the other side of the city, near the palace," he said. "Mother will be staying there this summer. During holidays, we can leave the academy and go and stay there with her."

I smiled at that. I was looking forward to spending time with Aunt Serena and Erien at their house, and it would be nice to get away from the academy when we had time off from school. It was also comforting to know that I had somewhere to go.

We rode up the side of the hill to the lofty white walls of the Academy of Magic. Once inside the academy gates, I was amazed at how beautiful it was. An immense walled complex, Evolon was like a little village of its own. Within the walls of the school, beautifully maintained gardens and shaded paths surrounded the academy on all sides. Court-yards with fountains and terraced gardens stretched back down to the cliff and the sea.

Serena took me to meet the Mastermage of Evolon, Elial Dekela. The mastermage's office was in a beautiful, two-sto-ried, white stone mansion with large, arched windows. Aunt Serena knocked on the stout door. A strong, stern voice bade us enter.

Elial Dekela was a small, aging man with long, salt-and-pepper hair tied back neatly in a ponytail. His sharp black eyes were deep set under bushy white eyebrows, and delicate spectacles rested precariously on his hooked nose. He looked like a very demanding teacher. He got up from behind his smoothly polished mahogany desk and came over to greet us.

"My lady," he said, bowing politely to Serena first, then straightening and turning to me. "So, this is Rory!"

Aunt Serena nodded. "Yes, and I want her to get settled in with as little fuss as possible. You understand how important it is that she not draw much attention," she stated.

"I understand completely. I'm glad we had a chance to meet before you started your studies here, Rory," said Professor Dekela, using my new name. "I am quite sure you will be happy here."

"It's imperative that her true identity remain hidden," said Aunt Serena to the professor, much to my surprise.

They didn't tell me that the old professor knew who I really was. How much did he know? Did he know I was a fae-mage?

Professor Dekela just nodded, walked over to the shelf and took down a scroll.

"This will help you get acquainted with the school and its rules and regulations, and it will also give you an idea about the grounds, in case you need some help getting to your classes," he said, handing me the old scroll. "I will send for you soon, so we can have a little talk after a few days have passed and you have had a chance to settle in."

I took the scroll and thanked him politely.

"Your aunt will show you to your house," said Professor Dekela. "She knows it well, as your cousin Erien has been here for a year already."

I followed Aunt Serena to my dorm house.

"Where did you go to school, Aunt Serena?" I asked while we walked down the flower-lined paths. The sun was setting, and I wanted to get settled in as quickly as possible.

"I was homeschooled," answered Aunt Serena.

"But why didn't you go to Evolon too?" I asked, confused.

Aunt Serena smiled, but I could sense sadness behind it. "Although I am born of a magical bloodline, I am one of the many not gifted with the magic of the mages."

I was stunned. I had never really thought about asking Aunt Serena about this. I always assumed she had magic like everyone else. It was going to take a while for me to get used to this world. There were so many things to remember and learn.

Finally we reached my dorm house. It was a fairly large stone house with ivy and creepers running all over the walls. It had a large gated garden and a picket fence with a sign that read, "Mulberry House." It was charming and quaint, and I was quite sure I would be happy here.

"This is where you will live for the year," Aunt Serena said. "Do not let the other girls convince you to break the rules. They do that to newcomers here sometimes. Professor Dekela is very strict about how you conduct yourself on the school grounds."

"How much does the professor know?" I asked Aunt Serena before we went in.

"He knows enough to keep you safe, but not everything," said Aunt Serena.

"But I thought Uncle Gabriel said not to tell anyone else," I said. "Too many people know."

"The mastermage only knows who your parents are," said Aunt Serena softly. "He doesn't know about your powers or the amulet. My father felt that it was important for the professor to know enough to keep an eye on you and see that you are safe. The Dekela family is a staunch supporter of your father. He will not betray you."

I nodded understanding and gingerly climbed the steps up to the large, white, stone house, which was to be my home for the next year.

My dormitory was full of girls of all shapes and sizes. It was buzzing like a beehive when I got there, but when I entered, everyone stopped to look at me.

The new girl!

I looked down at my feet. I hated people looking at me and talking about me; it made me feel very awkward.

A third-year girl in blue mage robes showed me to my room, which was situated on the first floor of the house where the first-year mages lived. Aunt Serena left me to unpack after a quick farewell hug.

My room was cute and airy, with a big window sporting green and yellow curtains. Two white, wrought-iron beds covered with comfy, white blankets with sunflowers embroidered on them, two wooden cupboards painted white, a matching chest of drawers, and a fluffy green rug completed the room.

I stowed the trunk that Aunt Serena had given me under the bed and put the rest of my things in the drawers and cupboard. I wondered who my roommate would be. Whoever it was already had her cupboard full and had taken the top two drawers of the dresser. At least she had left me the last two.

After I finished unpacking, my roommate walked in. She was the same age as me and also in the first year. She had long, wavy golden-brown hair the color of fresh honey and was wearing green robes over thick tights and a long, white shirt belted at the waist.

"I'm Vivienne Foxmoor," said my roommate, taking off her robes and flinging them over a chair, "and you are?"

"Um, Rory," I answered. I felt like kicking myself for hesitating.

"Hi Rory," said Vivienne bouncing herself on her bed, which was by the window. "Where are you from? What house do you belong to?"

When I looked flustered, she elaborated.

"What's your family name?"

I explained to her that I was from Andrysia and how my parents had died and that now I was a ward of the duke.

"So you are a Silverthorne!" she said, raising her eyebrows.

I looked down. "Well, not exactly," I said. "I mean, I'm

only a ward of the duke, not really a Silverthorne."

She waved her hand in a shooing gesture. "Being a ward is like being his daughter or granddaughter here in Eldoren," Vivienne explained. "You are now a Silverthorne, so get used to it."

I nodded, not knowing what to say to this. Vivienne seemed nice, and she was quite knowledgeable about the city of Neris and the nobility. Her father was the fifth earl of Foxmoor, and she had two older brothers, Nathan and Fredrick. Besides her father, she was the only one in the family who had magic, so she had been sent to Evolon.

I was glad I had Vivienne to talk to, but I had to be careful to not give myself away.

"Come on," said Vivienne, after we had chatted for hours. "Let's see if there is still any dinner remaining."

We crept downstairs. The house was quiet and dark, and most of the girls had gone to sleep. Vivienne led me to the kitchen, where slices of cold roast beef and cheese lay waiting on the middle table.

The kitchen was a lovely, high-ceilinged room with a long wooden worktable and benches in the center. In the middle of one wall, the last embers of a fire were flickering in the large fireplace. Along the other wall were a brick oven and a large washing tub. We ate our midnight snack in silence, crept back upstairs, and climbed into bed.

That night I slept very little. I kept having dreams of standing in a classroom with everyone laughing at me. Then

Rafe was there, as he always was in my recent dreams, but I could only see his back. I called out to him, but he was walking away from me, on the arm of another girl whose face I couldn't see. They were laughing and cuddling as if they were having a marvelous time, and Rafe never even turned to look at me. I tossed and turned the whole night and was still awake when the sun rose from the Stardust Sea in the early hours of first light.

The next morning I got out of bed early, since I was already awake. The crisp morning air was chilly, and I dressed quickly, trying to figure out how my new uniform was to be worn.

The novices all wore the same thing: ankle-length robes with a white, full-sleeved shirt under a leather vest that was to be tied in the front with laces. This was worn over thick tights tucked into sturdy leather boots. The color of the robe depicted the year that the mage was in. Novices all wore green; the second-years wore red robes; third-years wore blue and fourth-years purple. When it was cold, we had a standard brown cloak that all the students wore. The professors were dressed in black robes lined with silver.

I was anxious about my first day and didn't want to be late. The dining table in my dorm house was laid with freshly cooked eggs and fruits with little pots of butter and jam interspaced about the table. Big jugs of cream accompanied the blueberries that were placed in tiny bowls. Jugs of different fruit juices and milk, and baskets of freshly baked bread, cakes, and fresh jam-filled pastries, along with bowls of porridge, cheese, and some sort of cured meats, filled in the gaps. A few of the girls were already there, eating and chatting away.

When I came in, they ignored me. Vivienne was already sitting at the end of a table eating. She waved me over, so I found myself a place at the end of the bench near her, sat down, and quickly ate my breakfast.

Vivienne and I had classes together, so that would be fun. I consulted my scroll as to where our first class was.

Evolon was like no school I had ever been to. Although the classes involved students and a teacher, that is where the comparison stopped. Most of the classes were held outdoors, in courtyards near fountains, under the shade of an old oak, or down in the gardens where a marquee was set up to shade us from the sun. And, as if the whole place wasn't confusing enough, the classes kept moving, so if you didn't check the board in the main hall every day you may have to end up trudging miles back from a class that had already moved. To top it all off, the classes were not all in the same structure.

There was a separate area on the grounds for warrior skills, a different house for healing studies and one for transformation and illusion skills. Alchemy was all the way on the other side of the campus because the students were frequently blowing things up. Ancient studies, history, and political studies were located in the best house of all, the library.

I checked my schedule; my first class was history. That seemed quite normal, except it wasn't really. I would be learning about the history of a world I never knew existed until a few weeks ago. One thing I was definitely looking forward to was learning about my heritage. I had read a few books when I was in Silverthorne Castle, and most of them mentioned my father or mother's name at some point, or one of their ancestors. It was quite fascinating, learning about my family in this way.

Vivienne and I walked along the flower-lined walkways that intersected in a maze of confusing paths, sometimes leading to a frustrating dead end. Finally we had to climb over three flowerbeds and under one bush to get to the broad avenue that led to the largest mansion on the property, the library of Evolon.

I was picking leaves out of my hair and smoothing my dress when I saw it. According to Vivienne, the library of Evolon was famous throughout the whole kingdom and beyond for housing the greatest collection of knowledge, second only to the knowledge of the fae, who had lived in this world longer than any other race.

It was a fantastic structure, which looked a lot like a sixteenth-century manor house. Wisteria had climbed the walls of the front façade, which was huge and imposing, and two additional wings led out at right angles towards the sea. It stood on the highest point of the university grounds, on a cliff overlooking the clear blue waters of the Bay of Pearls.

The main avenue leading to it was lined with cherry blossoms and was packed with scurrying students eager to get to their classes and not turn up late.

We hurried towards the massive structure, not wanting to be late on my first day. We climbed the large stone steps and stepped through the oak doors and into the library.

The inside of the library was just as wonderful; the foyer was a majestic, high-ceilinged room with a grand staircase and corridors leading to the classes on the first floor. The whole ground floor consisted of reading rooms, which all opened up into each other. Shelves upon shelves of thousands of books, worn and bound in brown leather, lined the walls reaching all the way to the top of the high oak-beamed ceiling. Small tables and benches had been placed in all the rooms, and students were quietly working at their studies while library monitors prowled the corridors. One big table where the chief librarian sat was placed in the center of the massive foyer.

I climbed the stairs and followed the signs to my classroom, which was all the way at the end of the west wing of the structure. I wanted to sit at the back, but Vivienne, who was obviously an extremely eager student, pulled me up to sit in the front with her. I was always very conscious of sitting in the front, not because I didn't want to learn, but because I was afraid the teacher might call on me or ask me a question, and I wasn't ready for that.

The class was already full, and the professor entered just

as the last of the students trickled in. "I am Professor Plumpleberry," she said, as she waved her hand in a flick and the door slammed shut behind her. I was relieved. If Penelope were teaching this class, I would be okay.

I noted a few girls giggle. Professor Plumpleberry did not hear them or simply chose to ignore them. I had to admit it was a funny name, especially since it suited her so well.

Professor Plumpleberry was not what you would expect of a history and ancient studies teacher. Although I knew she was fae, the others hadn't noticed yet. She looked so young and was suitably plump with curly, white-blonde hair. But I knew she was a very old fae and highly skilled at magic.

"Good morning everyone," Professor Plumpleberry said jovially, hovering two feet off the ground. Some of the others gasped. I grinned; I was happy to see Penelope.

"For those of you who have looks on your faces that would give the village idiot a run for his money," Professor Plumpleberry said, tucking her hair behind her pointed ears, "I am one of the fae, and I am three hundred and ninety-three years old. So, if any of you do not think I am qualified to teach ancient studies, you can go to another school. I hear Nerenor has a history teacher who is well into his fifties. I'm sure he can give you as much illumination on the state of our world two or three hundred years ago."

Everyone in the room was now quiet, and the giggling girls had promptly shut up.

"He can give you facts, figures, and embellishments written by biased men, but I can give you the truth," said Professor Plumpleberry.

"For instance," she paused dramatically. The class was now hanging on her every word. "I was there when Dorian the Fourth was king. I watched as his son, Tristan the Third, slew the Gorgoth with his bare hands."

I heard a few girls in the front gasp. Erien had told me about Gorgoths, men who had been turned into giant bats, abnormally strong, with dripping fangs and razor-sharp claws. I shuddered at the thought of meeting one of those creatures and hoped I never had to.

"I helped rebuild Kelliandria along with the dwarves when the great earth shook and destroyed countless lives," she continued. "That was a very long time ago, almost two hundred summers."

Some girls gasped again. I grinned. Mrs. Plumpleberry really was a very good teacher. And she knew how to keep the room quiet and her students interested.

"On a more recent note, I was there in the midst of the last mage war that took place on the plains of Eleth. It was a dark time for all of us. A rebellion of nearly a hundred fully trained mages, who fought against their king and had turned away from the gentle way of the mages, sought to take the kingdom for themselves."

Everyone was silent as Professor Plumpleberry looked around the room. For a fleeting second, she looked straight at me, her blue eyes twinkling, then she continued her story.

"I was busy healing a warrior-mage, and was present when Prince Azaren, the king's champion, Warden of the West, and the most powerful mage of our age, created a lightning strike so formidable that it burst through the approaching army, killing the traitor Joreth." She shook her head then went on. "With their leader gone, the traitors who called themselves the Black Mages surrendered."

I couldn't help myself; I felt a hot tear trickle slowly down my cheek. My father was a hero, a real champion. Everything that Uncle Gabriel had said about him was true. Not that I ever really doubted it, but hearing it here, in school as part of a history lesson, was amazing. Was he really the Warden of the West? I made a mental note to ask Penelope about that after class.

I got back to concentrating on what Professor Plumpleberry was saying. I was now quite sure which class was going to be my favorite. Everything I needed to know about my parents was here, in this classroom and in this library.

When the class finished, Penelope was busy talking to a student, and Vivienne dragged me along with her, so I decided I could talk to Penelope later.

After ancient studies, we all moved to another classroom in the same building. It was called "Social Structure and Government in the Seven Kingdoms", but it was essentially politics. Professor Ruthbridge was old and boring. He had a timid voice and shaggy, unkempt silver hair, which made him look a bit like Albert Einstein, I thought, as Vivienne and I found seats at the back of the class. Vivienne wanted to sit at the front as usual, but all the seats were taken. I was relieved.

I sat quietly while the professor rambled on and on about places I didn't know. He was spewing a litany of names, and I was completely lost.

"There used to be slaves in Eldoren too?" a boy called Reginald asked, interrupting the professor.

The old professor nodded. "The mages used them to tend their estates," he said. "The slave trading may be under control now, but our kingdom is still fueled by unrest. There is a huge underground network of cutthroats, thieves, and outlaws that roam these lands and prey on the helpless. The city guards are swamped with work, and the dungeons are overflowing."

"But what about the Blue Cloaks?" one girl asked. "Can't they do anything?"

Professor Ruthbridge shook his shaggy head. "The Blue Cloaks are powerful mage warriors, but there just aren't enough of them to go around. We must rely on nonmagical guards too."

My thoughts drifted to Rafe. He was an outlaw; was he also a part of this underground network that the professor spoke about? I knew so little about him. He could very well be dangerous, but still I didn't care, I couldn't stop thinking about him. Although he must have forgotten all about me after he left me at Greystone.

While I was busy dreaming about Rafe, political studies ended. I wondered what I had missed. I would have to take notes from Vivienne later. She was taking alchemy, and I had healing next, so we had to split up.

"See you later," said Vivienne, rushing off towards the alchemy house.

I had a few minutes before my healing class started, so I went over to the healing house early to meet Penelope. She was mixing some liquids in a small bottle and peppering it with some sort of silver powder. She gave me a huge smile when I came in. I rushed over and gave her a big hug, careful not to spill the contents of the bottle.

"It's so lovely to see you again, Penelope," I said, meaning every word. This was the first time I had been able to speak to her since I arrived. "How's Kalen? Did he come with you?"

Penelope shook her head, her golden curls bouncing. "No, my dear, but I will send for him soon, I promise. He wanted to come, you know how Kalen is, but it's just not the right time."

I was disappointed that Kalen had not come to see me; it would have been nice to have him around while I was getting used to this new school. Vivienne was sweet, but I couldn't talk to her about Morgana or the fae. At least I had Penelope.

"What are you doing?" I asked, fascinated. "What's that?" I pointed to the greenish liquid in the bottle she held in her hands.

"Getting ready for my next class," she said, smiling.

"Are you teaching healing too?" I asked.

"Yes," Penelope said. "Professor Dekela requested that I fill in for the healing teacher, who has gone on a year-long pilgrimage to the temple of Briesies in the foothills of the Silverspike Mountains."

"But I thought you were the ancient studies teacher?"

"I can teach both," said Penelope, her eyes twinkling as she bustled about the room, while I sat on a high stool. "Anyway, there are many other history teachers, I only teach ancient studies once a week and a few healing classes. Most of my time goes into assisting the academy healers when they have a particularly bad case."

"Tell me about healing please, Penelope," I pleaded. "Just a little before the class starts. I'm so behind all the other students in my class. They have all grown up around magic, but I can't even understand how fae healing and mage healing are different."

"They are not as different as you would think," said Penelope. "Fae healing is similar to mage healing in many ways, but the distinction occurs in the fae's capacity for healing."

"Which means?"

"The main difference is that mage powers diminish rapidly when you heal someone, and it takes the mage a long time to recover, depending on the mage's innate power."

"That makes sense," I said.

"Although most mages know how to heal," Penelope continued, "it is hard to do and exhausting to the mage performing the healing. But to the fae healing is instinctive, and we are better at it than mages. It is part of the nurturing trait of the fae. That is why in Eldoren most of the healers are fae and are very highly respected within the community."

"But then why do Morgana's guards hunt the fae?" I asked, wondering.

"It is only in Illiador where Morgana rules that the fae are being driven out," explained Penelope. "The common folk all over the length and breadth of Illiador have been suffering for years because all the fae healers have left, been killed, or been chased out of Illiador."

"Why does Morgana hate the fae so much?" I asked.

"Who knows what goes on in the mind of such a twisted person?" said Penelope, grinding herbs together and then performing some sort of magic on them until the green powder turned purple. "People fear what is different, and Morgana fears the fae."

"But how are fae powers so different from mage powers? I thought you said they were similar." I asked.

"Fae magic comes from nature, blessed by the goddess Dana," said Penelope. "There are five types of fae magic—earth, air, fire, water, and spirit. Some fae can command two or even three of those elements, but generally most fae can command magic from only one."

"And what is your magic?" I asked, fascinated.

"I am earth and air," said Penelope. "My magic is more suited to healing and glamour than fighting, although I can defend myself should the need arise, and I am very lucky to be gifted with two powers. But it is the fire-fae who are the most powerful warriors, and fire-fae that command more than one element are stronger still. Fae magic does not diminish like mage magic when used a lot; it can be replenished indefinitely."

"And those that have the power of spirit, what can they do?" I asked.

"The fae gifted with the magic of spirit are the most formidable. They are the only ones who can create portals and produce powerful glamour that can last for centuries, but they are rare."

"So what element could my mother control?" I asked.

"Elayna was earth, air, fire and spirit, one of the most powerful and unique combinations. Controlling four elements is very rarely seen among the fae."

"Is there anyone who can control all five elements?" I asked.

Penelope nodded. "Just one, and she is our queen and your grandmother."

"If the fae are so powerful, how come mages rule the lands?" I asked.

"In ages past, the fae were feared and revered by all races, but over the centuries—for reasons unknown—the magic of the fae has become weak," Penelope explained. "Most of the fae born now are either air or earth fae. Fire, water, and especially spirit fae are very scarce, and there is only a handful of your grandmother's fae-knights left to defend her kingdom."

I nodded. It was fascinating learning about the fae, but students had started filing in, so more would have to wait.

Healing was an eye opener. I never expected that I could use my powers to heal, and to such a degree, although it would take years of intense training to do what Penelope could do. In healing studies, we learned about different herbs and their properties to assist healing, how to combine them, and where they should be used and in what quantity. The most fantastic revelation was that I could actually learn to use my powers to heal a wound or a broken bone. It was difficult but possible, just with my will and magic alone.

If I were able to use my fae powers for healing, I would never deplete my power source. But I couldn't take the risk of even Penelope knowing that I was actually a fae-mage. Uncle Gabriel had explained the risks. So I went about my day learning what I could.

I was eager to test my powers and see what I could really do. I knew that in order to become a fully trained mage, I had to complete four years of mage studies at Evolon. I also knew that I didn't have that much time on my hands. The sooner I learned how to use my powers, the better. I had no idea what Uncle Gabriel had planned for me, but I needed to be ready to face whatever it was, and time was running out.

16
THE BLACKWATERS

THE NEXT DAY at lunch, I asked for directions and found my way to the school cafeteria. Until then I had only eaten in my dorm house where there was always something laid out for the girls to snack on.

My eyes went wide as I took in these new surroundings. The Evolon cafeteria was the most amazing school cafeteria I had ever seen. There were no benches or wooden tables for us to sit on. Instead, a vast and beautiful garden—more like a small park—stretched across the school grounds to the edge of the woods that surrounded the city. Everywhere, Evolon students were milling around, strolling the narrow flower-lined paths and eating their food on colorful mats spread out on the grass.

It was such a lovely concept, a picnic in the park. Even the stalls that served the assortment of food were unique. Standing barrels decorated with flowers were stacked with a variety of delicious-looking sandwiches, small meat pies, breads, and cheeses. Various picnic baskets were packed and displayed on a round wooden table, and students could just pick up a ready basket if they wanted a pre-set menu.

Colorful glass balls, which hung low from the trees, dispensed juice and water. The cut stump of a massive tree served as a wonderful dessert table, piled high with fabulous cakes and mouth-watering pastries.

I filled my exquisitely carved wooden tray and went to sit down on my own under a secluded tree. I was waiting for Vivienne, who was late as usual. I had soon realized that my roommate had absolutely no concept of time at all. Last night Mrs. Richbald, our housemistress, gave her a lecture for over an hour because she arrived late for dinner.

I was busy tucking into a flaky meat pie when someone came and stood beside my tree, blocking the sun.

"You are the Silverthorne ward, are you not?" said a haughty, nasally voice.

I looked up, squinting against the glare.

A blond-haired boy, who looked like he was about my age, was standing near me with his arms crossed. I nodded slightly. I was a little stunned that someone had come out of his way to talk to me. His voice was high-pitched for a boy, and he looked very arrogant. Although he was smiling, his smile never reached his cold blue eyes. He was quite good looking, but there was something about him that made me feel uneasy.

I nodded. "Why do you ask?"

"We thought," said the haughty boy, glancing over at his friends, who were sitting on a mat close by, "that, since you are so obviously alone, you should come and sit with us."

I was taken aback, he seemed quite full of himself, but it was better than sitting alone, and maybe it would be good to get to know some more people in the school.

"I'm not alone; I'm waiting for someone," I said, trying to salvage some of my pride.

He acted like I hadn't even spoken. "I am Damien, by the way," he said and gave me his hand.

I hesitantly took it and got up, brushing remnants of stuck grass from my robes.

"Rory," I said, almost under my breath.

"You can wait with us," said Damien, and, before I could reply, he had already scooped up my tray. And so I had no choice. I followed him to where his friends were sitting.

Damien sat down and gestured for me to sit beside him. A big, muscly guy moved over to make room on the mat, and he didn't seem happy about it.

"That's Zorek," he said, inclining his head toward the big fellow sitting next to him. "And Calisto," he gestured towards the girl in the group. She was blonde and extremely beautiful, but her eyes were black as coal, and I had to suppress the urge to retreat. Calisto smiled a catlike, sinister smile.

"How quaint, Duke Silverthorne's poor orphaned ward," Calisto said scathingly. "Damien, you do have a penchant for picking up strays. This one is the scruffiest one yet." She eyed me up and down.

I looked down, a little embarrassed. I knew I was not a

blonde bombshell like her, but I wasn't bad looking. With my long black hair and big green eyes I thought I was quite striking, but I soon remembered I now had short, mousy brown hair and eyes the color of mud. Still, I wasn't that bad. Was I? Obviously Calisto thought so.

I couldn't think of a retort to Calisto's mean comment, so I just said nothing. I think she expected a fight, and now looked disappointed that her jabs hadn't worked.

"My sister," Damien added, as an afterthought, as if it explained her behavior towards me. "She is in the second year here at Evolon."

I was confused. What did they want with me? Did they really want to be friends, or was this something else? I looked at Calisto and then at Zorek. They had resumed their banter and seemed to have forgotten I was there.

"So," said Damien, "it seems that we are in the same warrior skills class."

"Oh!" I said. I wasn't very good at conversation, especially with boys. I thought I had been getting better at it; obviously I had deceived myself. I was still a complete idiot when it came to these things. The strange thing was that I didn't even like Damien, I just wanted so much to be accepted that I didn't want to be rude.

He continued to chatter on about classes and some gossip about one of the professors. Mostly I had no clue who or what he was talking about. In a few minutes they all got up to leave.

"See you later at warrior skills," said Damien in a know-it-all manner, as if he was merely stating a fact instead of asking me.

I nodded and waved good-bye. Calisto and Zorek didn't even look back. I dropped my hand, embarrassed. What was wrong with me? I felt like kicking myself as I finished playing with the remnants of food on my tray.

Finally Vivienne ran over, huffing and puffing. "Sorry, sorry," she said, as soon as she saw my face. "I was in the alchemy house when one of the students blew up the whole classroom. We had to go and help the rest of the class and take them to the healers."

One of the girls from my dorm, the one who ignored me at the breakfast table, sauntered over. Her hair was flaming red and tied in a frizzy ponytail, but it was her massive nose that dominated her gaunt face.

"So, looks like Damien has taken a liking to you," she said, a silly smile spreading across her face.

"He wanted to be friends, I guess," I said, glancing at Vivienne who finally sat down next to me. She didn't say anything, but just started eating her food.

"And you said yes, of course," the girl squealed. "How lucky you are to get asked out by Damien Blackwater in your first week here."

"Oh, is that his full name?" I said, scrunching up my nose. "Suits him. And no, I did not agree to go out with him. I just sat with him for lunch."

"Same thing," she said, sitting down next to me. "Will you be seeing him again?"

I shrugged my shoulders. "In class, I guess," I said, hoping to look nonchalant.

"I would stay away from Damien if I were you," said Vivienne, raising her eyebrows at me.

"Damien doesn't talk to just anybody. He's the most popular boy in the school," the girl piped up. "I'm Celia, by the way. Celia Greendew. My father is a viscount, in case you were wondering."

I wasn't, but I didn't say that aloud. What was wrong with these people? Did they just become friends with me because of who I knew? And was it really necessary for me to know that her father was a viscount?

"Vivienne is right," Celia went on, tucking into a huge slice of apple pie. "Damien is a bit of a snob and very arrogant. Just because his father is a duke and his uncle is the archmage, he knows he can get away with anything."

"His uncle is Archmage Lucian?" I said. I didn't know that.

"Is there any other?" asked Celia, frowning.

I didn't know what to say. I glanced at Vivienne, who was also looking at me quizzically. I felt like kicking myself. I needed to be more careful.

"Well, you should know that he and the others hate all the Silverthornes," said Celia.

"Others?" I asked confused, looking over at Vivienne.

"Other Blackwaters. His elder brother Zorek and his sister Calisto are not to be trifled with," said Vivienne. "They are sort of royalty in the school. Cousins to the prince."

"They are?" I asked Vivienne, my eyes wide. I didn't know this.

"You don't know?" said Celia sharply. "You are the Silverthorne ward; you should know this."

I wasn't sure what to say. I had to be more careful with what I said. I could tell that even Vivienne was looking at me strangely, and I was sure she suspected something was wrong with my story.

"Celia," said Vivienne to my surprise, covering for me. "She has just recently arrived from Andrysia, so it is possible that they don't know much about the Blackwater's in the northern kingdoms."

Celia looked at me. "Maybe," she said. "But soon all of Avalonia will know about them." She moved closer and lowered her voice to a whisper. "I heard my parents talking, and apparently our crown prince is a wastrel. He spends his days sleeping and his nights in various unsavory taverns and gaming halls. They say that after King Petrocales dies, the Duke of Blackwater will overthrow the ruling Ravenswood Dynasty and take over Eldoren."

"Celia!" Vivienne gasped, her voice barely a whisper. "It's treason to talk like this."

Celia shrugged. "Well, it's true. Everyone is talking about it. The Prince of Eldoren is a complete rake, and he is not bothered about the kingdom at all. His father has guards following him now all the time just to make sure he comes home at night. But he somehow always manages to evade them."

Could there really be so much unrest in Eldoren as well? I had no idea how complicated the ties were within the nobility. There was so much to learn and so little time, and I had to be careful about my story. This time I was lucky, but if I slipped up again, someone would figure out who I really was.

"Oh no, we're late," said Vivienne, jumping up and banging her head on a low-hanging branch.

"Ow," she squealed, rubbing her head.

Celia rolled her eyes. "When are you not late, Vivienne?" she said tartly.

Vivienne just made a face, ignored Celia, and gathered her things.

I laughed and got up. "See you later, then," I said to Celia. "I've got to go too. Don't want to be late for my first warrior skills class." I turned and hurried out of the outdoor cafeteria.

"Do you think Celia is telling the truth?" I asked Vivienne as we walked to class. "Maybe all these stories about the prince are rumors, did anyone ever think of that? I don't think he could be all that bad."

Vivienne shook her head. "Celia's right, I have also heard my parents talking recently, and apparently the Eldorean nobles have already been moving their allegiance from the ruling Ravenswood dynasty to the Blackwaters. Father says King Petrocales has pinned all his family's hopes on the Silverthornes. Your guardian is the most powerful lord on the royal council, and Father says that, without Silverthorne, the Ravenswood dynasty will come to an end. It is the Duke of Silverthorne who is the real power behind the throne. He is chief advisor to the king, and the Blackwater's hate him. So be careful."

"Why should I have to be careful?" I said. "I haven't done anything."

"It doesn't matter to the Blackwaters," said Vivienne. "You are a Silverthorne. If I were you, I would watch my back."

We walked down open corridors, past gardens and fountains, to the eastern grounds of the academy. A large marquee was set up in an open field, overlooking the sea. This was to be an outdoor class, and it seemed like it would be fun. The cool sea breeze ran across my face. I could hear the waves lapping on the shores of the beach, below the steep white cliff. I was early, and only two other boys, whom I recognized from my healing class, were whispering to each other on one side of the marquee.

Soon the rest of the students came in twos and threes, and finally Damien Blackwater and a group of boys and girls I hadn't met before walked in. He had such a smug look on his face that I felt like smacking him. I was not too happy to be sharing a class with Damien, and especially this one.

Warrior skills would be the most important if I were going to learn to defend myself. I had only just learned to put up a shield and even then I couldn't hold it for long.

"All right, everyone," said a big, booming voice. "My name is Professor Tanko, and you may call me Baron or Sir. Is that clear?"

I looked up to see a massive man with plaited red hair, wearing a leather breastplate under the black robes that swirled about him as he strode into the center of the marquee. He carried a huge sword at his hip.

"Now, I understand that most of you have no training in warrior skills at all. But no matter; you are here to learn, and I will teach you what you need to know. The basic skills are easy to practice and should hopefully be enough to defend yourself should the need arise," said Professor Tanko. "Advanced magical warrior training is quite another matter. I know that all of you have the potential, or you would not be in this school, and we shall find out soon enough. Now, I want all of you to pair up."

Unfortunately we were not allowed to choose our own partners. Professor Tanko paired everyone up, and much to my disdain I was partnered with Damien.

"Now, I want all of you to take a defensive position," said the Baron, his voice drowning out the sound of the waves. "Shielding will be our first lesson. I presume everyone here has read the theory about shielding, chapters one through four, and knows how to create a shield even if it hasn't been successful. If not, I expect you to do the needful by tomorrow's class."

The professor went through the groups checking our shields.

"Now, keeping your shields up, I want you to pick up a pebble and throw it at your opponent."

I did as I was told, and concentrated on keeping my shield in place. It was easier this time because I had done it before. I flung my pebble at Damien, and it bounced effortlessly off his shield. But suddenly I felt a pain on my shin, and I collapsed on the ground. My shield had wavered, and Damien's pebble, which was more like a large stone, hit me hard.

Professor Tanko came over to me. "Your name?" he said.

"Rory, Baron. I mean, Sir Baron," I said, getting up and rubbing my shin. That hurt a lot.

The big professor smiled at me. "Just Baron or Sir is fine," he said kindly. "Rory, you must remember that concentration is the key. The first rule is: always keep your shield up, no matter what. It gives you time to think, to decide what to do. When you attack your opponent, your shield must not waver. It is the main novice mistake. At the time of attack, your shield is at its weakest."

He turned to the rest of the class. "If your shield is strong when you attack, it will not break. Nothing can penetrate the shield unless you let it," he said. "Now try again. Shields up!"

I calmed down and drew my magical shield around myself. I concentrated on holding the shield while I did other things. We practiced this for a whole hour, and by the end of the class my shield was getting better, but I was tired, and Damien kept taunting me and breaking my concentration. Sometimes my shield would waver just enough for him to get a hit in.

"All right, that's enough for the day," said Baron Tanko.

Illusions class was more fun. Our professor was a young man, probably in his thirties or so, and quite an entertainer. For our first class, he made six illusions of himself and walked them around the classroom. We had to try and recognize which ones were illusions and which one was really him.

They all looked the same. Short, curly blond hair, eyes the color of a shallow lagoon, and a wide toothy smile. Each one was dressed exactly alike, in black robes lined with silver. One girl touched the arm of one of the illusions, and it dissipated in a puff of smoke.

"Very good, Marietta," said Professor Swindern, from the other side of the room. "That, as you just saw, is one way to tell if it is an illusion or not. Illusions are not real. Transformation, however, is a different thing altogether, and much harder to do. Although it is taught as one class, transformation and illusion are not the same thing."

I raised my hand for the first time since I had come to school. I had a question.

"Yes?" said the professor, squinting against the light to see me at the back.

I stood up. A few people turned to look at me, probably noticing me for the first time.

"Is it possible for a mage to change the appearance of a person?" I asked. "Like, say, hair color or the color of your eyes?"

The professor nodded as the four remaining illusions dissipated into tendrils of smoke.

"Absolutely," he said. "It can be done. Many of the ladies of the nobility pay handsomely for these services. Some want their hair color changed, and some want different colored eyes; some even want their lips permanently reddened. In fact, many mages who leave the university get jobs doing precisely this."

I nodded, sitting back down on my bench. I was confused. If mages could do all that, then why did Rafe take me to see the old fae lady Magdalene and get her to use fae glamour on me?

I decided to ask Penelope after class.

"Mages use illusions to change things into what they want them to be. Some illusions can be temporary, and some can last for years. It all depends on the will of the mage who performs the transformation or creates the illusion," Professor Swindern was saying to the whole class. "Now, can everyone please turn to pages six and seven in your books, and we can begin."

It was a warm evening, and the leaves rustled gently as I walked down the flower-lined paths of the academy. I was looking for Penelope, so I went to her room in the professors' house.

I knocked gently on the stout oak door.

"Come in, come in," said Penelope, opening the door and smiling as she always did. "What is bothering you, my dear? Come and sit with me and tell me what happened."

"Nothing has really happened as such," I said, sitting down next to her on the comfortable cream couch. "It's just that I wanted to ask you a question."

"Yes," said Penelope patiently, giving me her full attention. "What is it you want to know?"

"If mages can change a person's appearance, why did I have to go to the fae lady in the woods to do it? Rafe or even you could have done it. Now how will I get rid of it when I want to? Will I have to go back to Magdalene to have it removed?" I asked, all in one breath.

"Firstly, my dear, you had to change your appearance before you traveled to Neris, or even Greystone," said Penelope after a moment of silent contemplation. "And I was not with you."

"Okay," I said, "but then why didn't Rafe or even Uncle Gabriel do it?"

"Because," said Penelope, "fae glamour, though it is similar to mage illusion, is undetectable by mages. If Rafe or your granduncle had put the illusion on you, or even if you did it yourself, the mages would be able to sense it."

Oh! I thought inwardly. That made sense.

"But can someone else remove it, or will I have to go back to her?" I asked.

"I can remove it for you when you wish it," said Penelope. "Do not worry, my dear, for now you know that it is better to leave it as it is. I will remove it for you when the time is right."

I was relieved. I said good night to Penelope and thanked her for all her help. I was exhausted and aching all over, so I had a long, hot bath and got into bed. I was too tired to go for dinner, and Vivienne very sweetly brought me a baked potato and an apple to eat in my room.

Celia came over to say good night, but I suspected she was only being nice to me for a chance to get to know Damien. Vivienne had told me earlier that Celia had been trying to get Damien to notice her for years; everyone knew that she had a huge crush on him. But I was too tired to be bothered about that just then. Tomorrow would, hopefully, be better.

The next day, I tried to ignore Damien and the other Blackwaters. I just grabbed my breakfast and ate on my way to class. Vivienne was busy in alchemy and would be the whole day. Damien cornered me after my healing class.

"Are you trying to avoid me?" he said. He looked more amused than angry. "I was just teasing you in class yesterday.

I hope you didn't take all that childish banter seriously."

"No," I said, looking him straight in the eyes.

I was still irritated with him and just wanted him to leave me alone. He was mean and selfish. But I realized that this was a perfect opportunity for me to get close to Damien and find out more about Lucian and Morgana's plans. If I pretended to be friends with him, I may overhear something of importance that could help my granduncle.

Damien's voice interrupted my reverie. "So are you coming or not?" he asked abruptly, probably nonplussed that I wasn't hanging on his every word like half the other girls in the school.

"Sorry, I didn't hear the question," I answered sweetly. I was enjoying his confusion. I wanted to upset him, but not too much. I needed to get friendly so I could find out what he knew.

"I asked if you wanted to come with us into town tonight," Damien said slowly, as if he was talking to an imbecile.

I fought hard to control my temper; he always brought out the worst in me. "But isn't it forbidden to leave the academy grounds after dark?" I said, and I immediately felt stupid for saying it. Of course they would be breaking rules. The Blackwaters didn't think that any rules applied to them.

"Yes," he said, "but what fun would there be if we were actually permitted to go?"

I thought about it for a moment. I could go. That would show him that I wanted to be friends. But I was apprehensive, and I was breaking school rules. If Professor Dekela found out, I would be thrown out of school in my first week. Uncle Gabriel would not be too pleased about that.

Why did the Blackwaters want to leave the academy at night? Where were they going and what were they up to? My curiosity got the better of me, and I had to find out.

"Sure," I said finally. "Why not?"

17
THE LION'S DEN

"YOU CAN'T LEAVE the academy after dark," whispered Vivienne, looking at me wide-eyed. "If the night patrol catches you, you will be expelled from school."

"Don't worry so much," I said to Vivienne, who was sitting cross-legged on her bed, and had already changed into her nightclothes.

"You can't trust Damien," she said in a whisper.

"I know," I answered, pulling on my supple leather boots. "I don't trust him, but I want to find out what he's up to."

"Why do you care what he's up to?" said Vivienne, watching me carefully. "Damien's a troublemaker and can be very dangerous if you get on his bad side. I really think you should be careful. Just stay away from him."

I knew Vivienne must be suspicious, and I wanted to tell her the truth, but it was too risky. I didn't know her well enough and wasn't quite sure where her family's allegiance laid.

I hugged Vivienne. "I will. Thank you. It's so sweet of you to worry about me, but I'll be fine. Don't wait up for me. I may be late," I said as I gathered my cloak and ran downstairs.

Damien came to get me from my dormitory after dark. He was waiting near the entrance, leaning against an old spruce and wearing a black cloak over a black robe, like the professors. I wondered where he had gotten it. Although most girls would find him handsome, I thought Damien looked more sinister than good-looking in the moonlight. He flashed me a wide grin, showing all his pristine white teeth. I shivered slightly and pulled my own brown cloak tightly over my shoulders.

"I thought you were going to back out," Damien said, a cutting edge to his voice.

"Wouldn't miss it," I murmured.

Calisto and Zorek were standing a little further away in the shadows.

"Come on," Calisto urged quietly. "We haven't got all night."

She glared at Damien and completely ignored me, as though I didn't exist. Zorek led the way. We followed him down shadowy paths, past the alchemy building, and round the back, until we came to the far walls of the university. How were we going to get out? There were guards at all the gates. Zorek then moved slowly along the wall, to a shadowy little grove surrounded by apple trees. He went towards a particular spot on the wall and moved his hand over it. As if by magic, which was exactly what it was, a little door appeared in the wall.

Calisto pushed past me and walked toward the door.

"But how?" I said.

Damien shushed me. I glared at him.

"Be quiet," he murmured under his breath. "We could still get caught."

Zorek chuckled; he didn't think much of it and seemed very confident. He was the eldest and had been here at the school for a while, and he had probably used this secret door many times before. Zorek had the door open before I knew it, and we all followed him through, out of the academy and into the city of Neris.

Lanterns lined the still-crowded streets, and busy people were going about their daily business. Some were walking down the broad avenues, whereas others were hastily hurrying home from work or simply strolling on the pavements. Shopkeepers were shutting down their shops, and street vendors had already packed up their wares and were heading out of the upper town.

I followed Calisto and Zorek through the broad streets, Damien walking behind me. We kept mainly to the shadows, and I noticed that we had turned out of the broad avenues of the upper town into a dark alleyway leading into the poorer sections of the city.

Across the bridge, on the other side of the sprawling city, the houses were massive, whitewashed stone structures of the nobility and merchants. But on this side of the river were housed the smaller lodgings of the workers, shopkeepers, and artisans. We were going still further into a maze of shadowy alleyways and dark streets.

A few drunk men were laughing loudly at the end of the alley, and a man and two women, with their cloaks wound tightly around them and their hoods up, brushed past us as they hurried to some unknown destination.

It was a dark and dingy area. The houses here were crammed close together, creating an unplanned maze of streets and alleyways, which you could easily get lost in. The stench was unbearable, and I had to literally hold my nose as we walked past the sewers and heaps of garbage that had piled up on the streets.

Calisto and Zorek came to a stop outside a shabby wooden door of an equally shabby looking inn with a sign overhead that read, "The Lion's Den."

The name didn't help my growing fear that something was wrong, and I grudgingly followed them inside. It was not like I had never been in an inn before. I had stayed in one in Greystone with Aunt Serena and Erien. But we had been traveling with Rafe, and with him I was always safe. If Rafe knew I had come here, he would be so angry, not to mention what Uncle Gabriel would do if he found out.

This place was nothing like the little inn we had stayed at. While "The Dancing Daisy Inn" was quaint and cozy, "The Lion's Den" was just the opposite. One long, rickety staircase wound underground, opening up into a very large square room with a high-beamed ceiling. The atmosphere here was loud and boisterous. Shabbily dressed men and women were drinking, dancing, and frolicking everywhere. Wafts of stale ale and equally stale and unwashed bodies enveloped me in humid folds. It was even more overpowering than the smell of the sewers. I suddenly found it hard to breathe.

We had to push past some big burly men, who didn't look like they wanted us to pass, but reluctantly stood aside. I wondered what business the Blackwaters were mixed up in to be friendly with these sorts of people. They all looked like they were ready to start a brawl at any moment.

One table had a few suspicious looking men huddled in a group, and Zorek and Calisto were headed right for them. Damien gestured for me to follow him.

"Keep up," he said in his irritated voice, as if I had done something wrong again.

I was going to protest at his rudeness, but thought I'd better wait till we were safely out of this place.

Damien and Zorek sat down on the bench opposite one of the hooded men while the others moved slightly to give them some privacy, I supposed. Calisto stood right behind Damien, and I tried to stand as close to Calisto as she would let me.

"Keep your hood on at all times," she whispered. "Mages are not exactly welcome in the ghettos of the underworld."

I froze, and Calisto smirked at the obvious reaction it was having on me. My eyes darted around the room. Talk about walking into the lion's den, literally. But why had they brought me here with them? I was not getting a good feeling about this. My palms had started sweating, and my heart rate had accelerated. I really wanted to get out of this place, and fast.

Zorek and the hooded man had finished their transaction, and the man gave Zorek a small leather pouch. I wondered what was so precious that we had all come down into this horrible place to get it. Even the Blackwaters, untouchable as they were, didn't seem to be at ease around these people.

Professor Ruthbridge had dedicated a whole lesson to the Eldorean underworld. And this was it, or at least part of it, that I was sure. The man in the hood looked like one of their leaders, because everybody seemed to defer to him or simply stayed out of his way.

Zorek slipped the pouch into his pocket and got up, Calisto and Damien right behind him.

Damien brushed past Calisto, and I heard him say in a barely audible whisper, "Leave her."

I was still confused, but my fears were realized soon enough, when Calisto grinned at me evilly, turned on her heel, and followed Damien and Zorek out of the inn in a flash. I turned to go after them, but they were already gone. They had left me there at the mercy of those vile men.

Dirty, dreadful faces moved in front of me, touching my hair, staring at me. I brushed a few hands off me and tried to move towards the door. But it was so far away, all the way at the other end of the huge room. My heart started hammering in my chest, and my hands started shaking. I didn't even want to think about the nasty things that these men must have in store for me. How could Damien have just left me here to die or worse? Were the Blackwaters really that evil?

My eyes darted back and forth. I felt like a trapped deer, and the lions were converging on me. What was I supposed to do now? I tried to remember my lessons, but all that seemed like a faint memory just now. A magical shield would not protect me from those filthy hands. I tried to think, but I was so scared that I could barely breathe. I felt like I was going to faint. The room started spinning, and I stumbled backwards.

Someone grabbed my shoulders from behind. I struggled, but it was impossible to escape. The steel grip that held me did not falter. My mind suddenly went into overdrive as I covered the possibilities quickly. I had to do something, and I had to get out of here. I hadn't even learned stun strikes so far, and even if I did manage a powerful enough stun, I couldn't stun all of them, and the rest of them would be upon me like a pride of lions.

My legs trembled, and I caught the edge of a table to steady myself. I took a deep breath and concentrated on my power source. Nothing! I was too scared, and I couldn't concentrate enough. I opened my eyes and stared back into the face of the hooded man.

The leader removed his hood and came to stand in front

of me. Underneath his cowl was a sinister worn face, more wrinkled due to his expression than age. Dark, shaggy black hair surrounded him like a mane, and I instinctively knew now where the name of the inn had come from. His eyes were black and angular, with bushy eyebrows as their ghastly frame.

I stopped struggling. It was useless; this man was not going to let me go. It was better I played along until I could find out what he wanted.

"So," said the lion-haired man, stroking his shaggy black beard. "A Silverthorne! Well, that's a first. I guess the Blackwaters are getting better at this." He chuckled, but it sounded more like a cackle.

"Why?" I asked, trying to sound brave and defiant, but it came out like a squeak. "What do you want?"

"Let me introduce myself, my lady," he said, trying to sound gallant, but failing. "My name is Fagren. The Blackwaters and I have a deal. Every few months they like to play a little game with the novices at the academy." He cackled again, rubbing his hands together. He gestured to the man behind me and his grip loosened, but it was still firm enough that I couldn't run.

I felt a wave of nausea wash over me as he said that. What did he want from me? How was I going to get away this time? No one even knew I was here; I would vanish into thin air and never be found again.

"Why, why would they do that?" I asked, trying very hard

not to let my fear show in my voice. "And what did you give them? I saw you give Zorek a pouch."

At least I could try and find out something since I was here. And talking was a good way of stalling until I figured out what to do.

Fagren shook his wild head. "Aren't you more concerned about what we want?" he said, looking a little amused.

I shook my head. "No, not really," I said, trying to make my voice seem casual, and hoped nobody noticed my legs trembling. I couldn't show them that I was scared; that was what they wanted.

To my surprise, Fagren laughed. "Well, that's a first," he cackled. "Usually those who are brought here, especially the women, are in hysterics by now." He paused and came closer as if to examine me. "You are quite entertaining. It has been a while since I met someone as intriguing as you. If you weren't one of those filthy scum mages, I would ask you to join my people." He grinned.

The way he said that sent chills up my spine. As if I would join him. Fagren laughed again. He gestured to his men, and the one holding me let me go.

That was unexpected. I didn't know whether I should make a dash for it. But I knew I would barely make it halfway across the room before they easily grabbed me again. There were too many there. I decided it would be better to try and talk my way out of it.

Maybe he wouldn't hurt me. I tried to convince myself

of that, but my knees were still shaking, and my heart was hammering like a set of drums inside my chest. My hands were clammy as Fagren gestured for me to sit opposite him where Zorek had sat just minutes ago. At least he was being civilized, in a way.

I walked slowly over to the bench and sat down at the long table opposite Fagren.

"What I would like to know," said Fagren, "before I answer your questions, is how did they manage to get one of you Silverthornes? You people are usually one step ahead of the Blackwaters."

Now I felt really stupid. I had been made a fool of, lured and trapped inside a lion's den. Of course the rest of my family would never fall for a trick like that. I tried to shrug it off.

"Maybe no one cares what happens to me. I am just a ward of the Silverthornes, not really family." I thought that maybe if they thought I was not important enough they would let me go.

"I doubt that," Fagren said, his forehead creased as if he was trying to think and it was proving to be a massive pressure on his brain. "But it doesn't matter. We have you now, and what a prize you are." He grinned; black, rotting teeth flashed before my eyes.

I looked away.

"So what was it you wanted to know?" he said. "What the Blackwaters were doing here? It is all a game to them. I detain their, um . . . " he tried to find the right word, " . . . victims for a night, and they pay me well to do it. A sneaky bunch, all of them, the Blackwaters."

It started to dawn on me. "You're saying that they lure unsuspecting new kids out here and give them to you to keep for a night?"

"That's about the bones of it, yes," said Fagren, his eyes lighting up.

I was now worried. This guy was not going to let me go. It may be a game to the Blackwaters, but I was scared, and that was exactly what they wanted. Would these men really hurt me?

"But you gave them something too," I said. "I saw the pouch."

Fagren grinned again. "Perceptive little one, isn't she?" he said to no one in particular. Now his face was covered in an almost maniacal grin.

Suddenly strong arms gripped me again, but this time it was very rough, and whoever it was yanked me up from the bench and threw me onto the floor at Fagren's feet. My knees were bruised and my hands were cut from fallen shards of splintered wood.

"Now that's more like it," he said, his black, dirty teeth looking like fangs in the dim light of the flickering lanterns.

"Respect, that's what I want from you stinking people, if your kind could even be called that. And I will get to all of you, if it takes me a lifetime to do it, one by one," said

Fagren.

"Why? Why do you hate mages so much?" I asked. This was not going well at all. I stated to panic again. How could I have been so stupid?

"Ask that bitch Morgana," he spat. "She murdered my whole family; she didn't even spare my infant son," he said, standing up. "You mages think you rule the world, but I will prove you wrong. Torturing a Silverthorne is going to give me more pleasure than I could have ever hoped for."

I winced at the word torture and tried to push myself up, managing to stand on unsteady feet.

"Take her to the cellar," Fagren said angrily. "I will deal with her personally."

I felt sick. So much for trying to talk my way out of it. It had backfired. Rough hands dragged me across the crowded room towards a back door. I struggled, but it was no use; Fagren's men were all around me.

Suddenly I was dragged to a stop. The crowd tensed, everyone turning towards the entrance to the inn. I couldn't see what they were looking at.

"Let the girl go," said someone in the crowd.

I didn't have to look up to see who it was. Even in this situation and as scared as I was, I would know that voice anywhere. A wave of calm washed over me, and I felt safe. Even the hands that held me roughly seemed to waver slightly.

The man holding me turned me around roughly to face the newcomer.

"I said, let the girl go, or you will have to answer to me," said Rafe, as he walked purposefully through the crowd of Fagren's men towards me.

They moved to let him pass, and no one tried to stop him.

What was he doing here? I didn't really care; I was just so relieved to see him. I knew he would get me out of here. His walk was like a panther: slow but sure. His obsidian-black cloak rippled about him like water as he moved. He was wearing his mask, and in a few strides he was standing beside me.

The other man let go of my arm as if I had burned him.

Rafe's grey eyes were fierce, and he looked straight at me as he spoke. "You do have a way of getting into trouble wher-ever you go, my lady," he said, an amused tone to his voice, despite the circumstances.

I felt my heartbeat quicken, and it wasn't from fright this time. He looked at me as if he could see right into my head. His face was hard and set in a mocking smile, but I could see the anger behind the façade.

"Are you all right?" Rafe asked softly, his voice more serious.

I nodded quickly.

"Good," he said and turned towards Fagren and his men.

He put his arm around my waist gently, as if I would fall down at any moment, and I was grateful. Even though my legs had stopped shaking, I was still feeling uneasy. I could feel myself blushing despite the circumstances. Rafe was here now, and nothing could touch me.

"Fagren," said Rafe, inclining his head in a sort of greeting.

"Ah, the Black Wolf," said the lion-haired man, looking menacing but somehow afraid of Rafe. Yet how could he be? He was surrounded by at least twenty men, and Rafe was alone. "What a pleasure to see you."

I turned my face to look up at Rafe. His eyes did not betray a hint of emotion.

Why had he come? How did he know I was here?

"She's coming with me, Fagren, and there is nothing any of you can do about it," said Rafe, an edge to his voice that I hadn't heard before.

"I wasn't going to do anything to the girl, you know," Fagren growled. "She was part of my payment for services rendered. I was only going to detain her for the night and let her go in the morning."

"Who paid you?" said Rafe.

"The Blackwaters," said Fagren promptly. It seemed his loyalty wavered with a threat to his safety.

"You could have refused," said Rafe scathingly, his hand resting on the hilt of his sword. "You should learn to stay away from the Evolon students. One day the mastermage is going to have your head on a pike."

Fagren laughed. "Right you are, my boy. I will await the day in anticipation." He waved us past. "Go. Take the girl. I got my money anyway."

"Come on," Rafe said lightly in my ear.

My heart was hammering in my chest, and I prayed that he couldn't hear it. I couldn't believe he had come for me. Despite the whole horrifying situation, I smiled. No one moved towards us as the Black Wolf guided me slowly though the crowd and out of that terrible place, one hand round my waist at all times.

18
FIRST LOVE

BEFORE I KNEW IT, we were outside. The fresh air was a blessing, and I inhaled deeply, instantly feeling better. Rafe led me down the dark alleys, keeping to the shadows, his arm fastened securely around my waist. I didn't protest. He was walking so fast I needed the support to keep up.

When we entered the upper town, Rafe pulled me into a shadowy corner, took off his mask, and held me up against the wall, his one hand resting on the stone wall behind me.

"What do you think you were doing?" he scolded in a loud whisper. His beautiful, grey eyes looked angrier than I had ever seen before.

My own emotions wavered, and my gratitude turned into anger. Who was he to ask me what I was doing?

"What were you doing there?" I asked, anger building in my voice. "I mean, not that I am not grateful for you rescuing me, but how did you know I would be there? What is it that you are not telling me? Are they the people you hang around with?"

"Hang?" he asked, an amused tone to his voice.

"Keep company with," I retorted quickly. "Murderers and

thieves . . . they didn't even stop you, and they seemed to know you very well. Who are they, your friends?"

He was looking down at me with those deep, searching eyes of his, and I was acutely aware that his one hand had still not let go of my waist. I suddenly couldn't remember what I had been saying.

"Are you quite finished, Aurora?" he said. His face was hard, but his eyes danced, and he looked like he was trying to suppress a smile.

"Yes, I think so," I muttered, feeling a little stupid and embarrassed.

I should have been thanking him, but instead I was fighting with him. What was wrong with me? The truth was that I just didn't want him to know how much I liked him and how glad I was to see him, because he would probably just laugh at me. I had suspected for quite a while that he was some sort of fugitive or outlaw, or something to that effect, but it didn't matter. Every time he looked at me, smiled at me, or even showed up, my stomach would start doing cartwheels and my heart would begin fluttering like a hundred butterflies had taken up residence there. I couldn't understand why he had this effect on me, and it was starting to get most inconvenient.

"Good!" he said, finally letting go of me and crossing his arms across his chest.

When he withdrew and moved away from me, I felt a wrenching feeling in my chest, as though I would never be happy until Rafe put his arms around me again. I pulled my woolen cloak tightly around myself and shivered slightly.

"Firstly, I would like you to know that those are not the people I hang around with," he said. A hint of a smile curved slightly on one side of his handsome face. "I am not friends with them. Fagren owes me a debt for sparing his life once. In any event, even if they were my friends, what I would like to know is what you, a mage and clearly an untrained one at that, were doing in Fagren's den. It's the most notorious clan of the underworld of Eldoren."

I stared at him. Was he serious? Here I was, nearly killed, and he was interrogating me as if it was my fault. Well, it sort of was my fault for being so stupid and following Damien, but still. I suddenly realized that Rafe thought of me as nothing more than a spoiled child. My heart sank, and all my romantic fantasies went straight out the window.

I had enough of this. I spun on my heel, hoping dearly that I wouldn't fall, and walked towards the academy. In a flash, he was beside me. Again he put his arm round my waist and half-dragged, half-carried me into a side street.

"What do you think you're doing?" he hissed. "Do you want to be caught by the night patrol?"

"The what?"

"No underage mage is allowed outside the academy after dark. You know the rules. If the night patrol catches you, they will have you expelled," Rafe said quickly but sternly. "Come on, Aurora. I'll get you back into the school tonight, and you can tell me what happened on the way. I have heard that the Blackwaters take it upon themselves to harass and intimidate new mages. This was a silly game they have played before. But how they agreed to get you to go willingly with them is quite a mystery."

"I was trying to find out what Morgana and Lucian's plans were," I said. "Fagren gave them something in a small pouch, and they paid him for it."

"Did they discuss it or say anything?" asked Rafe.

I shook my head. "No. All I saw was a small, brown leather pouch. They took it and left me there."

Rafe cursed darkly under his breath.

"You should stay away from the Blackwaters. They are nothing but trouble," he said, resuming our walk through the now deserted streets of the sleeping city. "If you had been harmed . . . " He broke off, shaking his handsome head and muttering to himself. "When you are back in school, maybe you should tell the mastermage and have them expelled."

"No," I said again, a little calmer. "I have to learn to deal with this myself. If I get the Blackwaters expelled, they will come after me and start looking into who I really am."

"You really need to stay away from them, Aurora," said Rafe. "How do I make you understand that the Blackwaters are dangerous?"

"Don't you want to know what they came all the way down here to get?" I said.

"I will look into it," said Rafe. "You just concentrate on

staying out of trouble."

"But I can help," I insisted. "I can find out what's in that pouch."

Rafe shook his head. "No, Aurora. It's too dangerous. If the Blackwaters find out that you have been spying on them, they won't think twice about getting rid of you."

"Don't worry. Once they know I'm not going to say anything to the professors, they will leave me alone," I said, trying to convince myself. "They just think I am some insignificant ward of the Duke of Silverthorne. If I become friends with them, I can find out what Lucian's plans are. Won't Uncle Gabriel want to find out what they are up to? The pouch may contain some clue." I sounded more confident than I felt.

"You may be right," said Rafe, but he still didn't look convinced. "Be friends with them, but I don't want you looking for the pouch. I will handle it."

I nodded and kept silent. Rafe didn't think I was capable of doing anything, but I would show him. I would find out what was in that pouch, and then he would have to admit that I was not entirely useless.

He led me into a large house on a side street off the main avenue. The door was locked, but Rafe had a key.

"What is this place?" I asked.

"There are many routes in and out of the academy," he said cryptically, a hint of a smile on his face.

Rafe opened his fist and held up his hand. A ball of light

quivered and swirled in it, lighting up the darkened house, just as he had done in the dungeons of Oblek's castle. He took my hand in his as he led me through the shadows. As his warm hand closed about my fingers, I felt my heart flutter again.

This was getting to be very inconvenient. What was I going to do when he went away again? And he would go away, he always did, and as usual I would have absolutely no idea where he was. There was no real future for us, and he was so obviously not interested. That thought saddened me, and my heart sank.

The huge house looked like it had not been lived in for a very long time. Dust covers obscured all the furniture, including the chandeliers and statues. I could only imagine what this place would have looked like all clean and lit up. It was like a mini palace. Rafe led me up the massive marble staircase and down a long corridor to the last room.

"Is this your house?" I asked, amazed that he knew his way around so well.

He smiled. "One of them," he said. Even in the darkness of this eerie house I felt safe, as long as he was with me.

Who was he to have a house this big and never use it? I wished he would tell me who he really was. Not that it mattered. I would still be crazy about him. I had never felt this way before, and that was what terrified me the most.

"This house belonged to my mother's family," he said finally.

"And no one lives here?" It was a silly question, but it was out of my mouth before I realized.

His face darkened. "No. Not since she died," he said abruptly.

He looked like he didn't want to answer any more questions, so I kept my thoughts to myself.

"I'm sorry," I said sadly, feeling bad for his loss. "About your mother, I mean. At least you got to meet her. I can barely remember what my real mother even looked like."

His gaze softened, and he gave my hand a small squeeze, but he didn't say anything more.

The last door at the end of the corridor was unlocked. Rafe led me inside a small room where bookshelves lined the walls. The only other furniture in the room was a large mahogany desk and an old worn leather sofa. He went over to one of the shelves and pulled out a book. Part of the bookshelf moved inwards, revealing a dark passage.

I was so used to secret passages now that I didn't even flinch. I had half-expected it. How else was I going to get back into the school at night? Calisto and Damien must have closed the magical gate.

"This leads directly to the cellar of your dorm house," he said.

Was that just a coincidence? My head could not process any new thoughts at the moment, so I just held Rafe's hand and let him lead me through the passage.

The fairly large, arched passage was dark and gloomy.

The grey stone walls were cold and damp, and I could hear a dripping sound in the distance. I fervently hoped that there were no rats down there as we walked deeper under the city of Neris and towards the academy.

I wondered when I would be able to see Rafe again. He always came and went so mysteriously, and I had no idea when he would turn up. I wished there was some way I could meet him more often.

"Can you teach me to fight?" I said unexpectedly. If I learned from him, he would have to spend more time with me.

"What?" said Rafe. Obviously he hadn't expected that.

"Well, since you say I keep getting into trouble," I said slowly, not wanting to anger him, "I thought it would be good for me to know how to defend myself."

"And you want me to teach you?" he said as we walked quickly through the eerie passage, back to the school.

"Yes," I said.

"And how am I supposed to meet you?" he asked, amused.

"Well," I said. I had not really thought about it, so the words spilled from me abruptly. "Maybe I could sneak out here some nights."

"Sneak out!" said Rafe, stopping to look at me, his lips arching in the cutest smile I had ever seen. Great, now he was laughing at me again. "No, I won't have you breaking the rules and getting yourself into trouble. Don't they teach you to fight in warrior classes?"

I had to shake my head to stop myself from staring at him as I hurried after him.

"Yes, the magical stuff is fine. I can manage that, but fighting with a sword is so cumbersome. I want to learn to fight with knives," I said finally.

"Knives!" Rafe looked amused again. "Why knives?"

"Well," I said, still holding his hand, following him through the secret passage, "knives are easy to conceal. You can carry more than one on your person at all times, and you can throw them. Erien said you were faster with knives than you are with a sword, which is impressive, since I've seen you fight."

"We shall see," was all he said. He didn't preen or look proud of himself, and I liked him even more for that.

We had reached the end of the corridor. Rafe gave a simple push on the right stone in the wall, and a door opened into the cellar of my dorm house. I stopped and turned to look at him. He had paused, too, and was staring at me; our faces were only inches apart, and his grey eyes flickered in the dim light. I thought for a second that he was going to kiss me.

"Good night, Aurora," he said finally, moving back. "I will be gone for a while, so please stay out of trouble."

I blushed and looked down. He was going away again.

"Where are you going?" I asked, trying to keep him there for as long as possible.

"I don't want to burden you with all the boring details,"

270

he said, grinning, "but I have some work I have to do for your uncle. How much do you know about what is going on in Illiador?"

"Not much," I said. "I know that Lucian is trying to invoke an old law naming Illiador as the High Kingdom and Morgana as High Queen."

He nodded. "Yes, and there is unrest all over the seven kingdoms. Your granduncle has gone to Andrysia and Kelliandria to make sure that they don't succumb to Morgana's threats."

"Yes, he told me," I said, "but do you think they will?"

Rafe shook his head again. "Who knows? Morgana has now allied herself with the Drakaar, and Andrysia and Kelliandria are right in the middle. They may not have a choice. If it comes down to force and numbers, Morgana could very well take over the whole North. The fae that are left in Illiador are suffering. I must help the ones who want to leave to move south."

"When will you be back?" I asked.

He shrugged. "I don't really know," he said.

My heart sank, but I nodded nevertheless. "Good night, and take care of yourself."

Imagine my surprise when he pulled me against his chest and kissed the top of my head. I melted into his arms and put my arms round his waist. I wished I could have stayed there forever. I couldn't bear the thought of something happening to him while he was gone.

"I will," he whispered into my hair. "And I want you to stay safe too. You really scared me today, Aurora. I don't even want to think what could have happened if I hadn't got there in time . . . " His voice broke off.

I was elated. Rafe did really care about me; it wasn't all in my head.

Finally Rafe gently backed away, took my hand in his, kissed it, and gave a short bow. He pressed one of the stones on the wall, and the door started closing on its own.

"Till we meet again, my princess," he said gallantly and turned to walk away.

My heart was crying for him to come back. But all I could do was stand rooted in my place, watching his back disappear into the shadowy recesses of the secret corridor. That's when I knew for certain that what I had felt for Alex Carrington was just a silly crush. I was falling in love with Rafe, and it didn't matter who he really was. There was absolutely nothing I could do to prevent it.

I sneaked back to my room and opened the door slowly, creeping on tiptoe towards my bed.

"Where were you?" Vivienne whispered, lighting a small candle and sitting up in her bed. "I was worried."

"I'm sorry," I said quickly. "I just lost track of time."

Vivienne raised both her eyebrows. "What are you not telling me?" she said, jumping off her bed and coming over to sit next to me.

I finally relented and told her about the Blackwaters and

how they tricked me.

"I told you Damien was dangerous," Vivienne said after I had finished my story.

I nodded.

"And how did you escape?" she asked, wide-eyed.

"The Black Wolf saved me," I said, with a stupid grin on my face.

Vivienne gasped. "The Black Wolf! Is he as handsome as they say he is?" she asked, nearly swooning.

"More," I said, grinning.

"Who is he?" Vivienne asked, leaning closer.

I shrugged. I guess it was better that I didn't know. Then I didn't have to lie.

"No idea," I said, "but it makes no difference. He's just wonderful."

"And dangerous," said Vivienne, looking like a stern professor again. "You don't even know him, Rory. I have heard stories about the Black Wolf that would make you shiver. He may be very charming and handsome, and ladies all over the lands practically swoon at his name"—she lowered her voice to a whisper—"but some say he has killed members of the Shadow Guard, and anyone that powerful is not to be trifled with."

"It doesn't matter," I said, ending the topic. I really didn't want to get into the "you don't know him. He is dangerous," conversation. "What's really important is what the Black-waters have in that pouch they bought from the thief lord."

"I don't think we should get involved, Rory," said Vivienne. "If we get caught, there's no telling what they might do to us."

"I can't forget it, Vivienne. Whatever is in that pouch is probably something that my guardian would like to know about. Please help me. I need someone to be a lookout while I search for it."

"You want to search Zorek and Damien's rooms?" said Vivienne, wide-eyed. She shook her head. "No, no, I can't. If I get expelled from school, my father will disown me."

"Please, Vivienne," I begged. "I really need to do this."

"Why?" she asked, crossing her arms and looking at me very sternly.

"What?"

"Why do you really need to do this? Your guardian has many people working for him who are more qualified spies. Just send word to the countess, and she will handle it."

"No!" I said, "I have to do this myself. Please just trust me. I would tell you if I could, but I can't. Not right now."

"Then when?" said Vivienne, more softly this time. "Rory, ever since you came here I've known that you're not telling me everything. I'm your friend, and I want to help, but if you don't tell me anything, how can I do that?"

I looked down at my feet. What could I say? I wanted to tell her who I really was, but what if she told her parents?

"You're right," I said. "I haven't been completely honest with you, but there are reasons. And I will tell you. Just give me a little more time. I need to find out what is in that pouch. Please help me, and I promise I will tell you everything."

Surprisingly Vivienne hugged me. "I'll help you, but we'll talk about it in the morning. I'm exhausted," said Vivienne, climbing back into her bed.

I lay down on my bed and covered myself with my blanket. "Thank you, Viv. Good night."

"Good night."

"Vivienne," I said tentatively.

"Yes, Rory."

"I hope you won't say anything about this," I said, "about the Black Wolf, I mean. I don't want Damien finding out how I got back."

"Your secret is safe with me," she said, closing her eyes and snuffing out the candle.

I lay in my bed, looking at the dark ceiling. It would be dawn soon, and I hoped I could get a few hours of sleep before I had to wake up for class. But I couldn't get Rafe's face out of my head, and I kept going over everything he said in my mind until dawn broke.

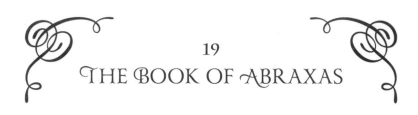

19
THE BOOK OF ABRAXAS

THE NEXT DAY, I walked with Vivienne to the library. Classes were just beginning, and countless students were milling about, trying to navigate their way through the library as quietly as they could. Library monitors were constantly shushing those who were being too loud.

"Isn't that Damien, talking to Zorek?" Vivienne whispered.

I looked over to where Damien was standing, at the far end of the library, where the older books were kept. He was talking to his brother, but they didn't see us.

"Come on," I said softly, pulling Vivienne along with me. I wanted to hear what they were saying.

We wound our way through the shelves and stopped on the other side of the bookshelf, where Damien and Zorek were standing. I moved closer, and I could see them clearly if I peered through the space between the books.

I saw Zorek pass the mysterious pouch to Damien.

"Keep it safe," Zorek said. "Lily goes through my things sometimes. I don't want her to accidentally find it."

"Lily Brentstaff is a such a social climber," said Damien with a trace of disgust in his voice. "You know she's only with you because of who you are."

Zorek shrugged. "I don't care why she's with me, as long as I get what I want." He grinned at the thought.

Damien shook his head, opened the pouch, and took out a small triangular piece of bronze. I couldn't see it clearly from where I was hiding, but it looked like it had some strange symbols etched into the metal. He inspected it, turning it around in his fingers.

"Fine," Damien said, putting it back into the leather pouch. "I'll keep this safe until we can deliver it to Father." He patted his pocket. "Did he tell you what it is?"

"Yes," said Zorek, "but I don't know much. All he said was that it was the key to some book."

"A book?"

Zorek nodded. He came closer to Damien and lowered his voice. "I overheard Mother and Father talking, and I heard him mention the 'Grimoire of Abraxas.'"

"What's that?" asked Damien.

The Grimoire of Abraxas. I had never heard of it. I looked over at Vivienne, who shook her head.

"No idea," Zorek shrugged.

"It must be very valuable if Father is being so secretive and paying a king's ransom for it," said Damien.

"It is, but I would not get involved if I were you," said Zorek. "I suspect our uncle the archmage has some hand in this."

I had heard enough. I moved away from the bookshelves

and gestured for Vivienne to follow me. The triangular piece in the pouch was a key, a key to a book. I had to find out what exactly the Grimoire of Abraxas was and what it could do, before one of the Blackwaters figured out how to use it or, worse still, gave it to Lucian and Morgana.

Vivienne and I hurried to our classes; we were so late. We didn't get a chance to talk about it until later in our room.

"I really don't think that we should get involved in this, Rory," said Vivienne. "This sounds like something to do with the dark arts. It is forbidden."

"We're not learning dark magic," I said, removing my cloak and hanging it up in the cupboard. "We're just finding out what the book is and why it needs a key for it to open. If it has something to do with Lucian, then it's entirely possible that Morgana is behind all this. I have to find out what she's up to."

"Why?" asked Vivienne, sitting down on her bed and glaring at me with her arms crossed. "I'm not going to help you do anything if you don't tell me what is really going on here. Why are you so interested in what Queen Morgana is doing?"

I sat down on the bed next to Vivienne. I could tell she was upset, and I wasn't sure what I should say. She was the closest thing I had to a best friend, and she had helped me so far without telling anyone.

"I'll tell you everything," I said finally, "but you have to promise to have an open mind."

Vivienne nodded, but she didn't smile. I took a deep breath and proceeded to recount my story. She listened without interrupting me, but only until I gave her my real name.

"Aurora Firedrake, the lost princess of Illiador," said Vivienne, her eyes wide like saucers. "Are you serious?"

I nodded. This was it; I had told her. Now I just had to hope that she kept my secret. I was struggling with deciding to go one step further and tell her that I was also a fae-mage, but I think some remnants of good sense prevailed, and I kept that part to myself.

"But Princess Aurora died nearly fifteen years ago," Vivienne insisted, shaking her head. "It's not possible. Everyone knows that Azaren's family was completely wiped out."

"Well, everyone is wrong. I'm still alive," I said. "Somehow my parents managed to save me by sending me to another world. I am Azaren's daughter and Morgana is my aunt."

"So that means," said Vivienne thinking, "that you are actually the Queen of Illiador, not Morgana. That's why you want to find out what she's up to."

"Exactly," I said, happy that I didn't have to spell it out for her. "I'm sorry I didn't tell you sooner, but you can understand why."

Vivienne nodded and leaned over to give me a big hug. "Of course I understand, " she said. "You don't have to worry, Aurora, you can trust me."

I smiled. "I think it's probably better if you still called me Rory."

Vivienne clapped her hand over her mouth. "Oh no! Sorry, sorry."

I laughed. "It's okay, Viv. I know it's a lot to take in, but you'll get used to it."

For days, Vivienne and I searched through dozens of scrolls and books in the library for any mention of the Grimoire of Abraxas, but there was none. We didn't want to ask any of the professors, since dark magic was forbidden in Eldoren.

I continued to work hard at my studies, and I could hold a shield against all nonmagical attacks. Stones and other flying objects would just bounce off my shield. Magical attacks were more difficult to defend against, but I was learning fast, and my magic and concentration were slowly getting stronger. I had warrior skills class almost every day, and my attacks were getting better. I could stun a mouse from a hundred paces, and I even learned how to push someone away from me using only my magic, which was called a push strike.

We also learned how to control the intensity of stun strikes, luckily not on each other, but on targets set up for practice. I found out about other types of magical attack: fire strikes, crushing strikes, and even lightning strikes. We were still not allowed to use these outside class, as they were too dangerous.

I remembered the magic Oblek used on me when he was

dragging me to his castle. He had used a crush strike on my neck. Now I finally understood how it was done, and if I ever met Oblek again, he was going to be sorry he'd ever laid eyes on me.

Every other day I had healing lessons, where I learned about different kinds of herbs and plants and their uses and dosage. In Avalonia, the plants were different, so I had a lot of catching up to do.

The most difficult of all healing classes was magical healing. I learned mainly by assisting the university healers with their patients. I was amazed at what some of them could do just by using the powers within them. Mending bones, regrowing tendons, even knitting flesh.

Weeks passed, and we still had no idea what the Grimoire of Abraxas was. I finally decided to ask Erien. He always had the highest scores in ancient history, so maybe he could shed some light on this whole situation. That day after classes, I went over to see him in his room.

"Erien, I need your help," I said, shutting the door behind me.

Erien was lying on his bed reading. I pulled up a chair and told him everything that had happened.

"I've never heard of the Book of Abraxas," said Erien, "but if it is a grimoire, then it must be one of the forbidden texts. You won't find anything about it in the school library."

"But isn't there some way to find out about this book and what it does?" I asked, leaning forward. "Erien, if Morgana and Lucian are behind this, then we have to find out why she needs the book."

Erien nodded. "There is a way. But we should tell grand-father about it first," he said. "If this has to do with dark magic, then we shouldn't get involved. We could get expelled from school."

"But Uncle Gabriel is in some faraway kingdom," I insisted. "We are not doing anything wrong. When he's back, we can tell him what we've found out."

"Anything that has to do with black magic is wrong," Erien said.

"Please, Erien," I begged, "you know how important this is to me. Morgana ruined my life. I need to know what she's planning to do next. The only way I am going to survive is if I stay one step ahead of her at all times."

Erien sat up in his bed and rubbed his palms over his face. "All right, Aurora," he said finally. "I understand why you want to do this. I will help you, but remember I can't make any promises. The forbidden texts were lost or destroyed centuries ago. We still may not find anything."

"I couldn't find anything in any of the books I looked at," I said.

Erien shook his head. "You won't find anything in the ordinary books, " he said. He came closer and lowered his voice. "But there is a secret library that lies underneath the school. Most people think it is a myth, but I've seen it, and the professors know it exists, but only the Mastermage of

Evolon holds the key."

My eyes widened. "A secret library. But how do we get in?"

"Leave that to me," said Erien, pulling on his black leather boots and cloak. "Meet me outside the academy library tonight after dinner."

I nodded. "I'll be there. Thank you, Erien."

"You don't need to thank me, Aurora. We're family," Erien said, coming over and giving me a big hug.

I hugged him back. It was so nice to finally be part of a family that accepted me for who I was.

That night, Vivienne and I sneaked out of our room after everyone had gone to sleep and met Erien outside the library.

"I said, 'come alone,'" Erien whispered when he saw Vivienne.

"We can trust her," I said. "She knows who I really am."

Erien's eyes widened. "You told her?"

I nodded. "I live with her, and she became suspicious."

"I hope you didn't tell her everything," he said so only I could hear.

I shook my head. Even Vivienne might not take too kindly to living with a fae-mage.

"Good," said Erien, ending the topic. "Come on. We only have a few hours." He opened the library door with a key he had with him.

"Where did you get that?" Vivienne asked.

"I help the mastermage with research," said Erien. "He

has a key that can open any door in the academy, and I just happen to know where he keeps it."

Vivienne looked impressed.

The library was dark and eerie at this time of night. Muted moonlight threw shadows on the walls and floor that seemed to move according to the whims of the cloudy sky. Bookshelves stretched into darkness on both sides of me, and an unnerving silence seemed to settle like a thick shroud over the vast structure.

Erien's hand lit up, pushing back the shadows. We had been taught how to do this in class. I concentrated my magic into the palm of my hand, slowly pushing some of it outward and rolling it between my fingers. A ball of white light swirled, lighting up the aisle in front of me. Vivienne still hadn't managed to master this concept, and her light kept flickering and going out. Finally she gave up and stuck close to me.

We wound our way through the countless aisles to the far end of the library. Erien shifted a section of the bookshelf, and it opened inwards like a door, revealing a hidden stone staircase that led downwards, spiraling into darkness.

"Follow me, " said Erien, holding his hand out in front of him.

Vivienne took my hand, and the two of us navigated our way behind Erien. A few hundred feet down, we came to an old wooden door. Erien used the master key, and it opened, the creak of the wood echoing through the silent library.

We stepped inside, and I held out my hand. The ball of light in my palm cast an eerie glow over the cavernous room. I looked around. We were standing at the top of a massive grand staircase that descended into a huge room that seemed to have no end. Row upon row of books lined the shelves, stretching two stories high all the way to the beautiful vaulted ceiling. The musty smell of leather and dusty books permeated the still air as I walked down the staircase, following Erien.

This looked like an impossible task. The secret library was huge. How would we ever find the right book?

"Do you think the Grimoire of Abraxas could be here?" Vivienne asked.

"No, I don't think so," said Erien. "The Book of Abraxas sounds like a forbidden text, and the mastermage would never allow a dark grimoire in the school. It's too dangerous; anything could go wrong if used without the correct knowledge. But we may be able to find out more about it in some of the other, older books."

"How do you know so much about all this?" Vivienne asked Erien, lighting a candle.

"I'm going to be a historian," said Erien, puffing out his chest a little. "The mastermage said that I could even be a professor someday."

Vivienne laughed. "But you're a noble. You can't become a teacher."

"Professor Tanko is a noble," Erien argued.

"He's the only one," Vivienne insisted. "In any case, Professor Tanko is just a baron with limited holdings. You are presently the Earl of Everdale, and after your grandfather, you will be the next Duke of Silverthorne."

"I could do both," Erien said, taking a few books off the shelves and putting them on a nearby wooden table.

"Not if you're on the royal council," Vivienne said, crossing her arms.

"You seem to know a lot about the way the kingdom is run," said Erien.

Vivienne shrugged, picking up a book. "Father tells me stuff," she said. "I listen."

For hours, we searched through all sorts of books, from ancient symbols and languages to the genealogy of kings, but there was nothing that even mentioned the name Abraxas.

"We should go back," said Vivienne finally. "It's going to be dawn soon, and people will start coming into the library."

Erien nodded and started putting books back onto the shelves. "I agree."

"No, just a few minutes please," I said, desperately wishing I would find something.

The sound of a door closing echoed through the secret library. All three of us froze in our tracks. Someone was coming, and there was nowhere to hide. I looked over to the stairs leading down into the vast room. A ball of light was moving steadily towards us hovering in the hand of a shadowy figure in mage robes. As he came toward us, the light illuminated his face.

Professor Dekela!

"What is the meaning of this intrusion?" said the master-mage, raising his hands and sending sparks flying into the air, lighting the candles on the chandelier that hung from the high ceiling. The room lit up. "Erien, you know better than to be down here. I expected more from you, and I showed you this library because I thought you were more responsible than the rest. The books here are not meant to be read by students. You know that perfectly well."

"I know, Professor. I'm so sorry," said Erien, hurriedly putting back the remaining books on all the wrong shelves. "It's not what you think."

Vivienne just stood there, staring at the professor, and looked like she was about to burst into tears.

"It's my fault," I blurted out. I didn't want Erien and Vivienne to get kicked out of school because of me. "Professor, this has to do with Morgana and the Book of Abraxas."

The old professor did not look surprised. He assessed Erien and Vivienne for a second and turned to me. "Explain."

I told him everything that Damien said about the key. I didn't tell him about my night visit to the city with the Blackwaters though. I only said that I overheard them talking in the library. I didn't need to get myself into more trouble than I was in already. The old professor listened carefully and didn't interrupt until I finished my story.

"This time the Blackwaters have gone too far," the mastermage said. "The Book of Abraxas must never be opened."

"Why?" I asked, my eyes going wide. This sounded serious. What was Morgana up to now?

"It is only because of who you are that I am telling you this," said Professor Dekela. "And it seems that you obviously trust your cousin and your roommate here, so I will allow them to hear what I have to say, since I think you will probably tell them everything anyway."

Embarrassed I looked down. He was right, of course.

He looked at Vivienne. "I won't say this again, Ms. Foxmoor. I hope you know that whatever we talk about here must never leave this room."

Vivienne nodded fervently.

"The Grimoire of Abraxas," said Professor Dekela, turning back to me, "also known as The Book of Power, is considered to be the most dangerous and mysterious manuscript of all time. It contains magic thought to be long forgotten, magic that existed before the age of the first kings, even before the fae came to this world. Many believe it to be only a legend, but the Grimoire of Abraxas does exist. It was locked with four magical keys, which were hidden in remote locations all over Avalonia to prevent it from ever being opened. The key that was stolen is one of them."

He took out an old, worn leather-bound book from one of the shelves and opened it on the table in front of us. "Is this what the key looked like?" he asked pointing to the page.

I looked at the diagram drawn in the book—four triangles, all of them fitting together to form a larger one. "This is it," I said. "Damien had one of these triangular keys."

"Why it is so dangerous?" Erien said, moving Vivienne out of the way to get a better look at the page.

"The Grimoire of Abraxas, gives the one who opens it the knowledge to control demons," said the professor, closing the book.

"Demons!" I repeated. "Are you serious?"

Professor Dekela nodded solemnly and continued. "And not just any demon, but the Book of Abraxas contains the secret to controlling the most powerful of all demon lords ever to have lived—Dragath."

"Is that even possible?" I asked, horrified. "Uncle Gabriel said that Dragath has been gone for thousands of years, trapped in a magical prison."

"That is what the legends say," answered Professor Dekela.

"But, if Dragath is gone," Vivienne said, looking pale, "how can Morgana control him with the book?"

"I don't know," said the old professor, shaking his head. "Maybe she doesn't intend to control Dragath himself. But there are other demons and demonic beings that exist in other worlds that are connected to ours, and the Drakaar can summon them. If Morgana manages to open the book, she will possess the knowledge to control the demons and make them do her bidding. That will be the end of our world as we know it. Demon magic is much more powerful than the magic of the mages or even the fae. A mage who can control demons can rule the world."

"Do you think that Morgana already has the book?" I asked. "Or do you think the Blackwaters are doing this on their own?"

Professor Dekela shook his head. "The book is safe for now," he said as we put everything away and climbed the steep staircase to the school library. "But I don't think that the Blackwaters would pursue magic this powerful on their own. The only ones who would be able to wield this sort of dark magic are Lucian and Morgana."

"But how do you know the book is safe, Professor? Morgana or Lucian might already have it if they are looking for the keys," I asked following the professor.

"There is something else you must know," he said, halting at the top of the stairs and turning around to face me. "Remember, I told you that there are four keys."

I nodded.

"When the book was locked, the keys were given for safe keeping to four magical families. The locations of the four keys and the Book of Abraxas have been passed down through generations. The Silverthorne family and my own have been guardians of the book for centuries now."

My eyes went wide at this piece of information. "Erien is a Silverthorne, and he didn't know about the book," I said, glancing at Erien, who looked just as surprised as I was.

"He would have found out eventually," said Professor Dekela, "it was because of you that he learned about it sooner than he was supposed to."

"Oh!" was all I could say.

"That is how I know that the Grimoire of Abraxas is safely hidden and so are the other three keys," continued Professor Dekela. "I only just got word that one of the Guardians has disappeared. Now I know why. I will inform your grand-uncle about this new development," said the professor, opening the secret door that led back to the school library. "This is very serious, Aurora. If Morgana wants the book, it is only a matter of time before she finds what she is looking for."

"I know," I said. "We can't let her succeed in her plans. We have to get that key back from Damien."

"That may not be so easy," said the professor. "The Duke of Blackwater came to visit his children today. They must have given it to him already. I will have his house searched, but we will have to be careful. Accusing the duke of theft may not be the right move just now. We need to find out more before we can bring him in front of the Mage Guild."

I nodded. I was glad the mastermage had it under control and it was one less thing to worry about. As it was, I'd had so much on my plate, and there were not enough hours in the day to learn everything I needed to defend myself against Morgana. Things had become too complicated. It was one thing trying to stay away from Morgana and trying to learn how to use my powers. But dark magic and demons were a bit more than I could handle at the moment. I hoped Uncle Gabriel would come back soon. He would know what to do.

The sun was just rising over the city of Neris as we hurried back to our rooms. I was exhausted from not sleeping the whole night, but I had to go to class. We would be having tests soon, and I didn't want to make a fool of myself. I had been so busy worrying about what the Blackwaters were doing that I wasn't concentrating on my studies. If I failed my first tests, Uncle Gabriel was going to be livid.

20
NERIS

A FEW DAYS LATER, a messenger arrived from Everdale House. Aunt Serena had invited me over for a few days, as the university was shut for the summer solstice festival, and those who had places to go could leave the school.

I was excited at the prospect of staying in Aunt Serena's Neris townhouse. Vivienne was also going home, and Foxmoor House was just a few streets away from Everdale House.

"I'll come to see you once you are settled in," said Vivienne as we packed our trunks. "There are so many places I want to show you."

I nodded and hugged Vivienne before leaving.

Aunt Serena sent a carriage as she had promised, and Erien and I climbed in. We crossed the main streets of the upper town and went on beyond the bridge to the other side of the river, where the nobility had their mansions.

The carriage pulled up in front of a massive stone structure.

Everdale House was a two-storied mansion with enormous bay windows and a huge mahogany front door. The horses had barely halted before Erien threw open the carriage door and bounded out eagerly. He ran up the steps, and, before he could even knock, the massive door opened, and the butler, a thin old man with slicked-back silver hair, let us in.

"Good afternoon, Your Lordship," said the butler to Erien.

"Good afternoon, Figgins," said Erien. "Is Mother home?"

"Her Ladyship is waiting for you in the morning room, my lord," said Figgins, divesting us of our cloaks and luggage.

I looked around in wonder, still unaccustomed to the ways of the Eldorean nobility. The front door opened onto a massive foyer tastefully decorated with ornamental furniture and oak paneling. A grand staircase with a richly polished mahogany banister wound up to the upper floors of the house under a gleaming crystal chandelier.

We followed Erien to the back of the house, where the morning room was situated. Aunt Serena was waiting for us. It was a light and airy room, done up in cream and gold, with huge French doors that opened out onto a terrace that surveyed the gardens and the river beyond. She hugged us and ushered us both in to sit down.

"First things first," Aunt Serena said, turning towards me. "We will have to take you to a dressmaker to fit you for clothes. You certainly can't wear that green dress every day."

I looked down at my green day dress; it was one of Aunt Serena's from Silverthorne castle. She was right; I didn't bring much with me.

"We will also have to get something suitable for the harvest ball at the palace, which will be held later on in the year," said Aunt Serena.

"A ball at the palace," I said, wide-eyed. I would love to go to a ball, but I had no idea how I was supposed to behave in front of the rest of the nobility in Eldoren.

"Yes, every year the king holds a huge ball at the start of the harvest festival," said Aunt Serena. "And we are all invited, of course. Tomorrow night, the Blackwaters are having a dinner party. And we will be attending, so you will need something to wear."

"The Blackwaters," I sneered. "I don't want to go to their house."

"Yes, I'm sure you don't," said Aunt Serena, raising her eyebrows. "I heard about your midnight trip to the tavern, young lady, and I have been waiting to talk to you about that."

"You heard?" I asked, glaring at Erien. I knew Professor Dekela had already met with Aunt Serena and told her everything we had learned about the Blackwaters and the Book of Abraxas. But he didn't know about me leaving the school at night. Erien must have told her.

Erien sheepishly looked away, getting up to pour himself a glass of juice. I felt like smacking him over the head for his stupidity.

"Yes, my dear, I certainly did," said Aunt Serena, putting her hands primly in her lap and sitting as she always did, perched at the edge of the chair, her back straight as a rod. "You could have been in a lot of trouble. You are lucky that your granduncle had instructed Rafe to keep an eye on you."

I hung my head. Even though I knew Rafe was just looking out for me out of some sense of duty, it hurt every time I heard someone say it out loud.

"But if I hadn't gone I would never have found out about the key and the book," I argued. "Now at least we have some idea about what Morgana is planning."

"She is right, Mother," Erien piped up.

Aunt Serena ignored her son. "You were lucky this time, Aurora," she said, unconvinced by my reasoning. "I want you to forget about the book for now. There is nothing you can do. I have spoken to the mastermage and sent word to my father. He will be returning soon, and you must let us handle it."

"But we can't just sit here uselessly while Morgana is looking for the book," I said, standing up.

"We won't allow her to get it," said Aunt Serena. "You have to trust me." She got up and put her hand on my shoulder. "I really want you to forget about this for now and concentrate on learning how to use your powers, Aurora. Or have you forgotten why we sent you to Evolon?"

I lowered my eyes. She was right; I had been neglecting my training, and if I was going to survive, I had to learn as much as I could, and fast.

"Now, my dear," said Aunt Serena. "The Blackwaters have

invited you specifically. I think their son Damien told them about you. I must say I was quite surprised myself, but if we try to keep you from them, they will wonder what we are trying to hide. I have already informed Sorcha, the duchess of Blackwater, that we will all be attending."

I slumped in my chair. I guess what I wanted didn't matter. I wondered if I could fake a headache tomorrow so I didn't have to go. Why was Aunt Serena insisting I go? What if someone recognized me?

A kind-looking middle-aged woman came in.

"Ah, Ms. Rikley, please show Lady Rory to her room," said Aunt Serena. "Once you freshen up, come downstairs for some lunch, and then we can go into town."

I nodded. "Thank you, Aunt Serena," I said politely and followed the housekeeper up the stairs to the second floor of the house, where my room was situated.

It was a bright, cheery room with a big mahogany bed and gleaming hardwood floors strewn with plush carpets. Rich, rose-colored curtains framed the large windows, and I leaned over the side to see the lovely formal gardens of Everdale House, which led down in tiers to the river. Vivienne had once told me that all the best houses were overlooking the river. I wondered where Foxmoor House was and how I could get a message to Vivienne to come over.

I washed my face and hands with the little porcelain bowl and jug in the room and went downstairs to join Aunt Serena and Erien.

Lunch was served in the dining room, a large rectangular space with a massive, finely polished wooden dining table that could seat at least twenty people. Two crystal chandeliers hung from the frescoed ceiling, and four large, arched double doors led out to the gardens of the house.

The food was heavenly. There was a creamy mushroom soup, a fish in a delicate sauce with nuts, a whole assortment of vegetables, roasted game, different cheeses and fruits, and a honey pudding with thick yellow cream.

I ate so much I was stuffed, and all I wanted to do was crawl back into bed and go to sleep. But Aunt Serena was insistent that we had many things to do that day, and going to the dressmaker was one of them.

We climbed into the Everdale carriage, which was very spacious and comfortable, with the Everdale coat of arms emblazoned on the side. The dressmaker's shop was not far away, and the carriage rumbled down the broad paved streets of the city of Neris.

This area of the city was very different from what I had seen before. I peered out of the curtained carriage window and glimpsed a host of fashionable people walking around, shopping or chatting as they came across an acquaintance or friend on the street.

The shops in this area were also different from what I had seen before; they were bigger and more ornate. There were no blacksmiths, masons, or carpenters here; the shops were mainly jewelers with big, decorative shop windows, and dressmakers with their latest creations on display. There were also shoemakers, tailors, barbers, headdress makers, wine sellers, spice merchants, and a few luxurious bakeries.

The carriage stopped in front of a big dressmaker's shop with a purple awning. Above the front of the shop, in big gold letters, was written, 'Lady Charlotte's Creations.'

We got out of the carriage. I could smell the wonderful aromas coming from the bakery next door.

"Can we go in there first?" I asked Aunt Serena, pointing to the little bakery with delicious-looking cakes sitting on the windowsill.

"No! We are running late as it is," said Aunt Serena.

I followed the countess into the shop to meet with the dressmaker. She was a thin, little lady with stern black eyes and a hooked nose. Her white hair was tied back securely in a severe bun.

The shop was a dream of fabric heaven. Bolts of rich velvets, shimmering satins, silks, luxurious brocades, and tulle in a myriad of colors and designs were resting on the tables. Lady Charlotte gestured to one of her shopgirls to bring out some more.

"Lady Charlotte is the best. Her designs are the most coveted by the nobility of Eldoren and beyond," said Aunt Serena, trying to appease the stern little lady, who looked extremely peeved to have been kept waiting. She couldn't say anything in front of the countess, so she kept quiet.

She measured me in so many places that I was exhausted

by the end of the session. Lady Charlotte draped me in different fabrics in a variety of colors and designs, pinned me, and poked me again and again. I was convinced that all the poking was done deliberately as my punishment for keeping her waiting. Getting fitted for a ball gown seemed to be the most strenuous work I had ever done.

"We also need a ready gown for a dinner party tomorrow night," said Aunt Serena to the dressmaker.

The stern little lady nodded. "I have just the thing," she said in her heavily accented voice as she snapped her fingers to call one of her girls and send them scurrying to find what she required.

They brought out a shimmering, cream satin gown, with a fitted bodice exquisitely embroidered with beautiful pearls and cut beautifully in a wide off-the-shoulder cut. The dress was trimmed with three rows of pearls, which cinched my waist like a belt and cascaded down the side of the dress. It was absolutely gorgeous.

We thanked Lady Charlotte, who said she would have the rest of my clothes ready in a few days, and left the shop.

We went into the little bakery next door with the bright yellow awning. It was cute and homely, and little tables with yellow-and-white-checked tablecloths were placed near the windows. Beautifully decorated cakes and pastries, in a range of colors and flavors, lined the counters and were stacked in tiers, forming elaborate designs. I tasted something called a honey burst, and it was delicious. It was like a crisp biscuit ball, and when you bit into it, all the delectable honey melt-ed into your mouth. I couldn't resist sampling some more of the delicacies the bakery offered, and so I also had two tiny lemon cakes and a lovely strawberry-cream cupcake.

Aunt Serena dragged me into another shop. I looked up at the sign: 'Headdresses, Veils, Diadems, Circlets, and Tiaras.'

"I need something for the harvest ball," she said as we entered the shop.

There were a few customers already there, trying on the wares. One was a beautiful blonde girl, with long golden hair elegantly pinned up and cascading down one shoulder in a shower of perfectly curled ringlets. She was wearing a yellow day dress, artfully embroidered with flowers along the neckline and cuffs.

"Oh, I don't think the prince will like this one," she said in a high-pitched and bitter-sounding voice, trying on a hideously expensive gold diadem studded with massive diamonds.

The other girls were nodding like puppets.

She turned towards us. Her eyes were a beautiful, icy blue, but they were cold and full of malice. She didn't look like a very nice person.

"Ah!" she said, looking at Aunt Serena and then at me, "if it isn't the Countess of Everdale."

"Good evening, Leticia," said Aunt Serena politely.

"And who is this?" Leticia said, eyeing me up and down as if I was some lowly peasant not fit to be in her company.

"This is Rory," said Aunt Serena. "She is my father's ward."

Leticia dismissed me once she decided that I wasn't important enough to merit her time.

"Well, we will see you tomorrow night at the Blackwater's dinner party, Countess," said Leticia to Aunt Serena, completely ignoring me, as if I didn't exist.

"Yes, Leticia," said Aunt Serena, "we will all be attending."

"Oh good," said Leticia, her smile not reaching her eyes. "I shall see you all, then."

She flung the offensive diadem down, much to the dismay of the little bearded shopkeeper, stuck her nose up high into the air, and walked out of the shop with her friends following like little ducklings behind their mother.

"Who was that?" I said to Aunt Serena after the blonde girl had left.

"That is Lady Leticia, daughter of the Earl of Glenbarry," said Aunt Serena. "She is her father's only heir and is betrothed to the crown prince."

"She's going to be Queen of Eldoren someday?" I asked, horrified at the prospect.

"Looks like it," said Aunt Serena. "No wonder that poor boy keeps running off for days on end. Who would want to be shackled to the likes of her?"

The poor boy being the crown prince, I surmised.

On our way back to the house, I asked Aunt Serena some more about the noble families and the aristocracy of Eldoren and Illiador.

"I wish I didn't have to come with you to the Blackwaters' house tomorrow," I finally blurted out.

"You must," said Aunt Serena. "As I explained to you, no one will know who you are. As long as you are in plain sight, no one will question why you are here."

"Well, you know how Damien and I don't get along," I said. "I don't think he would even want me in his house."

"Nonsense," said Aunt Serena. "Damien will do as his mother says. Childish rivalries in school do not matter in the greater scheme of things. The Blackwaters and the Silverthornes have a tumultuous history, but we all have to keep up appearances for the sake of the realm."

Aunt Serena explained that Damien's hatred for my granduncle and all the Silverthornes stemmed purely from the political rivalries of our families. Apparently, Uncle Gabriel was the richest noble in all the kingdoms. He was far richer and even more powerful than the King of Eldoren, and his lands and estates outweighed those of the crown. His army was the largest and fiercest in all the lands, and they were loyal only to him.

I was slowly starting to get the feel for politics, and I couldn't believe that my uncle actually thought that I would be able to fit in in this snake pit of treacherous nobles and jealous families fighting for their place in society. I was not used to it, and I wondered if I would ever truly understand how it all worked. I had to try, though. I was, after all, the only true living heir of Azaren, and Morgana was not fit to rule Illiador. I had seen that now. I really hoped that Aunt Serena was right and that they had some sort of plan to stop her.

I shook my head at the unfairness of it all. Secretly I wished I really had the courage to take back the kingdom from Morgana. I still had four years of studying, though, until I was a fully trained mage. And then I had to learn to use fae powers as well. Being a fae-mage was not all it was cracked up to be. Even if somehow Uncle Gabriel's army defeated Morgana's and the armies of Maradaar and finally put me on the throne, what would I do? I couldn't run a kingdom or be queen. I had no idea where to begin.

The carriage rolled to a stop in front of Everdale House. I climbed the steps, and Figgins opened the door to let us in. I was informed that Vivienne was waiting in the informal drawing room.

"Which one is that again?" I asked Figgins, still confused by all the rooms.

"Down the corridor and on your left, my lady," said the ever-helpful Figgins.

I followed his directions and hurried to meet Vivienne.

"There you are," she said, jumping up from the sofa and coming over to hug me. "Where were you? I have been waiting for ages."

"Sorry, Viv, I was at a dress fitting with Aunt Serena. I have to go to a party at Damien's house tomorrow night," I said, scrunching up my nose.

"Oh no," said Vivienne, suitably upset at the situation. I knew she would understand immediately.

"So, where's Erien?" Vivienne then asked, quite unexpectedly, her eyes scanning the room.

"He's out," I said. Why did she care?

"Oh!" said Vivienne, her face falling.

"Viv," I said carefully. "Do you fancy Erien?"

"No, no, of course not. Don't be silly," she said, jumping up off the sofa. "I was just asking."

I smiled. Vivienne definitely had a crush on Erien. It was sweet, and I thought they would make a cute couple. I wondered if I could set them up.

"Did you tell your aunt about the book?" asked Vivienne, changing the subject.

I nodded. "She knows; Professor Dekela told her."

Vivienne sat back down next to me, and I proceeded to tell her everything that Aunt Serena had said.

"How can I just forget about the book?" I said to Vivienne finally. "If Morgana gets all the keys, she will open the Book of Abraxas and take over the whole of Avalonia. No one will be able to stand in her way."

"Your aunt and the professor are right," said Vivienne. "You can't prance around the kingdom looking for the keys; they could be anywhere. If you don't learn to use the powers you have, it won't matter if Morgana has the book or not, she's going to kill you anyway. Now that your granduncle knows about it too, she can be stopped from ever getting the book or the rest of the keys. You have already done enough and alerted them of Morgana's plans. If you are going to be a queen, act like it. You need to learn to delegate responsibility. You have to let them handle it."

I nodded. She had a point, and Vivienne always had a way of putting things in the correct perspective. I had to concentrate on my studies and learn all I could. I couldn't stay hidden forever, and I needed to prepare myself for what was surely coming. Again, I thought about telling her my other secret, but I decided that this probably wasn't the right time, and I kept my mouth shut.

The next evening, I admired myself in my new evening gown. The creamy satin shimmered in the candlelight, and one of Aunt Serena's maids did up my horrid, mousy hair into an elaborate coiffure of ringlets and pearls, all elegantly pinned up and set beautifully.

As the carriage pulled up to Blackwater House, I was amazed. It was a huge, three-storied stone mansion at least twice the size of Everdale House and richly ornate, but frankly overdecorated, I thought. The inside was even more impressive, with a marble foyer, huge columns, and statues everywhere.

As liveried servants escorted us to the drawing room, I glimpsed intricate tapestries, massive windows draped in silk, gilded frames, and portraits that lined the gleaming mahogany walls.

The drawing room was full and bustling with chattering ladies in all their finery, as well as smartly dressed men in their evening doublets and highly polished boots. It was brightly lit with fragrant candles burning in massive silver candelabrums and a huge crystal chandelier gleaming overhead, hanging from an ornate and intricately carved ceiling.

"Ah, Serena, how lovely to see you," said a beautiful lady, with chestnut hair spun with gold. She was wearing a rich maroon velvet dress, which clipped her tiny waist before falling to the floor. It was thickly embroidered with gold flowers, and she had matching flowers adorning her elaborate hair.

"Sorcha," said Aunt Serena, greeting the lady warmly. She then pulled me forward. "Rory, this is the Duchess of Blackwater," my aunt said.

"Your Grace," I said with a small curtsey.

Serena had taught me most of the ways I should address people. I was still confused about ranks. I knew a duke was the highest ranking noble after the king and prince, but then was it a marquis or an earl, a viscount, and then a baron, or the other way around? It was all very confusing.

"So this is Rory," said the duchess. "Damien has told me about you. I am so sorry about your parents. It is unfortunate and such a huge loss for a young girl your age."

The duchess sounded genuine and was not at all mean

like Damien, but I reminded myself to be careful; after all, this was the archmage's sister I was talking to.

I was introduced around, and most of the people paid me only a passing greeting. I was relieved that no one was too interested in me, as I was not very comfortable answering questions about myself, since I had to lie so extensively.

Soon dinner was announced, and we were led into the dining room, which was also larger than the one at Everdale House. The massive hardwood dining table was highly polished and could easily seat fifty people. White-gloved and liveried footmen, who accompanied us everywhere like shadows, showed us to our seats.

Somehow Damien managed to seat himself next to me. I don't know where he turned up from. I hadn't seen him the whole evening. Calisto was seated opposite me near Zorek, but luckily a huge flower arrangement hid me from her view. I was not in the mood for Calisto's cutting remarks. Next to me, much to my horror, was the Lady Leticia Glenbarry, who looked just as peeved to have been seated next to a nobody like me.

I was plowing through the first of ten courses when Aunt Serena gave me a glare from across the table. I soon remembered that she had warned me that proper young ladies don't eat as though they have never seen food in their life. Women are supposed to only pick, chew a lot, and make innocuous comments about the sauce.

There were courses of everything from soups and roasted

vegetables to fish in an array of sauces, extraordinary concoctions of some meat, and poultry done in a dozen different ways with cream, nuts, and honeyed apricots. The desserts were just as elaborate: delicious spun sugar concoctions, hot berry puddings with creamy sauces, cheeses, fruits, and more chocolate than you could possibly imagine.

We were halfway through dessert when the man next to Leticia spoke up.

"Lady Leticia," he said, fawning over her, in obvious hopes of being noticed by the lady who was betrothed to the Prince of Eldoren. "When will the prince return from his travels? I have an urgent matter to discuss with him."

"I cannot divulge that information, Lord Mornington," Leticia said, smiling sweetly, but her eyes flashed with anger.

"She has no clue where my cousin is," whispered Damien meanly in my ear. I could tell he didn't like Leticia, but she was a very difficult person to like. "He prances off whenever he wants, and my uncle has to constantly send guards to bring him back from whatever inn or tavern he is holed up in."

I was taken aback; Damien really hated his cousin, the prince. It wasn't only in my family that jealousies ran rampant. I knew that if the Blackwater's had their way, they would overthrow the king and take over Eldoren. Were all these rumors true about the prince?

Across the table, a conversation was turning into an argument.

"You cannot possibly think that the Black Wolf is anything more than a thieving outlaw," said an old earl loudly, sitting up straighter in his high-backed chair. "He must be caught and brought to justice."

"But he saves so many innocent lives," said a plump, middle-aged lady who I recognized as the Countess of Dewberry. Aunt Serena had introduced us earlier in the drawing room. "He should be awarded a knighthood if you ask me, Marcus."

"A knighthood," spluttered the old earl. "Have you gone insane, woman? When that outlaw is finally caught, he should be hanged. I shall bring this to the notice of the council. Outlaws cannot be permitted to take the law into their own hands."

"But he does so much good," the countess insisted, holding her ground.

"What good is he to us?" said the old Earl, now going red in the face and looking like a ripe tomato ready to burst. "All he does is save those heathen fae. If you ask me, I think I quite agree with Morgana, that the fae should go back to Elfi and stay there."

The countess gasped and turned away from the earl, refusing to even look at him.

I was so engrossed by their conversation that I didn't notice the man next to Leticia trying to get my attention.

"So!" said Lord Mornington, looking at me. "Rory, is it?"

"Yes, my lord," I nodded.

"And you are a mage in training at Evolon?"

I nodded again.

"Yes, yes, very good, all the Morningtons have been to Evolon too, you know. Except myself. Sadly I was not graced with the magic you possess," said Lord Mornington, leaning back in his chair and fondling his wispy beard. "Young Damien here must be teaching you a few things, eh?" He gave me a lewd wink.

What did he mean by saying that Damien was teaching me? There was definitely nothing I wanted to learn from him. And what was that wink about? Did he think I was dating Damien?

"No, my lord," I said, as sweetly as I could, even though I was fuming inside. "It's more that I could teach Damien a few things—in magic, that is."

The bald, paunchy lord laughed so loudly at my answer that he dropped his silver wine goblet, and red wine splattered all over the table and over Lady Leticia's obviously hideously expensive dress.

She jumped up, screaming.

"You clumsy clod, you," she screeched at the mortified Lord Mornington, who was clumsily trying to mop up the wine from her dress with his napkin and, in the process, proceeding to spread it around, creating an even more messy stain.

"Stay away from me," screamed Leticia, swatting Lord Mornington's hands away from her.

Footmen rushed to assist the screaming lady. The Duchess of Blackwater got up as well and tried to pacify her, but it was no use. Leticia Glenbarry, the future queen of the kingdom, gathered her skirts in a huff of stained satin and marched out of the dining room. I giggled to myself. She deserved it, the snooty thing.

Lord Mornington was apologizing all around, and he sat back down at his seat while the footmen miraculously dried everything and replaced the offending goblet with a new one, filled only halfway this time around.

I turned to Damien, but he did not look like he was laughing.

"Who do you think you are, anyway?" he said, his eyes flashing with malice.

I was momentarily taken aback. All this time Damien had been cordial, and now suddenly he hated me again. What had I done?

"How dare you tell Lord Mornington in full hearing of everyone else that you could teach me," he ground out between clenched teeth so no one else could hear. "I am a Blackwater. My blood is one of the most magical in the whole kingdom and beyond. You are nobody, a little girl from a faraway town that no one has even heard of. You think you can teach me anything, I will show you what it means to cross a Blackwater."

"I'm sorry," I said quickly, glancing around. I didn't want a scene now, especially here. "I didn't mean it like that. I was just trying to make a joke."

"Well, it wasn't funny," said Damien, his beady blue eyes full of hatred.

Luckily, the duchess announced that the men could retire to the drawing room, and the ladies would go to the parlor. Everyone got up from their seats and headed out of the dining room.

Damien gave me a dark look and brushed past me. "See you in school," he said, smiling his usual sinister smile.

I shivered at his words. Damien was definitely up to something, and I was quite sure I was not going to like whatever it was that was surely coming my way.

21

DAMIEN

THE NEXT FEW DAYS passed in shopping and spending time with Aunt Serena. Vivienne came over a few times,
and we went for walks in the little wooded park behind Everdale House. Soon we had to return to Evolon, and I was not
looking forward to that at all. I would have to see Damien,
and I was quite sure the Blackwaters were planning something nasty for me.

I thanked Aunt Serena and climbed into the Everdale
coach that was to take me back to Evolon. Erien got in with
me, and we waved good-bye to my aunt, who was standing
at the door to see us off.

Classes were interesting as usual, and I didn't see Damien
the whole first day I was back. He wasn't even in warrior
skills that day, which was a relief, but I wondered where he
was.

I fiddled with my amulet while I walked back from my
evening history class, through the gardens to my dorm. I
looked at it again, as I had done countless times before. It
looked so delicate and harmless, just a flat, round, gold disc
with strange etchings embossed into the gold. Quite extraor-

dinary that it held so much power. I slipped it back into my shirt.

It was getting dark, the sun had set, and the early hint of twilight filled the gardens with shadows. I quickened my step, pulled my mottled green cloak closer, and hurried on. It was getting cold. I could hear faint footsteps behind me. I looked back, but there was no one there.

Suddenly, out of nowhere, a dark shape appeared, moving steadily out of the shadows. I recognized who it was instantly.

"Damien!" I said, trying not to let the panic in my voice show.

He had threatened to teach me a lesson, and this was it, I presumed. Now he was here in a dark, deserted corner of the grounds with seven or eight of his minions, and I was all alone. Even if I shouted, everyone was too far away.

Calisto also came out of the shadows. Damien and his friends surrounded me. I looked for a way to run, but they were everywhere and had surrounded me on all sides.

I was scared now. If Rafe had taught me to use knives, like I had asked, I might have had a better chance of defending myself. But who was I kidding? Even with knives, one against eight was not exactly a fair fight.

"What do you want?" I asked. I hated that my voice was a little shaky; I could feel the fear rush in. Whatever Damien had planned for me tonight was not going to be pleasant.

"I want to see if you are as brave as all the other disgusting Silverthornes," he said, with a sneer. "Stay where you are and you may get a chance to defend yourself." His tone was full of malice, and his dark eyes bore down on me. "You are nothing, a commoner from a distant kingdom, yet you think you are better than me, Damien, son of the Duke of Blackwater, one of the noblest and most magically powerful families in the kingdom. You don't deserve to be in this school. I told you I'd teach you a lesson. Let us see what you're made of."

While I was distracted, one of Damien's minions surprised me with a stun strike. It was weak, but it hurt, and I was dazed for a few seconds. I quickly put up my defensive shield, although it was shaky at best.

I tried to calm my racing heart and slowly shook off the stun. I strengthened my shield just in time, as five more stun strikes hit my shield and bounced off. It held, but only just. I drew more power and infused it into my defensive barrier. Damien and his friends didn't stop their barrage of magical strikes. Attack after attack, stun strike after stun strike hit my shield and were thankfully deflected. I tried to think, but the attacks were coming at me so fast, I had no time to react except to shield myself. If I channeled my power into striking, my shield could drop.

The attacks were starting to become fiercer. At first, they were one at a time, but soon they were combining their strikes against me. I was getting tired; I'd never had to hold out to a magical attack for so long before. And even then it was against one person with Professor Tanko looking on.

One fire strike managed to get partly through my shield and scorched my leg before I could seal the breach. The pain was agonizing, but I held my ground.

I tried to remember everything Professor Tanko had taught me. "Keep your shield in place at all times. Don't forget to seal the top and bottom as well." I concentrated on the area and closed the break in the shield. I was getting tired. My legs had gone weak, and I fell to my knees, but still I drew more power into maintaining my shield. I just didn't know how long I could hold out. My leg was hurting where the fire strike had hit me. It throbbed, and my skin was red and burning.

"Come on, get up Rory," sneered Calisto. "You think you are so important because you are a ward of the Silverthornes. Well, let me tell you, your peasant blood is nothing compared to ours. We are Blackwaters, our magical bloodline spans generations, and no one even cares where Andrysia is."

She hit me with a strong fire strike.

My shield was weakening again. I felt fear rush in, and her strike hit me on my shoulder. Pain shot through my arm, and I cried out in alarm. I put my palm over the area and reinforced my shield, drawing more power into it. I could feel my power source depleting. Soon I would have none left, and, if I tried to do too much, I could die.

I knew I would have to eventually fight them physically; my magical shield was about to fall. I wondered if I should take off my amulet, but Uncle Gabriel's warning resounded in my head. If I took off the amulet, Damien would know who I really was. He would inform Lucian, and Morgana would come after me immediately. For now I was only safe because she had no idea where I was.

I calmed myself and got ready for the final blow. I was not going to let them defeat me. I was a princess, daughter of the greatest mage of this age, a fearless warrior, and the true King of Illiador. The thought gave me strength to further reinforce my shield, but time was running out.

Suddenly I heard Damien's voice. He sounded panicked. "Let's get out of here. Someone's coming."

They all left as quickly as they came.

I collapsed in a heap on the floor, my shield still defensively around me.

"Rory, are you all right?" a worried voice said.

I looked up to see Professor Dekela, the mastermage, crouching over me. I was safe, and I let my shield drop, but I was too exhausted to get up, let alone walk. Professor Dekela carried me through the mage quarters to his study and lay me down on a comfortable leather sofa. He was quite strong for an old mage.

He handed me a cup of what I recognized as snowberry milk, and I took it gratefully. Snowberry milk was wonderful for calming the nerves and restoring strength to the body, as well as aiding sleep.

The mastermage sat down on a matching leather armchair near me. He looked serious, and I was not sure how much I should actually tell him. If I squealed on Damien and his friends, they would hunt me down, and the next time I may not be so lucky.

"Who was responsible for this, Rory?" Professor Dekela asked slowly, but his eyes showed that he was very serious and concerned.

I shook my head. I didn't want to lie, and so it was better to just keep quiet.

"If you don't tell me, I will punish every student in this school until you do," he said, in his usual matter-of-fact way. "I don't think your friends would appreciate it, when all you have to do is to tell me who the aggressors of tonight's attack were. I will not have any of my students behaving this way."

I weighed the options carefully in my mind. It was no use lying; he would find out eventually.

"It was the Blackwaters, Professor," I said finally, unable to keep it in. "Damien and Calisto, along with some of their friends. You cannot let them know that I've told you or punish them. If you do, they will make my life hell, and you said I don't want to bring attention to myself."

"I will think about it," said Professor Dekela. "Tell me what happened, and then I will decide."

"There were about seven or eight of them, and they attacked me out of nowhere," I started. "I was stunned once. It was a weak stun, but then I got my shield up and held it. They didn't stop. I got scared, and my shield dropped for a minute. That's when the fire strike hit me on the leg."

I showed him where I had got burnt.

"Are you saying that they used fire strikes on you outside of class?"

I nodded. "Mainly stuns, but a few fire."

"We will fix that," he said simply. He put his palm over the wound and closed his eyes. I had learned this in my healing class but had never done it myself. The pain vanished almost instantly, and the skin started to heal, although I knew it would take a few days to restore itself to normal. I showed him my shoulder too, where Calisto's fire strike had hit me. He healed that as well.

"Now, let me get this straight," said Professor Dekela, when I was feeling a little better. "Eight students attacked you out of nowhere and used stun and fire strikes on you."

"And push strikes too," I added, remembering my ordeal.

He frowned. "And you held your shield against so many magical strikes one after another?"

I shook my head. "At first it was one after another, but then, when they were not getting through my shield, they all struck together, maybe four or five at a time. I think they were trying to break my shield from all sides. I didn't have enough power to strike back, so I concentrated on holding my shield."

Professor Dekela was rubbing his chin, and his eyes were wide. "Are you trying to say that you held your shield against so many multiple strikes at a time for, what was it, about ten minutes?"

I nodded.

"And this is the first time you have created a shield against a real magical attack outside of class, am I right?"

I nodded again. What was he trying to say?

The mastermage rose. "That, my dear Rory, is quite impressive. There is only one mage I have seen who had so much power at your age." He stopped, a faraway look on his face; he seemed hesitant to continue on that subject. "Nonetheless, this kind of behavior will not be tolerated in my school. Use of fire strikes on one of my students, ambush on school property . . . these students have to be dealt with in some way."

There was a knock on the door.

"Ah, Penelope and Miss Foxmoor," said the mastermage, looking over at the door. I turned to see Professor Plumpleberry and Vivienne walk in.

Vivienne ran over and hugged me. I winced when she touched my arm. "What happened?"

"Damien happened," I said simply.

Penelope looked livid.

Professor Dekela cleared his throat. "I summoned your roommate and Professor Plumpleberry when I brought you here. They will take you back to your room, so Penelope can tend to your wounds. I expect you don't want to be alone tonight."

I nodded gratefully. I would never have asked. I didn't

want to sound like a scared little girl, but I was glad that I didn't have to walk back to my dorm on my own.

"And there is something else," said Professor Dekela.

"Yes, Professor," I said.

"After you are feeling better, come and see me. I would like to arrange some extra classes for you. It seems you have a lot of untapped power, and it would be a shame for it to be overlooked." He glanced at Penelope, who I noticed nodded slightly.

"Thank you, Professor," I said gratefully, following Penelope and Vivienne out of the room.

As we walked along the flowering paths and down the main avenue of cherry blossoms, I told them what I had told Professor Dekela. Vivienne shared Penelope's anger, but they both agreed with me that, if the mastermage expelled Damien, it would definitely bring the Blackwaters down on my head, and I didn't want them snooping around into who I really was.

I felt humiliated. How could Damien do this to me, eight against one? He was always a coward, bullies usually are, and that's why he always had his cronies following him about. I was sure I could beat him one on one, even with my binding amulet on.

I decided that I was going to give more interest and time to my studies and training. I was suddenly extremely determined to be better than him. I knew I could do it, but I needed help. And now the mastermage of the university was willing to look into my studies personally. If I applied myself and worked hard, I was sure that I could challenge him to a public duel and beat him in front of the whole school.

I hardly slept that night. Nightmares of Damien and his cronies hunting me down plagued me every time I tried to fall asleep.

I woke up in a cold sweat. It was still dark, and Vivienne was sound asleep on the other bed in the corner of the room. A light sea breeze wafted in as moonlight shone through the little window and the trees threw rustling shadows on the bedroom floor. A shadow moved near the curtains, and my breath caught in my throat. Had Damien come to finish off the job, or had Morgana finally found me?

"Rafe!" I whispered, relieved beyond belief as the moonlight finally lit up his face. He wasn't wearing his mask.

Rafe came over, knelt down by my bed, and hugged me.

"Are you all right?" he asked softly, holding my face in his hands, his grey eyes glittering in the moonlight.

I nodded, lowering my eyes. Did he really care what happened to me, or was he just upset that he wasn't there to save me this time?

"What are you doing here?" I said, trying to keep my voice low. "What if someone sees you?" I glanced over at Vivienne's side of the room, but she was still sound asleep.

"Penelope told me what happened," Rafe said, holding both my hands in his. He spoke quietly, and Vivienne didn't wake up. "I had to come and see how you were. I thought I told you to stay away from the Blackwaters."

"I tried," I said indignantly, "but they cornered and attacked me when no one else was around. What was I supposed to do?"

Rafe muttered something about needing to teach them a lesson.

"You can't do anything about it, Rafe," I said. "Promise me you will leave it alone. The Blackwaters are powerful nobles, related to the king. If they catch you, you will be hanged."

Rafe laughed. "Don't worry, Aurora. I can handle the Blackwaters." He got up and sat beside me on the bed. "The only person I can't seem to handle is you. I wish you would learn to listen, especially when it's for your own good."

I tried to look offended, blood rushing to my face. I was lucky it was dark and he couldn't see my embarrassment.

Vivienne stirred in her bed.

"I should go," Rafe whispered. "But I want you to meet me tomorrow night in the cellar of your dorm house."

"Where are we going?" I asked, but only because I was curious. The truth was I would follow him anywhere.

"Well, you said that you wanted to learn how to use a weapon," Rafe said, smiling. "And I think it's about time you learn how to protect yourself, with and without magic."

My eyes lit up. "You're going to teach me?"

Rafe nodded. "I will see you tomorrow. Get some sleep," he said, getting up and moving towards the window. "And please stay out of trouble, for a few hours at least."

I smiled and, in a dance of shadows, he was gone.

I sat in my bed and thought about what he'd said. I finally realized that now was the time to enhance my training. Rafe was right. I had taken things too lightly so far. I was enjoying learning to use magic, but I'd never understood what having all this power really meant.

Damien and his friends were just students with limited capabilities. But Morgana, Lucian, the Shadow Guard, and especially the Drakaar were another case altogether. They were all experienced mages and sorcerers, and I would have to learn to do more than cringe under a defensive barrier if I was going to face them.

Ever since I found out who I really was, I had been trying to run from my destiny. But the reality was that, whether I liked it or not, I was the true Queen of Illiador, and I had a responsibility to my people to free them from Morgana's tyranny. I had to stop running. I had to turn and face my life head on. It wasn't enough being like everybody else; I had to be the best, and I was going to show everyone what I was truly made of. I was done with being a terrified princess, constantly waiting to be saved. I was going to be a queen, and, like Vivienne said, I had better start behaving like one.

22
QUEEN IN TRAINING

THE NEXT MORNING I got up, dressed early, and went down to Professor Dekela's room. He had requested to meet me before I started my classes. He was ready and having his morning cup of something steamy and hot, which smelled a lot like coffee.

"Well, Rory, you know why I have asked to see you. Your training is not satisfactory, although it is no fault of yours. I think that you need to be challenged far more. You have shown an extraordinary use of power for someone so young and inexperienced. I must say that I am not completely surprised. After all, you are Azaren's daughter," he said softly.

I nodded.

"I want you to cease worrying about the Blackwaters. I will keep an eye on them, and for now I will not expel them from this school. I understand that it is necessary to keep your identity secret. But now it is even more important that you learn all you can, as fast as you can. Your power must be properly directed and controlled. I also think you are ready to learn some more advanced skills, and unfortunately you don't have the luxury of time like the other students."

He stopped and leaned forward a little. "You may or may not know, but Morgana and the archmage are readying Illiador for war with Andrysia, and when and if that happens, even Evolon will be under threat."

"Why? I thought we were safe here. Uncle Gabriel said that you would be able to protect me," I said.

"Yes, that is true. We are safe for now. But the archmage has always been against me, and he wants me to give him warriors from the school to assist with his campaign. Naturally I said no, and he is obviously not too happy with me. He has given the king an ultimatum: give him an army of warrior mages of Eldoren or he will wage war on us too."

"Can he do that?" I gasped.

"Lucian has become very powerful. And he is the leader of the mage guild. Even in Eldoren, some are afraid to go against him openly," said Professor Dekela. He paused and looked me straight in the eye. "I am telling you all this because of who you are, or who we hope you will grow up to be. You must be updated on the politics of the kingdoms, as well as excel in your studies. Therefore, you will have classes with me every day after school. I don't want anyone getting suspicious, so we will just say I am tutoring you at the behest of your guardian, who feels that you are lagging behind in your studies."

I didn't like the sound of that. Damien would have a field day. Just the fact that I was getting extra lessons would make everyone presume that I was falling behind in my classes.

But I had no choice. And I had made up my mind; I was going to show Damien that I was not afraid of him or anyone else.

"Professor Penelope and Professor Tanko will also give you extra classes in healing and warcraft respectively. One day you may be in a situation where you will not have anyone to protect you, and you will have to defend and heal yourself. Now return to your classes. I will see you in the evening," said Professor Dekela.

I nodded. "Thank you, Professor," I said as I rushed away. I was already late for fae studies, and we were going on a small field trip to meet a family of dryads who had moved to the woods just behind the gardens of the school, relocated from Illiador.

I had already met dryads with Kalen in Pixie Bush. Dwelling on that caused me to wonder how he was doing. It had been a long time since I had seen my friend or heard from him, and I hoped he was all right. I reminded myself that I must ask Professor Plumpleberry when she would send for him. I missed Kalen and his incessant chatter.

I missed Snow, too. Uncle Gabriel had taken the Pegasus with him, as his journey was long and tedious, and Snow had offered to take him more speedily to Kelliandria. I even missed Uncle Gabriel. He was strict, but when he was around, I felt safe.

That night after dinner, I lay on my bed, waiting for Vivienne to fall asleep so I could go and meet Rafe. I knew she would disapprove, so I decided it was best not to tell her.

"Aren't you late to go meet your boyfriend?" said Vivienne tartly, rolling over in her bed to face me. Vivienne was sharper than I gave her credit for.

I was startled. I thought she was asleep. "I don't know what you are talking about," I said.

Vivienne sat up in her bed and tried to light a candle. But her fingers only sparked and went out. "Oof," she said, throwing her hands in the air and giving up.

"Could you please light the candle?" she said sheepishly.

I laughed—poor Vivienne. She was an amazing person and very intelligent, but unfortunately she didn't really have much potential for magic.

I pointed my finger at the candle and it lit up. Vivienne was just sitting there on the bed, her arms crossed, glaring at me.

"What's the problem, Viv?" I said.

"The problem is that you still don't trust me."

"Of course I do," I said quickly. "I've told you everything."

"I saw him last night," Vivienne said.

"Saw who?" I retorted, but I had a pretty good idea who she meant.

"It's the Black Wolf, isn't it?" said Vivienne.

I nodded; it was no use lying anymore. I had to tell her the truth. "You saw him without his mask. Did you recognize him as anyone you knew?" I asked tentatively.

Vivienne shook her head. "No, it was too dark. I couldn't see his face clearly."

I breathed a sigh of relief. Although I wanted to know who he was, I didn't want him to get into trouble just because he came to see me.

"You are being very reckless, Rory," said Vivienne. "You're meeting him alone, in the dead of night, without even knowing who he really is."

"I know he has a dangerous reputation," I said carefully. "But Rafe would never hurt me."

"So it's Rafe now, is it?" said Vivienne, raising her eyebrows. She did that so many times that I was surprised they didn't stay that way.

I smiled and started pulling on my boots. "I've got to go. He must be waiting." I took my brown woolen cloak and opened the door.

"Be careful," said Vivienne.

"When am I not careful?" I called back, closing the door gently and hurrying to the cellar.

Rafe was waiting for me with the secret door open. I lit my hand and followed him through the passageway.

"I heard that you finally found out what was in the pouch," Rafe said as we walked through the damp passage. "I don't know how often I should stress that you need to be wary of the Blackwaters."

"I wanted to find out what Morgana was planning," I

said. "Isn't it better that we know now?"

Rafe nodded slightly. "We would have discovered it eventually."

"But it may have been too late," I said. "Anyway, it's done. We know what she's after. The question is, what are we going to do about it?"

"You," said Rafe, "are going to do nothing."

I huffed at his answer but decided to keep quiet for now. I had to concentrate on learning to defend myself; that was my first priority now.

We came out in the study of the abandoned mansion. Rafe took me through the house and out into the garden overlooking the river. It was a beautiful night and soft moonlight lit the water, covering it in a sheet of silver. Rafe pulled out a sleek-looking sword, held it horizontally in both his hands, and presented it to me.

"I had it specially ordered for you," he said, as I took the sword from his hands. It was light and fast, a perfect sword for a person of my height and build. The hilt was beautifully inlaid with three large rubies, which looked like it would have cost a fortune. "It was forged by the dwarves of ancient Stonegate themselves."

"Thank you, Rafe. It's lovely, but I hope you didn't steal it?" I asked before I could stop myself.

Rafe laughed, and I was relieved that he wasn't offended or angry that I'd said that.

"No, I didn't steal it," he said, taking out his own sword.

"You really should have more faith in me, Aurora."

I blushed. "Sorry, I just presumed, since the jewels on the hilt look very expensive."

"They are," Rafe said simply, coming over to me. "Now let me see your grip . . . "

The next month was filled with grueling days with the professors and even more grueling nights with Rafe, learning to be a warrior. Besides learning to fight with a sword, he taught me to use knives in a fight, one in each hand, and I was getting better at throwing them. I hardly slept, but I pushed myself. I had to discover what I was capable of and what my limits were.

On top of my regular classes, which were four a day and one hour each, I also had an hour with Professor Dekela where we discussed politics of the kingdom, etiquette of the court and the royal families. The professor told me about the jealousies and the rivalries between the various noble families, the histories of these families, and their role in the government of the country. We also discussed the mage guild, the royal council consisting of the lords of Eldoren, the council of thirteen in Illiador, their duties, qualifications, who they were, and what families and factions they were loyal to.

He also told me a lot about Morgana and Lucian. "Know your enemy," said Professor Dekela countless times.

So I had to study Morgana's life thoroughly. I learned that Morgana was born a few years after my father's mother, Queen Fiona, died. Driven by grief, the old King of Illiador, my grandfather Ereneth, married again, this time to a woman he barely knew. Her name was Lilith.

"Morgana is the daughter of Lilith?" I asked.

Professor Dekela nodded. "Yes. But Lilith was no ordinary woman. Your grandmother Fiona was gentle and kind, as well as a powerful mage and healer. But Lilith, well, Lilith was not what she seemed at first. Your grandfather was captivated by her beauty and married her without thinking. When Morgana was born, Lilith's true nature became clear. She plotted and schemed against her own husband and was even partly responsible for the last mage war."

"No one has mentioned her in my history class," I said.

"Well, history is not always accurate. Lilith orchestrated the whole thing from behind the scenes, providing information and money to help their cause. If the Black Mages had succeeded in taking Illiador, she would have killed your grandfather and taken the throne for herself. But finally the king realized what she was about and ordered her to be arrested. She flew into a rage and tried to kill your grandfather. It was Azaren who stopped her, and she tried to kill him too. Azaren had no choice but to defend himself and end Lilith's life."

Realization dawned, and my eyes widened. "That's why Morgana hates my father and me so much. My father killed her mother."

Professor Dekela nodded gravely. "Now, let's get back to your studies, shall we?"

Three times a week I had extra healing with Penelope, in her private rooms. She taught me higher levels of healing than were usually taught to the novices. Penelope showed me how to heal myself from the inside, to shake off effects of magical strikes. I had already done this unintentionally when Damien and his goons attacked me. But now I knew exactly what I was doing. I learned how much power to use to heal myself without dropping my shield. I also understood about special fae herbs and potions that were Penelope's particular secret. I absorbed everything like a sponge, and I seemed to have a natural affinity for healing, becoming rather good at it.

Six times a week I had very strenuous lessons with Professor Tanko, who, although formidable in the regular classes, was jovial and friendly in our private lessons. I also found out that he was a very dear friend of my father's. I wished I could tell him who I really was, but Penelope had warned me that we still didn't know who to trust. And Aunt Serena was still very angry with me for telling Vivienne as well.

Professor Tanko taught me how to perform and block stun strikes, crush strikes, fire strikes, and lightning strikes. I practiced my basic push strikes until I could control the intensity of my striking power.

Soon I could hit a moving target with my lightning

strikes. And after every session, I had a whole host of game in a heap at my feet, which were sent to the kitchens, on Professor Tanko's orders.

I was becoming stronger, physically and magically as well. Even with the amulet on, my powers were resilient. The professor would also make me run for two hours every day in the woods on the outskirts of the city of Neris to build up my stamina and strength.

"Your powers are strong, Rory," said Baron Tanko one day, as we were resting after an extremely strenuous lesson. "I can understand now why the mastermage wanted you to have extra lessons. It's not that you are lagging behind, but in fact you are too strong. And with powers like yours learning to control them is very important."

I was still wearing my amulet at all times. I thought it would diminish my power, but it didn't feel like it. My strikes were fast and powerful, and my shields were strong. Could I really have more power than this? Was it even possible for one person to possess so much power?

Uncle Gabriel said that people were afraid of fae-mages. It sounded absurd that anyone could be afraid of me. But I was definitely getting curious about how much power I really had, and many times I contemplated taking off the amulet just to see what I could actually do.

Professor Tanko went on talking. "There is a very important lesson I want you to learn, Rory," he said.

I listened intently. I was determined to be the best, and I

would have to be if I wanted to achieve anything at all.

"Learning to control the intensity of your strikes is one thing, but what I want to teach you now is considered High Magic and only taught in the third and fourth years at the academy. Normally a mage of your age would not need to learn this technique yet, as their powers are still not strong enough to kill a person with their strikes."

"Kill," I gasped. "I don't want to kill anyone."

"I should hope not," said Baron Tanko, looking amused. "In any case, the lesson here is, how do you know if your strike can just wound a person or kill him? What I am trying to say is that the intent behind your strike is as important as the intensity of the strike itself. A powerful lightning strike can kill a man if the intent is there to kill. But you can perform a lightning strike that will temporarily paralyze your opponent if you so intend. The same goes for fire strikes. A novice would only be able to cause a slight burn when he or she performs a fire strike. But a fully trained mage can burn a man alive with it. Or he could only scorch somebody, depending on the intent. These strikes not only work against people, but on objects as well. A small fire strike can light a candle, but a strong one could burn down a house. This is the reason students are not allowed to use strikes outside classes. A wrong strike with wrong intent can cause severe damage."

I nodded, understanding dawning. Professor Dekela was preparing me for anything, not just for the school tests.

I still met Rafe every night and practiced everything I had learned so far. In the time that we spent together, we talked about everything. I told him all about my childhood, my adoptive parents, how they died, and my life with the Darlingtons. Rafe also opened up a little, and I got glimpses into his life as a boy and his relationship with his parents. He told me amusing stories about his younger years and spoke very fondly about many of his friends. I got a sense that he didn't really get along with his family, but he still never told me who he really was.

On occasion, Rafe would take me down to a secluded area of the docks, in the early hours of the morning, while the city was asleep, and I would haul boxes and crates onto a wagon, lifting them with magic. This sort of magic required a lot of precision and strength, and Rafe explained that exercising my magic was as important as exercising my muscles. I would leave my nightly classes exhausted, with barely any energy to eat, and fall into my bed.

Still, I was happy spending so much time with him, and my heart yearned for him to feel the same about me, but I was never really sure of his motives for helping me. And every time I thought that he might have feelings for me, he reminded me that he had a debt to repay my father.

So I tried to push him from my thoughts and immersed myself in my studies. I spent my free time at the library reading the histories of Avalonia and the politics and societies of all the seven kingdoms. I memorized the names of the kingdoms and their rulers, the names of the noble families, what they did, and who they were. I learned about the different guilds, the merchants and artisans, and how they sold and traded. Where all the main trading ports were and what cities and towns sold what, how many shops they had, and the prices of certain tradable items. I even spent hours poring over maps of the seven kingdoms and making extensive notes.

Professor Dekela was going to be giving me a test, and I intended to be ready for that, so I could prove to him and everybody else that I was ready for anything. After all, I was supposed to be the most powerful being in all the seven kingdoms: a fae-mage with unlimited magic. If I didn't prove myself now and be the best, how could I ever hope to run a kingdom and be queen?

23
THE FIRST TEST

THE GARDEN CAFETERIA was a gaggle of voices and chattering students. Autumn had arrived early, and stray brown and gold leaves scattered beneath the soles of the students' boots. I couldn't believe it had been only three months since I had come to Avalonia, and I had finally regained a sense of belonging that had disappeared when my adoptive parents died.

Professor Dekela strode into the garden; his very presence enough to quiet the cafeteria. His dark eyes flashed, stern and commanding.

"As some of you may know," he started in a strong, calm voice, "over the next few days we will be having our annual tests. All the students enrolled at the academy must pass these examinations if they want to proceed with their magical education."

Immediately, the chattering and whispering started in full force, like a wave rising and breaking against the shore.

"Please be quiet," said Professor Dekela, an exasperated look on his face.

One of the teachers handed the mastermage a sealed

scroll.

"I will post this on the information tree," said Professor Dekela. "Everybody please check the time and place of your tests. If you don't show up on time, you will fail at that subject."

The night before the first tests, I met Rafe in our usual place and he presented me with a pair of beautiful jeweled daggers.

"Because every queen needs a set of these," Rafe said, smiling when he gave them to me. "And they can be easily concealed."

"And how do you know what every queen needs?" I asked, trying to sound stern, but suppressing a smile.

Rafe's eyebrows arched upwards, and he grinned. "Do you really want to know?"

I shook my head and laughed. "No, not really. Thank you so much Rafe," I said, throwing my arms around his neck and giving him a big hug and a kiss on the cheek. "They are beautiful. I love them." This time I didn't ask where he got them.

He hugged me back. "Also not stolen, in case you were wondering."

"Not funny," I said, swatting him on his arm.

"I thought it was," said Rafe, still chuckling as we made our way back to the school before dawn broke.

When the day of the first test arrived, I was very nervous. I barely managed to stuff a piece of bread into my mouth as Vivienne accompanied me to the testing area.

The south field was splendidly decorated. Marquees and stands were set up to form a rectangle, and in the middle an open space loomed—the arena. Four tents were set up in the middle of the testing arena, which I presumed was the place the first test was to be held.

When I went to the professor to give him my name, I realized to my utter horror that Damien and I had been teamed together for the first test—Healing.

I had no idea what I was up against, and having Damien on my team was not reassuring. What were the teachers thinking? They knew better than to team Damien and me together, I mused. Everyone knew about our enmity. I just hoped he behaved himself while the examinations were on.

"I hope you know what you are doing," said Damien rudely, as he strode past me into the arena. "I don't want to lose because some amateur forgot how to do things."

"You're the one who needs to keep up," I said.

Professor Dekela strode in as everyone lined up.

"Let the test begin," boomed Professor Tanko's resounding voice.

Healing was the first test. There were four tents, one each for different levels of magic. We had to go in the tents provided and create a remedy for the patient in the tent who had been poisoned.

We waited for our turn.

"We're up next," said Damien, coming to stand next to me.

Finally it was our turn, and Damien and I went into the tent. A pale girl was stretched out on the bed. Her head was sweaty, and her face was deathly white.

"She has been poisoned by hemlock," stated Damien, in his usual irritating know-it-all manner. But he was wrong; healing was not Damien's strongest skill.

"No, I don't think so," I said, checking the patient. "I think it is more subtle than that."

I felt the girl's head. She was burning with fever, her eyes were closed, and her breathing was faint at best.

"I think it's a poisonous mushroom, but not just any mushroom. It seems to be the deadly Andrysian mushroom called the Shadow of Death," I said finally. "Look at the purple tint around her lips."

Damien thought for a moment. "Maybe you're right," he said. "After all, you are from Andrysia."

I was surprised that he agreed with me so easily. I thought I would have a fight on my hands.

"Well, that is an easy remedy to make then," he said, full of himself. He went about making the concoction. I wondered what he was doing. It didn't look right.

"I don't think you should add any more of the purple dragon-flower seed," I said. "The girl could die."

"You dare to question me," said Damien, smirking. "I

know exactly what I'm doing."

A professor was standing quietly in the corner. Only inspecting, no advising. I was alone. Damien had confused me, made me think I was wrong when I was so sure that I had been right. I remembered studying this with Penelope.

Damien spooned the mixture into the girl's mouth. Instantly she started turning white, and her breathing became even more labored.

"She's dying," I said aghast. It was as I expected. Damien had made the wrong antidote.

Even the old professor looked worried when I glanced over at him, but he offered no words of help.

Damien looked confused. "But it was such a simple remedy," he said to himself. "Maybe you were right about the purple dragon flower seeds." He started to look panicked. "What do we do now? You're supposed to be such a good healer, heal the girl! What are you waiting for?"

That made me lose all concentration, and I could feel the fear rushing in. What if I was wrong? What if I made the wrong remedy and the girl died?

I had to take a chance; time was running out. I mixed the herbs together as I had been taught. Everything I needed was there in the little kit that had been provided in the tent. Damien just stood there, doing nothing to help.

"If you are wrong, she could die," said Damien. "Not that it really matters. She is a peasant girl and of no consequence."

I faltered. No! I said to myself as I pulled myself together.

I wasn't going to let him get to me. And I wasn't going to let the girl die either, peasant or not. A life was a life, and everyone deserved to be treated the same. I knew what I had made was right. I poured some of the liquid down the girl's throat and waited. Her breathing was still hardly visible, but soon the girl's eyelids fluttered slightly.

The professor came and checked the patient. He smelled the contents of the liquid cure that I had made and then took the girl's pulse, but she was still not waking up.

"This is correct for the first poison," said the professor, "but I am afraid your partner here administered another poison into her blood. We must call in Professor Plumpleberry to heal her, or she will surely die." The professor looked extremely worried and left the tent.

Did that mean we had failed the test? Damien was smirking at me, but his eyes looked worried. What if Penelope did not get here in time? I hadn't seen her in the arena. What if the girl died before she could heal her? I thought about it, and if Professor Plumpleberry could heal the girl, then it could be done. I had to try something; time was running out.

I placed one of my palms on the girl's head and one over her heart. I closed my eyes and concentrated, just how Penelope had taught me.

"What are you doing?" hissed Damien. "Do you really think you can heal her with just your powers? Only the professors know how to do that. You will wear yourself out before you can even begin."

I shut out Damien's voice and concentrated. I could feel the faint heartbeat of the girl, and I concentrated on my own power source. I pushed some of that power into the girl through my palms and went about searching for the poison. It was easier than I had imagined at first, but soon my power started to fade. I could feel the amulet working, making me ordinary. My mage powers were not enough. I needed more to heal this girl.

I searched around me. I could feel magic in the air and under my feet buried deep in the earth. In fact, now that I was looking for it, I felt magic all around me, not just within me. I pulled some of it into myself and pushed it through my hands into the girl.

I knew instinctively that I was using fae powers instead of mage, but it didn't matter. The only thing that mattered right now was that the girl lived. I pushed more power into the girl, and the blue-white light spread through the girl's body like a forest fire, expelling and destroying the poison and cleaning her blood.

It was done.

I opened my eyes, and so did the girl.

Damien was shocked. "How did you do that?" he asked incredulously.

I was shocked at myself. What had I done? I had used fae magic. I was sure of it. Had I revealed myself? Did Damien know?

The tent flapped open, and in strode the old professor and Professor Plumpleberry. Penelope immediately went to the girl and checked her thoroughly. When she was finished, she turned and smiled at me, but her eyes looked worried. "It seems I am not needed after all," she said.

The professor who was overseeing the tent was spellbound. "But, but, I was sure she was dying. There are no herbs that could have saved her."

Penelope laughed and tried to sound flippant. "Maybe you didn't check thoroughly, Sebastian," she said, trying to ease the tension.

But then Damien piped up. "I saw what she did," he said, pointing at me. "She healed that girl with her powers alone."

The old professor scoffed at Damien. "Impossible, no one has so much power at so young an age, and even if she did, a healing like that would have sapped all of her powers. Only the fae can heal like this. You must be mistaken, my boy. I think the potion Rory made expelled both the poisons. Good, good, I must make a note of that for the guild."

"But I saw her," said Damien lamely. "I saw her. She healed the girl. She put her hands on her head, and she healed her."

"I do not like liars, my boy," said the old professor sternly, turning away from Damien and walking out of the tent. He gestured for us to follow him. Penelope stayed behind to check the patient.

I sneaked a peak at Penelope, and she was looking at me very suspiciously. I think she knew. The question was, what would she do about it? Would she support me? Uncle Gabriel said most people are afraid of fae-mages. Would Penelope turn me over out of fear? Or would she keep my secret?

It was done now; at least the professor didn't believe Damien. I knew Damien would not leave it. He was suspicious, and it was only a matter of time before he figured out the truth.

Damien was out of the tent first. I stumbled behind him into the sunlight.

Vivienne ran over. "What happened? Why was Professor Plumpleberry called in?"

Celia Greendew came over too. "Yes, Rory," she said, pouting. "I thought you were so good at healing, all those extra classes and all. Hope you don't fail your first test."

I hung my head. What could I say? I couldn't tell them what I really did. I had already raised Damien's suspicions, and Penelope must have realized that the magic I used to heal the girl was fae magic. It wasn't long now before someone found out and revealed my secret. And that someone would probably be Damien.

The next day of the tests went well. It was the illusions and transformation examination, and I had the highest marks in the class. I managed to turn Vivienne's hair pink and gave her fae ears. I thought she looked very cute. Even Professor Swindern was impressed and clapped when I performed my illusion. Luckily Vivienne just scraped through her test, since she tried to turn my hair green but only succeeding in coloring half of it.

The last day of the testing was upon us. I was so nervous the whole night I couldn't sleep. I tossed and turned in my bed and replayed all that had happened again and again in my head. I didn't see Damien at the Illusion test, and I hoped he had dismissed his suspicions about me. I dressed quickly and hardly ate any breakfast. My stomach was doing cartwheels, and I felt unwell.

The south field was completely transformed; in the center was a round, open arena, surrounded by stands that rose in tiers all around it. It looked like a mini coliseum. I looked up; there was a huge turnout today, and everyone had come to see the final tests—warrior skills.

Baron Tanko announced the opening of the day's examinations and signaled for the testing to begin. He then read out the names of everyone's opponents. It shouldn't have come as such a surprise when I was pitted against Damien. The teachers knew of our dislike for each other, but they also knew that I was the only one who was as good as Damien in warrior skills. They seemed to want a public duel, and I was going to give them one.

"I did some checking up on you, Rory," Damien said, coming up to me, a jeering tone to his voice. "I have searched all the archives for some mention of your family, and there is none. Every noble family is listed, even the obscure ones.

You are a low-born imposter, probably of peasant blood, and I am going to prove it."

I walked away from him, my anger boiling. How could I have been so stupid? I risked everything to save the girl, and now Damien was looking into my past. Once he found out who I really was, he would go straight to Lucian.

I couldn't think about that right now. I had to concentrate, or I would fail the most important test. Damien must have known that and was taunting me on purpose, but I wasn't going to let him get the better of me. I would show him.

The fourth, third, and second years went first, as they always did. It was quite wonderful watching the more advanced students matched in magical duels. Their strikes were fast, and their shields were strong.

It was finally my turn. Damien and I took our places opposite each other in the center of the arena. We took ten steps away from each other as instructed.

Baron Tanko's voice sounded across the arena. "Shields up!" he boomed. "Begin."

Damien turned before me and shot a stun strike at my head, but my magical shield easily deflected it. There were three rounds, and the best of three won. Confident that my shield was strong, I channeled my magic into attacking Damien. I hit him with a stun strike, but his shield held. I gathered more power and performed a push strike, which succeeded in making him stumble. I beamed. I had got a hit in and had won the first point. If I won the next one, I would win the duel.

Damien was looking at me with such hatred in his piercing blue eyes that a shiver ran down my spine when I remembered how he and his friends attacked me. But I was not the same person I was then. I was stronger, faster, and adequately trained to take him on now. I had to concentrate; I had to beat him.

As I was musing and patting myself on the back for winning the first round, I lost concentration. That was all Damien needed, and a powerful stun strike broke through my shield and hit me on my leg. I staggered and fell to my knees.

I channeled my powers into healing myself from the inside. Penelope had taught me how to do this. I shook off the effects of the stun immediately and without much effort. There were murmurs from the crowd, and I realized that I was not really supposed to know how to shake off the effects of a stun strike and heal myself, since I was still considered a novice. I had no choice, though. The stun would have left me too disoriented to have continued with the final round, and Damien would win by default.

I tried to clear my head and concentrated on the last round. If I lost this, Damien would win the duel.

He came slowly closer, circling and taunting me, as I tried to stand up. "You think you're so great because you are good at healing," he said meanly. "It takes more than healing powers to make a great mage."

I was finding it more and more difficult to concentrate with him badgering me. I was upset and frustrated that Damien had made me lose the second round, and now he was going to try and do it again. I ignored him and concentrated on holding my shield.

Damien started hitting me with a barrage of stun strikes and push strikes. I was maintaining the shield, and his strikes just bounced off it, but I was getting tired.

I could hear one of the crowd whispering, "She might as well give up now. The Blackwater boy is quite obviously a better warrior."

I willed myself to stand up, even though my leg was throbbing from where the strike had hit me. This was my last chance.

Damien's strikes were getting fiercer. I realized that he wanted to end this and was giving it his all. I gathered my power and strengthened my shield. In his frustration, Damien even tried a lightning strike on me, which was against the rules. It was weak, and it effortlessly bounced off my shield and fizzled out, but no one stopped the match or disqualified him.

I cleared my head and calmed my racing heart, taking deep breaths. I shut out the voices around me, just as Uncle Gabriel had taught me in my first concentration lessons. I was now more than determined to do my best and to show everyone what I was made of.

I knew I had been told to keep a low profile, but I didn't care; at this moment all I wanted to do was to win. I wanted to win to prove Damien wrong, and most of all I wanted to prove to myself that I was worthy of my father's throne. I had been holding back my powers for so long. I knew I was not supposed to show I was special, but the fact is that I was, and I was tired of hiding.

Uncle Gabriel's warning resounded in my head, but I pushed it from my thoughts and concentrated on the task at hand. A well-aimed push strike would send Damien flying a few feet, and the match would be over. I knew I could perform a formidable push strike. Professor Tanko's lessons had made my magic stronger. The more I used it, the more powerful I grew.

"Give up, Rory," Damien was saying. "You can't defeat me. I will always be stronger than you."

Damien was still trying to taunt me, but this time I ignored him and looked deep inside myself. The white light was growing fainter, but it was still there. I knew there was only one way to finish this. I pushed away the nagging warnings in my head, clasped the necklace that lay around my neck, removed my amulet, and put it in my pocket, all the while holding my shield and never taking my eyes off my opponent.

Instantly, my magic started to grow. Power rushed into me from all sides, even up through the earth, one of the greatest sources of fae magic. White light pulsed through my veins, and I was overwhelmed by the rush of power that was rising like a tidal wave inside me. I knew what I had to do and how to do it, but my magic was still growing. Power coursed through me, and I instinctively raised my arms in front of me, with my palms facing Damien.

I had intended on a simple push strike, but suddenly I couldn't control my power. My fae magic was mixing with my mage magic and fueling it. I tried hard to get it under control, but it was useless. It was still growing, like a huge ball of light that was ready to burst out of me, and I was shaking from the concentration it took to try and control it.

At the back of my mind I heard someone shout. "Can you feel that? I have never felt such power before!"

Someone else said, "Look at her, she's glowing."

Unexpectedly, and much to my utter dismay, I lost complete control over my powers. Powerful bolts of raging silver fire exploded out of my palms. It shattered Damien's shield and hit him directly in the chest. He went flying a few feet and landed on his back, screaming in terror as silver fire enveloped him.

I looked down at my hands; they were still spitting silver sparks. Penelope had told me that silver fire was the weapon of choice of fire-fae warriors. I was horrified. What had I done? When I looked down, I was hovering a few inches off the ground. I panicked and fell back down on my knees.

The whole school was in an uproar. Penelope was tending to Damien, whom I had just set on fire. Luckily, she had already put it out.

Professor Dekela's voice reverberated through the arena. "Please do not panic. Our healer has this under control. The student will be fine."

Shouts of, "She's no mage, she's fae," were resounding through the arena.

Another shouted, "She is no ordinary fae. Can you not feel the power she is emitting? She is a fae-mage."

As he said that, all hell broke loose.

People started screaming. Girls were screeching, and many began to run away, as if I was some monster who was going to destroy them all.

I got to my feet, quickly slipped my necklace back on, and ran out of the arena. After the disaster at the testing, I was afraid to go back to my dorm in case someone called for me to be detained. So I hid and waited until Professor Dekela was alone. And I went to see him.

"There you are, finally," he said when I caught him walking back to his rooms.

I was anxious as to how he would react. "You aren't scared of me?" I asked, feeling stupid as I said it.

Professor Dekela laughed at me. "No, my dear child, I am not scared of you." He chuckled again and shook his head. "Imagine that! A fae-mage living undetected under my very nose. Marvelous. I never thought in all my years that I would ever get an opportunity to meet one. I must say I am honored, Princess Aurora."

"So you are not angry with me?" I asked, looking down and feeling very awkward.

Professor Dekela frowned. "Now that is another matter entirely," he said. "You should never have revealed yourself like that. Everyone saw you; this story will spread like wild-fire through the seven kingdoms. Morgana will be looking for you even more fervently now. She will want to get rid of you before you can learn to master all of your powers. Now that everyone knows that you are a fae-mage, Morgana will think of you as an immediate threat. She will send her best after you. The school will not be able to protect you against her. You must leave the academy tonight. There is no time to waste."

I nodded. He was right. What had I done? I hung my head. "Where will I go now?" I asked.

"Go to the king at the Summer Palace. You must get the support of Petrocales. If Eldoren stands behind you, you will have a chance against Morgana."

"What if he says no?" I asked. "I saw how people looked at me. They think I am some kind of monster." I suddenly felt very sorry for myself.

"That is because two of the six fae-mages turned to dark magic to enhance their powers even more," said Professor Dekela slowly. "The world is still reeling from the death and destruction that they caused."

I looked at him aghast. "Uncle Gabriel didn't tell me that part."

"So he knows, does he?" Professor Dekela asked.

I nodded.

"I can see you are wearing the Amulet of Auraken. Where did you get it? Did Silverthorne give it to you?"

I shook my head. "It was my parents who made me wear it. It was around my neck when I was sent away to the other world. It was all I had with me when my adoptive parents found me," I explained.

Professor Dekela adjusted his robes. "I think you now know that it is probably better that you keep it on."

I nodded again. What could I say? My ego got the better of me. I shouldn't have done it, but I did. I had learned my lesson, and I hoped it was not too late. I felt terrible; even though I hated Damien, I was only intending to hit him with a push strike, which would have just made him fly a few feet.

"What will happen to Damien?" I asked the professor.

"Damien will be fine," he said kindly. "I know it was not your intent to unleash silver fire. I could see you lost control of your powers. Luckily for all of us, Penelope somehow pre-empted what would happen just before you struck, and she sent out a fae counter shield. He was only left with a few burns, which can be easily soothed and mended."

I was so relieved. At least I wasn't a murderer.

"But," he went on, "I hope you have learned your lesson. You must learn to control your fae magic soon, Aurora. You now understand the severity of the situation. Today you unleashed silver fire; only the deadliest of fire-fae warriors use this power. If Penelope hadn't been there, and your strike had hit Damien directly, it would have not only killed him, but turned him to ash in seconds."

I stared at him, wide-eyed. Was he serious? That was way too much power for me to handle. I was never going to take the amulet off again.

The old professor put his hand on my shoulder and said kindly, "Be strong, Princess Aurora. The mages of Evolon will always be at your service should you ever need us."

I thanked Professor Dekela for everything he had done for me. I went to my dorm while everyone was at dinner, gathered my stuff from my room, found Erien and Penelope, and left Evolon in the dark of night.

24
THE SUMMER PALACE

IT WAS DARK, and we rode quickly through the city streets. Professor Dekela gave us the use of three of the academy's horses. Luckily Penelope and Erien were accompanying me to the palace. I was relieved, since I was quite nervous about going there by myself. I'd heard from Penelope that Uncle Gabriel was on his way back and would be joining us at the palace.

Penelope had come to terms with the fact that I was a faemage. Her suspicions were raised, just as I suspected, when she saw how well the girl in the test was healed. Much to my relief, she was not afraid of me.

I was too scared to face Vivienne, and I had no idea how she would react to this, especially after I had lied to her time and time again. That was why I left Evolon without saying good-bye to her. I couldn't bear the thought of her rejecting me, and I was worried that I had lost my best friend.

When the palace came into view, I was taken aback by its magnificence. It was an enormous structure that stretched the length of a football field. Although I had seen it from a distance, since it was situated on the other side of the city, I had never seen it up close.

As we rode up the massive tree-lined path leading to the palace, I wondered what the King and the Crown Prince of Eldoren were like and was very apprehensive about meeting them. Would they accept me and support my claim to the throne of Illiador? At this point I desperately needed allies.

The Summer Palace of Eldoren was a fantastic piece of baroque architecture. Perched high on a white cliff overlooking the Bay of Pearls, it looked similar to pictures I had seen of the royal palace of Versailles, but painted in the Eldorean colors of blue and white. The front colonnaded façade was at least fifty feet high and decorated with massive windows that lined the front of the palace. The towering columns interspaced with the windows were trimmed with gold leaf, creating a dazzling sight for those who laid eyes on the palace for the first time.

I was shocked. I thought all the castles and palaces of Avalonia would be like Silverthorne Castle, all medieval stone and battlements. Imagine my surprise when I discovered that the Summer Palace looked almost eighteenth century. Even after living here for three months, this world never ceased to amaze me.

The splendid Summer Palace shimmered in the moonlight as we entered the massive gates into the palace's outer courtyard. We were led through the great central arch of the north façade and into the inner courtyard, where Aunt Serena was waiting for us.

Erien jumped off his horse, ran to his mother, and hugged her. I followed, sliding off my horse most inelegantly, and hugged my aunt.

"I've missed you, little one," Aunt Serena said. "Welcome to the Summer Palace, my dear."

I smiled. I was happy to be here. And I would definitely be safer here than at Evolon.

"Are you all right?" she asked genuinely. "After Professor Dekela sent me a message telling me what happened, I immediately came here to speak to the king. He has given his permission for you to stay at the palace, under his protection, until my father gets back and decides what to do."

I nodded. "Thank you, Aunt Serena. I'm sorry I acted stupidly. I shouldn't have taken off the amulet."

"What's done is done," said my aunt. "We cannot change that. The truth had to come out sometime. It's just that we wanted you to be ready, and in full control of your powers, when that happened."

I looked down, ashamed that I had let her and Uncle Gabriel down. He was going to be so angry when he heard what I did.

"It's nice to see you again, Penelope," said Aunt Serena to Mrs. Plumpleberry.

Penelope curtseyed. "It's always a pleasure to be of service to you my lady," she replied deferentially.

"Come," said Aunt Serena to me. "I will show you to your rooms. You will be staying with us in the west wing of the palace where the Silverthorne family resides while we are at court."

"Your room will be next to mine," said Erien, "overlooking Cherry Blossom Grove."

I smiled; I loved the names of all the places in Avalonia.

The foyer was an enormous, high-ceilinged room with a white marble floor that gleamed under the light of magnificent crystal chandeliers. Gilded columns stood like sentinels guarding the way as I followed Aunt Serena up a great marble staircase and through an immense hall lined with huge mirrors. Beautiful, intricate tapestries decorated the walls on one side, and big French doors led out onto white balconies and the gardens beyond.

We walked down exquisitely decorated corridors with portraits of what I assumed were royal ancestors, past ornamental rooms, and closed doors, to the west wing of the palace.

My room at the Summer Palace was a luxurious haven, which was even bigger and more spacious than my bedroom at Silverthorne Castle. Compared to this place, Silverthorne Castle could be called rustic.

A massive four-poster bed, hung with beautiful cream and gold brocade curtains and raised on a platform, could be reached by climbing four carpeted steps. The floors were white marble, and dozens of exotic carpets were placed tastefully around the room. Comfortable chairs, a gold brocade sofa, and elegant chests of drawers created a lovely entertainment space. Gilded frames and massive mirrors decorated the walls. A great crystal chandelier hung from the impossibly high ceiling, which was carved with intricate designs. The massive chandeliers were already lit with glowing candles, and it spread a warm glow over the whole room.

I washed up and went across the corridor to Aunt Serena's parlor. It was a beautiful room with blue and gold walls. A huge, blue-and-gold brocade sofa dominated the parlor, and Aunt Serena was lounging on it reading something.

When she saw me, she called me to sit beside her.

"Come, my dear," she said, warmly patting the plump cushion next to her.

Aunt Serena looked at me with a kind smile on her porcelain face. Sometimes I couldn't help staring at her. She was so beautiful. Perfect skin, beautiful blue eyes, long golden hair—she looked every inch a countess.

"The king is having a ball two nights from today," said Aunt Serena. "I brought you some clothes so you will have something suitable to wear in the day, and your dress for the harvest ball should be arriving shortly."

She showed me my new wardrobe, and I was quite speechless at her generosity.

"Thank you so much, Aunt Serena," I said, giving her a big hug.

The next day was extremely hectic. I was woken up by one

of the palace maids at the crack of dawn and told that Erien had asked me to join him in the courtyard for his morning ride. I dressed quickly in my green riding clothes, slipped on my soft riding boots, and followed the maid through the extremely confusing corridors, down the great staircase, and into the inner courtyard of the castle where Erien was waiting with a huge white pegasus.

Erien grinned his silly lopsided grin. He waved to me and said, "Surprise!"

"Snow!" I cried and ran towards my pegasus. I hugged her round her large neck and stroked her white mane. "I'm so glad you're back."

"I am glad to be back, little princess," said Snow in my mind.

"She got here last night with Grandfather," said Erien. "You should have seen his mood. He was so angry. I figured you could use some flying time before you have to meet with the duke."

Poor Erien. He was so sweet, and he looked quite worried. I could imagine what Uncle Gabriel must have looked like when he found out what I did and that everyone now knew who I was. I wondered who told him. Must have been Aunt Serena; no one else would have been brave enough.

I knew I was in trouble, but what was done was done. I did regret hurting Damien so badly. It was not my intention, but the truth had to come out sometime, and I felt like a great load of lies and deceit had been lifted from my shoulders. In some ways even though Morgana was hunting me, I felt freer than I ever had in my life. It was time to stop hiding, take my life into my own hands, and make my parents proud.

I held onto the leather strap that was wrapped around the pegasus's middle and hoisted myself up onto her huge back.

"Snow, have you grown since I last saw you?" I said in my mind.

Snow laughed her musical laugh. "Yes, my princess. I am still a young pegasus, and I will continue to grow for a few more years. Soon I will be able to fly you across the Stardust Sea to Elfi with no problem whatsoever."

Snow cantered a little, flapped her great wings, and soared into the sky.

"Why Elfi?" I asked. "I thought I was going to stay here."

"Your uncle has been planning to send you to Elfi for your safety. To your grandmother Isadora, queen of the fae."

"Sounds like Uncle Gabriel has already made up his mind," I said.

I knew I had a fae grandmother and that she was queen of the fae. But I had gotten so involved in my mage life that I hadn't thought much about my mother's family. And if what Penelope said was true and she was very powerful, I would be safe from Morgana in Elfi. Right now I was a sitting duck. Morgana probably already knew I was here.

"Will I really be safer there?"

"Queen Isadora is an Immortal and extremely powerful,"

said Snow as we soared over the azure sea. "It is only because of her that Elfi still exists. Morgana fears your grandmother and will not attack her kingdom directly."

"If Morgana fears her, then why is she attacking the fae in Illiador?" I asked. "Why doesn't my grandmother help them?"

"Morgana knows that Isadora cannot leave Elfi, as it is only her power and her presence that keeps the kingdom of the fae safe. She is trying to draw Isadora out, leaving Elfi vulnerable to attack," Snow replied.

I nodded. It made sense that Uncle Gabriel would try and send me to the safest place in the seven kingdoms, but I wasn't really sure if I wanted to run away and hide all over again. Although going to Elfi to learn to use my fae magic was probably not such a bad idea. I didn't want another incident where I lost control. I hoped we would be able to stay at the palace for a little while, though; I really wasn't looking forward to another long journey trying to evade Morgana's minions.

We soared over the landscaped gardens of the Summer Palace, over the cliffs, out to the open sea, and back. Snow flew abruptly out of the sky and cantered to a stop inside the palace courtyard. My neck was jarred with the impact of hitting the ground.

"Sorry," said Snow, "I've been used to the duke's weight for so long that I misjudged my landing."

I got off Snow and patted her on her neck as the grooms

came scurrying to take the now sweating pegasus for a cool down and then back to the royal stables.

"Did you enjoy yourself?" said Erien enthusiastically as I came over to him.

I smiled, my mind racing. I was going over what Snow had just said to me. "It was fun, yes," I said absentmindedly. "Thank you Erien."

I followed Erien into the palace, through the great halls and massive corridors, to the west wing, where our rooms were. Aunt Serena was waiting for us.

"Well," she said sternly, "where were you two?" She looked angry again.

"Aurora was just flying on Snow," grinned Erien.

But Aunt Serena was scowling at him.

"What did I do now?" he asked, his face falling.

"I have expressly forbidden you from taking Aurora out of the palace grounds. What part of that sentence do you not understand?" said Aunt Serena.

"In actual fact we were not really outside the grounds, or anywhere on it. She flew over the sea and came back," said Erien, still oblivious as usual.

I wanted to throttle him. He was just making matters worse, and he had no clue. Aunt Serena was getting angrier by the minute.

"Aurora has been summoned by the king to meet him this afternoon, and I have to get her ready," she said, pulling me towards my room.

I went back to my room and changed out of my riding clothes and into a pale blue chiffon dress with silver embroidery on the neck and cuffs. It was cinched at the waist with a wide silver sash. Aunt Serena had said that I was to meet her in the outer chamber of the throne room at noon, where I would be presented formally to Petrocales, King of Eldoren and to the crown prince as well.

I followed an old footman, who had come to escort me to the throne room, which was situated just under my rooms, in the west wing of the palace. Aunt Serena was waiting for me in the outer chamber.

I was a little nervous. What was the king like? Would he accept my claim to the throne of Illiador? Would he help me?

The massive doors to the throne room opened, and we were summoned inside. Aunt Serena led the way, and the doors shut behind me with a thud. The herald announced the Countess of Everdale, and I walked stiffly behind Aunt Serena.

The throne room was a cavernous hall, long and rectangular, with white marble floors. Huge pillars, spaced out at regular intervals, lined the two sides of the enormous room. The ceiling here was two stories high and decorated with magnificent frescos; huge arched windows bathed the room in sunlight. A long gallery ran along the first floor of the room, and a few lords and ladies of the nobility were standing around, whispering in low voices.

My hands were becoming clammy, and my heart had started hammering in my chest. Was this going to be a formal audience, in front of so many people? What if I slipped up? What if I said something wrong? All these people would laugh at me.

When we reached the dais where the king sat on the throne, Aunt Serena curtseyed and gestured for me to do the same. I immediately dropped into a clumsy version of a curtsey that I remembered from ballet class. Aunt Serena had been teaching me, but I wasn't very good at it.

The king looked pleased. He was a big, burly man with deep-set eyes and closely cropped salt-and-pepper hair, which peeped out from beneath his crown.

The king looked over to one of the guards standing on the side of the throne. "Where is my son?" he asked, his voice booming across the throne room. "Did I not expressly give a command that he was to be here for this audience today?"

The guard looked embarrassed. "I am sorry, sire. The prince got away from us again," he said in a soft voice. "We have no idea where he is."

"Probably out in a tavern, holed up with some wench as usual," said the king loudly, his voice laced with disgust. "Just find him. I want him here for the harvest ball tomorrow."

"Yes, sire," the guard said, nodding, and backed away into the shadows.

Some of the ladies in the crowd snickered and giggled. It looked like the reports about the crown prince were true. He sounded like quite a rake.

The king dismissed the sniggering, smiled, stood, and offered me his hand. "Come, my dear," was all he said, as he led me through a door behind the throne room into a smaller, more comfortable room. This was the private audience chamber of the King of Eldoren, and I immediately felt more at ease.

We sat across from each other, Aunt Serena and I perching ourselves on an elegant settee, while the king sat on a high-backed chair opposite us.

"The countess has informed me of who you are and why you are here," said the king. "We are glad to have you with us." He smiled. "I wanted our first meeting to be private, but later we can have a meeting with the council."

I must have looked startled, because Aunt Serena put her hand on my leg. "Don't worry, my dear. I told you we will not do anything you do not want. My father has arrived, and once you have had a talk with him, we can decide what is to be done."

I nodded. I was dreading meeting Uncle Gabriel. He was going to be so angry with me.

The king looked disconcerted. "I thought that fae-mages were a myth," he said, "but Serena has informed me that you are being taught to control your powers."

"Yes," I said meekly, looking down at my hands. I was still embarrassed about the fiasco at school.

"It also seems your powers are exceptionally strong, like

your father," King Petrocales said. "It would be a shame to see such potential go to waste, so we must get as many nobles as we can to support you if the war comes. You will need troops, and you need to be ready to face Morgana and Lucian."

"But . . . " I said, trying to get a word in.

The king held up his hand to silence me.

"Let me finish. When the time comes, we can decide what is to be done. I understand your hesitation. Serena had informed me that you are reluctant to rule Illiador."

I nodded again, more fervently this time. The king's brows scrunched together as he rubbed his temples.

"Nonetheless, you need to understand that we cannot permit Morgana to rule, nor can we permit her to invoke the old law of Illiador as the high kingdom. If Azaren were king, it would have been a different story altogether. I do not know how much your aunt and granduncle have told you about your father," he said, looking at Aunt Serena and back to me.

"After so many years, we had given up hope. You must be the one to ascend the throne. If you do not claim your right, the other noble families of Illiador will rally to someone else's banner, there will be strife in your kingdom, and your family name will disappear. Illiador is your kingdom, and you are its true heir. Do not shun your destiny because the way ahead seems too hard. You must embrace who you are, take your life into your own hands, and win back your kingdom in the name of your father Azaren and the great Firedrake dynasty."

I knew what he was saying was right. It was my duty to hold the kingdom for my father. He would never have wanted Morgana to destroy the kingdom like this. But why was this king helping me? Couldn't he just take over the kingdom himself? I thought all kings were power hungry.

"Your father was a dear friend of mine, Aurora," said the king, obviously sensing my confusion. "I do not want his legacy to go to ruins. When my own kingdom was in strife, Azaren was the one who brought troops into Eldoren to quiet the rebels. He was a kind and just man and would have made a wonderful king. I owe it to him to see his daughter restored to her rightful place on the throne of Illiador."

Hearing the King of Eldoren say all these things really drove the point home. And, even though I had decided a while ago not to run from my destiny and to accept my role as queen, I still had doubts as to whether I would be able to succeed in this monumental task. Morgana would not give up her throne easily, and there were no guarantees that I would even survive long enough to sit on the throne. But I was willing to try. I owed my parents that much.

"What do I have to do?" I said finally.

"At the moment, you need to advance your training and strengthen your powers. No one will follow a weak queen. Although," he paused, and then he went on, "you being a fae-mage will rally many to your cause, but only if you learn to control your magic."

"When and if Morgana attacks us, I intend to be ready," I said, now resigned to the idea, but sounding more sure than I really was.

Serena got up, came over to me, and hugged me fiercely. "I knew you would soon come to understand your responsibilities," she said smiling.

"Azaren's name itself will rally most of the nobles to follow your banner," said the king, standing up and indicating this meeting was over. "In the meantime, I want you to enjoy yourself here as well. Just stay within the walls of the palace, and you will be safe for now. I will leave you to meet your uncle. What's done is done. Now that everyone knows your true identity, it is futile to try and hide it."

Serena stood too and curtseyed, and I did the same.

"Know this: you have the support of Eldoren, should you choose to stand against Morgana. After the ball, we can meet with the council."

"Thank you," I said simply. What else does one say when someone gives them an army?

The king nodded and opened the door. "We shall see you on the morrow," he said and left the room.

We followed him, curtseyed again, and were led out of the throne room.

People were whispering and giving me strange looks. A group of ladies in ostentatious dresses, heavily adorned with jewels, were whispering something about the Duke of

Silverthorne.

I followed Aunt Serena to Uncle Gabriel's rooms to meet him. As we entered, I rushed in and immediately went and hugged my granduncle. I had genuinely missed him, and his big gruff presence was comforting.

"So!" said Uncle Gabriel, after he hugged me back and sat down next to me. "It seems you have been extremely busy since I have been gone, young lady." His tone was affectionate.

I smiled. "It was a tough few months, but I'm still here," I said, trying to sound flippant. I was relieved. At least he wasn't shouting at me.

"Yes, you are," said Uncle Gabriel, suddenly more serious, "but that does not mean that I approve of your behavior. You showed the extent of your powers to everyone. People have already started talking about you."

I nodded. I didn't want to argue; what I had done was stupid. I had revealed myself when I had been told not to. Now I had to deal with the consequences.

"I also heard about your other escapade at Evolon," went on Uncle Gabriel. "Sneaking out of school at night, and with the Blackwaters . . . what were you thinking? I should have warned you about them." He had an exasperated expression on his face.

"That's what Rafe said," I said.

"And what else did Rafe say?" Uncle Gabriel asked, amused.

"Nothing," I said blushing, and looking down at my feet.

"Well, it was a good thing that he was there to help you," Uncle Gabriel said with a twinkle in his eye. He raised one bushy eyebrow. "Serena also told me that you were the one who discovered the Blackwaters' plans."

I nodded. Now I was really going to get it.

"That was very resourceful of you," he said, to my utter surprise. "And I am glad that while you were at school you did not forget your responsibilities as a queen. This shows me that you have the potential to recognize a threat and act on your suspicions. Due to your information, we are now aware of Morgana's plans to collect all four keys. I have alerted the other Guardians, and three keys, including mine and Elial Dekela's, are secure and hidden in secret locations. Unfortunately the mage who was entrusted with the fourth key was killed before I could get to him."

"So Morgana now has one key?" I said.

"Yes," he said. "I had the Blackwater's house searched, but we found nothing. They must have already given it to Lucian. We have spies in Illiador keeping an eye out for that fourth key."

I nodded. At least I had done something right and three of the keys were safe. But one question was still bothering me.

"So where is the Book of Abraxas now?" I asked Uncle Gabriel.

"In the safest place it could possibly be," said Uncle

Gabriel.

"Which is?" I asked.

"It is better you do not know," said Uncle Gabriel. "I have made sure the book is hidden. And, without the Book of Abraxas, the key to open it is useless."

I was not convinced. Morgana wasn't the type to back down. If she wanted the book, she would find a way to get it.

"Now," he said, getting back to business. "I want to discuss what we are going to tell the council."

Serena looked over at her father. "Do you really think it's a good idea? Once the council knows, we cannot go back," she said.

Uncle Gabriel shook his head. "It is already too late for that. The time has come to start building alliances. I'm afraid we may soon see a war."

"War!" gasped Aunt Serena, her hands flying to her lips, unsuccessfully covering her horrified expression.

"Yes," said Uncle Gabriel grimly. "Andrysia is not strong enough to withstand Morgana's army. I spoke to Queen Maya; her sons are hotheads and want to go to war. Andrysia is already readying their troops in anticipation of an attack. If the threat of Eldoren attacking from the south does not deter Morgana from her plan to rule the North, then we will have to make good on our threat and go to war against her. We cannot let Morgana's rule continue. When and if we do stop her, we need someone to put on the throne, someone who has a blood claim to the throne of Illiador."

"But what do I do until then?" I asked. "I can't go back to Evolon. Everyone knows who I am now, and they are scared of me too."

"You will go to Elfi," said Uncle Gabriel. "Isadora, your grandmother, will teach you the ways of the fae. Only when you have mastered your powers will you be ready to remove your amulet."

"Tomorrow night at the ball we will announce you to Eldorean society as the king has said," Uncle Gabriel continued. "The king will also publicly state that he supports your claim to the throne of Illiador. That will keep you safe from everyone else in Eldoren, but not from Morgana."

Uncle Gabriel opened the door and looked at me. I got up and so did Aunt Serena.

"Make the most of your time in the Summer Palace, Aurora. I have some work I need to finish in Eldoren, and then in a few days we will leave for Elfi," he said.

"You're coming with me?" I asked, extremely happy that he may be accompanying me. I always felt safe when he was around, and I was also apprehensive about meeting my fae grandmother and the rest of my fae family.

"Yes," he said, smiling. "Can't have you traipsing around Avalonia on your own, can we? Who knows what trouble you will get into?" He chuckled to himself.

I laughed, too, as I followed Aunt Serena out of the room. It was time to reveal my true identity to the world. But first, I had a royal ball to attend.

25
THE ROYAL BALL

THE GRAND HALL was brilliantly lit with enormous crystal chandeliers that hung low and were interspaced along the length of the great ballroom. Rainbow-colored specks of dancing light wove along the marble floors like dancers in the midst of a crowd. One whole wall along the length of the massive room was decorated with gilded mirrors and elegant brocade settees. Huge, cream-and-gold, silk-covered, high-backed chairs were placed tastefully and strategically around the room just in case one of the many dancing couples wanted to rest their tired feet.

The opposite wall hosted magnificent arched French doors that opened out onto a white marble balcony, which overlooked the pristine manicured gardens of the Summer Palace. The gardens at the front of the palace descended in tiers down to the very edges of the white cliffs, which dropped hundreds of feet down into the azure depths of the Bay of Pearls.

The royal herald stood at the top of the grand staircase, announcing the guests. He had been instructed what to say when he introduced me.

I walked forward on Erien's arm, my Lady Charlotte creation swirling around me in a sapphire-blue, satin confection. Penelope had reversed the glamour the old fae lady Magdalene had put on me, and the color of my hair and eyes were back to normal: glossy black curls and shining emeralds. My hair was elaborately styled with a cascade of silver flowers woven expertly through the tumbling waves, which reached my waist. Aunt Serena had given me a beautiful diamond diadem to wear in my hair, and it looked lovely.

Kalen, who had just arrived that morning, walked behind us, leading Mrs. Plumpleberry.

"His Lordship, Erien, Earl of Everdale!" announced the Herald.

Everyone turned to look at us.

I started panicking. My heart had started beating fast, my palms had become clammy, and I looked around at the sea of faces that swept across the grand ballroom of the Summer Palace. I felt faint; I hated people looking at me.

"And," the herald said in a deep, booming voice. Everyone was quiet. "Her Royal Highness Princess Aurora, heir to the Firedrake Dynasty of Illiador, daughter of the royal house of Gwenfar-Ith-Aran of the Fae, and Princess Royal of the kingdom of Elfi."

I heard gasps in the crowd. Everyone was looking at me and whispering. Garbled chattering broke out, and everyone was moving forward to try and get a better look at me. I felt like a gallery exhibit.

I glanced around the room once and walked carefully down the great marble stairs, holding onto Erien's arm for dear life. I tried to gather my thoughts and concentrated on not falling down the stairs in an embarrassing heap of satin and taffeta.

I had a whole load of titles, which was pretty cool. But now people had started swarming towards me like a pack of flies towards an uncovered pizza. The ballroom was already packed to bursting point. All the nobility of Eldoren were there, and they all wanted to meet me. Aunt Serena had briefed me on the etiquette of attending a ball. We had also gone through a whole list of people whom I was supposed to meet to get their support. I had met a few of them already at the Blackwaters' dinner party.

I knew that the Blackwaters were also attending, as were other lords and ladies of the nobility that I hadn't met yet: the Hartfields, the Rothguards, and the Greystones. I had studied all these families with Professor Dekela, and I knew who hated whom, which noble house was trying to gain power, and which ones were loyal to the king. After the Blackwaters, the Silverthornes, and the Glenbarrys, these were the prominent houses and titles of the aristocracy of Eldoren.

Aunt Serena came up to Erien and me and led us around the room, introducing me to everyone. A big, burly man with salt-and-pepper hair and twinkling blue eyes, whose doublet was near to bursting its emerald buttons, came up to me, took my hand, and gave a sweeping bow. I could smell the alcohol on his breath as he raised himself up from his tottering bow.

"May I be the first to introduce myself, Your Highness?" he said, in a deep but kind voice. "I am Derek Sutton, Earl of Rothguard. It is an honor to meet you, and may I be the first to say we are delighted to find that you are indeed alive."

"Thank you," I said genuinely. He was a nice man, and I liked him instantly. He was one of the families Uncle Gabriel said would definitely support me.

"Your father was a very dear friend of mine. Anything you need from me, you only have to ask, and it will be done," he said gallantly.

I smiled, and thanked him again. It felt good to meet a friend of my family; maybe later I could speak with Lord Rothguard about him. There were so many things I had been meaning to find out but didn't know who to ask.

Another man, about the same age as Lord Rothguard, came up to meet me. "Julian Fenton," he said, bowing and kissing my hand. "The Marquis of Greystone at your service, Your Highness."

He was tall and impeccably dressed, with chiseled features and an aristocratic nose.

"Rothguard," he said, looking at the Earl. "Good to see you again."

Lord Rothguard smiled and gave a short perfunctory bow. "Julian, I thought you were in Andrysia."

The Marquis just ignored Rothguard and ran a hand through his wavy blond hair.

Aunt Serena came up to me and caught me by the elbow. "There you are, dear. I have been looking all over for you. There are so many people who want to meet you. You must come with me or we will never finish."

I followed Aunt Serena into the throng of chattering Eldorean nobility. I met old lords whose names I tried desperately to remember, I met their wives, the marchionesses and the countesses, and I had to rack my brain for the correct way to address them. I didn't want to make a fool of myself from the very start.

I spotted Vivienne and raised my hand to wave at her. Vivienne smiled and turned to walk towards me, when an older lady—whom I presumed was her mother—glared at me and pulled Vivienne away, disappearing into the crowd. I turned away, tears pooling in my eyes. It seemed I had lost my best friend.

Suddenly the trumpets sounded. Uncle Gabriel was being announced.

"His Grace, Gabriel, Duke of Silverthorne, commander of the king's army, and protector of the realm," boomed the herald.

Slowly a hush grew over the room, washing gently like a wave across the great hall, when they saw who had just walked in after the duke. The women had suddenly started giggling and whispering to each other like a bunch of crazed lunatics.

I also turned to see what everyone was staring at, and, if I could have fainted, I would have. But I decided that fainting at this moment would really not be a good idea.

Standing at the top of the stairs, looking his usual dashing self, was Rafe, and he was gazing straight at me. He was dressed formally in a midnight-blue doublet and hose with silver embroidery on the cuffs and collar. His boots were high and polished to perfection. And, as usual, he looked devastatingly handsome.

I felt my heartbeat quicken. I wished I could do something about this infuriatingly erratic part of myself that I couldn't control. Secretly I was pleased that he had picked me out of a crowded ballroom almost immediately. But what was he doing here, at a ball in the Summer Palace, underneath the nose of the king?

The Herald hesitated for a second before announcing, "His Royal Highness, Prince Rafael of the Ravenswood Dynasty, heir to the throne of Eldoren, Duke of Calos, Marquis of Shadowvale, and Earl of Killanon."

I could have sworn I saw Rafe wink at me as he walked confidently down the grand stairs towards us.

"I thought he was an outlaw," I whispered to Kalen, who was standing beside me, still not taking my eyes off Rafe. I couldn't believe he was actually there.

Kalen was grinning stupidly. "Oh yes! I must have forgotten to mention that, in Eldoren, he has many other titles."

I looked at Kalen incredulously. "And you just forgot to mention that one little part, did you?" I said, scathingly. "You made me keep believing that he was a wanted man."

Kalen shrugged. He was still grinning, and he seemed to find my reaction entertaining. "Rafe didn't want you to know," he said truthfully.

"Why?" I asked. "Did he think it would have made a difference?"

"I don't know," said Kalen. "Ask him yourself. He's coming over here."

I looked up as Rafe and Uncle Gabriel came over to meet us.

"Glad to have you back, Grandfather," said Erien, coming over and hugging Uncle Gabriel; he looked over at Rafe. "You too, Your Highness."

Rafe nodded, smiling, "Erien, Kalen."

Uncle Gabriel gave me a short hug and a kiss on the cheek. "Is everything all right?" he asked, looking concerned.

I nodded. I guess I must have looked so shocked that even Uncle Gabriel had noticed something was wrong. I felt like such a fool. How would I ever talk to Rafe again? How could Kalen not have told me that Rafe was actually the prince of Eldoren? I caught Rafe looking at me with that amused look on his face once again. And, for about the hundredth time, my heart took a quick somersault.

Rafe bowed formally and planted a chaste kiss on my hand. "Princess Aurora, always a pleasure," he said, smiling the most dazzling smile I had ever seen. I couldn't seem to keep my eyes off him, even though I was terribly embarrassed.

"Rafe . . . I mean, Your Highness," I said, suddenly remembering where I was.

"I must say, you look exceptionally beautiful tonight," he said softly, straightening, but still looking into my eyes and holding my hand. I blushed.

He finally let go of my hand when Erien butted in. "Let's go and find Mother," he said quickly to me.

Rafe scowled but didn't say anything.

"What's the rush?" I asked, irritated that I had been pulled away from Rafe.

Erien didn't answer as he took me by the arm and led me through the crowd.

"What was all that about?" I said, when he finally stopped with me behind a potted plant at the far end of the ballroom.

"Rafael," Erien said abruptly.

"What about him?" I said, trying to sound nonchalant.

"He's no good for you," said Erien sharply. "He may be a great warrior-mage, and he is the crown prince, but he is not the type to be tied down. It will only end in heartache, mainly yours."

I tried to look astonished, but failed miserably. Erien was right—Rafe may not be an outlaw, but he was definitely dangerous. And Kalen and his mother had warned me about that side of Rafe. Even his own father seemed to be exasperated with him.

Then I thought back to everything Celia and Vivienne had said about the crown prince. It was a different picture from how Rafe really acted. But which one was his real self? Was he the hardened warrior who traveled the kingdom helping the poor and helpless, the outlaw who was the bane of Morgana's guards? Or the spoiled princeling who was only interested in wine and women?

"I know that," I said, sighing. "Don't worry. I'm not going to mess up my future because of some guy, even if he is a prince." Although I wanted to mean what I said, I wasn't sure how much truth there was in that statement.

Erien looked relieved. "That's good to know," he said, becoming his usual jovial self again. "In any case, there is so much none of us knows about him. There are things about the crown prince that are a mystery to even those who know him best."

I nodded. I knew I had to stay as far away from Rafe as was possible. The more I saw him, the more I wanted to be with him. In hindsight, spending so much time with him training every night was probably not the smartest thing to do. I knew that, prince of Eldoren or not, Rafael Ravenswood was definitely not good for me.

Erien walked off to mingle with the guests. I declined to go with him, as I was still anxious about slipping up and saying the wrong thing. I looked around the room, searching for Kalen. When I saw him, I waved him over. He came over by the plant where I was hiding with a big grin on his face.

"It was kind of your uncle to permit me to stay at the palace with my mother," Kalen said enthusiastically, looking around at the whirling dancers. It was his first time inside the Summer Palace. "I am having a marvelous time."

I smiled at him from behind my plant. It was so good to have Kalen to talk to again.

"Why are you hiding behind a plant?" asked Kalen. "Let us go and meet Rafe. Don't you want to talk to him?"

"No!" I said, catching Kalen's arm and pulling him back behind the plant before he could escape again. "That's exactly who I am trying to stay away from."

"By hiding behind a plant?" asked Kalen, looking at me as if I had lost a few brain cells along the way.

"Sort of," I said, biting my fingernail.

"But why? I thought you liked Rafe," said Kalen, again looking confused.

"I do," I said, now getting exasperated with Kalen. "Too much. That's why I have to stay away from him. Don't you see?"

"No, I don't see," said Kalen, "but if you say so."

I rolled my eyes. Kalen could be oblivious sometimes.

"And don't you think you should have mentioned that the Black Wolf was really the prince of Eldoren?" I whispered.

"Shhh," Kalen hissed. "Be careful. If anyone overhears us, Rafe's life will be in danger."

"But how could you not tell me?" I asked again, trying to keep my voice to the softest of whispers.

"I told you when you asked me the first time—he didn't tell you because he didn't want you to know," said Kalen.

I hung my head. Rafe didn't trust me. That hurt more than it should, and I turned away so Kalen could not see the tears that swam in my eyes and threatened to fall.

"Oh, it will be fun to watch Rafe when he realizes his betrothed is here," said Kalen blithely, scanning the room.

I thought I was going to faint again.

Betrothed!

Rafe was engaged!

Oh no, Leticia! How could I have forgotten?

My eyes whipped about the room, and I spotted Rafe almost immediately, standing rather stiffly in front of Leticia. She had her back to me, and her beautiful golden hair, woven with glittering diamonds, cascaded down her back. She was dressed in a dazzling confection of baby pink and silver satin. She turned, and I noticed her icy eyes shone with anger and that she was directing that anger at Rafe.

I wanted to find out what they were saying. "Tell me about her," I whispered to Kalen.

Kalen was busy looking around the room and was obviously getting bored standing with me behind the plant. I could tell by the look on his face that he was glad to spill some gossip.

"That's Leticia, the daughter of the Earl of Glenbarry," said Kalen quickly.

I nodded, urging him to go on.

"She is his only child and will inherit everything after her father. The estates of Glenbarry are enormous. I heard some people saying that Rafe's mother and Leticia's mother were best friends. And, apparently," Kalen looked around once and lowered his voice to a whisper. "Apparently, his mother made him promise on her deathbed that he wed Leticia. Rafe agreed, to please his mother, but I guess he now regrets his decision to marry that shrew."

"What do you mean?" I asked. "Isn't she nice?" I already knew she was horrid, but I wanted to know what others thought about her.

Kalen snorted. "Ha! Nice is the opposite of Leticia. Poor Rafe only found that out once she was officially betrothed to him. I heard from the palace servants that he keeps putting off the wedding, but I don't know how long she is going to let him get away with that."

I pulled Kalen's arm as we wove through the crowd, towards Rafe and Leticia. I kept stopping and trying to hide behind statues and people along the way so that Rafe didn't notice me. When I finally reached eavesdropping distance, I pulled Kalen and sat down on a high-backed chair next to where Rafe and Leticia were standing. Kalen perched himself on the arm next to me. The chair was turned away from the crowd, so Leticia did not see us, but I was sure Rafe had spotted us already; he never missed anything.

"What are we doing exactly?" asked Kalen, confused again.

I rolled my eyes for the millionth time. "Shhh," I said, trying to listen.

" . . . And you just go off and leave me," hissed Leticia quietly to Rafe.

"Leticia," said Rafe slowly, as if it was taking all his power to keep his anger in check. "I told you I was away. I cannot be at your beck and call all the time."

"But we are to be married, and I want to know where you were for so long," she said sharply, "so you better get used to it. You gave your word to your mother, and I know even you would not go back on that promise."

I tried hard to hear Rafe's reply to that, but a gaggle of chattering women had approached and were accosting the prince. I turned around. Leticia looked peeved, but Rafe seemed to be relieved and was now enjoying himself, flirting openly with all the women who were fawning over him.

I got up quickly from my chair, and Kalen followed. A young man, quite cute, who introduced himself as Viscount Steele, stopped me and asked me to dance. Aunt Serena had tried teaching me the intricate dance of Eldoren, which was very similar to a waltz. I was not very good at it, but I decided to give it a go.

I took the viscount's hand as he led me onto the dancefloor. He wasn't a very good dancer, and I tried to follow his lead, but he made it very difficult. The musicians were playing a lively melody, and my spirits lifted with the music. It was no use feeling sorry for myself and following Rafe around like a lost puppy. I was upset that he hadn't told me that he was engaged. He just let me fall for him without a thought as to what would happen when I found out about Leticia.

Despite my anger, my eyes searched for Rafe, and my heart leapt when I found him. He was leaning against a far wall of the ballroom, his powerful arms crossed across his chest, watching me. Our eyes locked, but he didn't smile.

The viscount was still obliviously whirling me around the dancefloor and stepping on my toes while he was at it. I winced each time and finally stopped dancing. The viscount apologized profusely, but I wasn't paying attention. I looked back to where Rafe was standing, but he was gone.

The music stopped, and the viscount begged me for another dance. But I'd had enough and turned to leave the dancefloor, when my face collided with a rock-hard chest covered in expensive, midnight-blue fabric.

"May I have this dance?" said the voice I had come to love and trust.

I looked up at Rafe. His reassuring presence and piercing grey eyes were so familiar that I couldn't help but smile.

"But, Your Highness," said the viscount, interrupting and standing close to me. "You never dance."

"I do now," said the Prince of Eldoren, never taking his eyes off me.

Rafe held out his hand, and I took it, just as I had dozens of times before. He led me to the center of the dancefloor, and overdressed nobles moved out of the way to let us pass. The musicians started playing a haunting melody, and Rafe swept me up in his arms, holding me close and gliding across the dancefloor. He was a wonderful dancer, and I didn't even have to think as I followed his effortless steps.

As we danced, Rafe said nothing, but he looked at me as if I was the only person in the room, and in that moment a flame in my heart ignited and my soul woke up, recognizing its other half for the first time. For some unexplainable reason, I knew beyond a doubt that I had finally found a permanent place for my heart.

Everyone was watching us as we danced, but I didn't care. I was in Rafe's arms and that was the only place I wanted to be. The music stopped, but Rafe didn't let go of me immediately. I knew people were staring and whispering, but I couldn't look away.

Erien came over and pulled me away into the crowd. "What do you think you were doing?" he chided in a whisper. "Everyone is talking about you and Rafe. He's going to be married; you have to stop this now."

"You don't think I know that?" I snapped, irritated that Erien was absolutely right. "It was nothing. We were just dancing."

"It didn't look like nothing from where I was standing," said Erien.

"It's my life. I'll do what I want," I said, turning from Erien's angry gaze. I wanted to be alone; I had to leave the ballroom.

But before I could disappear into the crowd, Leticia stopped me, and Rafe was too busy to notice. Leticia ignored Erien and glared at me. If looks could kill, I would have been dead a thousand times by now.

"Calisto told me about you," said Leticia, sniffing with her thin, pinched nose as if she smelled something horrid. "We thought you were just Silverthorne's orphaned ward. It looks like you deceived everyone, Your Highness."

Leticia was quite beautiful, but as soon as she opened her mouth, all that beauty just vanished. Leticia Glenbarry had a shrill, nasal voice, and her words were acidic and deadly. She was definitely someone I wanted to stay away from.

"You may think you can deceive everyone else, but you don't fool me. I just thought I would inform you that Rafael and I are to be married very soon, so don't start getting any ideas," said Leticia snidely. "Just because you have discovered that you are a princess, doesn't mean that the prince will leave me for you. He doesn't care about that sort of thing. He is mine, and there is nothing you can do about that."

I looked down, embarrassed. Surely she couldn't know how I felt about Rafe? No one did, or so I thought. But I guess the spectacle I had just made of myself was hard to ignore.

"I saw you and Rafael dancing," said Leticia. "It is quite plain to see that you want him. If you don't stay away, you will be sorry."

Kalen pulled my arm, but I didn't budge. Who did this woman think she was, talking to me like that?

"I have no interest in the prince," I said, trying to sound all grown up. "He is close to my granduncle, that's all. And for your information, Rafe knew who I really was months ago."

Leticia's mouth fell open.

Let her chew on that, I thought to myself, as I turned on my heel and walked away quickly. My heart was beating heavily, and I felt like crying. I had intended to stay away from Rafe anyway, and now that I knew he was to be married, I thanked my lucky stars that I did not get any more involved with him earlier or tell him how I felt. I would have looked like such a fool. Even if he did have any interest in me, it was just the way he was with any woman. He was gallant and kind and every bit a prince, and the more I thought about him, the more I wanted him. But it could not be, and I was definitely not the type to go after someone else's fiancée. That dance was the last one we would ever have.

I was feeling claustrophobic. There were too many people chattering around me and to me. I didn't even bother listening to what they were saying as I wound my way through the crowd. I had to get out of that room. It was too stuffy. I walked out onto the balcony and leaned against the marble balustrade. I gazed out at the now brightly lit gardens of the Summer Palace, took a deep breath of the fresh night air, and immediately relaxed.

I could think properly out here.

I walked down the wide steps leading to the garden. I just wanted to be alone. A few minutes of walking quietly would make me feel better, then I would just unobtrusively slip in one of the side doors and go up to my room, and no one would even notice.

In a few days we would leave for Elfi, and I would never have to see Rafe again. My heart ached with the loss of my first love, but I knew now that it was not meant to be. He was getting married to someone else, and anyway he had never even said that he liked me. I was just imagining that he did because that was what I wanted. I realized that now.

I looked out at the beautiful, moonlit gardens. There was no use in thinking about Rafe.

"Why are you out here alone, Aurora?" said an extremely familiar voice behind me.

Talk of the devil. I whirled around so quickly that my foot got stuck in the irritatingly billowing skirt of my Lady Charlotte creation. I could feel myself falling, but there was nothing I could do about it.

Suddenly, strong hands gripped my arms and prevented me from making a complete fool of myself. When I looked up, I was staring into the beautiful grey eyes of the Prince of Eldoren himself, and, to make matters worse, he was laughing at me.

I gathered myself and stood up shakily. Rafe was still holding me by my arms in case I stupidly fell down again,

I supposed. He was looking at me intently, and I quickly brushed away a few stray tears that had unexpectedly stained my cheeks.

"You have been crying," said Rafe. He looked angry.

I shook my head. What could I say? That I cried every time someone was rude to me? Rafe would really think I was a useless idiot.

"Did someone hurt you?" he asked again, more gently this time.

I shook my head again. I didn't even look up into his eyes, as I was afraid of what he would see in them. According to Leticia, it was obvious to everyone around me, and she was right. In only a few short months, I had fallen completely in love with Rafe. It was useless denying it to myself, and as much as I tried to stay away from him, it made no difference; he was always on my mind. But he was betrothed and lost to me forever. My only hope now was to forget about him and hope that I succeeded.

I steeled myself, looked up at Rafe, and smiled. "Oh, it's nothing," I said, trying hard to sound flippant. "I just got some dirt in my eye, that's all."

"Oh!" said Rafe, coming closer. "Let's see."

I could only stand still and watch, spellbound, as Rafe brought his face so close to mine that our noses were almost touching. Looking straight into my eyes, he smoothed a stray lock of hair away from my face and tucked it behind my ear. Rafe entwined his fingers through mine, brought them up to his mouth, and brushed his lips over my fingertips in the lightest of kisses.

"Why did you lie to me about who you really are?" I asked softly, looking up at him.

Rafe looked to the side and avoided my eyes but didn't let go of his hold on me. "I guess I just wanted you to like me for me."

"Why did you think it would have made any difference?" I asked.

"It has in the past. Every girl or woman I am with usually wants the title that comes along. Even Leticia is only with me because she wants to be queen," said Rafe.

"Well, I am not like that," I said, pushing him away and folding my arms across my chest. "I was already in love with you when I thought you were an outlaw."

Rafe smiled. "You were? You are?" he asked, a little apprehensive, as if he couldn't believe what he was hearing. But he still didn't say anything about how he felt. He was always so mysterious; I had no idea what he was thinking.

"Yes, you silly fool," I said, now waving my hands about. "I think I fell in love with you from the first minute you walked into that dungeon. I didn't even know at that time if I could trust you or not."

Rafe strode over to me, grabbed my arms gently, and pulled me to him. He looked into my eyes for a soul-searching moment, and his lips descended onto mine in the most urgent of kisses. I melted into his arms as he pulled me closer to him, his arms tightening around my waist. I wrapped my arms around his neck and closed my eyes. In that moment, I felt the whole world melt away. There were only Rafe and me and a world of possibilities before us. I never wanted this moment to end. It was everything I had wished for and more.

Finally I broke off the kiss, which had left me gasping for air. When I looked back up at him, his grey eyes were focused and staring straight into my own with an intensity I had never seen before.

Rafe held me close. "You are the most beautiful, courageous, and fascinating girl I have ever met," he said. "I cannot help the way I feel. I know it's wrong. But ever since I met you, you are all I think about."

"What about Leticia?" I asked breathlessly, my heart leaping at the possibility that Rafe really may have feelings for me.

"Leticia is my betrothed only in name. It was a promise I made to my mother before she died, when Leticia and I were still very young," Rafe said.

"But you cannot go back on your word," I stated. I knew the answer before I even asked the question.

"No, I cannot. There is no way I can change the course of these events. Leticia and I will be married next spring," he said.

I disentangled myself from Rafe's arms and pushed him away.

"Then why did you kiss me?" I asked, stunned.

"I couldn't help myself," he said truthfully. "Ever since I saw you in that dungeon at Oblek's castle, wearing those funny clothes, I was completely besotted. I wanted to get to know you before I revealed who I was, or my feelings for you."

"I quite doubt that," I said, now hiding behind my anger, which had started building up slowly but steadily.

I didn't believe him. And I absolutely refused to be someone he had on the side, with Leticia as his bride-to-be. Then it hit me. I had been so stupid; of course he was only toying with me. He never intended to give up Leticia for me. It was the most humiliating moment of my life, and my heart was crushed, smashed into little bits. I was not sure I would ever be able to fit it back together again.

Rafe looked confused. Why was it that men never thought anything of being unfaithful? I thought to myself.

"I can't do this," I said finally.

"What do you mean?" he asked carefully.

"I mean that you are betrothed to Leticia, and I know that you cannot break your vow to your mother. I respect you for that, but I cannot be with you and kiss you knowing that you are to be married."

Rafe was silent.

"And what about after you finally get married, what then? I will not be your dirty little secret. I will not let you treat me like some tart," I said, trying very hard to keep my voice under control.

He suddenly looked more confused. "Tart?" he asked. "What kind of tart?"

If I were not so angry, I would have laughed. "Not that sort of tart, silly," I stormed, but in a whisper, because I didn't want anyone to hear us. "I won't be your mistress, or girlfriend on the side, or whatever you were planning. I won't do that."

Rafe looked upset for a second, but he soon composed himself and had that charming smile back on his face.

"I never asked you to be my mistress, Aurora," he said. "I would never presume to do so. I am sorry I offended you. What can I say? I lost my mind for a moment. And as for the feelings I have for you, well, there is nothing we can do about that. You are right; we can never be together. I am betrothed, and nothing I can do will change that."

I just clutched my skirt and stared at him.

"I guess this is good-bye. I will take your leave, Princess," he said formally. He bowed briefly and took my heart with him as he turned and walked away through the flower-filled garden and into the autumn night.

I tried not to cry, but my heart was breaking, and I watched Rafe longingly as he disappeared into the crowded ballroom, leaving me standing confused and alone in the moonlit gardens of the Summer Palace.

26
THE COUNCIL

THE NEXT DAY, I lazed about in bed the whole morning, nursing my broken heart. Since I didn't want to meet anyone, I ate in my room.

Finally I pulled myself from my slump and dressed carefully in a pale-grey silk dress, with a high collar and long sleeves. I wanted to look older, as I was to meet with the council. The king was going to announce that he supported my claim to the throne of Illiador, and Uncle Gabriel had said that there was to be a meeting to discuss the upcoming war. Would Rafe be at the council meeting? I hoped so. I knew that, if I had any sense, I would stay away from Rafe. But the thought of never seeing him again was too upsetting to even think about.

"I'm ready," I said as I stepped out of my room.

There were two guards posted outside my door, and I felt a bit like a prisoner, even though Aunt Serena had said that they were only there for my protection. One of the chain-mail-clad guards grunted a response and gestured for me to follow them.

Two footmen in blue-and-white livery opened the huge

double doors to the council chamber, and the guards posted themselves on both sides of the massive door. Did I have to enter alone? I hesitated a moment, but I didn't want to let everyone know how scared I was. I had to meet the council, the lords of Eldoren; they, along with the king, would decide my fate. If Eldoren refused to accept my claim to the throne of Illiador, then I would have nothing: no army, no kingdom, probably no life.

Even if I did manage to stay one step ahead of Morgana, what would my life be like? I would have to run and hide forever. I would never be able to have a family, as they would constantly be under threat from Morgana. This was the only way. Even if I didn't end up as queen, Morgana had to be stopped.

I entered the room slowly, dragging my feet, so I had some time to look around. The council chamber was a huge, bright room overlooking one of the inner courtyards of the palace. Benches rose in tiers on two sides where the lords of the council sat, and the king was seated on a raised platform facing me.

Lord Rothguard was there, as was the Marquis of Greystone, my father's friend. Uncle Gabriel sat next to two extremely old lords who didn't look like they could even stand, let alone hold a sword. I noticed, much to my dismay, that the Duke of Blackwater, Damien's father, was also on the council. Leticia's father, the Earl of Glenbarry, was among the gathered lords. These were the people who would decide my fate. I noticed one chair closest to the king was empty. Was that meant to be for Rafe?

Where was he? Why wasn't he here?

I stopped in front of the benches as everyone stopped talking and turned to scrutinize me. Lords Rothguard and Greystone smiled at me reassuringly. Aunt Serena told me that I didn't have to curtsey anymore. I was royalty, and no one would follow a queen who bowed to others.

"Let us proceed," said the king loudly so everyone could hear. "We are pleased you are alive, Princess Aurora. And Eldoren would like to offer you our support against the forces of Morgana."

The Duke of Blackwater stood up. "If I may, Your Majesty," he said, in a soft, slimy voice. "How can we be sure that this person is indeed the Princess Aurora? Last I heard, Morgana massacred the whole family and all of Azaren's friends and supporters. She could be a shapeshifter sent by Morgana herself to find out our plans. She may even be an assassin, Your Majesty."

I snorted very inelegantly at this. "Assassin, oh please!"

Uncle Gabriel, who had remained quiet until now, stood up. "I have inspected her myself, Devon," he said to the Duke of Blackwater, "but if you are not satisfied with my word, would you like the princess to remove her amulet and show you who she really is?"

The Duke of Blackwater didn't look too pleased at his answer. "You saw what she did to my son in Evolon," he said, pointing his bony finger at me. "She is a monster and should be locked up."

"It was a mistake," I said, interrupting. "I didn't mean to hurt him."

The Duke of Blackwater ignored me. "All we know for sure is that she is a rogue fae-mage and wears the amulet of Auraken," he said, glaring at Uncle Gabriel. "That doesn't prove that she is Azaren's daughter."

I wiped my sweaty hands discreetly on my dress. I was getting worried. What if they refused to support me because of what I had done? After all, Damien was from an important noble family, and now it looked like many people were actually scared of me. I wanted to be liked, not feared, and I didn't particularly like being called a monster. But I figured no one wanted an episode like what had happened at the test in Evolon. Everyone had now heard about it, and the whole city was abuzz with the news that I was alive and well and here at the palace.

"Well, she does look a lot like Azaren," said the king, looking at me. "And Morgana too, actually."

Suddenly the doors swung open, and Rafe sauntered in. I tried to look away, but I lost that battle quickly. He was dressed casually in tight breeches and high leather boots; his sword hung from his belt at his side. He was wearing a sleeveless leather doublet belted over a white shirt with the cuffs rolled up. His shirt was open at the neck, and he looked heartbreakingly handsome.

"Good morning, Father," Rafe said as he nodded to Uncle Gabriel and took his place beside the king. He looked at me as he sat down; for a second our eyes locked, and I quickly looked away.

"Where have you been? The council meeting started a while ago," said the king to his seemingly wayward son, going red in the face. "And what are you wearing? Have I not made it a rule that you must dress formally for council meetings?"

"I was detained, Father," said Rafe casually. "I did not have the time to change."

The king didn't look pleased, but he knew this was not the time or place to fight with his son, so he looked away.

"Now, where were we?" said the king. "Ah yes, Princess Aurora is to be given the full support of the council and its combined forces. If and when Morgana attacks, we must be ready. I want all of your troops prepared for an invasion; every last soldier must be alert. Professor Dekela has assured us of the support of Evolon and all his warrior-mages as well as the healers."

The Duke of Blackwater, realizing that his objections had been dismissed, quickly sat back down in his chair.

"If I may, Your Majesty?" piped in the Earl of Glenbarry. "How can we be sure that the princess can control her powers? We all heard about what happened at Evolon, and I have it from a high authority that she lost control of her magic. How can we be sure this will not happen again inside the palace? It would put many innocent lives at stake, like my dear daughter—soon to be your daughter-in-law."

Rafe laughed at this. "I do not think the princess will pose a problem, Glenbarry. As long as she has the amulet on, her powers are in control. But if you feel so strongly about the safety of your dear daughter, maybe you should let her stay at Glenbarry House in the city instead of here at the palace," he said.

"No, no, Your Highness," said the pompous Earl of Glenbarry, sitting back down in his seat. "I am sure you will see to it that my dear Leticia will be safe."

Rafe did not answer and chose to ignore his soon to be father-in-law.

"But what if she decides to take the amulet off again?" said one feeble old lord with a long white beard and a balding head, who looked like he had just woken from his slumber. "There are many who now fear her, and many who feel that she should not be here in the palace, at least until she has mastered the use of all her powers."

"Are you afraid of a seventeen-year-old girl, Lenard?" said Uncle Gabriel, addressing the old lord and getting up from his seat.

"No, no, of course not," sputtered the old lord, "but there are many who . . . "

"Your Majesty!" said Uncle Gabriel, ignoring the old lord and turning to face the king. "Princess Aurora will not be a threat in the least. You have my word."

"And that is quite enough, as far as I am concerned," grinned the king, as he adjusted the heavy crown resting precariously on his head.

"Thank you, Your Majesty," said Duke Gabriel, giving the king a short bow.

"Well, if that is it, we have many other things to discuss with the council," said the king. "Aurora, you may leave. You are free to do as you wish; stay within the palace grounds and you will be safe."

I nodded and withdrew from the room. They didn't even let me get a word in. But I preferred to keep to myself for now. There was no need to tell them what I was thinking. I decided to just let them think that I was meek and easily moldable. When the time was right, I would show them who I really was, and God help anyone who tried to stand in my way.

I wandered around a bit and walked through the tiered gardens of the Summer Palace, down flowering paths and mossy steps, to the very edge of the white cliffs that plunged like huge white walls into the sapphire depths of the Stardust Sea.

I inhaled deeply. The smell of the salt air and sea wind took me back to happier times when my adoptive parents would take me on holidays to a little shack we had on the seaside. When I thought of them, my heart still ached from my loss. They may not have been my real parents, but they loved me like a daughter, and frankly they were the only parents I had ever known.

Now that life seemed so far away, almost like a dream. I had finally accepted that Avalonia was my home and Illiador was my birthright. My aunt had stolen it and betrayed my parents in a horrible act of treason, and now it was up to me to see that my parents' legacy did not die with them. I was going to be seventeen in a few days, and it was time I grew up and faced my responsibilities. It was up to me now to do what was expected of me, to do my duty, and to do what was right.

I sighed and turned to leave, when strong arms gently enveloped me from behind. I was momentarily startled, but I didn't have to turn around to know who it was. I would know him anywhere.

Rafe leaned forward and brushed my cheek with a soft kiss. I didn't pull away, even though I wanted to. Just being in his arms again made me feel like everything was right with the world. I couldn't understand the connection between us. I didn't want to feel this way, because I knew it would ultimately lead to heartbreak, mainly mine. But I couldn't help it. I was in love with him, and nothing he said was going to change that.

I leaned back on his broad chest and rested my cheek on his arm. We stood like that for a few minutes, not saying anything, just looking out at the vast sea.

Finally Rafe broke the silence.

"I am sorry about last night," he said gently, and sincerely. "I shouldn't have left you in the gardens and walked off."

"It's all right," I said, still not looking at him. "It's better this way anyway. You and I can never be together. In a few days, I will be going to Elfi, you will get married, and we will probably never see each other again."

He turned me around to face him. "I wish I could change the way things are, but I cannot. Do you have any idea how many nights I have thought of you and wished that our circumstances were different?" he said seriously, looking me straight in the eyes. "I have tried to stay away from you, but I can't. I even went away for a while, hoping that I would be able to forget about you, but all I could think about when I was gone was when I would see you again."

I hugged him and rested my head on his chest. His strong arms wrapped me in their warmth, and I closed my eyes and wished that Rafe and I could be together always.

"It was just not meant to be," I whispered, choking on the words as I said them.

His embrace tightened as he gathered me closer to him, kissed me on the head, and smoothed my hair.

"I don't believe that," was all he said.

He let go of me and held out his hand. "Come," he said gently, as I intertwined my fingers through his, "I will walk you back to your room."

"Thank you," I said, "but I had a pair of guards following me around. I don't know where they went." I looked around. The scruffy guards had miraculously disappeared.

"I sent them away when I came to see you," Rafe grinned.

"I thought you would still be at the council meeting," I said.

"I will find out what I need to know when I speak with your granduncle later today," said Rafe, shrugging.

"So Uncle Gabriel knows who you really are?" I asked, quietly glancing around to make sure no one heard me.

Rafe nodded. "He knows the real identity of the Black Wolf, yes."

"Why does your father think you are running around in brothels and taverns and wasting your life away?"

Rafe laughed. He came closer and spoke softly. "My father had refused to send an army to help the fae against Morgana, so I do what I can for the ones who are left in Illiador."

"Then why are you letting him and the rest of the court think you are some wastrel, spoiled prince with too much time on his hands?" I asked, because it upset me whenever anyone spoke badly about him.

Rafe winced at that. "Is that what they are saying about me?" he said as we walked into the palace through the east wing entrance to the gardens. I followed him down a long gallery lined with gold-framed portraits of the kings of old. He still held onto my hand, and I didn't want to let go.

"Yes," I said, looking at one particularly large king who appeared too big to fit on the throne. "And what's more, some think that after the king, you will be too weak to rule this kingdom, and the Blackwaters will take over."

Rafe laughed out loud at that. "Just let them try," was all he said with a twinkle in his eyes.

"So why don't you tell them what you're doing?" I said.

"And go openly against my father's wishes?" he said, shaking his head. "People would see that as dissension in the family. My father does not want to break the treaty and send troops into Illiador. Morgana may see it as an act of war. No! It's better they all think of me as a rich prince with a head full of fluff and no ambition. It will serve me better for now. The Blackwaters will never see me coming."

He led me to my room and hugged me close. "I will see you tomorrow," he said gently.

I nodded, and Rafe left.

I sighed, opened the door to my room, and went inside. It was no use thinking about Rafe again and again. There was no hope and no future for us. If I continued like this, I would never be able to wipe him from my mind. But I loved spending time with him, and I just couldn't seem to stay away. My heart yearned for him, but soon I would leave for Elfi, and maybe it would get easier. Although, from the constant ache in my heart, I wasn't entirely sure I would ever get over him.

I was so engrossed in my world of Rafe that, at first, I didn't notice that all the candles except one had gone out. Someone had left the window open, and a chilly wind was blowing the curtains astray. I went over and closed the widows before my last candle blew out. I looked at the woods beyond my window. Twilight was setting in, and dark shadows seemed to have entered my room.

I whirled around as I saw something move from the corner of my eye.

"Who's there?" I called out.

But there was no answer, only silence and the elevated beat of my heart. My breath caught in my chest as shadows started moving towards me from the corners of the darkened room. I opened my mouth to scream, but nothing came out. I was rooted to the spot, and a cold dread washed over me as I saw what the shadows were. My skin prickled, and a deep, clawing dread ripped my courage to shards. The Shadow Guard! Here in the palace? How did they get in?

I knew powerful magical wards sealed the palace from intruders, so they had to have been let in. But who would put the whole palace at risk? Then a smaller shadow walked out of the darkness, her hair sparkling in the candlelight in golden hues.

Leticia!

"Hello, Princess Aurora." She said it with so much venom in her voice that I was taken aback.

"You!" I said, my voice cracking. "You are the one who betrayed me."

"In order to betray you, we would first have to be friends," said Leticia meanly, "and that was not possible with you having your beady little eyes on my prince. Take her away." She gestured haughtily, as if she were already queen.

"But how did you remove the magical wards protecting the palace?" I asked, in the midst of my panic. "You have no magic."

Leticia sneered at me. "I have friends," she said, her voice dripping acid.

Another shadow dislocated itself from the darkness. Damien!

"You!" I said glaring at him. "You were the one who let them in."

Damien just grinned evilly at me; he seemed completely healed. "Bind her wrists," he said to the Shadow Guard. "Don't let her take her amulet off, it is what is suppressing her powers."

I gathered my magic and shot a stun strike at a Shadow Guard, but he easily put up a shield to deflect it. Another guard caught me from behind and bound my hands. There was nothing I could do; I was trapped.

"You will not get away with this, Leticia," I said, sounding more confident than I felt.

"Oh, I think I already did," said Leticia, cackling, as the Shadow Guard bound and gagged me.

"I told you I would get back at you," said Damien, finally amassing the courage to come closer to me once my hands were bound. I always knew he was a coward. "My uncle, the archmage, will be so proud of me once he knows I am the one who delivered you to his queen."

I tried to cry out, but the gag was cutting the sides of my

mouth.

Suddenly, a dark shadow descended onto the room. I turned towards the window to see a monstrous shape with obsidian black wings and razor-sharp claws perched on the windowsill. A Gorgoth. I had heard of them but had never seen one before. My eyes widened in fright. Were they going to feed me to that thing? Its face was a contorted mix of man and bat, and its red eyes glowed like hot coals.

"Queen Morgana is waiting for you, Princess," rasped the guard who was holding me. "She wants to deal with you personally this time."

Two guards clasped my arms and pulled me towards the window. I kicked and screamed but to no avail. The Gorgoth caught me in its razor-sharp claws and lifted me up like a leaf. Its great leathery wings beat the air as it pounced off the window ledge, holding me roughly in its talons. It flew me swiftly up into the darkening sky, towards Morgana and my impending doom.

27
MORGANA

I LAY ON the cold stone floor of the dungeons at the ruins of Tinerea Castle. I had heard the guards talking and discovered that we were up in the hills, far away from the city of Neris. The Gorgoth was gone. It had dropped me in the ruins, and the Shadow Guard were there to capture me again.

I sat up and looked around me. It was a dark and horrific place with chains and manacles fastened to the walls. Dust and cobwebs hadn't been disturbed for years, and, above all else, there was an eerie silence. I had an inkling that I was the only prisoner here.

I had learned in my ancient history class that, according to legend, this castle was haunted, so no one ever came here. It had been destroyed, along with a mage who had turned to dark magic.

I couldn't believe I had come full circle—back in the dungeons, tied, trapped, and waiting to be taken to Morgana.

I was so angry with Leticia and her sly attempt to get me out of the way. I should have known she would do something like this; she'd made it very clear she hated me. It was clever of her to go to Damien for help; she must have known how much he hated me too.

I heard a click at the door. I panicked. Had they come to get me? Had Morgana arrived? The guards opened the door, and another prisoner was roughly shoved inside. The door banged shut, and I could only roughly make out the figure that was standing before me. But then, in the darkness, I heard a familiar voice.

"Sorry I took so long, Princess."

"Kalen!" I whispered. "How did you get caught? Why did you come here?"

"I followed you, and I was looking around when the Shadow Guard caught me," said Kalen, smiling and looking very pleased with himself. "They brought me straight to you."

Was Kalen mad, risking his life like this?

"Morgana is on her way here. She will kill you if she finds you here. You must go, please," I said fervently.

"I'm not leaving without you," he said plainly.

"How did you get here so fast?" I asked, trying to think of a way to get him out of here. I had resigned myself to the fact that, this time, there was no hope of escape. The Shadow Guard were everywhere, and they had said that Morgana was on her way herself.

"Snow," he said. "I was in the stables, and Snow suddenly started going mad, banging her stall, and trying to get out. I got onto her somehow; she was so distressed that she didn't seem to mind. I freed her, and she flew me here."

"Snow is here?" I said, hope rising in my heart.

Kalen nodded. "I also alerted your granduncle, and hope-fully he is on his way. I flew on ahead. I need to get you out of these ruins before Morgana arrives."

"How?" I said pessimistically. "There is no way out. The Shadow Guard are everywhere." I hoped Uncle Gabriel would find me in time. I couldn't live with myself if I got Kalen killed because he was dragged into my mess. "Where is Snow?"

"She is circling the castle," said Kalen. "I don't think the guards saw her. If we can just get to her, maybe we can escape."

The door to the dungeon opened suddenly, and four black-robed Shadow Guard came in.

"Make sure her hands are secure," one guard with a raspy voice said. "Do not let her remove the amulet."

Two Shadow Guard grabbed me, and the other two grabbed Kalen. We both struggled, but they were strong, and I could feel evil magic radiating from them. They checked my hands to see if they were still tied. Even with my hands bound behind my back, the Shadow Guard had their magi-cal shields up, as if I might suddenly break loose and kill all of them.

I hadn't forgotten about the amulet, but how to take it off? All this time it had been round my neck, and now it seemed it would be the thing that got me killed. I had no idea what would happen if I did ever get to remove the amulet again. I remembered the rush of power and the overwhelming fear of helplessness when I couldn't control my magic. But now I didn't even have the option to choose; my hands were tied, and so were Kalen's.

We were dragged up an old, crumbling stone stairwell covered in vines and wild, gnarled creepers that invaded the stone walls and clung to them like parasites, and into the moss-covered ruins of the old castle. Parts of the castle had completely caved in, and moonlight streamed into the rooms, lighting up the usually dark stone corridors.

We were led into an open courtyard, surrounded on three sides by the crumbling ruins of the castle and leading to a sheer drop down the side of a mountain crag upon which the castle had been built.

I looked over to the end of the courtyard, amongst the dilapidated ruins and fallen stones. There, at the edge of the cliff, the wind whipping at her dark, glossy hair that flowed about her shoulders and bled into the blackness of her robes, stood the usurper, my aunt and archnemesis, Morgana.

I was pulled forward, stumbling across the moss-and-weed-covered floor of the crumbling castle.

One of the Shadow Guard hit Kalen on his shoulders and pushed him to the ground "Kneel before the High Queen of Avalonia, you worthless fae," he sneered.

Kalen fell to his knees.

The Shadow Guard behind me did the same thing, and

pain shot through my shoulders and knees as I was roughly shoved to the ground at Morgana's feet.

"So!" said Morgana, her green eyes flashing and staring at me as if I was a little bug. "Azaren's little whelp. Did you think you could run from me forever?"

I pushed myself off the ground and got to my feet, but Morgana backhanded me, and two Shadow Guard pushed me down again. I felt something wet on my chin; my lip was bleeding, and I tried to wipe it on my sleeve, but it was difficult with my hands tied behind me.

"You will kneel before your queen, you insolent wench," said the Shadow Guard behind me.

"And so will your little fae friend," Morgana said, looking over at Kalen and then back at me. "Did he think he would, what, help you escape again? I know the fae were involved in the escape at Oblek's castle. Well, this time you will not be so lucky. I will make you watch as we kill your little friend slowly."

"Let him go," I said, sounding much braver than I felt. "He has no part in this. You wanted me, and now you have me. Kalen has nothing to do with it."

"No," said Kalen, struggling with his jailers. "You won't get away with this, Morgana, the Duke of Silverthorne is on his way here as we speak. He will destroy you if you hurt her."

Morgana laughed. "Silverthorne is a doddering old fool," she said. "His powers are no match for me. I look forward to his arrival. But, as long as my brother's heir lives, my claim to the throne will always be weak. The girl must die, for there can only be one Queen of Illiador."

As she said that, she raised her right hand and hit me with a push strike so forceful that I flew a few feet. I hit my head on the wall and scraped my back. I could feel blood trickling down my neck from the gash on my head. My head was throbbing, and I could barely see straight. Kalen cried out and tried to get to me, but the Shadow Guard swarmed around him and held him back. One guard held a knife to his throat.

My head was swimming, and I was dazed. I instinctively put up a hasty shield around myself. Then I went about healing myself from the inside. I knew my mage powers were not enough, so I pulled magic from the earth, mending the gash on my head, as I had done before in my healing test.

I looked over to the other side of the courtyard. Four Shadow Guards were pulling a struggling Snow. She was tied with coarse ropes, and even her wings were bound so she couldn't fly off. She was covered in terrible, red cuts all over her beautiful, white wings. I was horrified. What had they done to her?

"Snow," I whispered faintly in my mind. "What have they done?"

"I am all right, little one," said Snow, "do not be afraid. I am much stronger than you think. Concentrate on Morgana. Never take your eyes off her."

My hands were still tied, so I couldn't even get up properly. I managed to maneuver myself off the ground and tried to stand up on my now very shaky feet.

"Very impressive," said Morgana, her hands on her hips. "I can see your power is strong, little princess, even with the amulet on. But you are no match for me."

I knew I was going to die; there was no way out. My palms were sweating, and I was shaking. I had to pull myself together. If I could create some diversion, maybe Kalen could escape. I knew there was no hope for me.

"Looks like you have your father's foolish courage, Niece," Morgana said scathingly. "But that will not help you now."

With the amulet on and my hands bound, I was no match for her, and she knew it. It was then I realized that Morgana was a coward, and she was afraid of me, afraid of my powers. I quickly put up a stronger shield. I would die fighting, not quivering in the corner like a weakling. At least I didn't need my hands to shield myself.

Morgana laughed and hit me with fire strikes that bounced off my shield, but they were strong. Her strikes kept pushing me back, and she was advancing upon me slowly. I knew she was toying with me, and I reinforced my shield. My power was waning, and Morgana was hitting me with alternate lightning and fire strikes.

I concentrated all my power on keeping my shield intact. I kept telling myself that I would not let her kill me with magic; I would not let her beat me. But all that was useless.

She just kept coming at me. Beads of sweat had started forming on my forehead, my heart was racing, my palms were clammy, and I could feel raw terror welling up inside me. I didn't have enough power to stop her. Morgana was going to kill me, and there was nothing I could do about it.

"You are brave, little princess," Morgana said as she hit me with another lightning strike. It broke my shield and hit my left leg.

I fell to the ground on my knees in pain.

"Yes," said Morgana, "kneel before your queen." She cackled.

A wind had picked up, and Morgana's hair whipped around her face as she held up her hands, palms facing outwards, to deliver another blow. She struck me with a fire strike that burst through my shield and burned my arm and leg, but it was not a killing strike. She was still toying with me. I screamed in agony and fell face forward onto the hard, moss-covered floor. My nose was bleeding, and shooting pain ripped through my left arm and leg.

"It is unfortunate that you got away from me the first time, Aurora," said my aunt with a sneer. This was the first time she had called me by my name. "Your mother used up the last of her powers to stop me from getting to you."

She hit me with another burning fire strike while I was on the ground, and fresh pain shot through my body again.

"It was she who made the portal and sent you away to the other world," Morgana went on. "If you were not wearing that cursed amulet, I would have found you much sooner."

I barely had any strength left. I tried to heal myself, but only a flicker of magic now remained in me.

I maneuvered myself to my knees, blood streaming from my nose and leg. My arm was burning, and I pulled at the magic around me to try and create some semblance of a shield. I could feel the magic surrounding me, but however much I tried to pull it into me, it wasn't enough.

"I stabbed your mother through the heart myself," cackled Morgana. "And it took nearly ten Drakaar assassins to kill your father. But he was finally cut down as he tried desperately to save you both. If your mother's power weren't concentrated on trying to save you, she could have saved herself and him."

Morgana hit me with a crushing strike. I screamed in agony and would have clutched my chest if I could, but my hands were still bound behind my back.

This was too much. I couldn't bear it anymore. I could picture my mother giving her life to save her only child, and my father, who must have tried to save his family only to be cut down by dark magic. My dream flashed in my mind. I could see my mother standing still, eyes flashing silver, protecting me with her magic as Morgana came at her with the curved dagger.

Morgana was the one who had destroyed my life. She was the cause of all my pain, and she was the one who took my parents from me and destroyed my family. She was a monster, evil to the core, and she had to be stopped.

This thought gave me strength to fight on. I faintly heard Kalen's voice calling my name. I tried to get up, but I was hit with another lightning strike that shattered my shield and left me writhing on the floor in excruciating pain.

Morgana was laughing at me. "Yes, get up, Fae-Mage," she goaded, "show me what you've got."

The Shadow Guard were also laughing, while Snow called my name in my head. I barely heard them. I had had enough. I shut out the voices, the fear, and the terror that were invading my mind and looked inside myself, to the safe place where the source of my power lay. A faint light was still flickering and struggling to stay alight.

I tried to sense the magic around me, but I had no strength to pull it to me. I couldn't even remove my amulet. But I had to do something. I couldn't just give up and die. People were depending on me. And, for the first time in my life, I felt a sense of responsibility. I was no ordinary person. I was the true Queen of Illiador. I was a fae- mage with unlimited power. But where was that power now?

I closed my eyes and silently called out for help. I had no idea if there was even anyone to hear me. Imagine my surprise when I actually got an answer.

My eyes snapped open. It wasn't Snow. I would recognize her voice anywhere. I had no idea who it was, but this voice was deep and distinctly male, and a sense of calm washed over me as I listened.

"Rise, Aurora," said the voice that only I could hear. "You are a fae-mage. The amulet doesn't control you; you control the amulet."

I tried to make some sense of this in my already fuzzy mind. "What do you mean?" I asked the voice, still trying to push myself up from the floor. "My hands are bound. I couldn't take off my amulet if I wanted to."

I had long since ceased to be surprised by mind communication, and this voice seemed to know what it was talking about.

"Your powers are different from others. You can do what no one else can," said the voice. "You don't need your hands for magic. It is your mind, your will, and your innermost soul that control your power. Imagine the amulet disappearing from your neck and put it somewhere else."

"How?" I asked quickly.

"Do not try to pull the magic to you," said the deep voice. "Open yourself to the power around you, and you will see what I mean."

I pushed myself to my feet with all the energy I could muster.

Morgana looked at me with her eyebrows raised. "Back for more, little niece?" she said, grinning manically.

But I ignored Morgana and concentrated on the deep voice that was speaking only to me.

"Imagine the amulet has disappeared from your neck. Push all your magic and your will into that thought," said the voice.

I did as I was told; I gathered my magic and pushed my will into imagining the amulet disappearing. Nothing happened, and I tried again.

"Who are you?" I asked silently, but the voice was gone, and I got no answer.

Morgana hit me with a fire strike. The pain was excruciating, and my skin was burnt all over. Angry, red welts had formed on my arms and legs. I was in agony, but I concentrated harder. I calmed my mind and imagined the amulet gone from my neck. I pushed the last of my magic into that thought.

I glanced at Morgana, who was now raising her hands and gathering all her magic to deliver the final blow, the magical strike that would kill me instantly. But I didn't break my concentration. I held the thought firmly in my mind and braced myself for whatever Morgana had in store for me.

Suddenly, much to my utter astonishment, the chain around my neck started to get hot, as if it was resisting my magic. It vibrated faintly, but finally my magic held out, and the amulet disappeared from around my neck.

It was like a veil had been lifted from my magic. I quickly drew my shield around me and searched outside myself for fae magic. I was not surprised this time to find the power that lay around me just waiting to be tapped. I gradually opened myself to it, careful not to force it. Magic started flowing into me in gentle waves, filling me with power and strengthening my shield. Morgana raised her hands to deliver the final blow. Lightning was sizzling in her palms. I opened myself wider to the magic surrounding me. Power filled my senses, and my shield grew in strength.

Morgana hit me with a powerful lightning strike, which would have killed any who stood before it. But my shield was resilient, and it was still growing.

Morgana looked surprised for the first time. "How is this possible?" she said faintly, more to herself than anyone else. She looked furious, and she shot numerous fire and lightning strikes at me. Morgana was powerful, but her magic didn't even shake my shield.

In the same way as I had done with the amulet, I imagined my ropes gone. They immediately disappeared, and my hands were free.

"No, no, no," Morgana screamed. "This is impossible. I was watching you. You never removed the amulet. How did you free your hands?"

I shrugged, offering her no more explanation.

Morgana had her shield up, and I lashed out at her, shattering her shield and hitting my aunt with a powerful push strike. She flew backwards and landed in a heap against a crumbling stone wall. Morgana shrank back under a hastily constructed shield.

I could see from the look on her face that she was getting worried, and my power was still growing. Magic was seeping into my very pores, flowing into me in waves of potent power. My feet left the ground. I could feel the magic all around me, lifting me up, and it was all mine to command.

"No, no, this is not possible," Morgana kept saying, over and over again. "You were wearing the Amulet of Auraken. It is impossible."

"Nothing is impossible," I said without emotion, advancing on her slowly, a ball of silver fire growing steadily in my palm.

"Kill her, kill them, kill them all!" screeched Morgana to the Shadow Guard as she scrambled backwards and away from me.

I turned from Morgana for the briefest of seconds to see Kalen being hit on the head by one of the guards. He fell to the ground in a crumpled heap. I looked on, horrified, as another Shadow Guard slit Snow's neck.

Fresh, crimson blood streamed down the pegasus's beautiful white mane and coat, and she collapsed onto the moss-covered floor of the ruined castle, the life slowly draining out of her.

"Nooo," I screamed in terror, and moved to run towards them.

In the split second that I was distracted, Morgana took the opportunity to disappear.

I was left alone with the Shadow Guard, who had slowly started advancing on me. There were more than twenty of them, but now, suddenly, I had no fear. I had faced my greatest enemy, Morgana, and won.

My mind shut off the rising tide of despair that was grow-
ing inside me. All I wanted to do was to get the Shadow
Guard out of the way so I could attempt to heal Kalen and
Snow, if they were still alive.

I gathered all the power swirling within me. Waves of
shining white light were coursing through my veins, and I
lashed out at the Shadow Guard with all the magic I could
muster. Silver fire exploded out of my palms and struck two
of them, the ones who had slit Snow's neck. They screamed,
and the acrid smell of burning flesh stung my nostrils. I
watched, a little horrified at what I was capable of, as two of
the Shadow Guard were enveloped in sheets of blazing silver
fire.

Immediately my shield was bombarded with red bolts of
energy, and I was momentarily pushed back. I turned to the
rest of the Shadow Guard, who had now started advancing
on me.

I strengthened my shield and moved towards the Shadow
Guard. They may have been men once, but the dark magic
that they practiced had changed their features. Soulless eyes,
black as night, and white, skeletal skin barely covered the
last vestiges of humanity that they had left.

The Shadow Guard were relentless and powerful, but
with my amulet now gone, my shield was slowly becoming impenetrable. Strikes of red energy blasted at me and
bounced away.

I looked down. My feet were inches from the ground. I

could feel the magic in the air all around me, helping me. I was now completely surrounded by the Shadow Guard, who were trying to get through my shield.

I was filled with an overwhelming need for revenge for what had been done to Snow and Kalen. I gathered my power, letting the fae magic flow into me, fueling my mage power and strengthening it. The lingering Shadow Guards shrieked in terror when I unleashed the full intensity of my powers and struck them down with wave after wave of silver fire until there was nothing left around me except smoke and ashes.

28
RETURN OF THE
DARK QUEEN

I RAN OVER and checked Kalen's pulse. It was faint, but he would live. Snow, on the other hand, looked like she had breathed her last. I left Kalen and knelt down next to Snow, tears streaming down my face as I held her lifeless head in my arms. She had no pulse, and there was so much blood. What was the use of all my powers if I couldn't save the ones I loved?

I buried my face in her mane and wept. My mind was trying to go over everything I had learned in healing class. I had to try and do something; maybe she wasn't completely gone.

I put my hand over the gash on her throat and proceeded to try to heal her. I opened myself to the power around me and channeled it into Snow. She was still lifeless, and I concentrated harder, searching around in her body, concentrating on trying to find some sort of life to start the healing. After an agonizing few moments of frantic examining, I found it, a faint flicker of white light. It was like a silk thread, so fine that I had to strain to catch it.

I concentrated harder and pushed more magic into Snow. My hands had now started glowing, and slowly whatever I was doing started working. Veins began mending themselves, muscle and tendons regrowing. Bit by agonizing bit, Snow's neck began to heal.

Suddenly the deep voice in my head spoke, and this time it was even more urgent. "Stop this, Aurora. It is forbidden."

I stopped, but only for a moment. I then continued my healing as I spoke. "Why should I? If I can use my powers to heal her, why shouldn't I try?"

"The pegasus is on the threshold to the otherworld. If you bring her back now, and I am not sure that even your powers are strong enough to accomplish this task, there will be a price to pay," said the voice sternly.

"I don't care," I said stubbornly, refusing to listen. "If I can somehow heal Snow and bring her back, whatever the cost is, I will do it."

"Then let it be so!" said the deep rumbling voice. "But you have been warned, Princess Aurora. This kind of magic always demands consequences."

"I will deal with it when the time comes," I said, determined not to let Snow die.

The voice was silent again. I turned my concentration back to what I was doing. My magic was slowly starting to heal Snow's neck, and now the last bits of tendon, muscle, and skin were reforming. I pushed more healing power into Snow, and her eyelids fluttered. I sagged with relief and decided it was all worth it when Snow opened her eyes, got up, and shook her beautiful white mane.

"Thank you, Princess," she said simply. "But I fear you don't fully understand the magnitude of what you have just done. The magic you performed here has never been performed before. Even Auraken Firedrake has never been able to successfully bring someone back from the otherworld."

I laughed with joy, and happy tears rolled down my face. I didn't care. I had done it. Morgana was gone, and Snow was alive.

"What have you done?" said Kalen, horrified, scrambling over the stone courtyard towards me.

I looked up at his terrified face.

"This is dark magic, Princess," he said, shaking his head, "and all dark magic comes at a cost."

"Whatever the price, it will be worth it," I said stubbornly again, but I was relieved that he was all right.

I didn't want to think about the consequences just yet. It was done now, and I couldn't take it back. Whatever happened, I hoped I would be able to live with myself. Even the mysterious voice in my head had warned me about using my magic like this.

Suddenly the ruins were filled with voices and lights from wooden torches.

"Aurora," said Rafe, as he rushed over to me, closing the distance between us in a few huge strides. He pulled me towards him, and I let myself melt into the safety of his arms and rest my head upon his chest.

"Are you all right?" he said, gently kissing the top of my head and smoothing my hair.

"Sort of," I mumbled and nodded into his chest. I had only now begun to feel my injuries, and parts of me were still numb.

"I don't know what I would have done if anything had happened to you," he said, his voice rough and strained with emotion.

"I'm fine," I said, looking up at him.

Suddenly there was a flash of lightning, and a dark form arose in the middle of the courtyard. I looked on in horror as the shadow moved slowly towards us. A hideous creature that was unmistakably a woman with blazing red eyes and a tattered black robe was floating a few feet off the ground. It was more wraith and shadow than any real form. Rafe moved instinctively in front of me, shielding me from whatever that thing was.

The wraith spoke, its voice a rasp. "Finally you have released me from my prison, young fae-mage."

"Who are you?" I whispered.

"Lilith!" said Uncle Gabriel in a barely audible whisper as he came to stand beside me. He was looking at the wraith with a horrified look on his aging face.

"Yes, Gabriel," said the shadow wraith.

"But how?" Uncle Gabriel asked. I had never seen him look so upset. "Azaren killed you."

The creature Uncle Gabriel called Lilith spoke, its voice like nails screeching against a blackboard. "When the pegasus was brought back from the threshold of the otherworld, the fae-mage inadvertently opened a portal for me to come through. I have been waiting for this for a long, long time," it said.

Suddenly, the wraith screeched and flew at me, trapping me within shadows that clasped around my throat. I fell backwards, hitting my head on the stone floor. I thrashed and kicked, struggling to breathe, as I could slowly feel the life draining out of me. It was like a huge crushing weight was sitting on my chest, and rotting shadows pressed at my throat.

"Heir of Azaren," rasped the specter, "you shall pay for the crimes of your father."

Uncle Gabriel and Rafe were watching with terrified looks on their faces. From the corner of my eye, I could see Rafe moving forward to help me, hands raised to attack Lilith.

"No, Rafe!" I heard Uncle Gabriel call out. "Do not strike the wraith. You could harm Aurora instead. Lilith is made of shadows; your magic will only pass through her. Aurora must do this herself."

I had not come so far only to die here today. My mother had died for me so that I would be safe. My father had defeated this thing once, and I was more powerful than my father ever was. So I concentrated hard, blocking out all sensations, even the feeling of not being able to breathe. Slowly,

I opened myself to the magic around me and let it flow into me.

The white light within me started to glow and move outwards, creating a shield around me. I concentrated on pushing it outwards from the center of my chest. White light coursed through my veins, and I started glowing all over, the light of my magic piercing the shade that held me in its grip. Much to my surprise, I didn't just create a shield around me; I was the shield.

Lilith shrieked as if she was in pain, and the shadows let go of me as sheets of white light emanated from my body and pushed Lilith away from me. The dark wraith queen rose over us, hovering just out of reach.

With hollow eyes flashing the color of blood and shadows swirling, it spoke again. "Your power is very strong, young fae-mage, but once I have regained my body, not even you will be able to stand in my way," Lilith shrieked and flew away in a haze of darkness and shadows.

My shoulders slumped as my light dimmed. I searched my pockets, and, finding my amulet, I put it back on. The light went out.

Rafe came and put his arm gently around my waist, helping me to my feet. "Come, my love, let me take you home," he said simply.

Rafe gathered me up in his arms and gently put me onto his horse sidesaddle. He jumped up behind me and held me in his arms the whole way back to the Summer Palace in silence.

At some point I must have fallen asleep in the saddle, and I soon found myself resting on a soft bed in my room at the palace. I had no idea how long I had slept. Penelope had healed all my injuries, but I was still aching all over, and the burned skin would take a few days to heal completely. But, for all intents and purposes, I was fine and, most importantly, still alive.

I had a bevy of visitors in my room, from Kalen and his incessant chattering, to the king, who came to tell me he was pleased that I was still alive. Kalen was hovering around the whole day, and Penelope had to keep sending him away, saying that I needed to rest.

Rafe never came to see me, but Vivienne did.

She came into the room in a bustle of green silk skirts and promptly hugged me. "How could you not tell me any of this?" she said, settling herself beside me on the bed. "I could have helped, you know."

"You're not angry with me?" I asked tentatively. I was relieved; at least I still had my best friend.

"I was," said Vivienne, pouting her lips, "but only because you didn't tell me. You are my best friend. I don't care that you're a princess and a fae-mage who can kill me with a simple swipe of your hand. Although my mother thinks you might murder me in my sleep."

We both fell into a fit of giggles, and I hugged Vivienne again. It was good to have her here and finally know the whole truth.

"So is it true that you killed Morgana's whole Shadow Guard all by yourself?" asked Vivienne, wide-eyed.

I nodded faintly and silently cringed. I was not proud of what I had become, someone who everybody feared.

"That is nothing short of amazing," said Vivienne. "It was thought that the Shadow Guard could never be defeated. They have been terrorizing the people ever since Morgana came to power. This news has already spread throughout the kingdom. They are calling you Avalonia's Savior."

I didn't want to be a savior. I had so much to learn, and everything seemed so hard and complicated. The road ahead didn't look like an easy one. I may have defeated Morgana, but she escaped, and now, with Lilith on the loose, I had no idea how to proceed.

Vivienne's voice snapped me out of my reverie.

"I saw the prince hovering outside your door a while ago," she said, leaning in closer.

"He was?" I said, trying my best not to smile.

Vivienne nodded. "What else are you not telling me, Aurora?" she said, her voice becoming sterner.

I always thought that she would make a good professor; she always made me feel like a child. She was right most of the time, but I didn't want to think about that now. I looked away, but only for a second. How did she know? Was I that obvious?

"It's nothing," I said finally. "The prince is a friend, and he's going to be married soon, anyway."

I sounded so lame, even to myself. And Vivienne didn't believe me for a moment. She raised her eyebrows at me in a perfect impression of Professor Dekela.

"Everyone is talking about how the prince was looking at you the night of the harvest ball," said Vivienne, grinning now. "Apparently the prince never dances with anyone. Leticia was so angry, she looked like she was going to self-combust."

I shrugged, but I was grinning inside.

"The prince only had eyes for you. Apparently Leticia is going crazy and taking it out on everyone around her."

"But he's going to marry her anyway," I blurted out. "He kissed me, and then he told me he was still going to marry her."

"You kissed the prince?" said Vivienne, wide-eyed.

I nodded and finally broke; I told her everything, even about who he really was.

"Prince Rafael is the Black Wolf," she said, in a stunned whisper.

"Shhh," I said, sounding like Kalen. "You can't tell anyone. Don't even say his name in the same sentence, you understand?"

"Okay, okay, I won't. I promise," said Vivienne quickly. "You can trust me, Rory. I mean Aurora."

I smiled. It would take Vivienne some time to get used to using my real name.

"So," Vivienne said, making herself more comfortable on my bed. "Tell me everything."

We talked late into the night, and it was good to have someone to talk to again. Kalen was my friend too, but he was a boy and didn't understand what I was feeling. Vivienne, on the other hand, was full of sound advice and support. I felt I could trust her. Otherwise I would never have taken the chance of telling her about Rafe's secret identity. I hoped—no, I knew—she would keep my secret.

"So, now the two of you aren't talking?" asked Vivienne.

"We are," I said quickly, "but it's no use. Leticia has her claws in him, and his vow to his mother makes it all the more hopeless."

"Sorry to say," said Vivienne, a little tartly, "his mother is dead. Can't he just break off the engagement?"

"No!" I said, shaking my head. "He won't do it."

"Then just tell him it was Leticia who was the one responsible for letting the Shadow Guard into the palace."

"I can't," I said, shaking my head again. "It's her word against mine, and Damien will side with her. Rafe will never believe me. He will think it's some sort of tactic to get him to break his engagement to Leticia."

"I think, after all you have told me," said Vivienne, after thinking for a moment, "Rafe will definitely believe you over Leticia. Ever since they brought you back, the prince hasn't left your bedside," said Vivienne, a huge smile on her face.

"Why?" I asked. I wanted her to spell it out.

"It doesn't take a fool to see that he was distraught about what had happened to you," said Vivienne. "I heard one of Leticia's ladies talking, and apparently the prince hasn't slept since you went missing three days ago."

"I've been asleep for three days?" I said, aghast. I thought I'd just had a few hours of fitful rest.

Vivienne nodded. "Yes, and he was waiting to see you when you woke up, but I suspect there were too many people about. I arrived this morning, and he was pacing outside your room. Then, when he saw me, he walked off."

I sat there in my bed and thought about what she said. Rafe may have been concerned, but I didn't believe that he hadn't slept for three nights because of me. And this time I didn't agree with Vivienne about telling Rafe about Leticia's role in the whole Morgana thing. Even if he believed me, I didn't believe that he would go back on his vow to his mother for anything. It was pointless thinking about it, and it was starting to give me a headache.

I yawned, and Vivienne jumped up from the bed.

"Oh dear, I must let you rest or Professor Plumpleberry will have my head," she said looking around.

I smiled at the vision of Penelope coming after Vivienne with a broom, or maybe a huge stack of books to study.

"Now I have to go see Mother and help her. She is having one of her boring garden parties again," said Vivienne, rolling her eyes and opening the door. "Don't get into any trouble while I am gone."

"Why does everyone keep saying that to me?" I said, making a mock grumpy face. "I can take care of myself, you know."

"I can see that," said Vivienne, good-naturedly raising one eyebrow as she left the room.

Finally Uncle Gabriel came to see me.

"I am glad to see you are feeling better, little one," he said kindly, sitting down on a chair next to my bed.

"Thank you, Uncle Gabriel," I said. "I have to tell you it was Damien who let the Shadow Guard into the palace. You must tell the king."

"I know," said Uncle Gabriel, sighing and leaning back in his chair. "The Blackwaters have fled the kingdom, by ship apparently, so we have no idea where they are."

"They're gone?" I said. "All of them?"

Uncle Gabriel nodded. "The Royal fleet is on the look-out, but I doubt that they will be found," he said. "They have now openly shown their allegiance to Morgana and Lucian."

I couldn't help a smile spreading across my bruised face. I was glad Damien and all the Blackwaters had finally shown their true colors, but the guilt over what I had done was overwhelming me, and I had to talk about it.

"I am so sorry about what I did, Uncle Gabriel," I blurted out, "but I couldn't just let Snow die. I couldn't! I had to do something. I didn't know Lilith would come back like that."

Uncle Gabriel listened to me quietly. "I think you'd better tell me everything, young lady," he said finally. "Start from the beginning, and do not leave anything out."

I recounted everything that had happened to me that horrific night. Meeting Morgana, the fear and terror I felt, the anger about what she did to my parents, the voice in my head, Snow, everything except Leticia's role in the whole thing.

I had finally decided that, since she was going to be Rafe's wife, and Rafe would never go back on his vow to his mother, even if he hated the person he was married to, I didn't want him to spend his life hating his wife because of what she did to me. Technically, it wasn't her who let the Shadow Guard into the palace; it was Damien who had the magic, and it was Damien who openly hated me. So I resolved to say nothing. In any case, Leticia without Damien and his magic was harmless. Still mean, but harmless.

Uncle Gabriel sat patiently listening to me. His face looked troubled, but he said nothing. Finally he spoke. "I understand why you did what you did, Aurora, but I hope you now realize that all actions always have consequences. And the greater your power, the greater is your duty to do the right thing."

"The voice told me there would be a price to pay," I said quietly, hanging my head in shame, "but I didn't listen."

"Yes," said Uncle Gabriel. "Now about this voice. Has it ever spoken to you before that night?"

I shook my head. "No, only when I was nearly killed by Morgana."

"Well, I am glad the voice helped you," said Uncle Gabriel. "Nevertheless, you must be very careful. We don't know who it is."

"He has only helped me so far," I said defiantly. I don't know why I trusted the voice, but, strangely enough, I did.

"Yes, but if the voice speaks to you again, I want to know immediately," said Uncle Gabriel sternly. "We don't know who or what we are dealing with, and we must always be on our guard. Now, with Lilith back, our chances of defeating Morgana have become even less."

"Why?" I asked, wide-eyed. What had I done now?

"Because Lilith is half demon, she is immortal," said Uncle Gabriel. "That is why she was able to return. She is still weak in her wraith form. She needs a host, but she will not find it difficult to find some poor soul who will not be able to resist her powers."

I sat up straighter in my bed. "But that means that she could be anyone!"

Uncle Gabriel nodded. "Yes, although she will keep changing bodies until she finds the one that suits her purposes. And, if I am correct in my guess, the body she will choose to inhabit finally will be Morgana's."

I gasped. "Will Morgana let her do that?"

"We cannot possibly know for sure, but Morgana is hungry for power, and Lilith is her mother," said Uncle Gabriel. "Lilith's immortal demon magic will make Morgana's powers increase a hundredfold, and Morgana will be more powerful than ever. Once Lilith's wraith merges with Morgana's soul, she will be virtually unstoppable, even by you."

I hung my head. What had I done? Instead of helping, I had just made matters worse. I had to do something. This was my mess, and I was the one who should clean it up.

"There must be a way to stop Lilith and Morgana," I said, trying to think of something, but my mind came up blank.

"There might be," said Uncle Gabriel, thinking for a moment before going on, "but the answers we need are not to be found here. We must journey at the earliest to Elfi, and meet with Isadora. You must learn the true extent of your magic. The old magic of the fae is the only thing that can help us now."

"Then we will leave right away," I said, trying to be brave, but all I wanted to do was sleep for a week.

Uncle Gabriel smiled. "You have gone through a prolonged and horrific ordeal, Aurora. You will rest for a few days, until your wounds have healed completely. The journey to Elfi is long and arduous, and I would have you at your full strength."

Uncle Gabriel got up to leave.

"Rest now. You have been very brave, and I am astonished at what you have achieved in such a short time. Your parents would have been very proud to see the young fae-mage you have become," said Uncle Gabriel, leaving the room and shutting the door.

I smiled, tears pooling in my eyes and threatening to spill, as I sat on my bed and contemplated the rest of my life. I was no longer the scared little girl who was dragged through the tapestry in Redstone Manor. I had changed and grown up, finally accepting who I was and what my place was in this world. I was the true Queen of Illiador, descended from Avalonia's greatest dynasty, and I was at long last ready to fight for my kingdom and take back my throne.

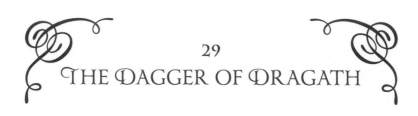

29
THE DAGGER OF DRAGATH

THE NEXT DAY, Penelope let me out of bed for a short walk, but now four palace guards followed me everywhere I went, and they had been instructed never to leave their posts for any reason. I made my way to the palace library, looking for Uncle Gabriel, since one of the footmen had seen him head there that morning.

I found him sitting on a chair, a pile of big, leather-bound books with yellowing pages, in various states of being read, lying all over the huge rectangular oak table in the center of the room.

I looked around.

The library was a wonderful two-storied room with a wooden gallery running along one side that could be reached by a large spiral staircase. It was bright and spacious, with shelves upon shelves of beautiful, leather-bound books adorning the walls. A set of doors led out onto a large balcony that overlooked one of the palace's inner courtyards.

"Is there something you needed, Aurora?" said Uncle Gabriel, looking up at me for a second as I entered the library before going back to studying his books.

"I was thinking, Uncle Gabriel," I said, sitting down in the chair beside him.

Uncle Gabriel closed the book he was reading, raised one eyebrow, and looked at me patiently. "Yes, well, that is never a good thing with you," he said, but his eyes looked like he was holding back a smile.

"It's just," I began, my hands fiddling with my amulet, "I've been thinking about my mother a lot after Morgana confirmed what really happened that night."

"Oh," said Uncle Gabriel, "and what is it you would like to know?"

"Penelope once told me that there are magical weapons that can kill an immortal. And that's probably how Morgana killed my mother."

"There are such weapons, yes," said Uncle Gabriel, "but no one has ever seen one in centuries. What is your point?"

"Can't we use one of those to kill Lilith?" I said.

"Possibly," said Uncle Gabriel, thinking, "but the only weapon we know of is probably with Morgana, and we don't even know what it is or what it looks like."

"I do," I said. "I know what it looks like."

"And how, may I ask, did you manage that?" he asked, raising his eyebrows again.

"I haven't told you everything," I began.

"I surmised so," said Uncle Gabriel sternly.

I was hesitant at first, but I finally told him about my dream. Having Morgana confirm that she stabbed my mother through the heart finally made me realize that the horrible nightmares I used to experience were a real memory, and I wanted to make sure my uncle knew the whole truth if we were to defeat Morgana and Lilith.

Uncle Gabriel heard me out patiently, but when I came to the part about the dagger, his eyes lit up.

"Are you sure?" he interrupted, quite unexpectedly. "In this dream, are you sure you saw Morgana stab Elayna with a dagger?"

I nodded. "Yes," I said. "I think so. She was about to stab her, but in my dream I am always pulled away at the last second, and then there is a blinding flash of light."

Uncle Gabriel nodded sagely, his hands stroking his clipped white beard. "You were being pulled into the portal. The flash was the portal closing after you went through. Such power is rarely seen. Only the fae can create such a gateway, but usually it takes over a dozen powerful fae to do what your mother did for you that day."

Again tears welled up in my eyes, and I brushed them away, determined not to get waylaid by my emotions. My mother was gone. There was nothing I could do about it. I had to concentrate on the task at hand, which was finding a way to defeat Lilith.

"About the dagger," said Uncle Gabriel, his eyes lighting up again, just like when I mentioned the weapon before. "Describe it."

"Well," I said trying to visualize it. "It was sort of curved

. . ."

"Curved, or sort of curved?" asked Uncle Gabriel sternly. "There is a difference."

I checked my memories again. "Yes curved, definitely curved," I said finally.

"Good, good. Go on," said Uncle Gabriel, sitting on the edge of his chair.

"And it was made entirely of gold, with a big red ruby on its hilt," I finished.

Uncle Gabriel stood up and abruptly walked over to the door.

"Guards," he bellowed.

I was startled. Why had he called the guards? The guards posted outside the door responded immediately.

"Summon my daughter and Mrs. Plumpleberry."

"Yes, Your Grace," said one guard as he marched off to do the Duke's bidding. To the other guard, Uncle Gabriel said more quietly, "Ask the prince to meet me here. Let him know that it is an urgent matter."

"Yes, Your Grace," said the second guard and scurried off in the opposite direction.

"Why have you called them all here?" I asked, now thoroughly confused. What had I done now?

Uncle Gabriel was not listening. He was rummaging around on the shelves and trying to find a book; which one, I had no idea. He refused to speak to me.

Serena and Penelope arrived a few moments later.

"Father," said Aunt Serena, "is everything all right?"

"It will be," said Uncle Gabriel, still rummaging the shelves for a book.

"Is there some reason in particular you have asked us here, Your Grace?" said Penelope, coming over to me. "Is Aurora in any discomfort?"

She checked me for the tenth time that day.

"Yes. No, I mean. Yes, I have a reason, and no, she is not in any discomfort," said Uncle Gabriel finally, pulling out a large, dusty, leather-bound book. "Found it!"

He opened the book. The pages looked worn and yellow, and Uncle Gabriel turned to a page that had a horrifying picture on it. A terrible, demon-like creature with curved horns, hooved feet, and reddish black skin held aloft a dagger, ready to stab it into the heart of a kneeling fae warrior. They were painted amidst a battlefield. And all over the page, bodies lay strewn in contorted poses and grizzly heaps at the demon's feet.

I looked away at first, but there was no mistaking the dagger the hideous evil creature held in his clawed hand. It was definitely the same dagger, the one Morgana used to kill my mother in my dream.

"This is it," I said, incredulously. "How did you know? This is the same dagger."

"I thought so," said Uncle Gabriel, closing the book and sitting down in the chair. Aunt Serena and Penelope sat down too. They looked perturbed; Aunt Serena would not even look at the picture in the book.

The doors opened, and Rafe walked in. "What's this about? Is Aurora okay?" he asked my granduncle.

"I'm here in the room," I said, getting irritated. "You could ask me yourself."

Rafe didn't seem perturbed and looked straight into my eyes. "Well, if you didn't run around the kingdom trying to get yourself killed all the time, then I wouldn't have to keep asking how you are, would I?" he snapped.

I huffed at his answer and could not think of a suitable retort. Even if Vivienne was right, and he was concerned about me, why didn't he come to see me? I was still angry with him. One minute he was saying how he couldn't stay away from me, and then he wouldn't see me for days. His moods were too confusing, and it was playing havoc with my emotions.

"Now, now, Aurora," said Aunt Serena. "I am sure the prince meant no harm in asking about your health, my dear."

Rafe smiled at me weakly. He did look a bit disheveled and not himself, but I was still upset that he hadn't even come to see me even for a few minutes. Especially after he called me "my love" at the ruins. Did he say that to all the girls? Was that just the way he got them to fall madly in love with him, only to move on to the next one? So I just huffed childishly again and looked down at my lap.

"Sit down, Rafe," said Uncle Gabriel. "This is important."

Rafe suddenly became serious and sat down immediately.

"What is that dagger you just showed me?" I asked expectantly.

"That, my dear," said Uncle Gabriel slowly, "is the Dagger of Dragath."

"Dragath," I said. "The same demon lord Dragath who ruled these lands before Auraken Firedrake?"

"The very same," said Uncle Gabriel, but he wasn't smiling.

"And what does the Dagger of Dragath have to do with Aurora and us?" asked Rafe, leaning forward in his chair.

Uncle Gabriel told Rafe, Serena, and Penelope about my dream.

Rafe looked astonished, a bit like he looked when I told him who I really was in the beginning.

"And you think Morgana used the Dagger of Dragath on Elayna?" said Rafe, his eyes narrowing.

"Precisely," said Uncle Gabriel, smiling now.

"But that would mean . . . " said Penelope.

"That Queen Elayna is still very much alive," finished Rafe, turning his head to look straight into my startled eyes.

I was stunned; I didn't know what to say. My mother was alive! How was this even possible?

"How?" I asked, my voice a small, hopeful whisper. "Didn't you just say that there are weapons that are capable of killing an Immortal?"

"Yes," said Uncle Gabriel nodding, "but the Dagger of Dragath is not one of them. The legends say that the dagger was specifically crafted by the demon lord Dragath himself to trap, not kill, the immortal fae."

"What do you mean?" I asked. Magic in Avalonia was so complicated.

"Before Auraken Firedrake defeated Dragath and trapped him in his magical prison, Dragath used that dagger to trap countless fae warriors," said Uncle Gabriel in disgust. "That was how he controlled them and their magic."

I just stared at Uncle Gabriel.

"Are you saying that my mother is trapped in that dagger like some, some, genie?" I said finally.

"That is exactly what I am proposing," said Uncle Gabriel. "That is why Morgana wants to open the Book of Abraxas. It all makes sense now."

"How does this make sense?" I said, completely lost.

Rafe turned towards me. "Morgana's plan is even more devious and elaborate than we had thought possible," he said, getting up from his chair. "If Morgana has the dagger of Dragath and has Elayna trapped inside it, she will be able to use Elayna's powers to release Dragath from his magical prison."

My eyes widened. "But Morgana trapped my mother almost fifteen years ago, why didn't she release Dragath then?"

"Because she has been waiting to get her hands on the Book of Abraxas," Uncle Gabriel answered. "That is why she wants the keys to open it. Only then will Morgana finally be able to control Dragath. If she released him without possessing the secrets to controlling him, Dragath would destroy the world along with her in it."

My mind had gone into overdrive, assimilating all this new information. My mother was alive, trapped and alone for over a decade. I had to find her. She had given up her life to save me, and now I must try and save her. Also, if I released my mother, then Morgana could not use the dagger to release Dragath. I had to do this for her, for my father, for his kingdom. Whatever it took, whatever the cost, I would find a way.

"If my mother is alive, I will find her," I announced to the room, my voice breaking slightly. "We cannot let Morgana use the dagger to release Dragath."

I had absolutely no idea how I was going to accomplish that, but I was going to give it my best shot.

Uncle Gabriel shook his head tiredly. "She will not release him until she has the book and all the four keys," he said. "We still have time, but we must make sure she never gets her hands on those three remaining keys. That's why we will take one of the keys with us when we go to Elfi. It will be safe with Isadora."

"But what about my mother?" I said, perturbed that no one was concerned about releasing her. "We need to go to Illiador and take back the dagger first."

"No, Aurora, you cannot go running off unprepared into Morgana's castle and take back the dagger. It is not so easy."

"But . . ."

"No buts, Aurora," said Uncle Gabriel, raising his voice. "Your parents did not give their lives to save you just so you could run straight into Morgana's clutches. I will not allow it. And have you forgotten about Lilith, or the throne of Illiador? It is your parents' legacy, the one they died to protect."

That was just about all I could take. I stood up, pushing my chair back so hard it nearly toppled over. "I'm tired of everyone telling me what I can and can't do," I said, shouting at all of them and none in particular. "And no, I haven't forgotten about Lilith. That's why I came to see you in the first place. But I will not go on an extended holiday to Elfi to see my long-lost grandmother just so that she can teach me more magic. I know enough. I fought Morgana once, and I can do it again. You all seem to think you know what's best for me, but none of you even know me. My real mother is alive, and you want me to just look the other way until I find a convenient time to find her. I can't do that."

Uncle Gabriel, Penelope, Aunt Serena, and Rafe were staring at me. This was the first time I had actually shouted at any of them. I hated to raise my voice, and I disliked being rude, but I was tired of being pushed around. Well, it stopped now. I was going to do what I thought was right.

I looked around and sat back down on my chair, feeling a little foolish after my rowdy outburst. But Uncle Gabriel had it coming. He rested his elbows on the arms of the high-backed, mahogany chair and pressed his fingertips together as he assessed me from under his bushy silver eyebrows.

Finally, after a few agonizingly stretched out moments, he spoke.

"I will take what you have said under consideration," said Uncle Gabriel, "but you have to understand that your education is in no way over, or even half done. The old magic of the fae is unpredictable and very complicated, even more so than the magic of the mages. Demon magic is even more powerful. It is ancient magic, and few have ever really understood it."

Granduncle Gabriel paused to see if everyone was listening, then, satisfied at the undivided attention he was receiving, turned back to me and continued.

"Even if you do somehow manage to travel through Illiador without getting caught by Morgana's remaining Shadow Guard and by some means manage to enter the castle at Nerenor, how will you defeat Morgana? How will you find the dagger? How will you know where it is? It could be hidden anywhere. It may not even be in the castle. Have you even thought of that?"

I kept quiet while my heroic dreams were smashed to bits. The hope of ever seeing my birth mother was fading away into the realm of the impossible. But Uncle Gabriel wasn't finished. He continued talking.

"Then, even if somehow you do manage to find the dagger, how will you get out of the castle? And say you even manage to do that, although I would imagine you would probably be dead by this point, I would like to know how you propose to break the ancient demon curse on the dagger and free your mother? Especially when you don't know the first thing about demons and the magic that they possess."

I hung my head. He was right; I was being foolish. How could I ever have thought that I would do all these things? I would have liked to think that I could, but the road ahead sounded impossible. Even with the powers I had, I would never be able to get into the castle, let alone find and steal the dagger and free my mother. I needed help, but no one was going to give it to me. I was on my own again, and I had absolutely no idea what to do next.

30
A PLAN

I WANDERED the long corridors of the Summer Palace for hours, thinking. What should I do? I knew what I wanted to do, but Uncle Gabriel had expressly forbidden me to pursue the dagger. I couldn't just forget about it just like that. My mother had given her life for me. After what I saw in the dream, how could I not at least try and save her? Uncle Gabriel could take one key to Elfi so that Morgana couldn't open the Book of Abraxas. And it made sense to go after the dagger at the same time. If we released my mother and destroyed the dagger, Morgana could never release Dragath.

I was supposedly the most powerful fae-mage since Auraken Firedrake, but I was not a legendary king. I could not command armies and lead battles; Uncle Gabriel didn't really need me. They only needed me as someone to put on the throne. I would be a puppet, answering only to Uncle Gabriel if he did manage it. I knew Uncle Gabriel and Aunt Serena and the king and everyone else were expecting me to be a queen. And even though I didn't think I was queen material, I would try my best, but only after I found my mother.

I knew it was hard. I knew what I was proposing was foolish, but there had to be a way. If only someone would help me. I needed more information. I couldn't understand why the dreams had only started after I turned sixteen. So I went to see Penelope. She wasn't in her room, and I finally found her walking in the gardens. When she saw me, she led me to a bench and sat down, gesturing me to sit beside her.

"Tell me, my dear," Penelope said kindly, "how can I help? I can see something is bothering you. I have to say, I hope you don't expect me to try and convince your granduncle to take you to Illiador. His mind has been made up, and nothing can change it. You have to understand he only wants the best for you and for the kingdom."

I nodded. "It's not that, Penelope," I began, "it's just that I don't understand why the dreams only started when I turned sixteen. Why didn't I remember any of this when I was younger?"

"Yes, I had thought about this earlier," said Penelope, "but I didn't voice my opinion. Maybe I should have."

"What do you mean?" I asked.

"Well," she began, "there is a certain sort of fae glamour that can repress memories until they are ready to be revealed. It is an ancient art, wielded only by the spirit fae."

"Which means?" I asked, still confused at what she was getting at.

"I have been thinking about this since you told us about the dream," said Penelope, "and I was going to speak to you about it at one point, but I cannot be sure if I am right."

"Right about what?"

"I have a theory," said Penelope slowly. "And it is just a theory . . ."

"Which is?"

"That Elayna knew she could only save herself or her child," she said and paused. "She chose you."

I nodded weakly.

"But Elayna was clever, and extremely resourceful as well as powerful. If she knew Morgana was going to use the Dagger of Dragath on her, she must have known she wasn't going to die, only be trapped within it."

"But isn't it the same thing if no one knows she's there?" I said.

"Not if the child she saved is a powerful fae-mage who can come back one day and save her."

"You mean," I paused, understanding dawning, "she wanted me to find her?"

"Yes, I believe she did," said Penelope finally. "I think she must have glamoured you into forgetting everything you saw and knew until you were ready. But that doesn't mean you get yourself killed in the bargain. You have to master your powers. Only then will you be able to take on Morgana and Lilith. Even then, the chances of us winning are slim. You must listen to your granduncle and go to Elfi. Your grandmother Isadora is queen of the fae, and Elayna is her daughter; she will definitely help you find your mother. I am sure about that. Go to her, see what she has to say, and then decide what you want to do. Elayna has been trapped for nearly fifteen years now. A few more months will not make a difference."

But it made a difference to me, a big difference. Everything was so clear now. It all made sense. My mother knew she would be trapped, she knew I was a fae-mage, and she knew, if I ever found my way back to Avalonia, I would find her and save her. And that was exactly what I was going to do. I didn't say anything to Penelope, though. I couldn't trust her not to tell Uncle Gabriel what I was planning.

"Thank you, Penelope," I said, getting up from the bench. "You have been a great help."

"Glad I could help, my dear," said Penelope, "and I hope you can understand why we all are doing this. It is only for your own safety."

I nodded. "I know. Thank you," I said and hurried off through a flowering garden path, back into the palace.

I went back to my room and started packing a few things in a leather satchel.

I had to leave soon. I had to get out of here before Uncle Gabriel took me away to Elfi. I had no idea how I was even going to get out of the palace, let alone the city, but I had made up my mind. If I didn't leave now, I would be forced to go to Elfi, and my chance of finding my mother would be gone. I knew Uncle Gabriel said he would help me find my mother, but only after I did as he wanted. If war came—and it was coming—the lands would be in turmoil. I might be stuck in Elfi for years, unable to cross the borders. I could not be sure if my grandmother would help me. My only chance was to go now.

"What are you doing?" said Kalen, as he came in the door. I whirled around.

"Don't you ever knock?" I said, relieved it was only Kalen.

"The door was open," said Kalen, looking apologetic.

"Well, shut it," I said, quickly trying to find some suitable things to take with me. I had no idea what I was doing and what I needed, so I was bustling around the room like an aimless chicken.

"Are you planning to go somewhere without telling me?" Kalen asked, a hurt note to his voice, but I barely noticed.

"Kalen," I said, putting a pair of warm woolen socks and a leather vest into my satchel, "if I tell you, you have to promise not to tell anyone, okay?"

"I promise," said Kalen, his eyes twinkling as he perched himself on the edge of the bed.

I wasn't sure if it was a good idea to tell him, but I had to tell someone. I was just so confused. So I told him everything about the Dagger of Dragath and my mother.

"Queen Elayna is alive?" said Kalen, his eyes growing wide.

I nodded. "And trapped," I added. "I have to get her back."

"So you are running off in the dead of night into a kingdom you have no idea about, all alone," said Kalen, narrow-ing his eyes. "A masterful plan that one, I must say, my lady."

"You don't have to be sarcastic," I said, pouting. "You sound like Uncle Gabriel."

"Your granduncle has a point," said Kalen seriously. "Even I can tell you that this is a hopeless quest, one in which you have absolutely no possibility of succeeding."

"I could," I said quickly, sounding more sure than I felt, "if I had some help."

Kalen's eyes widened. "You want me to go with you?" he said, quite obviously aghast that I had even mentioned it.

"Well, why not?" I said, trying to be practical. "You said yourself that I need help, and you know these lands, so you could take me to the Star Palace in Nerenor, couldn't you?"

"I could," said Kalen, "but I won't."

"Why not?" I asked, surprised. I was quite sure he would go along with me.

"Because I don't particularly want to get myself killed," said Kalen, standing up and crossing his arms over his chest. "I really don't think you should do this, Aurora. You should go to Elfi with your granduncle and meet your grandmother. I'm sure together you will all be able to figure out a way to get the dagger back and free your mother. You can't do this on your own."

"Then come with me," I pleaded.

I really did need someone with me, and I was apprehen-sive about going alone. But I had to do this; I had to find my mother. She expected me to. She was counting on me; I was the only one who could manage this. Morgana would be looking for me elsewhere; she would never think to look for me under her very nose. Kalen and I could disguise ourselves and pose as brother and sister. I had some money saved from what Aunt Serena had given me, and Kalen knew all the roads leading to the capital city of Illiador. It would be a long journey, but we could stay at inns along the way or camp outdoors if we had to. I couldn't take Snow with me, since she would be too conspicuous.

"You are really going to do this," Kalen asked, looking at me very sternly.

I nodded, saying nothing more; I moved to my dresser and went back to packing my things.

"Fine, then I shall go with you," he announced, after not too many moments of careful pondering. "Did you know that Rafe said I could take anything I wanted from the armory? I got myself a new bow, with a whole quiver of arrows and everything. And I have been learning to use a sword with Erien when he trains."

I smiled. Kalen was still the same, a little taller than when I had first met him, but he hadn't changed, and I was glad. He was a good friend, and I was secretly relieved that he was coming with me. At least I would have someone to talk to on the long journey, and, although I was pretty confident that I could protect myself and Kalen if it came to it, I had absolutely no idea how to get there.

That night, Kalen fetched me from my room.

"What did you say to the guards?" I asked.

"Didn't say anything," shrugged Kalen, "I just used one of my mother's sleeping potions on them."

"You drugged the palace guards?" I said, shocked.

"Well, how were you planning on leaving your room without four guards following you all the time?" said Kalen, scrunching his forehead.

I shook my head. "No, you're right," I said, being practical. "Now where?"

I crept out of my room and past the sleeping guards. Kalen must have given them a strong dose, as they were all snoring away with happy looks on their faces.

The night was dark, and a chill wind had crept into the palace corridors. I adjusted my old brown cloak and covered my head. I wore riding breeches and leather boots with a long shirt under a fitted brown leather vest, belted at the waist. I carried the sword that Rafe had given me, and I had even strapped a knife in my boot, just like he did. I wanted to try and pass for a boy, and so I tied my long dark hair back and hid it under my hood.

"We will go through the servant's quarters and out through the kitchen," said Kalen in a whisper, as we moved silently through the dark hallways.

"Do you know where it is?" I asked, feeling foolish. I

couldn't even manage to get myself out of the palace. How was I going to get to Illiador?

Kalen nodded, and I followed.

"Going somewhere?" said a voice from the shadows. I jumped, but I knew who it was.

"Rafe," I whispered, "you almost scared me to death."

He pushed himself away from the wall he was leaning on and stepped into the moonlight. His eyes quickly scanned the scene in front of him as he took in my choice of attire and traveling satchel.

"You were leaving without saying good-bye," he said. It wasn't a question, and his voice had an edge to it that I hadn't heard before.

I looked down at my feet. What could I say? If I had to say good-bye to him, I would never leave. It was better that I just went away and saved myself the heartache that would surely come when I saw him marry someone else. Either way I had to leave. Even if I went to Elfi, I would probably never see him again.

"Good-bye Rafe," I said, trying to sound like I didn't care.

Rafe ignored me. "Kalen, are you helping her in this foolishness?" Rafe said, turning slightly.

Kalen looked embarrassed. "She was going to leave alone," he said finally. "I decided that someone should go with her."

Rafe suddenly took two quick steps towards me, caught my arms, and pulled me towards him. Our faces were so close, our noses almost touching, but he didn't kiss me. His breath smelled of alcohol.

"Have you been drinking?" I asked breathlessly.

I could never think when he came so close to me. I wished he wouldn't do that anymore. It was getting harder and harder to resist him, and my conscience was slowly being bludgeoned to death by the persistent little voice that kept telling me not to give him up.

"Maybe," he said roughly, "why do you ask? It's not like you care."

I wiggled out of his grasp, and he let me go.

"You're right," I said, lying blatantly, "I don't care."

I had to push him away. I had to make him think I didn't love him, and then he would leave me alone.

"All right, then," he said finally, straightening the cuffs on his half-open shirt. "Go then, I won't stop you."

"Are you serious?" I said incredulously. "And you won't tell Uncle Gabriel?"

I was so sure he was going to try and convince me to stay and go to Elfi with my granduncle just like everybody else.

"He will find out soon enough without my help," Rafe said, shrugging again. "In fact, I think I am going to help you instead."

"You are?" I said, skeptical at his sudden change of heart.

Rafe nodded. "Yes," he said simply. "Kalen, what was your plan so far?"

"Well," said Kalen looking around the shadowy corridor to make sure no one else was coming our way. "We were supposed to leave through the kitchens, then out of the palace gates, telling the guards I had an errand for my mother to get some herbs from the apothecary, since Aurora is supposed to be her assistant."

"And then," said Rafe "how would you have left the city?"

"I hadn't thought about that yet," said Kalen, biting his lip.

"You hadn't?" I asked, turning to Kalen, "but you said you would sort it out."

"And I will," said Kalen to me, as if he were talking to a child. "I just don't know how yet."

Rafe rolled his eyes, and I was tempted to do the same. Kalen was so infuriating sometimes.

"Follow me," Rafe said.

We followed the prince through the palace corridors and into a closed room, which happened to be his bedroom.

I looked around. It was neat and cozy, but not overly plush or ornate like some of the other bedrooms in the palace. A large, wooden four-poster bed was placed in the center of the room, the carved headboard resting against one wall, which was hung with a worn tapestry. A warm, tan skin rug covered the floor and a dressing room was situated through a velvet-curtained doorway. A large writing desk and a high-backed chair lay along one side, next to a wooden chest ornately decorated with intricate carvings of magical fae creatures.

Rafe put on his cloak and took out his mask, which he had hidden in the locked wooden chest. He also filled a leather sack with a few things and belted his sword around his waist. Various knives were strapped on, and he snatched up a worn-looking satchel.

"What are you doing?" I asked, confused.

Kalen's eyes widened. "Are you coming with us?" he asked, grinning.

"I think it's a good idea," said Rafe. "You said yourself she is going to need help. So I'm helping."

"You can't come with us," I said, horrified at the prospect of spending who knew how long with him.

"I can get you to Illiador and help you get the dagger," he said, turning to me.

"Why?" I asked. "Why are you doing this? You don't have to come with me. I can do this on my own."

"Aurora," he said, more gently this time. "I understand how you feel. If I were you, I would also be out trying to find my mother, no matter what anyone said."

I was elated. Finally, someone who actually understood how I felt.

"I know that we cannot be together," he continued, taking my hands gently in his. "But I would really like for us to be friends. We are friends, right?"

I didn't know if being friends would ever be possible, but I was willing to give it a try. I knew that I should say no, that I should go with Kalen and never look back. But of course, my tired conscience was not even trying to wake up and chastise me for my stupidity. Secretly I was relieved. Rafe knew these lands like the back of his hand. He would get me to the Star Palace in Nerenor, of that I had no doubt.

I nodded weakly. "Friends. Yes, absolutely," I said, my heart breaking for the thousandth time.

"So friends help each other," he said, as if it was all settled.

I had no choice, and having Rafe come along suddenly made me feel like maybe I could actually succeed in this, perhaps together we really had a shot at finding the dagger. That was my main focus now. Find the dagger, and then I would worry about the rest, as it came along.

"But what about Leticia?" I still had to ask.

"The wedding can be postponed for a while," he said, grinning like he had just come up with a brilliant plan.

So that was his game, I mused. He wanted to come with me so he could get away from Leticia and postpone the wedding indefinitely. If that was his reason, fine, I could live with it. It was foolish to suppose he was coming because he wanted to spend more time with me and really did care about helping me find my mother. But I took what I could get; at least with him accompanying us, I had a real chance of succeeding.

"And what about your father, the king?" I asked. "Won't he wonder where you are?"

"I will leave a note for him that I had to go away on some urgent errand," said Rafe shrugging. "He will be angry for a while, but he'll get over it. After all, it's not like he's going to disinherit me and give the crown to the Blackwaters."

It sounded like he had it all sorted out. Rafe was very resourceful, and I didn't even know half of what he was capable of.

"So what's your plan, Rafe?" said Kalen. "Do we still leave the palace through the kitchen?"

"No," said Rafe, putting on his mask. "I have another way."

"Which is?" I enquired.

I was happy Rafe was in charge. Kalen was sweet, but his plans were really not properly thought out.

"How do you think the Black Wolf gets in and out of the palace at night with no one ever noticing?" he said, grinning behind the black mask and pulling on the hood of his shadowy cloak.

I grinned back at him. "Secret passage," I said without hesitation.

"Looks like you know me quite well," he said chuckling. "I do happen to know of many secret passages in and out of the palace, but only one leads outside the city gates. Follow me," he said, and we accompanied him down the silent corridors of the Summer Palace to the council chamber.

"So where is this secret passage?" I asked looking around the vast room but still smiling away.

Suddenly the door to the council chamber burst open, and two palace guards charged into the room, their swords flashing silver in the moonlight.

I whirled around. How did they find me? I couldn't let

them stop me now. I had to leave the palace tonight. "I thought you said you gave them the potion?" I said to Kalen, panicking.

"I did!" said Kalen, flinging his arms into the air.

The guards' eyes widened when they saw Rafe in his black mask and cloak. "The Black Wolf," said one Guard, recognizing the infamous outlaw.

Rafe took a step forward, and the Guards shrank back instinctively. But this was my fight and my only chance to find my mother. I wasn't going to let a pair of foolish guards stand in my way.

"I've got this," I said to Rafe, moving in front of him and raising my hands, palms facing the guards. This time I didn't need to make an effort; my magic was a part of me. The white light coursed through my veins and exploded in two perfect beams, hitting the guards in the middle of their chests. The force of my stun was so strong that they flew backwards hitting the wall as they fell to the floor unconscious.

"That was one fantastic stun strike," said Rafe coming up to me and grinning. "You combined a stun and push strike together even with your amulet on. I don't think I've ever seen that done before. Maybe I should hire you to protect my kingdom from now on."

I laughed and beamed at the praise, especially coming from him. "Anytime," I said. "But first, I have my own kingdom to defend."

"I'll wait," Rafe said, still smiling as he walked over to the mantelpiece above the fireplace and bent one of the candlestands forward. The wall behind the fireplace moved backwards, leaving enough space for a person to pass through on both sides.

"The Summer Palace was built over an ancient ruin," said Rafe. "This passage is as old as Auraken himself."

The passage beyond looked dark, and Rafe went first. His hand lit up with a tiny white ball of light that illuminated the grey stone walls. Magic had now become second nature to me, and I pushed some light into my hand, whirling it around with my fingers until it formed a ball.

Rafe silently took my hand and entwined his fingers through mine. This was it; I was really going to do this. From now on, I would not run from my destiny or my responsibilities. My mother was alive, and I was going to get her back. Morgana had better prepare to defend herself, for I was the last of the Firedrakes, and I was not afraid of her anymore. My life was my own and so were my choices. I just hoped I had made the right one.

I gathered my courage and walked forward into the dark passage that led from the Summer Palace of Eldoren out into the fascinating, magical, and dangerous world of Avalonia that lay beyond.

ACKNOWLEDGMENTS

First I want to thank God, with whose grace and blessings nothing is impossible.

My wonderful mother, Zinia Lawyer, who has always supported and empowered me to do what others thought I could not.

My amazing husband, Riyad Oomerbhoy, my pillar of strength and love of my life who has always believed in me and told me I could write, even though he has had to endure hearing me ramble on about my characters for the past ten years, and knows them nearly as well as I do.

My precious children who have always been my biggest supporters.

My wonderful family, my brother Rustom Lawyer, my sister and brother-in-law Roohi and Chetan Jaikishan, my father-in-law Rashid Oomerbhoy, my niece and nephew Amaan and Jehaan, my sister-in-law Shazmeen, and Shiraz Austin for their constant encouragement.

There are so many others I want to thank who have helped me bring this book to this point, so here it goes. To Hannah Dierker Cortese for all her help beta-reading. Basanti Didwania, Shweta Nanda, Navya Nanda, Farida Irani, Shernaz Vakil, Priya Nathani, Gayatri Shah, and Anita Vaswani who read a very rough first draft of the book and actually liked it.

My super-efficient assistant Kate Tilton, without whom I would not have met the wonderful women at Wise Ink Creative Publishing, especially Laura Zats for all her enthusiasm and unwavering support, and for giving me the chance and expertise to publish the best possible version of my book. My superb editor Amanda Rutter, who guided me throughout the editing process and helped create this final version. Thanks to the amazingly talented cover designer Scarlett Rugers for all her patience and wonderful creativity in designing this beautiful cover. I must also thank Jade Zivanovic for her beautifully detailed depiction of the map of Avalonia. I also want to thank Patrick Maloney for his meticulous proofreading, and Kim Morehead for her beautiful interior design, which has enhanced the written word and made the book more enjoyable to read.

There are a few more people I must not leave out who have all contributed in some way towards me publishing this book. My wonderful Wattpad group, the Wattpad Class of 2014, consisting of twelve talented authors who have been so kind, helpful, and supportive. I am honored to be one of you. And last but not least, my wonderful Wattpad readers who made me believe anything is possible.